PRAISE FOR THE NO

SMALL TOWN, BIG MAGIC

"The magical world of St. Cyprian is one readers will never want to leave. *Small Town, Big Magic* is an absolute triumph of a debut.... Hazel Beck has created the perfect blend of magic, humor, world-ending peril, friendship and romance, brewed into a spellbinding combination that readers will adore, and that will have them desperate for the next book!"

—*New York Times* bestselling author Maisey Yates

"Emerson Wilde is a smart, funny protagonist whose unshakeable belief in herself will charm the reader from the very first page of *Small Town, Big Magic*. A diverse coven of witches, an enchanted history, and a dangerous adversary all add up to an absolute delight of a magical tale."

—Louisa Morgan, author of *The Age of Witches*

"A fresh, fun, zany spin on paranormal romance, *Small Town, Big Magic* casts a big spell. Take one girlboss witch, add a magical journey of healing and self-discovery, and sprinkle in a dash of romance, and you've got an enchanting read perfect for fans of *The Ex Hex* and *Payback's a Witch*."

—Ashley Winstead, author of *Fool Me Once*

ALSO BY HAZEL BECK

Small Town, Big Magic

To learn more about Hazel Beck,

visit www.hazel-beck.com.

BIG LITTLE SPELLS

HAZEL BECK

ISBN-13: 978-1-525-80472-4

Big Little Spells

Graydon House
22 Adelaide St. West, 41st Floor
Toronto, Ontario M5H 4E3, Canada
www.GraydonHouseBooks.com
www.BookClubbish.com

Printed in U.S.A.

For sisters by blood and by magic, wherever we may find them.

BIG LITTLE SPELLS

YOU DON'T HAVE TO BE AN EXILED WITCH under threat of the death penalty should you cast the faintest little spell to feel the magic in Sedona, Arizona.

But it doesn't hurt.

The full moon is shining, high and bright, making the red rocks glow outside my little bungalow. The air is soft and dry instead of swollen with Missouri's trademark humidity, which I'm not sorry to leave behind.

If it was up to me, I would never have gone back to Missouri at all.

Because one thing exile has taught me is that magic is as much a habit as anything else. Unnecessary at best. Dangerous at worst. An addiction, in other words.

These days I am all about recovery.

Except for tonight. Tonight, admittedly, has been a bit of a relapse.

I breathe out and try to blow away the past while I do.

I'm standing out in my little yard, my head tipped toward

the Arizona sky and my shoes kicked off so I can feel the earth and as many vortexes as possible. Because I'm a hippie, I tell myself. Just a run-of-the-mill Sedona hippie. Hair down, feet bare, crystals hanging all around like every other New Ager around here.

Not magic, just vibes.

But before I manage to fully ground myself here, I feel something grab me, like a huge, magical hook around the center of me—but inside out. It's dark. Hard. Kind of slimy, really—and it makes my stomach heave.

This *particular* magical tug is a summons, yanking me out of the life I fought so hard to build, all on my own. Not for the first time.

Not even for the first time *tonight*.

Though this summons is harsher than the one before. Meaner.

I know instantly it's not *him*.

Because *he* yanked me back to St. Cyprian too, but it didn't hurt when he did it. It's not supposed to hurt at all, and he made it feel almost *good*—

But I stop thinking about the maddeningly beautiful, impossible immortal witch who ruined my life once already, and start worrying about me.

There's only one reason for me to be dragged back home against my will. And it's been a long night already. My sister, Emerson, who I haven't seen in person in a decade, formed her very own coven made up of our closest friends and one obnoxious immortal. Then, together, we all fought off a major, magic-induced flood that would have submerged the town of St. Cyprian and most of Missouri.

The final jerk makes Sedona disappear into a blur of red, then there's a *whooshing* sensation while whispered words fill the air around me.

Rebekah Wilde, come before us, the voices command me.

And I'm back.

Right where I don't want to be.

I'm standing outside a farmhouse across the river from my hometown. And instead of the terrifying wave of water and my sister ready to dive into the middle of it all like the first time I showed up here tonight, the river has settled down. The fight is over.

Or...maybe it's only just begun.

Because a quick glance around shows me that Emerson is standing outside in the cool April night, looking like the fierce Warrior she is, her eyes blazing gold with all her newly rediscovered power. Jacob North, our old friend and a Healer—and, I think, my sister's new love—stands with her and doesn't look any worse for the intense healing he did when we came much too close to losing Emerson earlier.

Behind them is Zander Rivers, my cousin, looking uncharacteristically grim for a guy who used to make the role he was born into—a Guardian—seem a lot more fun than the name suggests. Next to him is Georgie Pendell, Emerson's best friend, whose entire family has been witch Historians—and actual historians who run the town's local-interest museum—as long as anyone can remember. And last but never least, Ellowyn Good. *My* best friend. And also the Summoner who helped Emerson contact me once Emerson remembered she was a witch, despite the Joywood spell that took those magic memories away from her for ten whole years.

Across from them stand all the members of the Joywood, the ruling coven based here in my hometown of St. Cyprian, MO. The authoritarian, bullying, small-minded coven that cheated me out of the life I was supposed to have.

Seven dictatorial witches I had no intention of laying eyes on again.

I feel a rush of a very old, too-dark fury inside me—but stop myself. It's practically a reflex at this point. I don't do outsize emotion or high drama anymore. I don't do *dark*. That would lead directly to my death, and I've always been pretty clear about wanting to stay alive.

If I hadn't wanted to *live*—*my* life on *my* terms—I would have stayed here. I would have let these petty Joywood tyrants wipe my mind the way they wiped my sister's, taking away any hint of ever knowing magic.

I tell myself that I've forgiven them. I chant it inside me, *not* like one of the spells forbidden to me, but like a mantra. They were only doing their jobs, following their laws, as stupid as those laws might be. I forgive them because forgiveness is mine to give. I don't need to carry the bitter taste of St. Cyprian and its ruling coven with me. I chose to leave all of this behind. I still choose it.

Something—not quite a shadow—moves in my peripheral vision, and I see *him* too. Nicholas Frost, the one and only immortal witch. Some people call him a traitor.

I call him all kinds of things and unlike most, have done it to his face. But now is not the time to air *all* my oldest grudges.

His gaze from halfway across a field makes everything inside me…change. Not so much that dangerous black fury any longer. This is something else. A different kind of heat.

I don't want to acknowledge it. Or him. Especially not with this audience.

Even if, for a moment, it feels as if the two of us are all alone here.

I have to remind myself that we're not.

I forgive you, I think at him, in my smuggest internal voice. The best of a decade of recovery programs right there. And even though I can't—won't—use a witch's usual telepathic version of conversation, I suspect he hears me anyway. Because his dark blue eyes gleam.

From all the way across the tall grass.

"Rebekah Wilde," booms a voice I recognize entirely too well, even though I haven't heard it in a decade. Carol Simon, the Joywood coven's Warrior and therefore the leader of... everything involving witches the world over.

I force myself to look at her, hopefully without my feelings all over my face, and decide that teenage me was right. Her frizzy hair really is unforgivable.

"You have been summoned here, to the site of your infraction, to answer for your offense," she *intones*.

I finally take note of the fact that she and her cronies hauled me into this field, but not into the group of my friends and family who also *infracted* tonight. I'm standing halfway between them and the Joywood. As tempting as it is to think that's just carelessness, I know better.

They don't do careless.

I slouch where I stand, because even being across the river from my hometown makes me want to behave like the sulky teenager I was when I lived here. That's what Carol and her buddies likely see anyway, so why not live down to their worst expectations? I've always been excellent at that.

I lock eyes with Felicia Ipswitch, the Joywood's Diviner and my personal nemesis, and smirk a little. And just like that, it might as well be tenth grade when Felicia was the high school principal and I was a problem. A problem she thought she could solve with draconian detentions and the kind of punishments that would send human teachers to jail—but witch students heal up better.

Turns out I'm not over high school, which doesn't really do a lot for the sullen *peace and love* vibe I'm trying to exude here.

I look away from that evil old hag to find Emerson looking at me like I'm an answer. That's not unusual. My sister always thinks there is one. And better yet, that she can find it and implement it.

I know better, because I made my own way out in the world, relying on nothing and no one but me. I learned the hard way that life and the world often have no answers, no neat little bows. For anyone, witch or human.

I tell myself that it gives me great internal peace to accept this knowledge, and maybe it will, someday. I grit my teeth and think *peace, please.*

Especially when Carol starts to speak again. *Peace, love, light,* I chant inside me. No spellwork here. No witchcraft. Just words of power that anyone could use while anointing themselves in essential oils and rearranging their houses for better feng shui.

"I know you must think you did something big here tonight," Carol is saying, as if she's never heard anything dumber in her life. Her voice is so persuasive that I have to pinch myself to remember that no, we weren't giggling over a Ouija board, pretending we weren't pushing it while we clearly were. We actually fused together the way all the books say true covens should, fought some gnarly dark magic, and won. *Almost* at the expense of my sister's life.

"But I'm afraid all you really did, Emerson and Rebekah, is break the terms set down before you when you failed your pubertatum." She glances around. "And the rest of you broke *several* laws aiding them."

The word *pubertatum* has not gotten any less obnoxious in the ten years I haven't heard it spoken aloud. It's an ugly Latin word for a coming-of-age ceremony where witches in their eighteenth year are required to demonstrate their powers so they might take their places in witch society. Pass the test and you answer a few questions to be herded into one of the seven witchkind designations. Warrior, Guardian, Summoner, Healer, Historian, Praeceptor, or Diviner.

Fail the test, like Emerson and I did, and you get to be a zombie or an outcast.

"I have power, Carol. You can't deny that," Emerson says with her usual bouncy forthrightness, like she's flabbergasted at the possibility that Carol would bother *trying* to deny such a thing. When it's so obvious.

I really have missed my sister.

"You told me I had none." Emerson points to me now. "You told *us* we have no power at all. You were wrong. And then, all this power inside me you said I didn't have fought off *your* obliviscor."

I expect rage. Carol has never been one for being told she's wrong. Her mind wipe spell wasn't supposed to have failed. But Carol surprises me.

She titters, and her cronies all laugh along with her. I remind myself that it's *supposed* to make me feel wrong and stupid and vaguely humiliated. That's what they do. Better to rule us by making us hate ourselves.

"And you've turned a simple testing error into some... nefarious plot? I do worry, Emerson, that fighting off the obliviscor addled your senses."

"We just saved St. Cyprian and possibly all of witchkind, Carol," my sister says, and not angrily. Just like she's reciting facts, inviting Carol to come aboard. She even smiles. "You're welcome."

And I know hate is for the weak. Forgiveness is power. Blah, blah, blah.

But Carol Simon makes the case for blood feuds, forever. Especially when she rolls her eyes.

"We saved witchkind with no help from you," Emerson

continues, as if she doesn't see any eye-rolling. Because she won't give up. Emerson never, *ever* gives up.

Even when she should.

"As a concerned, dedicated St. Cyprian citizen who also happens to be chamber of commerce president, I have to wonder," Emerson tells Carol. But she also casts an eye over the rest of them, these fixtures of St. Cyprian and my witchy past that I did not miss at all. Like Maeve Mather, the Joywood's Summoner, who used to go out of her way to be mean to my grandmother. Just because she could. "Why, I'm asking myself, did the ruling body of all witchkind not only turn a blind eye to the obvious imbalance in our power source that's been making the rivers rise so dangerously, but also fail to help us fix it? Why did *we* have to stop it?"

"I assume because you wanted attention," Felicia says. It is a familiar sentence, meant to be pure condemnation. She used to use it all the time as a precursor to her nasty little punishments. My gaze moves across the dark field to find Ellowyn's, and I can tell from my best friend's expression that she's remembering the same thing I am.

All of high school, basically. When Principal Ipswitch dedicated herself to what she called our reprehensible, attention-seeking behavior.

What amazes me is how little I've thought about high school since leaving Missouri. Deliberately. And tonight, it's like I never left.

"I saw the darkness at the heart of the confluence myself," Emerson says with a great calm I certainly don't feel. Especially since I saw it too. That terrible, encroaching dark, eating the world whole. It had hunkered there where the three rivers meet, waiting malevolently. And then, tonight, it exploded. Emerson, with our help, destroyed it. My heart starts kicking at me again, a riot of panic, like it's still happening.

"Are you accusing us of something?" Carol asks, and she's scarily good at this. She sounds on the verge of laughter, yet somehow almost hurt. As if she cares deeply what Emerson thinks of her. Of them.

I worry this will work on my sister. Because the truth is, Emerson has no power here. She's too honest, and this is politics. Power. It's ego and control. Emerson is a lot of things I roll my eyes at all the time, but she's never been ruled by ego or greed.

Not like these witches.

"I'm pointing out facts," Emerson says, sounding patient now. My sister has never met a windmill she didn't try to charge head-on. "And the facts are, we saved St. Cyprian. You could have helped us, Carol. But you didn't."

"Oh, Emerson." Carol sounds sad. Legitimately sad, which would require emotions on her part. And I'm pretty sure velociraptors don't have emotions. "Why would we *deliberately* choose not to help save the place where we live? How does that make sense?"

Emerson blinks. "You tell me."

I want to give a short TED talk on gaslighting and master manipulators, but this is *not* the time. It's still not clear whether this is an execution or not. Carol did mention infractions of the pubertatum rules, and last I heard, me using magic the way I did tonight is a capital offense. Emerson wasn't supposed to be *able* to do it. I claimed I *could* do it, but was exiled because they said I had no real power—only the shameful, unsafe urge to use borrowed force. Either way, using witchcraft as an exile is about as forbidden as you can get.

I can always be counted on to rebel when it will do me the most harm.

There's a part of me that wants to turn to Nicholas Frost, the only other being here who isn't standing with a group. He's the one who came up with the goddamned pubertatum back when the earth was young, or so they taught us in school. He is considered the first Praeceptor—the teacher of all teachers, but not in a safe little classroom way. Praeceptors in his day taught armies of witches, then wielded them.

But I know better than to look to him for help.

Looking at him at all is fraught enough when you were once a teenage girl with a teenage girl's unwieldy crush. Those things are hard to vanquish.

"We saved St. Cyprian," Emerson says again, as if saying it enough will get through to Carol when as far as I know, *nothing* has ever gotten through to Carol.

"Maybe you did save the town," Felicia says, with her little sniff of disdain that I remember all too well. "But if you did, it was for your own gain and nothing more."

I want to say that at least that's better than doing it for attention, but I don't, because I'm evolved as fuck.

My sister's eyes narrow. And here's the thing that most people don't know about Emerson Wilde. She expends a lot of energy trying to convince the people around her to see the error of their ways. She embodies the notion that if you lead a horse to water in the right way, it really will drink.

But when she's done, she's done.

As her little sister, I know this better than anyone. So, I step in to stop the impending storm. "This seems straightforward to me," I say, doing my best to sound as if all this carrying on is a waste of energy, and I low-key resent it. And as if I'm some kind of authority here. "Emerson has some magic. Let her take the test again."

MY SUGGESTION IS MET WITH THE KIND OF silence that could freeze waterfalls in place.

Carol's gaze turns to me, and that's when I realize she hasn't really looked at me until now. Too busy playing games with Emerson, I guess—and I remind myself that it doesn't matter if nothing ever changes and everyone still treats Emerson like she's the only important Wilde sister. Because I don't live here and the way these people behave reflects on them and has nothing to do with me.

Not my circus, not my monkeys.

I have to chant that a few more times as Carol curves her mouth into a benevolent smile that makes my blood run cold. "And what about you, Rebekah?" she asks.

"Me?"

"You were warned not to use any witchcraft during your exile," she says, so very softly, and I don't know what Emerson sees when she looks at the creepy head of the Joywood, but all *I* see is my own impending death. I always have.

It's one of the reasons I knew I had power all along. And more, that I was a Diviner. I could see even the futures I didn't want to see.

It makes me shiver, though I fight it back, to realize the future I see in this woman hasn't changed at all since I was a kid. It's the same bleakness.

But I spread my arms wide and smile as if she didn't just threaten me. "And I haven't," I say. "I assume you already know that or I would have been called before you long ago. But this is home. Does participating in coven magic in St. Cyprian actually count as breaking the no-magic-in-exile rule?"

Clearly, I catch Carol off guard with this. It's far more satisfying than it should be. I like to talk a lot about *active recovery.* I like to consider myself clean. I put magic behind me, which, not to brag, I doubt any of the witches on this field tonight could do. I call myself *a cycle breaker* and I mean it.

But that old drumbeat of revenge still exists inside of me. The desire to take Carol Simon down every last peg and dispense some much-earned justice to the rest of her coven too, while I'm at it.

Collectively, they're responsible for almost all of my trauma. It would give me nothing but joy to return the favor, which I know is disordered thinking and sickness reasserting itself and so on. That doesn't make it any less true.

"I'm more than happy to head right back into exile, actually," I say as mildly as possible, as if I'm not emotionally invested in anything that happens here.

But I know I am, because an emotionally uninvested person wouldn't go to all the trouble I do to keep from looking over at Emerson, Ellowyn, or any of the rest of them. Including the glowering immortal witch standing almost directly across from me, the dark night draping itself around him like a cloak, not that I should notice or care.

Sadly, noticing him is an old habit and it makes me furious at myself, because I should know better.

I don't need to look at any of them anyway. I can feel their disappointment in me just fine. I should be used to it by now. I smile at Carol and remind myself that I'm not responsible for anyone's feelings but my own.

"Exile is always a choice," Carol agrees. But there's something in the way she studies me—in the way her dangerous, insidious magic swishes around me, looking for a way in—that tells me there's a catch.

Or maybe it's just that I know her and her cronies.

"You may choose it again, if you wish," she tells me. Then her eyes gleam with what is clearly malice. "After the pubertatum."

"I've already taken and failed the pubertatum," I point out, trying to sound anything but terrified. Because I choose my goddamned emotions and I choose *not* to be terrified by that stupid old test I couldn't pass when I was actually prepared for it.

"You were part of this." Carol waves her arm at the river flowing calmly before us, like it was all some childish prank here tonight. Not, you know, my sister sacrificing herself to save this stupid town that only cares about witch hierarchies and power. "You and Emerson exhibited power, according to your own accounts of what happened. You yourself suggested retaking the test, Rebekah." Carol studies me the way a scientist might study a corpse. A cold chill starts at my chest like *corpse* is a premonition. Maybe it is.

"I'm afraid we cannot let you back out into the world again without the proper test to check the extent of any abilities you might have," she says, sounding almost sorrowful, though I can see she's no such thing. "It wouldn't be safe. We must keep witchkind safe, Rebekah. You know as well as I do what happens when witches expose themselves."

No one says *Salem*. The pitchforks and hysteria are implied.

Still, I try to argue, because apparently I'm not that evolved after all. "You can't just—"

Carol sweeps her hand up and I cannot speak. She literally hexes me mute.

"You'll both be tested," Carol is saying, as if she regrets the necessity, yet thinks it's for the best. As if this is a *kindness*. "We'll investigate this river business. And we'll come to a verdict that, as ever, keeps witchkind's best interests at heart."

If you don't know Carol, you might think she sounds relatable and sweet. Humans think she's the best head of the town council they've ever had. But everyone here tonight is a witch, and we know who Carol really is.

"Then let's take this test," Emerson pipes up when Carol finishes speaking. Always ready to slay the dragon, no matter the cost.

"Em," Georgie says softly. Her voice is quiet, but there's a power in it. She's not the same shy Georgie I remember from high school. She lays a hand on Emerson's arm, and her gaze feels like the same kind of touch on me when it meets mine. "The adult test is different."

It's a warning.

Emerson's forehead wrinkles, and I imagine mine does too as we both look at Georgie. "The adult test?" we ask in unison.

Though all I actually do is move my mouth, with no sound coming out.

This is one of the things that used to keep me up at night. The *pettiness* of St. Cyprian witchcraft when it's *magic*. You could build whole worlds if you were Carol Simon, and instead you slither around hexing younger witches, just because you *can*.

Georgie eyes Carol, but then looks back to us. "There's recourse for when an adult spell dim witch finds some power. But it's much more difficult than the pubertatum. You'll need time to prepare. To study."

"You'll have until Litha," Carol says. *Litha* is what stuffy older witch types call the summer solstice. Then she intones, as I have heard her do many times before, "The longest day of the year, when we celebrate the light yet welcome back the darkness, and in so doing recognize the great gifts of witchkind in our young. The current class of fledgling witches will take their test then, as usual. You may take your adult test at the same time."

That last part is offered like Carol is doing us a great favor. As if the solstice isn't a mere two months away when the fledglings spend *their entire lives* getting ready for their supposedly easier test.

"I reject the entire paradigm of test-taking," I say, which is how I discover she's returned my voice to me. Everyone in the field stares at me. I smile. Okay, it's more of a smirk, and yes, I'm still slouching. "I mean, historically, I'm pretty bad at tests."

"What you were bad at was studying," Emerson says, frowning at me in all her big sister glory.

That brings back all kinds of memories, most of them ending in sisterly conflict, but *this is not high school*, I tell myself for the nine millionth time tonight.

"I'm sure your well-informed Historian will help you," Carol says in that slimy way of hers, complete with that insincere smile that's always been her calling card.

Then she turns her back, dismissing us. The Joywood disappear in an over-the-top display of light and power, but Carol's voice echoes after they've gone, like a thunderclap so loud it makes the trees shake.

Don't try to run away this time, Rebekah. We'll only have to drag you back.

I want to scream. Rage. Set something on fire like I may or may not have done the last time I failed—but I don't like to think about that night or what I did. I do know I want nothing to do with *tests.* With these witches messing with me, implying that I ran away like a baby instead of claiming the only path I could live with. With my overzealous, endlessly perfect big sister. With too much high school drama in the air and a brooding, unfathomable immortal like a cherry on top of a shit sundae.

I want to be as far away from St. Cyprian as I can be.

But as I stand there, fuming, Emerson comes over and twines her fingers with mine. Anchoring me here, maybe, but I can't deny that it comforts me.

Her hand doesn't feel the way I remember it, and I look down to see a ring on my sister's finger. Clearly an engagement ring, so I guess I have some catching up to do. I want to congratulate her, but something stops me. Because I have visions. I always have. Like all great Diviners, a universe of chances and paths not taken exists within me.

The light from Emerson's ring seems to blind me—but I know I'm the only one who sees it. The way I'm the only one who'll see what comes next. The magical alchemy of what a future might look like for Emerson.

Usually our shared blood—filled with generations of Wilde power no matter what the Joywood say—means my visions of Emerson come in pure and strong.

But something is wrong tonight. The visions come tumbling at me, too fast, and they're all…garbled. Cracked. There are too many lines, pictures, all scrambled. Nothing is clear. Nothing is *right*. It's neither good nor bad. It's nothing.

I'm used to visions coming at me full and clear, whether I seek them or not.

I focus on Emerson's ring. I try to see any one future line of events to completion. I even go so far as to whisper the old words I haven't dared say out loud in over a decade.

"I am the mirror, the Diviner, the crystal ball bright.

Scry me a future, let the path ignite."

But it's like a mirror that's been shattered into a million pieces. Static on an old TV. Something is wrong.

And even though I'm usually what's wrong in St. Cyprian, tonight I don't think it's me, or Emerson's future. It's... something else. Something bigger.

"I have the literature," Georgie is saying. "We can find out what kind of tests have been used before and practice for them, but there hasn't been an adult test in over a century. Firsthand knowledge would be better." Georgie's eyes dart over to the shadows. Over to Nicholas Frost.

Everyone turns to him, but his too-knowing gaze never leaves mine. Even if I was tempted—and okay, I'm tempted despite the fact I already know he'd betray me in a heartbeat, because he has—I wouldn't try to see his future. I have some concerns about the weight of his past. Anyone messing with visions knows you have to be careful. There's always the possibility they might move in more than one direction.

"I do not wish to take part in your study group, thank you," he says in that mocking voice. And something's wrong with me that I find it hot. Or maybe it's just the way he looks at me. Too long. Too dark. Like he already knows all kinds of futures I'm not ready to face. Like we're alone. "Welcome home, witchling."

Then, because he's Nicholas Frost, he disappears in a literal puff of smoke while a raven caws dramatically from the trees.

Show-off.

But for the first time, I almost feel like I'm home.

When everyone turns to stare at me—including Emerson right beside me, still gripping my hand—I smile like I planned this whole thing all along. Fake it 'til you make it, or something, because that's always been my philosophy and I'm still here.

"Well," I say, drawling out the single syllable because it's that or sob into the strange quiet that descends over us, here in the weird, fraught aftermath of the Joywood. And that whole saving our hometown thing we did earlier. And the mess that lies ahead of us, like it or not. "I guess we're having a high school reunion after all."

Around me, no one says anything, maybe lost in the horror of high school. Or possibly contemplating Nicholas's dramatic exit.

So I keep going. "I guess I need to collect my things if I'll be home through Litha," I say brightly. And maybe inside I'm tense like a fist, but to my sister and my old friends I'm going to keep on looking as cheerful as a daisy. My heart stutters over the *home* part, but I ignore it, along with the tears that threaten to sting my eyes. I will not let the Joywood steal my peace. And I will not show my soft underbelly in a field on a farm in Missouri, surrounded on all sides by my apparently as-yet-unburied past. Deep inside, I feel an old spark ignite. "Smudge won't care for being left alone in the wilds of Sedona."

Emerson's gaze flickers, a slight frown tugging the corners of her lips downward. "You still have Smudge?" She turns that frown at Jacob, who for some reason looks apologetic.

I remind myself that I'm a freaking *daisy* and smile. "Of course I still have her. Was I supposed to leave her behind?"

"The exiled and mind wiped aren't supposed to keep their familiars," Jacob says. Like he's reciting a rule book. Clearly perfect for Emerson in every way, and I'm suddenly remembering what it was like to go to school with all this perfectionism and overachievement.

Be a daisy, not a dick, I order myself. "Smudge is just your average house cat, Emerson." And thank the moon she isn't around to hear me say that.

Emerson blinks once but doesn't belabor the point before she smiles broadly. "You're cold. We're all tired. We'll all go home and regroup tomorrow."

As if I don't have a million complicated feelings about home. As if she's naturally in charge of all of us.

Emerson squeezes my hand, but she looks at Jacob. Where Emerson once only had room for St. Cyprian and leadership roles and community service and helping Grandma at Confluence Books, that ring on her finger suggests she now has space for an entire *man* she's going to share her life with.

If that's not evidence of change, I don't know what is.

But I also notice Jacob's subtle nod. There's a slight fidget of Emerson's hand, then the ring disappears.

Is it a secret? That doesn't make sense, but then again, the two of them are clearly having some kind of telepathic conversation the rest of us aren't in on.

Emerson reaches out for Georgie then, and Georgie for Ellowyn. Ellowyn clasps my hand tighter and smiles at me. I feel that smile like a key in a lock I didn't know was there. It's the same smile I remember from when we were little. Ellowyn smiling at me on the playground, just like this.

It feels like even if everything isn't going to be okay here, always a possibility with witches all over the place, we're okay again.

I'm more than a little shocked at how much it seems I need to know that.

We shoot up into the sky as if we're heading straight for the moon. Then we move over the river, and I catch my breath.

I used to be able to do this whenever I wanted. I assume I still can, though I haven't tried. Even the weakest witch can fly through a dark St. Cyprian night on their own. But I haven't *flown* in a decade.

Maybe there was a part of me that told myself I was making all this up. Or misremembering it. Maybe I had no choice but to tell myself that losing this wasn't torture.

Because flying again is sheer joy.

High in the sky, I can see Jacob's farm and the old cemetery where too many Wildes are buried, including my grandmother, who I can't bear to think about right now. I can see the two rivers that even humans agree cut through this part of Missouri and Illinois, but I can also see the third river that human maps claim never comes near enough to the other two for all three to mix.

But they do.

Our ancestors hid the real confluence when we settled here after Salem, because a confluence of three rivers means power, even to humans. Better to keep the real power to the witches who know how to use it well and let the occult-loving humans flock to places like Pittsburgh, where three rivers might meet but any power was drained long ago.

I haven't seen the three rivers that marked the first part of my life in a long time. Not from this angle. Not from up so high I feel like we're made of stars and the rivers underneath us are liquid silver.

Down below, St. Cyprian is spread out, a carpet of lights

set against the hills, the rivers, the marshland in the distance. Up here, I can't see the details of my hometown, though all its landmarks seem embedded deep inside me. From Nicholas Frost's falling-down house high on the bluff at one end, down along the cobbled streets past the brick buildings like my grandmother's bookstore, winding around to the house my ancestors built back when this was the great frontier.

Up here, in the dark, with the moon making tracks across the sky, I can admit that it's beautiful, my forgotten river town. And that part of it lives in me still.

Always, something in me whispers.

I find myself repeating the words my grandmother taught me long ago. *Time is mine until time takes me home.* It feels different now.

Because time really has taken me home tonight.

We're descending then, *whooshing* down from our impossible heights, and then we're standing in front of Wilde House. The others are talking as if this is all ho-hum and boring, flying around as we please, because to them it is. The same way it used to be for me.

It's funny, the little things you make yourself forget because that's the only way to move forward. Because if you don't move forward, you might drown.

That's how I feel as I stare up at my childhood home. It looms as large in real life as it does in my memories, or those odd haunted moments over the years when the past caught up with me no matter how fast I was moving.

The old house sits in its place at the end of Main Street—judging everyone who draws near. At least, that's how it always felt to me, forever on the outside looking in. It's all ancient brick and gleaming windows, elaborate trim and turrets, bay windows and flower boxes. Showy, some would call it. With great disdain, here where the local Midwest Nice culture forbids any direct commentary when a well-placed sniff will do.

I'm forced to accept that I've missed the passive-aggressiveness, elevated to an art form in these parts, and always by those who would describe themselves as humble homebodies at best. Felicia Ipswitch comes to mind.

I should follow my friends and sister inside. Georgie lives here. Ellowyn has decided to stay over. I should want to catch up with them, and Emerson too.

But it's too much.

The last time I was here, so were my parents. The last time I was here, my grandmother was alive. So sure I would make her proud.

Instead, I broke her heart. And my own.

But hearts mend. Forgiveness is a thing you can only give yourself.

I know this. I've spent years working on it. Still, I do not want to go into that house where my grandmother is not.

Emerson turns around. She leaves Georgie with Ellowyn as she comes and takes my arm again.

"You okay?" she asks.

"I just wish..." But that's a dangerous road to start down, in the middle of a very long night and me without so much as a pair of flip-flops. I settle on, "I miss Grandma."

"She's here," Emerson whispers. "When she needs to be."

I know she means that to be comforting, but the unfairness of it bites at me. I lost everything when I was exiled. I lost my grandmother that night, and then for good when she died a couple of years later. I've only felt her since then when Emerson pulled me back here—against my will, even in our dreams—when she was trying to figure out how to save St. Cyprian.

All this time, I've been pretending that Grandma was here.

That she was still here, right where I left her, in this town I wasn't allowed to come back to.

I don't know how to walk inside and face the fact that she's not.

There's a sob—maybe a whole lot of sobs—trapped inside me, but I don't intend to let it out.

I'm afraid that if I start, I won't stop.

I force myself forward. I try to tell myself that every step toward my old home is not a punishment in and of itself. I know Emerson will want to talk, to settle me in. But I can't. I just *can't.* And as we cross the threshold, I don't let myself look too clearly at anything. "I'm very tired," I say to Emerson. I don't look at her. I don't wait for a response.

I head up the stairs to the room where all these ugly feelings echo back at me the loudest, because they're the same ones I left here with.

Because this is where they came from.

I'VE LEARNED A LOT OF WAYS TO MAKE MYSELF fall asleep over the years. Ways that aren't magical but are still useful. Deep breathing. Finding my spiritual center. Certainly not contemplating dark, fathomless immortal eyes that spell nothing but betrayal and ruin…and too many heated dreams I pretend I can't remember.

Or scrutinizing every painful memory from my entire childhood and adolescence, over and over again.

But despite the noise in my head, I find sleep or it finds me. It's deep and strangely dreamless. It's only when I wake up the next morning that I realize that someone must have charmed the room for restful sleep.

Not someone, I correct myself. Emerson. I should be thankful. I try very hard to be thankful, because I choose what I feel.

I sit up in my old bed and look around. Everything I could want from my bungalow in Sedona is already here, neatly piled on the large table by the window with its stained glass in the form of the traditional witchy representation of the wheel of the year. Yet instead of the many symbols and words that are sometimes included, some ancestress of mine kept it simple. Just the suggestion of the wheel itself, with its spokes, unobjectionable to any human eyes that might see it from below in all its colored glass glory.

Smudge herself is curled up on my pile of clean clothes, looking like the outrageously fluffy, black stuffed toy she is not and never has been.

She blinks her yellow eyes open. *Kind of you to allow this* house cat *to tag along*, her raspy voice whispers inside my brain. She flicks her long black tail, a plume of floofy black. Because no, I was not supposed to be able to keep my familiar, but when I left here, so did Smudge. And she's been with me ever since.

Her choice.

Because even the most powerful coven in the world can't tell a cat what to do.

"Good morning and the sun's many blessings to you," I return in peak New Age hippie mode, ignoring her trademark grumpiness. "I suppose a 'welcome home' is in order."

Smudge stands and stretches. *It's about damn time.*

As if I've had any say in the matter. But she knows I made a life elsewhere because I had to, so I don't argue with her. We both chose our exile.

And despite what I suspect are my sister's fondest fantasies, being back in St. Cyprian doesn't mean I'm stuck here forever. I'm not Emerson. I won't be heading up any committees or spending every waking moment martyring myself to this thankless town. I'll pass the test, get my magic back, and then leave of my own volition.

I won't be chased away this time.

I get out of bed to find the sun is already warming up the room. It's proof that today's spring weather will do what it's meant to do. Bring the slumbering plants back to life. Make the green things grow as we march closer to summer. The Midwestern seasons are always so distinct. Even when they fall over each other trying to prove their dominance, they are fully and wholly distinguishable from each other.

I try to tell myself I haven't missed it. But there is something about knowing summer will come in with its heavy humidity, that the bright spring greens will deepen and darken. That the pastels of spring flowers will turn into the bright oranges and yellows of summer. And when all that's over, the leaves will turn and fall on the bricks, on the rivers, on Wilde House itself. And then winter will blow in, shaking the trees bare as they reach up to an impossibly blue sky made that way by the freezing temperatures that are not restricted to the dark.

I breathe in, then out, reminding myself that I'll be getting out of here before the worst of the summer heat settles in. No falling leaves and no winter wonderlands for me.

I remind myself I want it this way. That I chose it.

And that I will again.

I pad across the hardwood floor that generations of Wildes trod upon before me, and then kneel down in the center of the room while Smudge sits on one of the windowsills, cleaning her paws in a way that feels pointed. Because most of what she does is pointed. I ignore her.

The same rug is still right here in the center of the room. A great-great grandmother or some such ancestor braided it eons ago, weaving it with magic so it never fades, never thins. And better still, always hides what I want it to hide.

I pull back the edge of the rug and look at the wood planks beneath it. They look untouched, but I know better. It doesn't matter what tests the Joywood had me take, how little they thought my magic could do, I did have magic.

I did, I think fiercely.

And I still do. I've had magic all along, spells or no spells.

I close my eyes and take a deep breath. I hold my hands out and feel all the power that has been used in this room. You can cleanse it, try to erase it, but for a Diviner the echo of that power can always be felt.

If you know how. And though I've pretended I don't know how for a long time now, I do. Acknowledging that, finally, feels like its own homecoming.

"Reveal to me," I whisper, the words of the spell still so familiar no matter how little I've used them, *"what only I can see."*

The board before me twists, curls, and changes into a little door. I feel a rush of something inside me—relief, maybe? Recognition? I pull the knob and it opens easily. And there, beneath the floor, are all the things I once tucked away here. For a moment, I can only stare.

It's all still here.

I can accept, now, that I was worried my magic was so weak, so ineffectual, that someone would have stumbled upon this hiding place at some point. Though maybe the fact no one did has nothing to do with my abilities at hiding things and everything to do with no one caring to look for my hidden secrets.

What's worse?

I don't want to know, so I reach inside and pull out the box of treasures. The first is a ripped-out piece of notebook paper, where Ellowyn drew a particularly hilarious caricature of Felicia during a very boring detention period. Even all these years later it makes me bark out a laugh—the bulging eyes, dripping fangs, and terrible claws where the older woman's hands should be.

Beneath it there's a thick yellow thread from the scarf I was wearing when I received my first kiss. Kevin Gregory was not a witch, but he was an older boy who bussed tables at the Lunch House and flirted outrageously with all the naive teenage girls with daddy issues. Witch girls with daddy issues were *particularly* enthralled, not that Kevin knew the difference. But what's worse for an upstanding witch father from one of the oldest bloodlines in St. Cyprian than his daughter going around kissing unaware humans?

It's somehow both a pleasant memory and a painful one. Because I'm not sure anything I did ever really got through to my father. Except the one thing, there at the end.

But I push *that* intrusive thought away and focus on the rest of the trinkets. Other mementos to remind myself of various high school crushes and conquests. A friendship bracelet Ellowyn made me when we were kids. A sweet miniature incense holder Emerson gave me for my sixteenth birthday. A little spell book from Zander's mother, my aunt Zelda—then and now the only adult I could go to when no one else understood me. A birthday card from my grandmother that I hold for a moment, but don't let myself read. And so on. I considered these treasures worthy of hiding away forever.

That makes me smile.

The one thing that makes me pause is the ring that sits nestled at the bottom of the box. The gold shines as though it hasn't been tucked up under this floor for ten years. Instead of a jewel at its center, there's a tiny paper-white narcissus bloom—my birth month flower—encased in some kind of resin.

My grandmother gave it to me the day before my doomed pubertatum. Grandma loved flowers, plants, and herb magic. She had a green thumb, so her flower gifts were always beautiful, full of protection and her special kind of magic. An early birthday gift, she'd called the ring. I was sure it would bring me luck for my test.

But it didn't.

Because luck isn't real and magic might as well be a disease, I remind myself sharply. I put almost everything back in the box, shut it with a decisive click, then put it back under the floorboard. I stare at the plank for a moment, then shake my head.

"Let no eyes but my own,

Find this below."

The wood warps once again, the simple magic spell tingling through me. It's not strong magic, or much magic at all, and no doubt I'll be called to do far harder things. Like, say, saving the world, the way we did last night as our own little coven.

Still, doing simple magic feels good in too many ways I'm not prepared to dig into. Not cross-legged on the floor of my childhood bedroom on my first day back.

Smudge waits at the door with her yellow eyes fixed on me, though she could easily open the door herself. And I can practically feel Emerson's impatience echoing at me from downstairs, because she always did get up at the crack of dawn. On a sigh, I get myself dressed. The nonmagical way, because I actually *like* putting on actual clothes. That's revolutionary in St. Cyprian.

I like taking part in as many revolutions as possible.

I open the door and Smudge leaps out into the hall, straight for Ellowyn who's trudging toward the staircase. Her hair is rumpled, and she's wearing a colorful teacup-covered pajama set.

She crouches to scratch Smudge behind the ears, then grins up at me. "Seeing the past *is* generally my thing, but you being here in the present is weird as hell."

"I think the weird as hell is only beginning."

She straightens, still smiling. And though she doesn't say it—because she's Ellowyn, and she may be cursed to tell the truth but that doesn't mean she's keen on voicing emotional truths—I still *feel* all the ways she's glad I'm here.

I know it's not fair, but it doesn't weigh on me the way

Emerson's glad-I'm-here does. That's the difference between real sisters and chosen sisters. The real ones have all that family stuff between them, and whether anyone wants it or not, it always gets in the way. But the sisters we choose come without baggage. Where a blood sister might argue with a story you tell about your life, a best friend embellishes it.

I suppose it helps that we've stayed in touch this whole time. Testing the boundaries of what exile truly was. We didn't *magic* ourselves to each other or send little witchy messages. It was all very human. Texts. Phone calls. Emails.

I feel a pang of guilt at that, because the same can't be said about Emerson and me, but what could I do? I called once, right after I left, to check in and make sure she was okay.

But she wasn't my sister. She was what they did to my sister. She was so many parts of Emerson, but she couldn't remember the most important thing that had happened to us. I couldn't argue with her fake view of our world.

It broke my heart.

I hand Ellowyn the drawing so as not to dwell on all that old pain. She takes it and hoots out a laugh. "I can't believe you kept it." She clutches it to her chest. "I'm going to frame it for my shop."

"That'll win Felicia over."

"Nothing is going to win Felicia over," Ellowyn returns, then we wrinkle our noses at each other. Because Ellowyn can't lie, which means she's just announced that these next two months are already a little hopeless.

But Ellowyn links arms with me, a rare show of physical affection, and moves us toward the staircase. "This could be literally any morning from high school."

"Except today, praise Hecate, my mother won't be around for a rousing morning critique of my appearance." I sigh, only a little dramatically. "It makes me sad she's not here to enjoy the fruit of my facial piercing labors over the years. I bet she'd love them all."

We head down the stairs. "Men have pronounced Adam's apples," Ellowyn replies, in the way she does when she wants to tell a little white lie. But can't. "They have larger voice boxes that make the surrounding cartilage stick out more." She demonstrates a voice box with her hands. Then, when I laugh, she does too. "Your mother would hate your piercings with her whole soul."

And because she can say that sentence, physically, it means it's the truth.

This is not a surprise. I try to make that same perpetually appalled face that my mother has always worn naturally. Then I mimic her voice. "'Ladies, I am certain you do not mean to present yourselves in public looking like you have suffered a hexing.'"

Ellowyn laughs, and I keep up my impression of my mother all the way down the stairs. It helps me continue to ignore the house around me as we go. And all the ways not a damn thing has changed.

Including me.

HALFWAY DOWN THE LONG STAIRCASE, A LOUD knocking begins echoing through the house, the walls practically vibrating with it. And this is an old, sturdy house that has withstood centuries of river shenanigans and magical nonsense, so this means it's either a wrecking ball out there or someone is using a whole lot of unnecessary magic to announce themselves.

Ellowyn and I exchange a look, and even Smudge looks *almost* interested as she saunters for the door.

When Emerson doesn't come running to answer it, I shrug and move forward. I feel a little jolt as my hand skims over the dragon newel post at the bottom of the grand old staircase. I jerk my hand back because while it's hardly the first time that's happened, I used to think it was one of my mother's little land mines. Shocking the unwary so we would always stay on our toes in this house. It never occurred to me it was just…the post itself.

I stare at the dragon carving for a moment, but the knocking continues. Ellowyn beats me to the door and swears as she looks through the sidelight. "Maybe we can hide," she mutters.

"Why? Who is it?"

But I look out the window and see the answer myself, in all its horror. Especially at this hour.

Felicia.

"We could fly off to Tahiti," I offer.

"We *could*," Ellowyn says, but she clearly thinks I'm kidding. I know this by her rueful smile and also because she pulls open the door.

Felicia Ipswitch is standing on the front porch, looking as officious as ever and worse, holding a stack of white binders.

Hi, welcome to hell, I think. *All your enemies are here.*

"Rebekah. Ellowyn." She manages to say our names like they taste bad, then looks beyond us. Pointedly. I assume she's looking for Emerson and Georgie, or evidence of unsavory behavior that will convince her that Ellowyn and I are the delinquents she's always thought us to be. Both, probably. She continues to peer past us, but when we don't do anything but stare back at her, she lets out that *sniff*. "Here you are." She hands me a binder, then gives one to Ellowyn.

I'm not the only one who takes it automatically, but I hate myself for it.

"What is this?" I ask, but dread settles into my stomach at the sight of St. Cyprian High's familiar logo on the cover.

"It's your syllabus. Your work will begin in May if you have the faintest hope of readying yourself for Litha." Felicia makes it clear she has no such hope that I'll be ready for anything.

And still I laugh, because what I know is that laughing at bullies is one of the strongest weapons there is. Felicia, bully extraordinaire, is not moved to join me. I'm surprised that Ellowyn doesn't laugh along the way she usually does, but she's flipping through her much smaller binder. I decide not to give Felicia the satisfaction of opening mine.

Felicia sniffs again, then hands Ellowyn another slim volume like the one she's already holding. "You'll give this to Ms. Pendell."

"Will I?" Ellowyn returns, sounding like her old, insolent self. But she takes the second binder anyway.

"And you'll give this to your *sister*," she says to me, somehow making *sister* sound like *criminal*, which is hilarious when aimed at Emerson, of all people. Still, I notice Emerson and my binders are much thicker than Georgie's and Ellowyn's.

"You've been given a great opportunity here, girls," Felicia says sternly. *Girls.* When we are nearly thirty. "The Joywood have been kind enough to give you the time and space to prepare, to prove yourselves, little as some might think you deserve such consideration. *I* suggest that, for once, you two take that opportunity *seriously* and prepare for your test with the weight and gravity it deserves."

I flick my wrist, and the door slams shut in Felicia's face, leaving her huffing on the porch. "How about that for some weight and gravity," I mutter. I look over at Ellowyn, expecting a conspiratorial grin, but she's got her nose in the binder again.

I feel the faintest little trickle of foreboding, right down the length of my spine.

"It's like an assignment notebook," Ellowyn says, making a face. "A list of things we have to do as penance for our many infractions."

I look down at my binder, afraid to open it and find out why mine is thicker. Much thicker. Apparently, it turns out that proving you have magic when you're supposed to have none is *not* the boon you'd think.

Ellowyn is flipping through pages. Loudly. Then she makes

a *yelping* sound. "Holy shit. Rebekah, we have to go to Beltane *prom*."

I don't open my binder. I'm still stuck on the whole SCH logo on the cover, a symbol of the confluence I always thought looked suspiciously like a butt, like they *wanted* all that teenage sniggering. "Don't even joke about that."

"I'm not joking." She holds up her open binder and shows me the page. "It's listed in big, bold, underlined letters. 'For all who aided the exiled and mind wiped. Attendance *mandatory* to remind you of the importance of your place in the witch community.'"

I blink at the words, sure if I blink enough times it'll all go away. Or I'll wake up. But no. I can read the same words she does, complete with time and date. "I'm not reliving that horror. This is…" I struggle to find words beyond the renewed buzzing in my head. I expected, like, public hangings and blood rituals. Proper witch shit. Not reliving the torture of high school. "This is just petty."

"Yeah, funny how pettiness is damn effective in ruining my day," Ellowyn says darkly.

I'm forced to wonder if this is what keeps the Joywood on top around here. I spent years in exile turning over things like this in my head, wondering why the magical center of the world always seemed to devolve into petulance and spite and figured it was just people.

But now I wonder if the endless pettiness that is the Joywood's specialty isn't *despite* their power. The pettiness *is* their power.

I crack open the cover and begin to flip through my pages, and Ellowyn stands next to me, comparing. She's required to attend many of the same things I am—the hideous Beltane prom chief among them, to atone for her sins. But I have more things listed than she does—classes, practicums, all leading up to the grand pubertatum in June at Litha.

Worse, I remember all of this. It's exactly what they made us do as seniors.

Like...*exactly*.

I can only assume Ellowyn is spared the full scope of this humiliation because she already passed the test once. While us spell dim get double the punishment for being anything but.

"Looks like we're going back to high school," Ellowyn says, but then lets out a laugh. A bleak one. "Does that mean I have to dye my hair black again? I'm going to need to stock up on the eye makeup that makes me look like I'm bruised, I guess. I gave that up in celebration of my twenties."

I want to throw out my own joke in response to Ellowyn's, but I'm having trouble finding the humor here. This is meant to embarrass us. Humiliate us. Just because they can. At least if they wanted to kill me it'd feel like we were equals. Or at least like we were all adults.

Again, I think—if a bit distantly as I contemplate the horror of witch *prom*—that maybe that's the whole point.

But I really don't like it.

"You okay?" Ellowyn asks me warily.

I have no idea what face I'm making, but I can feel that dark black rage choke me. Worse, I recognize it. It's the same righteous fury that had me facing down the Joywood when I was seventeen, ready to prove to them exactly who I really was—and who Emerson could have been if Carol hadn't mind wiped her. Just like that. Cutting her down to size in a single, brutal second, not even waiting for the usual ceremony.

Emerson bustles in from the kitchen, followed by Jacob. He's holding a slim binder like Ellowyn's and Georgie's. His face is grim.

Emerson's expression is one of bouncing excitement. "Jacob

said Felix Sewell stopped by and brought him a binder that—Oh, is that mine?" she asks, practically rubbing her hands together at the prospect of the thick binder.

I hold hers out to her. "Apparently."

She takes it like it's a baby, smoothing over the cover and then opening it to gaze at the pages. She begins to flip through it—magically—frowning slightly like she's committing all the information to memory. Right now. She looks up at me, eyes bright and shining with excitement. "Isn't it great?"

"Great?" I echo.

Ellowyn just glares, as if too offended by the *smiling* to speak.

"It's a very clear to-do list of what we have to do to win."

"Em." Ellowyn shakes her head. "The enemy doesn't supply you the tools you need to beat them. It's almost certainly a trap."

Emerson looks wholly undaunted. "If we do everything to the letter, they can't punish us. It isn't about beating them." She considers, then amends. "Not necessarily. It's about proving we were right all along—not just to them, but to the next generation."

Now we are both staring at her as if she's lost her mind.

This is familiar ground, though. Maybe too familiar. Must everything feel like high school?

Except there's something to what she's saying that gives me that strange…disordered feeling. Like when my visions are fractured. I push the odd feeling away as Emerson waves a hand.

"We don't have to discuss it now, of course, but I think it's clear the Joywood can't go on. They're broken. Corrupt, maybe. At the very least they need some competition. Why not us?"

I can think of approximately twenty million reasons it

shouldn't be us, and especially not *me*, taking on the Joywood in Ascension—the ritual that decides the ruling coven. Ascension has always been a boring affair as much as I can recall, and the Joywood are never challenged. But I know that look in Emerson's eye. There's no talking her out of this current crusade, or any other wild idea she has, so we need to shift the topic. "And how do you feel about all this?" I ask Jacob, waving the binder at him.

Jacob clears his throat. "I think it's meant to embarrass us, so in that way, I think Emerson has the right of it. We shouldn't let it."

"And in what way does Emerson have the wrong of it?" Ellowyn demands. Earning a frown from Emerson and an uncomfortable look from Jacob.

"Well..."

Emerson glares at him, but he shrugs. "I agree with Ellowyn. They're not after helping us. They don't want you and Rebekah to prove you have power, to take your rightful places in witch society, or wield your magic openly. They'll find a way to make it not happen. This is—" he holds up his binder and shakes his head "—a distraction."

Georgie appears on the stairs, her curly hair in a messy red halo, wearing a thick, bright red robe with the bored-looking Octavius, her big orange cat familiar, following along behind her. She stops on the landing and blinks at us for a moment before she decides to come the rest of the way down. I note that she rests her hand on the creepy dragon post and clearly doesn't get a shock. "What did I miss?"

Ellowyn hands her a binder with far too much relish. "Felicia dropped this off for you."

Georgie looks intrigued at the prospect, but her smile dims as she opens it and begins to read. "This is insulting."

"But we can do it easily," Emerson counters. "I think we should look at it as an opportunity."

"An opportunity for what exactly? Abject humiliation?" I demand, wondering how my sister can be so...*herself* sometimes.

"Wait. If we all got one..." Ellowyn trails off.

As if she knows it's coming, when that's supposed to be my thing, she looks over at the front door as it flies open. I half expect Felicia, but it's Zander who storms in—and it is a whole storm. He's holding his own binder. He's also wearing black sweats and a black T-shirt that look like he slept in them. His eyes are bloodshot and a little wild, and his hair is a crazy mess. He looks more feral animal than the easygoing witch he pretends to be. "What the *fuck* is this?" he growls.

"I'll make breakfast!" Emerson offers brightly and then takes off toward the kitchen.

"I'll help," Jacob mutters. Georgie follows them, looking back at Zander once before disappearing. I make as if to go too, but Ellowyn glares at me and I stay put.

"I'm not going to Beltane prom," Zander belts out. "Someone must be drunk."

He doesn't look at Ellowyn when he mentions the prom, so I try not to either. But obviously all I can think about is what happened at Zander and Ellowyn's *actual* eighteenth-year Beltane. Which is still manifesting itself in all the ways they snipe at each other.

I push my free hand through my hair while Smudge does little figure eights between Zander's legs as if she'd like to comfort *him*, when shouldn't it be her job to comfort me? I sigh. "We should eat something. Let Emerson *rah-rah* us into complacency."

Ellowyn snorts. Zander does too, and again, they don't look

at each other. "Yeah, you're real complacent, Rebekah," he mutters. "You're known for that."

As if ten years hasn't changed a thing. Maybe for us it hasn't. Maybe it never will.

Ellowyn and I move in tandem toward the kitchen, Zander grumbling as he trudges behind us. When we get into the kitchen, Emerson is already magicking breakfast ingredients through the air. Jacob is acting as some sort of witch sous chef while Georgie sets the table.

I wish I could just be happy that we're all together. Instead, I feel full up on dread. I only *glanced* at that binder and I already want to forget this whole thing. Especially with a St. Cyprian High Beltane prom hanging over my head like a guillotine from hell.

Emerson murmurs spells, and as she does, a perfectly appointed breakfast begins to arrange itself on the old, scarred table where I used to sit and watch my grandmother weave baskets for her flowers with spells that made the air brighter. But I'm not ready to let myself think about Grandma just yet.

When Emerson sits down, she's so pleased with herself I can't help but smile. Then I remember that magicking a whole meal must feel completely *new* to her, still. Because it's only been a little while since she found herself. I feel the enduring ache of what the Joywood have done to us all over again. And maybe Emerson and everyone else sat here and had breakfasts while I was gone, but not like this. Not with magic, not with me.

The Joywood stole even something as simple as breakfast from us.

They stole *us*.

Somehow we're here anyway—the way we should have been all along—and it makes me think there's more hope to be found than there seems in the whole humiliation of it all.

I frown down at the binder in my lap and the offensive *St. Cyprian High* butt lettering, and think about Emerson wanting to prove to *everyone*, not just the Joywood, who we are. With a little revolution thrown in, just for fun.

"I don't get why I'm being dragged into this," Zander is saying in the same cranky way, loading his plate with enough food to set a bear up for several winters of hibernation.

"You've been a part of this from the beginning," Ellowyn retorts, using the sharp-edged athame she always carries on her hip to slice an apple. Clearly *at* Zander. "One could even argue you and Jacob started it, what with the whole hounding people about the imbalance in the rivers and everything else the past few years."

He scowls at her, but he doesn't argue. Instead, he nods at the offending binder he threw beside his plate. "Why waste their time slapping us down with pointless bullshit?"

"They don't think enough of us to pull out the pitchforks?" I offer. "Or even rustle up a decent mob?"

"I don't think that's true." Georgie cups her mug of coffee and looks like she's filled with less rage and more rational clear-thinking than anything I have going on. "This is a lot of performing if they really think that little of us. The binders. The delivery. The obvious attempt at humiliation, treating us like we're still kids. Is it really all that different than the stocks? The point is to embarrass—not just for us, but to prove to everyone all the ways they shouldn't cross the Joywood."

"It's performance with a purpose," I mutter. But it's more than embarrassment. It has to be. Emerson and I have broken the most sacred of witch laws.

"They don't want us to win, that's clear," Jacob says. "So whatever this is supposed to do, it isn't to *help* us."

"We can't just think about us. About how it feels for us. We have to think about this globally. They're performing *looking* like they're helping us," Georgie adds.

I think on that and the words seem heavy with importance. I can't move past them. It's about how this *looks*. It's about keeping up appearances. That means it's also about complacency. Around the Joywood. And maybe within us too.

"They want us back in high school," Zander throws out. "Like we're teenagers under their thumb all over again."

He's right, but there's something more to what he's saying. I frown. All that static in my head, all those fractured pieces—it's like they're still inside me. Trying to find purchase. Wanting me to somehow rearrange them. I place my hand on the binder, the Joywood's magic all around it, and try to *see*.

But I can't, and my head begins to throb. It's so loud it drowns out everything else. Beside me, Ellowyn puts her hand on my shoulder. She must say something to Jacob, because he reaches around her and gives my back a little pat and *poof.* The pounding inside me stops, and my head gets blessedly quiet again.

I force a smile. "Thanks." He nods.

"I for one look forward to my mother marching down to the school and giving Felicia a piece of her mind the first time Felicia decides to call me a half-wit again," Ellowyn says. She's smiling, likely at the memory of her mother barreling into the school with *actual flames* shooting out of her eyes. Ellowyn certainly didn't get her temper from the ether. "You know she'll be only too happy to reprise her role."

It's something about the image—both what happened then and how it might happen now, ten years later—that begins to whirl inside me like magic. Like *seeing.* "They want us back the way we were," I say, some of those pieces starting to stitch together, maybe. Something finally makes sense inside me, and it feels like a gift. "Powerless. Afraid. Humiliated.

So that everyone in St. Cyprian is on board with whatever they do to us."

"And Emerson wants us to *let them*," Zander says darkly. "Because she likes her binder."

"I don't want to *let them* do anything," Emerson replies steadily. "But I'm also not afraid of their little games. Or their tests. Or what people think. *We* stopped the flood." She takes a bite of cinnamon roll, but then continues. Because of course she continues. "Also, I could put together a *way* better binder. In my sleep."

I think about games and tests, and Emerson. Who was the perfect student back then and will be again now, no doubt. Who always went above and beyond. Who did everything that was asked of her and then some.

And who failed anyway, just like me, who did...none of that.

Now instead of just hanging us for treason, they want us to go back to the place where they won their unfair fight—where they wiped her mind and I ran away into exile. Because we couldn't *prove* what we both knew then. Everyone accepted that the adults knew more than the kids, the teachers more than the students. That those in power always knew more than their subjects.

Ellowyn always says that people like things simple.

But it's more than the fact that we couldn't prove ourselves ten years ago. That the Joywood didn't *let us* prove it. Not to them. It's been pretty clear to me for a long time that *they* know exactly what Emerson and I are capable of and what powers we've always had.

What they really didn't want was us proving that to *everyone else.*

Because that would also prove that the great Joywood

coven, who know all and see all, were completely wrong about the Wilde sisters.

For our entire lives.

And they can't have *that.*

"Emerson," I say. My visions are fractured and still don't make sense, but there's something in them. Something about being here after ten years of a break from St. Cyprian that lodges the idea inside of me. So deep, so true, I have to say it out loud. "Did it ever occur to you that we *didn't* fail the pubertatum?"

EMERSON'S EYEBROWS DRAW TOGETHER. "WHAT do you mean?"

"We have magic, Em. I always knew it. And look at you—whipping up breakfasts and ghost power points. Killing *adlets*." The scariest monsters in all the fairy tales we were ever told as kids. The ones that aren't supposed to be real but she, the spell dim disappointment who earned her mind wipe, fought them off anyway when they attacked her last month.

She shakes her head, but she doesn't look as certain as she usually does. "It was the adlets and their attack that awakened my power, and then Jacob and I got together and that cemented it." She looks over at him, but he's frowning too.

"Do you really think that you just came into your power? Randomly?" I ask.

"It wasn't random." She blows out a breath, but it doesn't sound the least bit steady. "It's a Confluence Warrior thing. That's how the book made it sound."

"If all of that power was in you all along, why didn't the

Joywood try to help you?" I ask, reasonably enough. I think. When I didn't even know this argument was simmering inside me. "I've always seemed to have as much magic as anyone else. And enough to help beat back a flood in the here and now. Why didn't they see that back then? Why wipe your mind and exile me?"

Emerson is blinking too much. "Because that's the law."

But she doesn't sound sure.

And no one else is eating any longer.

"It's divide and conquer," I say into the quiet, to all those stares. "A divided house cannot stand and all that. It's a *performance*, so everyone believes the Joywood have our collective best interests at heart. But what if they *don't*? And never have. They can't have us *challenging* them, can they? No one ever has. Isn't that what we're taught in school?"

There's an expression I recognize on my sister's face. "Were you actually listening during history class? That one time?"

But I don't take the bait. "We're supposed to believe no one stands against them because they're just that benevolent and good. *Are* they? They're sending us back to high school. Humiliating us. Belittling us. Playing their little mind games on us. And it's not like this is the first time. We believed them when they said we had no power as kids—everyone in town believed them. Our own *parents* believed them. Now, in addition to growing up as supposedly powerless witches, the objects of ridicule in this town, we've spent the past ten years paying *their* prices, not our own."

Silence descends around the table. It's not the censuring kind. I can tell everyone is filtering back through their memories, wondering if I'm right. If they fooled us back then. Lied to us. Took advantage of us.

I don't have to wonder.

There's not one part of what I've said that feels fractured or blurry to me. I *know* I'm right.

"Just what is it they think we can do?" Georgie asks. Her voice is raspy, and then she clears her throat. "If they want to strip your power and punish you again—and all of us, too—there has to be a *reason*."

"Can't it just be that they're assholes on a power trip?" Ellowyn asks, chomping on her apple irritably.

"This seems like a lot of work if there's no ulterior motive," Emerson says, clearly considering. "We're threatening." She looks back at me. "Specifically us. There are plenty of young witches—powerful or not—who they haven't wiped or exiled. It's something about *us*. We've always been threatening to them."

I don't have any interest in forming *covens* or participating in Ascension like Emerson, but this all makes me think she'd have a chance. A real chance to beat the Joywood. Why else would they care?

But before we can worry about what we might do in the future or figure out what happened in the past, we have to focus on the present. Last time, we accepted the Joywood's pronouncements because we didn't expect them. Everyone else accepted them because it seemed to follow the law, because we'd been *set up* to look like lifelong weaklings with no real power. Emerson and I were silly enough to believe that we could show the world they were wrong by passing our pubertatum. We thought it would be fair. That there were no decks stacked against us.

This time we know better. *All* the decks are stacked against us.

"We have to go back to high school," I say, trying not to wince. "Not to prove that they were wrong about us, but to beat them at their own game."

Zander lets out a long sigh that matches the pinched look on Ellowyn's face.

But Emerson, being Emerson, grins. She looks around the table at each of us. "And once we do, we can build a future that looks the way *we* want."

I know it's getting ahead of ourselves, and I know the future Emerson and I want isn't the same at all, but I can't help but smile back at her and all her optimism.

Because if I have to be home, might as well make it a home I don't hate.

We finish our breakfast, and there's much discussion of the differences in our binders. How much school Emerson and I will be required to attend, while our friends—the accomplices—only have to appear for the more social events of the season.

In so many ways, it's like the last ten years don't exist. Like I've been here, right here, all along.

Except it's so clear we're adults now. With jobs and responsibilities and, most notably, without my parents here to nitpick our every move. Jacob leaves to go take care of his farm chores. Zander mutters about getting some more sleep before his afternoon shift at the ferry and night shift at the bar.

And once they're gone, like she's been waiting to broach the subject until they left, Emerson turns her gaze to me. "Once you get ready, we'll go see Frost."

Just the name of my immortal makes little pricks of sensation break out deep inside. *Not* my *immortal*, I lecture myself, though the teen girl within disagrees. "Why would we be going to see Nicholas, ever, let alone at this ungodly hour?"

"We're as familiar with the pubertatum as everyone else is, but we failed last time." Emerson's voice trips on the word *failed* just like my heart did on the word *home* last night. "And

I doubt the Joywood will be teaching us what we need to know in these classes. So, we need help."

"A lot of help," Georgie agrees.

"If anyone can prepare us," Emerson continues, clearly her plan and her mind already made up, "Frost can."

"Nicholas is not the friend you seem to think he is, Emerson. He told you no last night." I'm careful to keep my tone even. And not at all as intense as I actually feel about my immortal nemesis. I look at Ellowyn, because surely she'll back me up. She usually does.

Ellowyn rubs her palms over her face. "I don't trust that arrogant bastard as far as I can throw him. No one becomes immortal for good reasons."

"But?" I supply for her, because I can feel the *but* lingering there, and it's irritating enough to poke at.

Ellowyn's gaze holds mine. "But he brought you home when we needed you. Even though he said he wouldn't."

"And he helped in the flood ritual," Georgie adds, as if she feels *compelled* to be fair. "We needed everyone. Like it or not, he's part of this."

I want nothing to do with him. Despite the reaction I always have to him. But I also know that going along with Emerson's plan will be much, much easier than fighting it. I sigh, and Ellowyn smiles at me, because I'm sure she knows where my mind is going.

We did a lot of giving in to Emerson back in the day, because it was easier. And she was often, annoyingly, right. Apparently none of that has changed either.

"All right," I say, trying to sound as if I've come to a place of peace with this decision even though I really, really haven't. "We'll go ask the ancient immortal, known for offenses great and small against all of witchkind, for his charitable help. I'm sure that's on offer."

Emerson only smiles, but then, she probably knew she'd win either way. "Do you want to go get ready? I'll put some coffee in a thermos for you."

"Oh, I'm ready. And I don't do caffeine. I've transcended the need for artificial stimulants."

"But…" Emerson presses her lips together and looks at me as I stand there, leaning against Ellowyn's chair. She doesn't say anything, but she doesn't have to. I'm more than familiar with my older sister's judgments.

She is not reacting to my deliberately assy comment about caffeine, which isn't even necessarily true. At the moment, what she does not approve of are my baggy sweatpants and the cropped sweatshirt I'm wearing that shows off the silver hoop in my navel.

I sweep a hand down the front of me. "I'm comfortable, and comfort is an important element of learning." I smile fondly at her, and it's only slightly put on. "I realized some time ago, Emerson, that societal expectations about what I should wear often chafe against my desire to be comfortable within myself. I've learned to value my own comfort first and foremost."

Emerson nods along. "I appreciate that," she says firmly. "It's very evolved."

I incline my head. "Just trying my best to be authentically me."

I say that partly because it's true. I do try to do that, generally speaking, because there's only so much authenticity a witch pretending to be human can claim on any given day. But the other reason I say it is because it will annoy my sister.

Bonus: that is also me being pretty freaking authentic.

Her nod at that looks a little more forced. "But maybe you want to grab a notebook or your laptop?" Because she just can't help herself, older sister that she is. No matter how she knows I'll balk at being told what to do.

I let my smile go saintly. "My mind is the only tool I'll need."

Emerson smiles back at me, but I can tell her teeth are gritted. Just like old times. Because a girl can love her sister, but is it really love if you don't also want to poke at her until she screams?

I glance at Ellowyn, and though she's not grinning as widely as she might have done when we were seventeen, a corner of her mouth is curled up in amusement.

"We should go, then," Emerson says briskly. "I have to open the store at nine."

Somehow, I forgot about the store. Confluence Books. Not just my grandmother's bookstore, but a building that's been owned by women in our family going back generations. Emerson always got into studying and memorizing those women. She could likely recite our family tree with absolutely no prompting.

I never could keep all the Sarahs and Marys and Rebeccas straight. I was happy to know they existed, that I might have been cut from the same cloth. But the bookstore—as a building or business—never called to me the way it called to Emerson.

You are my two sides of the same coin, Grandma always said. *First of the year, last of the year. Joined, destined. But that doesn't mean you're the same, or should be.*

I remind myself that never, in my whole life, did I think my future included me staying here. Much less working in a small-town book shop in the Midwest, in a place so out-of-the-way and unheard-of that I never tell people I'm from here. I just say St. Louis. Most coastal types find that hard enough to fathom.

This was never for me, this tiny little life, and I knew it from the start.

So there's absolutely no reason for me to feel sad that I'm not part of that long tail of Wilde women who inhabit the Confluence Books building in town, all brick and history. No reason at all.

We say our goodbyes, then Emerson is bustling me outside into the cool spring morning. She makes a little hand motion, and I know she's sending off some little magic love message to Jacob.

I don't want to feel sad, so I grin at her. "Save the town. Get engaged. All in a day's work for Emerson Wilde."

Her mouth curves and I don't know the look on her face now. It's soft and kind of sweet. It makes me want to smile myself, just as softly, even though I'm walking down Main Street in my own personal, cobbled hell.

"It was a long time coming," she says in a quiet voice that matches her expression.

"Why did you make your ring disappear?"

She blinks as if she's surprised I noticed. "Well." She takes an uncharacteristically long time to speak as she looks down at her bare hand. "So much is happening, and you're back, and I'd like to enjoy telling everyone. So I just thought... we'd wait."

"For what?"

Again she pauses, but this time she studies me while she does. I don't know if I can read her mind or if I just know her so well. She's giving *me* a chance to settle in, presumably without any more changes. She's giving everyone a chance to be happy to see *me*, and vice versa.

It's *for me*, and I hate it.

"Emerson," I say, trying to sound all the things I'm not in this moment—at peace, calm, *one* with what's happening to me, and in no way a sulky teenager. "Congratulations. I'm happy for you both."

"Thank you," she says, marching forward, still so...*Emerson*.

It releases that hard grip on my heart, just a little. I swing my arms more than necessary and question why I thought I needed to feel the cold morning breeze all over my abdomen. I look up at the bluff before us as we walk and tell myself the sudden chill I feel is my dedication to the crop top, nothing more.

That's not entirely true. I can see Frost House sitting there at the top of the bluff, perched so it can look down on the town and the rivers and probably the whole world. It has the glamour to end all glamours on it, making it look like the sort of disreputable, falling-down Victorian that scary Halloween movies are made about. Everyone knows that the immortal likes it to stand there like a festering eyesore. No one knows why.

I don't want to think about him. Or face him. At all. Here on these magical bricks of my hometown where the bricks aren't just cute, they also stand as a safe space for any and all magical beings.

Ten years of being away hasn't changed any of it. Ten years of Emerson not knowing hasn't changed anything for her either, it seems. Except...

"Do you ever feel..." The words come out before I can think better of them.

"Do I ever feel what?"

There are a thousand things I want to ask her. A thousand more I want to know that I don't know how to ask. I settle on the most obvious. "Ten years were stolen from us."

Emerson's expression goes dark. It surprises me, the strength of the bitterness I see on her face. "That's not a feeling. It's the truth. That's what they did."

"But you were here." I can't help but point out the difference. Maybe she didn't know what happened to us, but she wasn't an exile.

"I was. And I wasn't." Her eyes narrow as we reach the stairs in the hill that will lead us up to the fake eyesore that is Nicholas's mansion—because underneath that witchy glamour is a glorious, immortal-worthy mansion. *He* would never live rough. "I'll never let them take anything away from me again, no matter if they think they're doing the right thing."

Do they think they're doing the right thing? I wonder. Or are they, for all their magic and years, just like humans. Absolute power corrupts absolutely and all that. It's a tale as old as time.

We're walking up the steps that seem to grow in height and number as we go, slowing our progress until I'm nearly out of breath by the time we reach the top. And even though there's no way anyone can sneak up on an immortal witch like Nicholas Frost—something I know from personal experience—the glamour is still in place now that we're standing before it. Wheezing.

Up close, it looks even more like a haunted house.

Inside, I feel a kind of ticking. That restlessness that's chased me all over the country, most recently to Sedona. I was thinking it was time I headed around the globe, but the Joywood intervened.

I glare at the rotted-looking front porch. I note the fine touches of spooky mist and a potential incoming storm in the sky directly above it. *Only* in the sky directly above it.

"You can't accuse the guy of subtlety," I point out. "Why not just put up a neon sign that flashes A WITCH LIVES HERE? It's basically the same thing."

"When I was spell dim and came up here, I didn't think *witches*," Emerson says, and she says that in such a matter-of-fact way that I wonder why I've never *really* thought about what a vile term that is. *Spell dim.* I didn't like it when people said that's what I was. But I was sure they were wrong, so that was different. It actually wounds me to hear Emerson call *herself* that. It makes me want to...break things. Like this whole town.

"It was just unsettling. I never wanted to linger, despite the fact there's such a pretty view from up here. It just felt wrong. I think the haunted house thing is amped up for witches."

"I almost admire the lengths he's willing to go to for a *fuck you,*" I say, and I mean it. "And the commitment to keep it going."

"He's had a lot of practice, presumably." We grin at each other. Then she holds her hand out to me. "I can tell you that it takes a lot of effort to make the glamour fall. Say the words with me. Because our magic is here, Rebekah." She spreads out her free hand. "And here." She points to her heart, then mine.

I wish I knew how to resist that simple order, but no matter how clean a girl gets herself in human Narcotics Anonymous circles, there are some addictions that come with the thorny twists of family, of prophecy. Of who I really am.

"Reveal to me, what I should see," I say in time with Emerson.

She's right. The magic is deep within us. Unlocked at last for her, untamed in me. But our magic twining together is beautiful. It's that elusive peace I'm always seeking. Bright and golden, like hope and love and joy threaded together in goodness.

If we'd known all along we could do this, even with something as simple as this unmasking spell, what else could we have accomplished?

In the echoing glory of it all, the house's glamour falls, shimmering away into the April sunlight.

Instead of the skeleton of an old river Victorian, there is now a gleaming, stately brick three-story with ornately carved trim and rounded windows. Below the house is the river, flowing lazily toward the confluence, looking particularly pretty this morning.

Probably because we took the darkness out of its center.

Emerson and I look at each other. For all the ways we were sisters, did spells together, spoke our own languages, and accepted our grandmother's gifts, never has our magic *twined* like that before. We're glowing—her eyes a bright, astonishing gold.

"Wow," she says.

I can't speak at all.

Then there's a *noise*, and we both turn toward it.

6

NICHOLAS FROST STANDS THERE IN HIS DRAMATIC doorway with that ridiculous overcoat that flutters in his own wind like a cape made of weather.

Scowling, obviously.

It only makes him hotter. "Somehow I knew, no matter all I've done for you Wildes, that you'd keep turning up here to destroy my peace."

I think, *done* for *us Wildes or done* to *us?*

"Both, witchling," Nicholas says to me, out loud, though I know I didn't actually *speak aloud* to him. "It will always be both."

Emerson gives me a confused look, but I pretend I don't see it.

Luckily, Emerson has bigger fish to fry. Doesn't she always? "Good morning to you too. I'll ask you to pardon us. I'm sure that after last night's display you were tired and needed some rest," she says soothingly.

I think, *because you're very, very old*, and my reward is a twitch of one of his very dark, very acrobatic brows.

"But surely now that you've had some time to recuperate, to rest and regroup, you have to realize that the only reasonable thing for you to do is to tutor us. The Joywood certainly don't have our best interests at heart."

Nicholas's eyebrows get a workout with every word Emerson says. *Rest*, *recuperate*, and *regroup* seem to cause him the most agitation.

I want to grin at Emerson, who, once, I would have assumed doesn't know what she's doing. But maybe I didn't give her enough credit back then.

"And you think I do?" Nicholas asks.

Emerson studies him. "Yes. I do."

"I don't help, little Warrior. I'm an ancient, powerful creature, more myth than man. Obviously I have better things to do."

But he's standing here, having this conversation. Which is odd, as I know I wouldn't be anywhere near this place or this conversation if I didn't have my sister dragging me into it. What's his excuse? He could easily stay locked up in his immortal mansion, surrounded by the glamours he likes best—like moats or castle walls or giant, hideous spiders if he's feeling gothic—and never address us at all. He certainly has the power.

I have more power than you can possibly imagine, comes his voice in my head. And if voices have a taste, his makes me think of the sea. That immense. That all-encompassing.

That salty.

Surely, continues that voice, *you should already know this.*

"You have nothing better to do. I'm not sure you have anything to do at all." Emerson is shaking her head as if that makes her sad, personally. "Or you wouldn't be camped up here, year after year. Generation after generation."

"On the contrary, Em," I hear myself say, though I know I shouldn't. Humans shouldn't poke bears and witches shouldn't poke immortals. Everyone knows better. Then again, *shouldn'ts* have never been my strength. "I think he likes watching it all burn."

His mouth doesn't curve, exactly. I'm not sure what it does to signal a certain kind of amusement.

In my head, that big voice sounds like silk as he asks, *and you don't?*

Speaking of burns, that one hurts. And I walked right into it.

He doesn't sound any different out loud. "And if I help you, what—pray tell—is in it for me?"

"It's the right thing to do," Emerson says, because if my sister has a fatal weakness it is this. She can't get her head around the idea that some people don't want to do the right thing, even when it's presented to them on a silver platter. Some people don't care. Some people just want the platter so they can turn it for a profit.

But I speak this language. Fluently.

What wouldn't *you do to get what you want?* I demand where only he can hear me, and it's surprisingly easy to slide past ten years' worth of walls I put up to keep myself from slipping like this. *We both know you don't care about what's right. Or little, piddling things like common decency, friendship, or the truth.*

His gaze meets mine again, and I know it's pointless to hide physical reactions to someone this powerful, but that doesn't make it any less embarrassing that every last atom of me reacts. Just to his intense *attention*.

And not with the awe and fear and horror that a normal

witch would feel for him. All I feel around him, all I've ever felt around him, is this *heat.*

He flicks his gaze back to Emerson. "There is nothing either of you could offer that would entice me to be involved in this little farce. It will inevitably end with both of you turned into stones to mark the cemetery, as a warning to all."

Why not just turn us to stones yourself? I ask him, hoping I sound as nonchalant as he looks. *Why drag it all out into a drama?*

He looks amused, and inside my head, I hear his laughter.

I feel it. Everywhere.

I promised you long ago that I would take my time with you, Rebekah. Did you forget?

I haven't forgotten a single thing about him, and I tried my hardest.

I don't tell him that, but he knows. Of course he knows.

It will take as long as it takes, he intones grandly.

"There's a variation of a theme here. You say no. You help anyway," Emerson is saying. "Do you need a direct invitation? Fun fact—it's already official. You're part of our coven. No need to hide yourself away, alone."

For once he actually looks interested. Mildly. "Are you accusing me of being lonely?"

Emerson beams.

"You need a soul to be lonely, Emerson," I say.

This is a mistake, because his gaze is on me again, then. Dark blue and dangerous. So dangerous. And something deep within, somewhere in all that magic chaotically rambling around inside of me, sparks to life.

I have missed this. And worse, him.

This realization is absolutely mortifying.

"I wonder what you, of all people, know about souls," Nicholas says silkily, like he knows my deepest secrets. Because, of course, he does. "Should we find out?"

I feel certain that we should not. I wish I'd kept my mouth shut—a common wish I never manage to grant myself. I work instead at building those walls around me, brick by brick, made up of memories he can't access.

Witches call it shielding. I call it boundaries.

"I think you know that I won't stop." Emerson manages to make her voice sound both tired and indefatigable at once as she gazes at him. "You know I'm happy to make two months feel like a thousand immortal forevers."

And then she smiles again. Merrily.

I am beginning to understand how she ended up running the St. Cyprian chamber of commerce.

"Finally a compelling argument," Nicholas murmurs. "To get rid of you."

He doesn't move. He's just standing there with the cloak and the drama like he plans to stay like that forever. Like he already has. But he's considering this, I can tell. He's here. He's still not smiting us where we stand.

Or throwing us off his property, which I also know he can do. With a literal snap of his fingers.

He can feign indifference—I know all the signs—but he is not indifferent, no matter how he wants to be.

Join the club, immortal.

A corner of his mouth kicks up. *I do not* join *things.*

But he's looking at Emerson. "Before I can even consider helping you, there are some basic requirements you have already failed."

"Name them," Emerson says at once, already frowning because he said her least favorite word. *Failed.*

But he doesn't look at her. His gaze rakes up and down my entire body, as if he can see everything I've ever done or ever been. I don't shudder, though I want to. I can see by the way his gaze lingers at the silver hoop in my nose, then in my navel, that he's as traditional and boring as all the rest.

You are an endless disappointment, Nicholas.

I am endless, he agrees. *But what are you? A sad little teenage rebellion of one—again?*

Ouch.

"Requirements and failure," I say out loud, but I'm smiling. I'm going full-on daisy, immune to judgmental *looks* and private, rude comments. Even the ones that leave marks. "Do tell."

He suddenly looks something like…lazy. "Any witch—powerful or otherwise—should know it isn't wise to mar one's body with metal and ink."

I don't move. Or react, out loud or privately. Even though I would have happily sold my own teenage soul if he would ever pay that kind of close attention to my body. "How sad for you, Nicholas, to be in thrall to what's wise over what's best for you." I smile serenely. "I'm sure you have fond, personal memories of feudal systems, but in my world, a woman has agency over her own body and choices."

"You aren't in your world. You're in St. Cyprian. You've been sentenced to take the most difficult test known to witchkind." He matches my condescending smile with his, except his feels like knives. "I should know. I created it."

"Exactly my point," Emerson says, clearly trying to shift Nicholas's attention from me. I'm sure she's trying to protect me. Why does it bother me that she feels the need? "You know it. You made it. All roads lead to you. So help us."

His dark gaze gleams. "And how would I help you?"

She looks impatient. "Teach us what we need to know. You helped us before. Why is this different?"

"I'm not going to sit here and tutor you like Gil Redd, droning on in one of his cramped high school classrooms," he says instead of answering the question. It makes me think there must be something…important about the answer he won't give.

But then I'm considering Gil Redd, the Joywood's Praeceptor. Nicholas isn't wrong. The man could bore drying paint.

"How did you do it back in the Crusades?" I ask, not deferentially. I don't actually know if he was cavorting around then, but why not? The way he looks at me makes me feel entirely too many things I shouldn't, and I only wish I'd asked about Byzantium.

Careful. His voice is like smoke, curling inside me. *Be certain you actually want the answers you seek.*

"I was thinking more a study guide," Emerson says. "But sure. Epic battles could work."

Nicholas seems to look at me a long time. I pretend I don't notice. I think about Smudge grooming herself. The time she takes. The attention she gives every last spot on each of her paws.

We shield any way we can.

He flicks a hand. One very large, heavy-looking book appears in midair, then plummets. It lands with a thud on the porch. Neither Emerson nor I flinch at that, though it's a close call on my part. I glare at the book and the cloud of dust that puffs up all around it. It looks like the sort of thing Georgie would fall in love with at first sight.

Me, on the other hand? Hard pass.

"There's your study guide," Nicholas tells us, as if he's being helpful, which is a good sign that he is not being anything of the kind.

Emerson's mouth firms, but I can tell she considers this a win. I'm more stuck on how it looks a lot like homework.

"I suggest you study." Nicholas shakes his head sadly, as if we've already proven ourselves failures all over again. "If it comes to it, I suppose I could offer a few practice round tests. You'll probably fail."

"Unlikely," Emerson replies, and even I have to appreciate her tenacity—particularly when it's not aimed at me.

"This all feels a lot like Joywood propaganda," I say, because I am never more recklessly confident than when I'm charging straight into my own peril. "For all we know, he's in it with them. We already know we have all the magic they claimed we didn't. Why should we prove it to them or anyone else?"

Nicholas's gaze slides to mine.

And the ground beneath me seems to shift. Maybe even buckle, like this is California when I know very well it's not. We make our own fault lines here in the Midwest.

It's him.

Are you sure this is the tack you want to take? he asks me. When what I'm sure about is that I can feel each and every one of the nine hundred lives he must have lived already, swirling in me like another seismic event.

Like too many of them.

I'm sure, I tell him. *I already know what happens when you pretend to "help." You know what they say. Fool me once, fair enough, because I was a teenager and you're older than dirt, as well as an asshole. There won't be a* fool me twice. *I'm not actually masochistic.*

His dark blue eyes gleam, like he knows better.

"We might as well run a test now, then," he says in a low voice that moves down my spine like a touch.

"Great," Emerson says. "I can—"

"I know what the little Warrior can do. We all watched her fight last night." Nicholas does not acknowledge any connection to the Joywood. He does not acknowledge our past. He looks at me like he's never seen me before and I hate it, which tells me things about me I don't want to know. "But what about you, witchling? Can you do anything but run your mouth?"

WELL, SHIT.

It's not that I'm not capable of doing *something*, it's more that I don't want to have to prove anything to anyone—particularly him. *Tests* of any kind have never been a strength of mine. I don't like being judged.

Things I'm also not good at include: knowing when to quit, acting demure, and admitting I'm wrong.

"Your sister killed a host of adlets." He spares her a glance. "Allegedly."

"Allegedly?" Emerson lets out a cry of outrage, and I watch her fight with herself. I can practically hear her inner lecture. *Don't give him the reaction he wants, don't poke at the scary immortal*. But there are things Emerson is powerless against, now and forever, and being underestimated is one of them. "Don't forget that time I stopped a flood and saved the sacred capital of witchkind."

Nicholas looks unimpressed. "Typical Warrior things."

"Right, because Confluence Warriors are so *typical*," Emerson huffs.

But none of this is about Emerson. It's about me. He doesn't have to look at me directly for me to feel the force of his attention, though he does that now. It's like I'm in his high beams and he's not slowing down at all. "What designation do you fancy yourself these days, Rebekah?"

I narrow my eyes at him. There's a war going on inside of me, the kind I tried to leave behind. The kind I thought I *had* left behind, but something about his arrogance and what happened between us ten years ago makes all that growing I did seem to melt away. Like nothing's changed in me at all. "You know what I am."

I feel connected to the old me in a way I haven't in…maybe ever. Because beyond the shame of failure and the disappointment and that look on my grandmother's face I can't bear to recall, there was this.

Me.

The me that Nicholas Frost sought out. The one he offered to tutor and help guide, once upon a time. The me who was prepared to accept her exile until I *felt* what Carol did to my sister, abruptly wiping her mind of all magical memories without the courtesy of the traditional ceremony.

The seventeen-year-old me who stood up against what was obviously wrong, because of what they did to my sister. The scared kid who dared to try to fight against the Joywood—and particularly against Felicia.

And, okay, I didn't do that in a way I'm proud of—but I still *tried*.

I'm still *me*.

The same me who then watched this immortal bastard, who'd claimed he was only in my life to *help me*, turn his back on me when I needed him.

It doesn't matter that I lost that fight. All those fights. Or even that I crossed lines and shamed myself in the fighting, because I knew who I was then. I knew *why* I did what I did. I know now too.

Maybe I say that to him without meaning to, in this connected channel that shouldn't exist between us, because he almost smiles.

"Diviners are the rarest witches around," he points out, sounding lazy again. Which means he's anything but, especially when he shrugs. "Rarer still to be born of two Praeceptors, no matter the bloodline or pedigree. What makes you think some spell dim exile—"

"I don't appreciate that term, you know," Emerson interrupts, and I want to groan. I want to get this over with, not argue over a term I don't *love* myself. When it's an ugly fact of life here, thanks to the Joywood and their spells to supposedly preserve the peace. "It's pejorative *at best.*"

"You're not required for this, little Warrior. You can be sent home at any time."

Still, he's looking at me even as he speaks to Emerson.

"You will not send me away from my sister," Emerson retorts, sounding as threatening to him as he did to her. Her hands shake a little, but she curls them into fists. Because Emerson will always fight for me, no matter the opponent.

It occurs to me that she doesn't know I did the same for her.

No one knows, except Nicholas.

And really, does he even count as a person?

He definitely hears that, because the curve in his mouth deepens. I have to fight back a shiver.

"A true Diviner's simplest and most basic act is that of scrying," he intones, as if he's decided to start lecturing us despite claiming he wouldn't.

With a wave of his arm and a few muttered words, we're

suddenly inside. In a grand library so big it would make Belle weep. There are shelves packed with books straight up toward the domed ceiling. There is art everywhere, thick rugs tossed across a marble floor, and, oddly enough, what looks like a weasel in a Habitrail. It bares its teeth at us.

As I try to get my bearings without bursting into song about my provincial life or questioning Nicholas's choice of pet, a table appears before us. It's a high table, more like a counter. On top of it are all the typical tools for water scrying. Some fancy bowl, crystals—obsidian and quartz—and a wand. It looks older than Nicholas.

The wood of the wand is clearly ancient, but it gleams. The stone at its far end looks vaguely familiar, but for all my work with crystals I don't recognize it offhand. I have the immediate sense that it fits this house like a glove, even though there's no ornate carving all over it. Not like this library we're in that features scrollwork and carving everywhere, much of it ancient signs and runes. The wand is simple in comparison. Straightforward.

And I decidedly do not want to touch it.

Nicholas does something dramatic with his hand, reaching up and then out, swiftly. A window slams open, making Emerson and me jump, and then we both frown at the knee-jerk response.

I assume the point was to make us jump. His expression is far too bland.

A ribbon of water floats in through the window, shimmering as it twists and turns. It curls into a tighter circle in the air above the bowl before Nicholas snaps and it splashes down into the receptacle.

Like he made an invisible pitcher and poured it out.

"Ask the river for its wisdom," Nicholas suggests to me.

Not the way a teacher might assign a student a test. But the way some half-drunk, Revolutionary War–era fool might demand a duel. Except Nicholas is neither half-drunk nor a fool.

No matter how much I wish he was.

"Is this going to be on the *real* test?" Emerson demands, peering at the setup on the high table before us. She is probably taking mental notes *just in case*. I actually see her mouthing words, no doubt a spell to convert everything she sees into her teacher's-pet-type notes without her having to physically write them down.

Nicholas sighs. "You know, I *could* turn you into the buzzing gnat you are determined to be. It would take the smallest spell."

Emerson smiles as if that's a compliment. "I would think anyone who's been around as long as you, Nicholas, would know the squeaky wheel, or *gnat*, gets the grease."

"In my experience gnats are crushed by the nearest boot."

She shrugs. "I don't crush easily."

He makes a noise that is both dismissal and approval. Because somehow Emerson has managed to earn the immortal's approval, no matter how he dresses it up in irritation. Doesn't that just figure? All she has to do is show up.

Meanwhile, he's taunting *me* with the river. And requiring a demonstration when he is actually the only person alive, besides me, who knows exactly what I can do.

I remind myself that it's not my sister's fault that he's an immortal dick.

Emerson looks at me over the table. She smiles encouragingly. She doesn't give me a thumbs-up, but I feel one emanating off her just the same.

Emerson believes in me. Emerson believes in everyone she loves.

I believe that what I would like to do is drown Nicholas Frost in the bowl he's so thoughtfully laid out for me.

Many have tried, comes his laconic voice inside me. *Most recently, and notably, in Salem. Behold their success.*

I look down at the table instead of at him. I know how to water scry. I'm not worried about the results, exactly. Or rather, I'm not worried that I won't get any results, because I know I will. I'm more worried about what those results might mean.

His eyes are so blue it should hurt. "You'll need to rid yourself of your hinderances."

"No, I won't." He calls them hinderances, and I once believed that age-old witch adage myself. But when the ruling coven throws you out on your ass and you're a messy, self-taught Diviner who's been given absolutely no help, you learn to control what you have in all the human ways there are.

Meditation. Breath. Crystals.

Marring my flesh to dull the things that would otherwise overwhelm me, with piercings everywhere. The flashy septum piercing is for show, I grant you, but I keep the extra hoop helixes high on my ears to fend off stray spells, the daiths on both sides to center me, the bar on the top of my left ear to divert negative energy. I keep the metal circles in my nose and bellybutton, the stud in my eyebrow, the bar in one nipple, all to keep me solid and safe.

And I keep my most favorite one just for me.

If you know, you know.

I also plan to keep the tattoos that have taught me the control I need. The control that is the only reason I've survived long enough to come back here—after spectacularly losing control the night I left.

If I fail yet another test in this town, what do I care? The only test that matters is my own. I've been passing that one daily for a decade.

Pity that all this sentimental self-actualization will be interrupted when the Joywood strike you down and kill you, interrupts that immortal voice in my head.

I take a deep breath and work on blocking him again. The Joywood aren't here. This is between me and an obnoxious old witch who has no *real* power over me. What's a curse or a hex or a little toad-turning when I've survived exile?

I can do this. I do it all the time without trying. It happens to me whether I like it or not. In my sleep. In the grocery store. Seeing the future is never a problem—it's the stopping all those futures coming at me like a faucet of fate that I struggle with.

Sadly, he knows that too. He knows way too much.

But that's neither here nor there right now. This is a test, and no doubt something the Joywood will ask of me too.

I breathe, I center myself…this time, with all the forbidden witch words I grew up with. I let that hot ball of power within pulse in all the ways I've tried to avoid for a decade.

Much like outside holding Emerson's hand to drop the glamour, it's peace. It's homecoming. It's *me*.

I reach out and take the wand. It's been cleansed. Whoever it really belongs to, Nicholas or someone else, there's no hint of them or their magic. Even for a Diviner. It's light and feels just right.

I look at the bowl of water. Water from the confluence.

Ask the river for its wisdom, Nicholas orders me.

I can do that.

On a long, slow exhale, I touch the crystal tip of the wand—a precious opal, I realize, for amplification and hope—to the water in the bowl. I focus on the ripples. I focus on the water. I let the heat inside of me expand as the water moves and dances.

"Wisdom of the water, show me your light," I say, infusing the simple words with everything I feel inside me.

The power sings up my arm, all good—but it's hot.

Scalding.

Instead of me reaching out to ask for the power, it reaches inside of me and *burns*. There are flashes of images I can't make out. Blurry and fuzzy. Just like last night when I tried to see what the future held for Emerson. But this time with pain.

A lot of pain.

A sharp, burning, terrible pain that I can't control. It's racing through me, like it's the blood in my veins, and this isn't how it's supposed to be. This isn't right. Something else lances into my hand, so hot and painful I can't keep my grip on the wand and it falls to the marble floor with a clatter.

I like to think I don't make a noise, don't yelp at the pain—but Emerson is immediately at my side, so maybe I do.

"I'm all right," I assure her, inspecting my hand. It *feels* like it's burned, charred in fact, but it *looks* normal. I try to shake it off, even though that makes it hurt worse. "Things have just been a little wonky since last night. It isn't *in* me. It's something without."

"Wonky," Nicholas repeats in his cultured voice, as though the word is foreign. And absurd. But he studies me in a way that is more…considering than it was before.

Before I failed so epically.

And it's a good thing I'm not my sister, because *I* view failure as an opportunity.

"Fractured," I explain. "And no, it isn't my piercings or my tattoos."

Emerson is frowning at me. With worry, maybe, but something else too. Like maybe, for the first time, she's entertaining the thought we might actually lose this whole impossible fight.

It's not really a surprise that I'm turning out to be the weak link.

Which isn't to say her thinking it doesn't hurt almost as much as my not-really-charred hand.

"Try again." Nicholas sounds bored, but why would he tell me to try again if he's truly bored? It's that and that alone—the idea that I've somehow interested the greatest Praeceptor of all time, according to what I assume is his own, immortal propaganda—that actually prompts me to try again.

Once he turned his back on me, but he isn't sending me home today. Not yet. If I can prove to him…

These are old, disordered thoughts, I tell myself sternly. *You don't need to prove anything to anyone but yourself.*

"Try again," Nicholas says again, over some excuse Emerson is trying to make for me.

At the same time I say, "I'm going to try again." Like it's my idea.

Emerson clearly isn't happy about it, but when I pull out of her grasp, she lets me. She takes one small step back, which for her is pretty much the same as leaving me here.

I pick up the wand and frown as I study it. Maybe there's something wrong with it. Maybe Nicholas poisoned it to play some kind of trick on me, or the Joywood have imbued it with some sort of anti-Wilde hellfire.

If I hadn't had my own fractured vision last night, I'm sure I'd believe either one of those options. Happily. But I had that vision all on my own. Something is going on here, and it isn't in the wand. I'm pretty sure it's in me.

I focus not just on the water, not just on the answers I seek, but on controlling that blistering pain. And whatever it is that's fighting against me, cutting off my access to the visions that usually come so easily that I spent years learning how to keep them from swamping me completely.

I touch the wand to the water again. I focus. I chant the same words, simple but bright with power. *"Wisdom of the water, show me your light."*

The pain is instant. Just as sharp, just as hot.

I make myself repeat the words through the punch of agony, and the visions come—but they are even more fractured. So garbled I can't even make out details—no colors or people or messages, only flashes of light and pain.

So much pain it makes me think I might collapse. Or throw up. Or both.

I grit my teeth, hold the wand tighter, and let my gaze meet Nicholas's across the bowl.

His blue eyes are so dark they're almost black. And I think, *I need that.* That deep blackness. That textured *dark*. If I can touch it, harness it, use it, these visions will come together.

There are answers here. Somewhere in him, in us. Ones I didn't expect to find. Ones I didn't know could exist. I can feel them on the other side of that static. I only need to get there.

There is a flicker of something in Nicholas's expression. I'm not stupid enough to think it's concern, I just know it has some of the same markings as concern. Whatever that means on a soulless asshole.

"Stop," he grits out at me.

But I can do this. I know I can do this. I'm so close to something…something big. Like Emerson diving into the river.

Witchling, he says in my head. A warning, but also…almost as if that term that sounds so condescending is actually an endearment of some kind.

But I don't want his warning, and his endearment is clearly a foolish fantasy I've made up. I bear down. I reach for that space on the other side of all this static.

Crack.

There's a flash of blinding light. Everything involved in the test is gone—the table, the bowl, even the wand I had a death grip on. All gone. The library is smoky, and Emerson looks terrified while Nicholas looks thunderously angry—which makes me think he wasn't the one to make it all disappear.

I want to say something snide about that. Who knew the immortal witch could be played in his own house?

But I can't get the words out of my mouth, or even in the right order in my head. I have the terrible realization that the cracking sound I heard came from *inside of me.* And all the *me* is leaking out, so fast it's like some kind of riptide and I'm an empty shell—

Well, shit, I think again, or maybe I manage to say it, but then the world goes dark.

And not in a good way.

8

WHEN I OPEN MY EYES, I KNOW IMMEDIATELY I'm not at Frost House any longer. The ceiling is a little too simple. No scrollwork. No dramatic domes with frescoed ceilings like a witch's personal Sistine Chapel. Everything here is too…warm. Homey. I look around.

I'm lying in a cozy living room with a healthy fire flickering in the hearth. I know at once that I'm in a farmhouse. It's the exposed beams, maybe. All the furniture is oversize, comfortable-looking, and simple.

Emerson is sitting at my feet. I realize I'm lying on a couch. And Jacob is standing at my head.

I want to sit up immediately, but my body still feels… untethered. Yet much too heavy.

Emerson squeezes my ankle. "Don't try to do anything too suddenly. Ease back in. You fainted. I brought you to Jacob's so he could heal you."

"I don't *faint*," I reply at once. It's a knee-jerk response, sure, but I'm not the type to faint. I'm not all fluttery and fragile, thank you. I scowl at my sister, sure there must be another explanation.

Jacob laughs. "You Wilde women are very adamant about that, and yet…" He glances at Emerson, some secret smile on his face.

I also look at my sister, who is frowning back at Jacob. "You fainted? *You?*"

"I killed some adlets," Emerson replies with a tiny little sniff. "A lot of adlets, actually, because it turns out they're real. Exhaustion overtook me. I'm sure the same thing happened to you."

I'm not at all sure of that. Something happened inside of me when I looked into the water. When it looked into me. And I have no idea what. I look around the room, this time not to determine where I am, but because—

"He isn't here."

My gaze flicks to Emerson. Of course Nicholas Frost isn't *here.* I never thought he would be. Honestly. I can't even imagine him sitting in a comfortable armchair in Jacob North's farmhouse. Whatever happened back there in his ridiculous hidden palace on the hill was nothing.

I might have failed his test, but I don't care about that.

"You just sort of crumpled, and he had things to say, but I wasn't about to listen. I brought you to Jacob." Emerson is stubborn. Everyone who's ever met her knows this. But the bottom line is that if Nicholas *really* disapproved of her leaving, he wouldn't have let her go.

What could he have had to say?

"So what's wrong with me?" I ask of Jacob, because I'm sure something must be wrong if I *fainted* like some corseted drama queen. Besides, scrying magic is supposed to feel good. Maybe a little intense, depending. It's not supposed to *burn.*

"That is the question," Jacob replies, looking at me intently, like he's looking *into* me. "I've never seen exactly what I saw when Emerson brought you here."

I want to ask if there's a better, more established Healer around here. Not someone I went to high school with, because everything in me feels fragile and edgy. But I restrain myself. Partly because I don't want to be mean to the guy who's engaged to my sister, even if it's still a secret. That's no way to start off as in-laws. But also because he's always seemed steadier and more controlled than the rest of us, even when he was eighteen. I know without having to ask that if the issue was him not knowing enough Healer stuff, he would have found me a Healer who did. The North family is full of them.

"All the things that happened with Emerson over the past month are things I've never seen before," he tells me, and I don't love how that sits in me. Making me feel bad that I not only wasn't here, but I also tried my best to stay away. Even after Emerson asked me to help. But I try to concentrate on what Jacob is telling me instead of my favorite hair shirt. "Things Georgie couldn't even find in all the books. A mind-wiped witch unknowingly fighting her own obliviscor shouldn't be possible. If it's happened before, there's no record of it."

Obliviscor is another old Latin word I hate. I imagine all witches do, whether they've experienced it personally or not. A spell that wipes you of your magical memories isn't anyone's happy place.

But Jacob carries steadily on as if nothing gets to him, an admirable quality. "That's not getting into what happened to her, body and magic, in the water last night to stop the flood. Whatever's going on around us isn't usual. It isn't common. We have witches who are mysteriously sick."

Zelda, I think at once. My favorite relative in our parents' generation. My mother's sister, but happily nothing like my mother. For one thing, my mother calls me on my birthday and the major witch festivals every year, never more. Doing her chilly duty to her wayward exile daughter.

Aunt Zelda texts me all the time, and always has. Since the day I left home. When she's not suffering from her illness that no one can name or explain, that is. My hands itch to pick up my phone and tell her I'm home, so I can see her after all this time. So I can assure myself that she's okay.

But Jacob is powering on. "On the more positive side, Emerson isn't just a Warrior with a surprise power she's not supposed to have—she's a Confluence Warrior. There aren't too many of those. Throughout history."

"Pretty sure I'm the only one," my sister says cheerfully.

Jacob nods. "It stands to reason that what happened to you at Frost's today wasn't normal either. We're not dealing with *normal* anymore."

I'm not sure if I'm supposed to be excited by that. I'm not. Because when strange things happen *to me*, it doesn't lead to calm, peaceful happy-ever-afters in cozy farmhouses. Strange things involving me in St. Cyprian tend to end in shame, exile, and scorching fire.

Still, the way Jacob says the name *Frost*, like it's a curse, makes me think this brother-in-law thing is going to be all right. "Do you think he did this to me?"

I know he didn't. But I wouldn't mind someone to blame—and he has it coming.

No, that isn't healthy at all. Yes, it's 100 percent backsliding into old, terrible habits that did me no good. Today, following my *faint*, I'm okay with it.

"He wouldn't," Emerson is saying, and it takes me a minute—a cottony sort of minute that makes it clear I'm not right—to track that she's talking about Nicholas.

"I'm not so sure he *wouldn't*, just that he *didn't*." Jacob sounds grim. He does that intense *looking* thing again, like he can literally see my cells. I can't remember enough of my lessons on the Healer designation to be sure, but I think he probably can. "I don't see anyone else's magic. What happened to you today feels internal."

I nod sagely, but I'm remembering that *crack.* The water, the pain. The *burning.*

His fathomless gaze.

"Frost could have put it there," Jacob continues. "But mostly what I saw, what I healed, was your magic reacting with something. I'm afraid I don't know what it is just yet."

"Not just yet," I echo, because it sounds more hopeful than I feel.

"I'll consult with my grandfather. And we'll have Georgie look through her books. We'll see if we can find something that gives us answers." He smiles a little, in a way that feels like every doctor I've ever seen in my life. It's more soothing than I want it to be, I have to admit. "But for the time being, you should rest. Take it easy."

"I'll go make some tea," Emerson says, already on her feet before the words are out of her mouth. "You stay right here, Rebekah. I'm serious. Don't move *at all.* I know you hate being taken care of, but too bad."

I watch her charge out of the room, then turn to Jacob. "That doesn't get old?"

Jacob's brows raise. "Her taking care of the people she loves?"

A gentle admonition, and if I didn't love my sister so much, I might take against him for it. But I'm glad he'd take her side over mine. That he'd defend her like that, as if it's a reflex.

I smile at him. "So you're marrying my sister."

Maybe with some emphasis on the *my* part.

"Yes."

"Why?"

Jacob's expression cools ever so slightly at the question. I take that as another admonishment and smile wider, channeling daisies.

"I suppose the simple answer is I love her," he says. Almost formally. A faint smudge of color appears at his ears, but he doesn't look away. His gaze is direct and steady. "I always have."

This time my smile is full and real. "Good."

And I get a full, real smile from him in return.

Something deep and aching that has nothing to do with magic twists inside of me. My visions aren't getting any clearer so I don't see anything now, smiling at my future brother-in-law, and I wish I did. I wish I could tell him, and Emerson, how it's going to go for them. I can't.

Still, there's something hovering at the edge of what I can reach. I just wish it didn't involve dark blue eyes that have already seen a millennium.

I'd rather think about that thing that burned me up and spit me out than the future anyway. "Okay, so we don't know what happened to me at Frost House. But I'm good to go? No wacky magical time bombs or anything?"

Emerson returns with a mug of tea. "It's one of Ellowyn's blends with Jacob's herbs," she says, all but shoving it at me. "Drink up."

I take the mug and stare down at it. "I need a drink, Em. A real drink."

"This first," Emerson says, instead of what I expect—a lecture that will likely be both earnest and stern and all about the perils of using alcohol as a numbing agent, complete with spreadsheets and articles. Like the ones she used to give me all the time when I was sixteen and, granted, a little too rowdy.

"Then something hard?"

Emerson sighs and shakes her head, as if despairing of me, but I know she's faking. Emerson Wilde does not *despair.* Not even of her baby sister.

"We were thinking about going out to Nix tonight," Jacob says. "Everyone can have a drink. A kind of welcome home." He shares a look with Emerson.

"And an engagement announcement," I offer. And that is what I actually want. Not a welcome home. Not any talk about what happened to me or Emerson or all of us last night. Or back when. Not even the Joywood's high school punishment. Just friends getting together to celebrate something good.

"Maybe we shouldn't," Emerson says, looking at me worriedly. "You should rest. Settle in. Besides, there's all this studying—"

"No, Nix is just what I need. If you can convince Ellowyn."

Because Nix is a local bar down by the ferry, and the Rivers family has always run it, meaning Zander bartends most nights. And Ellowyn and Zander may have broken up in high school, but they still don't get along—or even try, if they don't have to, according to everything Ellowyn's told me over the years. Fighting off impending evil floods counts as *having to.* I'm guessing a random night out won't.

Emerson makes a face. "I was going to leave that to you."

I laugh a little. Because, like it or not, the way things around here don't change is comforting. I'm still in charge of convincing Ellowyn to do things. Emerson still thinks we should stay home and study. She just got engaged and I'm home for the first time in a decade, but everything else might as well be us at thirteen. Fifteen. Seventeen.

Even me getting hurt by a simple spell feels a lot like me messing things up back in the day. I sit up and wave a hand—the charred and yet not charred hand—over me, the blanket, the couch. "We don't have to tell everyone about *this*, of course."

Emerson's mouth firms in that way she has that reminds me a bit too much of our father. Not fair, because Emerson has all the warmth and care that Desmond Wilde IV lacks, but she sure can be rigid, just like him. I keep that to myself.

"I understand why you'd want to hide it," she is telling me. Rigidly, in my view. "Believe me, there were things I wanted to keep to myself these last few weeks." Jacob clears his throat and Emerson wrinkles her nose. "Okay, I *did* keep things to myself and that's why I can tell you that together is better than alone."

"That sounds like a slogan," I point out. "Did you put that on, like, town posters?"

She does not confirm or deny that. "We have to work together, Rebekah. And we have to know what we're working with."

"Or against," Jacob adds.

Or against. I think about the way something reached inside me, seeming to burn everything away. Was it real or a premonition? Was it the Joywood? Nicholas? All of them together? Or was it something else entirely? I don't want to ask, but Jacob's *or against* rings in my head like its own bad omen.

"Was I..." I clear my throat. "When you healed me—even if you don't know exactly what caused it, what were you healing?"

Jacob takes his time answering. When he flicks a quick, almost unnoticeable glance at Emerson, I get the sense he's trying to find words that won't freak her out. That he wants to cushion her a little bit.

I like that for her. She deserves a little softness after ten years in the dark.

"It's hard to explain," Jacob says. "Because it's the effects of magic, and while it might be *like* things we know or understand, it's also…not. In a way, whatever happened when you were scrying caused a kind of combustion, I suppose."

"Like…a burn?" I ask tentatively. My hand flexes on its own, as if testing for charred flesh.

He considers. "Sort of. Though, if I'm being honest, it was more like a…detonation spot."

Emerson gasps, dramatically of course. "Like an *explosion*?" she demands.

Again, Jacob hedges. "Yes and no. There was a reaction between two forces that caused something. Something magical, not of this world. So, I could liken it to an explosion, but it's not the same. It didn't blow up parts of her insides. It caused some damage, but it was healed easily enough, and likely she could have healed on her own, without me, if at a much slower rate. So, it wasn't a fatal reaction. Just a big one."

I don't like this no answers thing, but I look at Emerson, because no answers is her particular brand of nightmare. As expected, her eyebrows are furrowed. She has her arms crossed over her chest. Her toe taps against the wood floor.

"I don't like that at all," she says. "Frost will have to be way more careful about his little tests."

"You could also just avoid him," Jacob says, like this is a bone of contention. An older, more private argument. "And his tests."

Emerson does not respond. Because clearly she does not agree. "I have to go open the store." She frowns down at me, clearly still worried that I'm not all right. "I can drop you off at home, or you can come and stay with me at the store. I can have Georgie—"

"I think I'll head to Tea & No Sympathy and work on getting Ellowyn to come to Nix tonight," I say serenely, as if that was an option she offered. I turn to Jacob, because I know

Emerson won't trust me that I feel fine. "I've got a clean bill of health, right?"

Jacob nods, but speaks to Emerson—not me. Another thing that maybe shouldn't irritate me, but it does. "She's good to go. Promise."

I am my keeper. Not Emerson.

How many times and to how many people have I said that in my life?

I have to fight to keep the calm expression on my face, but I don't say it now. That's something.

Jacob gives Emerson a quick kiss on the cheek. "I've got some chores to see to. I'll see you at Nix tonight."

She nods and watches him leave the room. Really watches him, with a kind of gooey love-sick sigh that is so out of character that I'm about to comment on it. But then she looks back at me, her gaze clear and direct. All Emerson.

I stand up, and she reaches out to curl her hands around my elbows.

"I'm worried," she says simply. Honestly.

So honestly, I bristle. "Why? Because I messed up an immortal scrying ritual? Who knows where that water actually came from? He could have winged it in from the River Styx."

She squeezes my arms. "The way Frost explained it, you didn't mess up anything."

I want to shrug her off, knowing she won't like it, but I don't. Because the mention of Nicholas has me wondering how he reacted when I…burned. And collapsed. After all, he's spent more time in my head than I care to admit. I want to know what I missed.

Did he sigh as if I'd lived down to his lowest expectations? Was he bored? Did he wave a languid hand to keep me from hitting the floor?

Or did he actually try to catch me?

I can't imagine any of that. Or I'm imagining all of it, all at once.

I shouldn't ask. I shouldn't care. "I heard Jacob's explanation. What was Nicholas's?"

"He called it a negative reaction. That was after your eyes rolled back in your head, your knees gave out, and he caught you before you smashed to the floor. I couldn't stop it." Emerson slides a covert glance at me as she steps back and lets go, but I catch it. "I can't say I understand why he's allowed himself to get involved in all this. I like to think it's my amazing methods of persuasion."

"You *are* very persuasive."

"He gave me a book that explained Confluence Warriors last month. It led us to the ritual that stopped the flood that I didn't think he'd show for, but he did. Again, I'd like to think that was my convincing arguments at work, but I don't think he's open to any of the usual inducements." She eyes me again, this time not covertly. "He also brought you home."

"Against my will."

"He seems very…*intent* on you," Emerson continues, as if I didn't point out something that should have gotten her all wound up. The whole *he sucks at consent* thing. Then again, maybe this is typical of brooding, detached immortals who've been around for literally forever. I somehow doubt he's up on his wokeness.

And then, for a wild little second, I wonder if she knows. All those times in high school when Nicholas privately tutored me—all innocent, sure, but a secret. So many secrets I kept, that I was so sure she didn't know about. Has she known all along?

"Didn't you say you have to get to the bookstore?" I ask Emerson sweetly, because I desperately want to ask Emerson what she means. How he held me. How *intent* he is. All the things I know better than to believe are possible.

I hate Nicholas Frost. And he thinks very little of me.

The end.

Emerson makes a little noise of frustration, but also duty. She has things to do. And we both know she's constitutionally incapable of ignoring her responsibilities.

"Fine," she mutters. "But this conversation isn't over. Nix. Eight o'clock. Zander's shift starts at nine, so he can hang out for an hour before getting behind the bar. Do your best to convince Ellowyn, but if she's stubborn about it..."

"I'll get through to her." I say this with great confidence because even if I can't argue her into it, I know I'll be able to resort to guilt-tripping. Like any decent friend would.

"Are you sure you're feeling—"

I tap my wrist, an imaginary watch, and Emerson groans again. Then she leans in to give me a tight hug before flying off.

I'm now alone in Jacob North's farmhouse, which is weird. But what about the past twenty-four hours hasn't been weird? I give myself a moment to breathe, to really *feel*. I fold up the blanket that was over me and place it carefully on the couch. I take stock of my body, inside and out.

Nothing inside of me hurts or burns anymore. I flex my hand, but it looks and feels perfectly fine. I feel like me. Like that moment in Nicholas's mansion didn't happen.

What exactly *did* happen? For a moment, I consider going back. I could demand to know. I could demand that he tell me. No doubt he has answers.

But here in a Healer's house, alone, I face a truth I would have buried down deep if there was anyone around to see me.

I'm not sure I want those answers. I'm not sure I want to know what happened.

I'm not sure that fighting my way to whatever is hovering just out of my reach is going to be good for me. If it was, wouldn't I be able to see it?

Because I already know that there are things lurking in me that need to stay there. I already know the darkest parts of me a little too well.

I blow out a breath and text my beloved aunt Zelda instead. Guess what? I'm home. Yes, in St. Cyprian. And not in a Joywood jail. Can I come see you?

It takes a while. I see dots appear and disappear. I think about the fact that I could just talk to her the way witches do, now that I'm openly using magic…but I don't.

Because she could too. And she doesn't.

For the first time, it occurs to me that Aunt Zelda really might be sicker than she's let on, with her airy talk of good days and bad days.

Her text comes in.

I love thinking of you back home! I want to hear how this happened—and if it had anything to do with all the magic blowing up the skies of Missouri last night! I'm betting it did, she texts back. But today isn't a good day. Soon, sweet girl. Soon.

Zelda is the only one who calls me that. Possibly also the only one who thinks of me as anything even remotely sweet. Today that puts a lump in my throat.

Let me know when it's a better day and I'm there, I text back.

And then I'm just standing there in Jacob North's farmhouse, my eyes stinging. Missouri spring allergies, I assure myself. That's all.

So, Ellowyn's tea shop it is. I give myself a moment, bracing myself for something I haven't done alone in ten years.

Fly.

9

I LAND AT TEA & NO SYMPATHY WITHOUT ANY issues, confirming I am indeed the witch I always knew I was—but it's been a while.

"Check you out," Ellowyn says with a grin when I land in a rush out behind her shop, where she is breaking down UPS boxes with her absurdly sharp athame. "Like you were never exiled a day."

"Exile is in the mind," I reply as smugly as possible as I follow her inside. Even though what I want to do is engage in a few of my sister's signature celebratory fist pumps.

I manage to inform Ellowyn of tonight's plans in between her many customers. She isn't *happy* about it, but all it takes is telling her what happened at Nicholas's and she feels worried enough about me to be guilted into coming tonight.

As I knew she would.

And even though it feels like the past ten years were a blink of an eye, now that I'm back here—we're adults now. Everyone has jobs and responsibilities, and I do too. So, I say goodbye to Ellowyn and head back to Wilde House.

One of the things I learned out there in the *real* world was that I was not meant to work in an office with a boss breathing down my neck, witch or not. I learned to live on very little and do what I pleased. But in order to get there, I had to find a way to control my visions that didn't involve the sort of magic I was forbidden to practice.

I've handled them by bringing to life the most confusing ones. In the beginning, it was painting, sculpture. Big, huge, twisting art pieces of terrible and beautiful visions.

Over time, my projects got smaller. More controlled. I began to balance both my artistic and creative needs with the reality of needing to buy food. Lately, I've focused more on the easy and the portable with my computer. Digital illustrations and templates, mostly. I'm sure Emerson would laugh her face off if she knew her always late and double-booked sister was inspired to create planner templates thanks to her, and that they're now some of my best sellers.

I may never tell her.

Back at Wilde house, instead of holing up in my room—another dangerous memory lane route best avoided—Smudge and I go out to the balcony on the second floor, up over the street. I settle into one of the cozy patio chairs, drawing my knees up beneath me and propping my tablet before me. While I've definitely designed witchy-inspired things for humans impressed by that, it's usually from a very *human* standpoint. Brooms and pointy hats and black cats with accusing yellow eyes, all inspired by Smudge, of course.

Today, I let St. Cyprian inspire my art. Or I think I do. When I'm done doodling on my tablet, I look at the results and frown.

Haunted houses.

Ravens.

I might as well have written *Nicholas Frost* in big letters over and over again. Surrounded by hearts.

Like I did once upon a time, to my everlasting shame. The fact I was a teen girl doesn't excuse it.

I'm half-tempted to delete every last brushstroke, but even irritated I know they're great illustrations. I'll make them into stickers and planner pages and everything Nicholas Frost himself would sneer at.

But I'm still annoyed that's where my bitch of a muse took me.

You know, there might *be a lesson here*, Smudge intones from where she's sprawled out in a sunbeam, living her best life. In the spring sunshine outside the house where she and Georgie's cat familiar, Octavius, like to get together and *confer* about mysterious cat things they never share. *Something about running away and facing your fears.*

I glare at her. "I've unlinked my fear responses from shame and regret, Smudge. I'm pretty sure you were there for all thirteen of those sacred rituals. And let's not get into the ayahuasca retreats."

She flicks her tail in disdain.

I hear the squeak and groan of the front door down below and glance at the clock on my tablet. Hours have snuck by without my noticing it, but now that I do, I realize I'm starving. I can hear the faint echo of voices, and I recognize them as Georgie and Emerson, back from their pretty little lives here.

I should go down and join them. I should enjoy being with my friends while I can, but something holds me in place.

Smudge sighs. *I'm sure it's not your contrarian nature or anything.*

Not for the first time in my life I wonder why on earth this usually rude cat can mean so much to me while also being such a giant pain in my ass.

I suppose that also describes my sister, who I can identify by the sound of her quick feet up the front steps and into the house, always in a hurry. Since the day she was born, according to all reports.

My sister, whose engagement I'm determined to celebrate tonight. I stand up and work out the kinks in my neck I didn't feel while working. Then I head back inside to get dressed.

I don't have a lot of options, as it turns out, but luckily a witch-run townie bar in St. Cyprian doesn't have a dress code. In the end, I go with an impeccably hand-knit sweater I received as barter for one of my sculptures and a pair of loose pants that I'll no doubt regret when faced with the cold of a spring evening.

I make sure my belly ring is still visible, because I might want to celebrate my sister, but I also live to annoy her.

Then I do something I haven't given myself the pleasure of doing since I was a teenager. I do a cosmetic glamour spell, making my dark hair soft and romantic, my makeup just a hint dramatic.

I grin at myself in the mirror, because yes, I look good, and yes, I'm pleased with myself.

Happy engagement, Emerson. And happy return to your magic, me.

It's getting close to eight, so I decide to shock the hell out of Emerson and be ready before the appointed time. We'll call it her engagement present.

In the kitchen, Emerson is nowhere to be found but Georgie is sitting at the table, the big book Nicholas gave us this morning open before her. I'd forgotten about that book—perhaps purposefully—but Emerson clearly did not. I'm more than happy to let Georgie glean whatever is necessary from the old, dense pages and then pass it along. She's better than CliffsNotes.

She's also dressed up like she's ready to go. Her quirky style hasn't changed much since high school, all scarves and layers and *color.* She didn't live in our house back in those days, although she might as well have. While the Pendells are historically known to be dowdy, quiet Historians, her parents always found a way to be loud, dramatic and forever at each other's throats. Yet despite clearly not liking each other, they've always refused to call it quits. Georgie would end up here, where my parents would never dream of raising their voices.

Their preferred weapons were always encased in ice.

After a few moments, Georgie blinks up at me. Whatever worlds she's immersed herself in are still there in her eyes for a moment or two before she blinks them away. Then she glances at the wall clock. "Oh, it's almost time to go."

"Almost," I agree.

"Are you…early?"

"We all grow up, Georgie," I say piously.

Ellowyn waltzes in then, dressed in all black and a hell of a lot of leather. Her lips are painted a dark purple and her blond hair is piled up on her head.

"Wow," Georgie says to Ellowyn, drawing the word out. "You look dangerous."

Ellowyn grins. "The highest of compliments."

We all hear Emerson before we see her. She's coming down the stairs, muttering things, not exactly quietly. No doubt spells or notes that, somewhere, her planner is dutifully marking down. When she appears in the kitchen, she's dressed as the epitome of spring, sort of the colorful, floral opposite of Ellowyn's badass ensemble.

For a moment, all I can do is *look* at them as I realize, with a jolt inside me, that no one in the past ten years has meant as much to me as these three people. I don't let people in out there. Because how could I? That's the nature of exile, particularly from a place that's not supposed to exist. Not in all its true magical glory.

I actually feel a little teary again, and am glad no one is paying attention.

"We're all ready and on time," Emerson is saying. "What modern miracle this is?"

"I was going to say the modern miracle was you and Jacob going to Nix," Ellowyn replies with a teasing grin.

"Weird, I thought it was *you* going to Nix," Georgie chimes in, far too innocently to be believed. Ellowyn glares at her, but there's no heat in it.

Emerson beams at me. And she doesn't say it out loud, but I hear it all the same.

Rebekah is our miracle.

I most certainly am not. I'm only here because of vengeful witches and petty politics, but this night is about Emerson and Jacob. I am determined for it be about them. So I don't argue. I smile.

Emerson holds out her hand. Ellowyn takes it with no hesitation, and Georgie comes over and joins our little circle. I have no choice but to take Emerson's hand, then Ellowyn's.

I try to do it grudgingly, and Ellowyn's eyes gleam. Either the other two don't notice or, more likely, expect shenanigans from me and are ignoring them.

I feel simultaneously condescended to and comforted by that.

Emerson beams at us, all around our little circle. "We are four kick-ass women," she says, as if she's pressing those words into us like spells. Like charms. "And we are going to save St. Cyprian and witchkind as many times as it takes."

I don't want to think about fighting or saving anything. "Yes, yes, saving the world and all the witches by going back to *high school*," I say, squeezing Emerson's hand. "But that was last night. Tonight we're going to be women before witches. We're going to have a few too many drinks, have some fun, and laugh ourselves silly."

Emerson and Georgie share a glance I can only call worried, while Ellowyn laughs and presses her shoulder to mine.

And for this moment, in the bright light of the kitchen where all four of us once stood a million years ago in our bright white Beltane dresses, vowing to be better dates for each other to our witchy version of prom than any dumb boys could ever be—before said dates turned up, one of them evil, and there was a chinchilla incident I only talk about over tequila—everything is perfect.

Everything is *right*.

Or maybe it's that I am, because I'm here, with them again.

Where I belong.

We decide to walk down to Nix instead of fly. Though the air is cold once the sun is down, we keep each other warm with jokes and linked arms. It is like old times, but not. Because while I am filled with all sorts of *feelings*, it doesn't weigh as heavy as my teenage angst did. I remember the things I felt sitting on me like steel plates back then.

Maybe it's all the recovery work I've done. The time away to figure out who I am and what I really feel without all the St. Cyprian complications like family, friends, and three hundred plus years of witchery—whether I chose that time away or not. Then again, maybe it's simply that the longer you live, the better your armor gets. Whatever it is, I like it.

Toting steel plates around all the time is exhausting.

Once at the ferry parking lot, instead of waiting to board the ferry I can see making its way toward the dock through the dark water, we cut off to the side and follow the curving, poorly lit path that brings us closer and closer to the river. Until, just when you begin to think you might be about to go swimming, the bar comes into view. It's a squat but long blue building, the patio lit up with twinkle lights—though there aren't that many people out there tonight in the spring chill. In the summer, the entire place will be packed, inside and out. Music bumping, fans twirling up above, and minors only allowed until nine.

The sign out front reads Nix: On the Mississippi...and Sometimes in It.

Because you can't be a river town and not have some sense of humor about flooding, however black. There's also a tall pole out back, sunk into the river, that marks the river's water levels over the years. It's strange to see physical proof of what we did last night. The river is clearly much lower than it has been recently.

We file inside to the smell of yeast and an alarming amount of mixing perfumes, like too many potions gone awry. Zander and Jacob are already there, and Zander waves us over to the corner booth they've claimed. Emerson slides in next to Jacob and he drapes his arm over her shoulders, tugging her closer. Ellowyn crowds into the far corner of the other side and I press against her, so Georgie can squeeze in beside me. Zander pulls over a chair, and I share an eye roll with Ellowyn when he flips it around and sits on it backward.

For a moment, no one speaks. We're all here. Just like high school, when Uncle Zack would have been behind the bar and ready to kick us out at nine o'clock *on the dot*, because that's when the mysterious *adult things* happened.

But we're the adults now.

"I got us a round of beer," Zander offers, nodding toward the pitcher in the center of the booth's table and pint glasses stacked next to it. "Get the ball rolling for our little welcome home." He reaches over Georgie to give my shoulder a light punch, an old, affectionate gesture I don't realize I've missed until this very moment.

"But that's not all," I say, giving Emerson a look. She hesitates for a moment. Never let it be said Emerson might be accused of stealing my thunder.

But I don't want any thunder. Not tonight. I want to immerse myself in this evening. Soak it in. Marinate in the joy that I am here. With my people. And ignore the pending problems ahead.

Everyone else is looking at Emerson now. She smiles, a quietly elated smile I've never seen on her before and looks at Jacob.

"Emerson and I are getting married," Jacob says. It's a simple statement, as if he expects no fanfare.

But, oh, there is *fanfare* just the same.

Georgie squeals loud enough to draw stares and Ellowyn's *holy shit* seems to echo from the rafters. There are hugs. Even a few tears from Georgie and, okay, me too. Zander says something gruff, yet pleased on behalf of our broader family, then busies himself pouring drinks and passing them around.

We toast the happy couple again and again. They look happy and silly, especially when Emerson tries to toast us instead. Ellowyn is wearing a heavy statement ring to go with her whole goth thing tonight, and she raps it against her glass, claiming the couple has to kiss when they hear it even though it's not their wedding yet. Emerson makes it clear that she intends to deliver speeches about how much she loves her friends every time, kiss or no kiss.

One way or another, we down our beers in no time at all.

I order kamikaze shots for the next round while Ellowyn and Georgie ooh and aah with suitable awe over Emerson's ring that's once again visible, then tease Jacob for his impeccable taste.

Even Emerson and Jacob are cajoled into downing the bitter alcohol I order, and I know I should end the drinking here. I already feel too much, whether steel-plated or just joyful. I don't need alcohol conning me into thinking I should *share* the things I feel.

I glance at Zander, who hasn't really said anything, outside of some group cheering. There is something very…tense about him. He says all the right things when we all do, grins at the joking and the teasing, and wallops Jacob on the back a few times. Yet to my eye, he seems *even more careful* not to look Ellowyn's way.

Like, at all.

Not even when she's banging her ring against her glass, which has half the bar staring at her.

Honestly, the fact that ten years hasn't dulled the force of their mutual dislike has me wondering if Ellowyn really *did* tell me everything way back when. Because sure, teenage love hits hard and hurts worse, but at some point don't you evolve? Think back to all those dramatic moments fondly?

But what do I know? I've never once fancied myself in love. Not even when I was drawing hearts around names in my high school notebooks. Maybe Ellowyn and Zander's *All Too Well* ten-year situation is proof enough that what fades with time isn't real to begin with.

Or, possibly, that they're gluttons for punishment, because some people just leave the scene of the crime so as to avoid a decade of your ex in your face, but again. What do I know about it? I didn't leave here to avoid an ex. I just left.

That's as close to the truth of things as I care to get tonight, with bad decisions in the form of alcoholic drinks on the table and almost certainly more to come. I sit back and consider catapulting things to the next level in the form of a little

Jägerbomb action, elevating this situation out of the realm of piddling little shots with cutesy names and into true mayhem.

I decide this sounds good and even necessary to celebrate my one and only sister's engagement.

But the heavy outside door thuds open then, and there's a sudden murmur—a ripple of excitement you can practically *see* go through the bar.

I turn, and there he is.

Like I conjured him up myself.

10

"NICHOLAS FROST IS AT *A BAR*," GEORGIE WHISPERS, but loud enough to be heard back up on Main Street, like he's a priest walking into a strip club.

I wish I could manage something suitably snarky, but I can't. I can't exactly breathe as he walks toward our booth without seeming to look around, as if he knows exactly where we are without having to search for us. I decide I need to invest some time in learning a spell that can ward off my reaction to him—the sort of homework it won't kill me to do.

I'm sure I can hear him laughing in my head at that, but I ignore it. I tell myself it's the kamikaze shot I've already tossed back, doing its good work inside me.

Everyone in the bar is staring at Nicholas as he *strides* across the rough floor. I figure I might as well do the same thing. Just to fit in, because that's me. Known conformist.

He's wearing pants and a shirt like every other guy in here. No big deal. But it feels like a big deal. It's the *way* he's wearing just...a pair of dark jeans. Boots. A black T-shirt, because naturally he's impervious to the spring chill outside. There's no sign of a flowing cloak, a wizard cap, or a raven perched on his shoulder, and I will admit I feel let down by this. He looks like he forgot to shave—I remind myself that would be a glamour on a regular witch and on an immortal it's an affectation—and his dark hair is just long enough to make every single person in this bar imagine that *someone* must have been running their fingers through it. Recently.

But really it's those blue eyes that get me.

And, possibly, that rangy body of his that I just know is no glamour. That's him. Wide shoulders, narrow hips, lean and muscled everywhere.

If the goddess cared about me at all, she would have made immortality available only to trolls.

He seems to take ten hours to parade across the length of the bar to our booth, then stops before it.

In all his state.

I feel like there's an emotional cloak that billows behind him.

"Are you here for the engagement party?" Ellowyn asks with a smirk.

And I have to admire how unfazed she is by…all that. All *him*.

I'm also irrationally delighted that Georgie is sitting closest to him. Because she can act as body armor, I tell myself piously. It has nothing to do with my sudden, nearly overpowering desire to put my palm on what looks like it might be the finest male abdomen of all time.

Around our table, everyone is in various states of discomfort, which makes me feel slightly better about myself. Georgie is twisting her fingers together, looking anywhere but directly beside her. Ellowyn maintains the challenging expression. Emerson studies Nicholas, clearly trying to calculate the perfect response to his arrival. Jacob settles into a disapproving look, while Zander stands up from his chair—less to be aggressive and more to keep Nicholas from towering over him, I'm pretty sure—and goes with some glowering.

I have no idea what I'm doing. I chant at myself about peace and love, but my palm itches as if the fire that burned it was him. Maybe if it *was* him, it would feel good.

If Nicholas notices any of this, he gives no indication. His gaze moves over all of us as though we're inanimate objects, eventually landing on Jacob and Emerson. "Congratulations," he says. Aridly. "What a delight it must be to pledge your forevers when you are mortal and have so little time."

Obviously he does not sound the least bit delighted.

"Thank you," Emerson says regally, as if that was an offering of some kind.

Jacob frowns at the insult it actually was.

It makes me wonder what amount of time would count as forever to an immortal. Or if anything but *always* is frothy and insubstantial. For some reason, thinking about it makes me feel sad.

I tell myself I just need another drink. Or ten.

Nicholas is eyeing Emerson as if he expects that *thank you* to turn into a speech, which, you know, is fair. When it doesn't, he looks away from her.

"I need to speak to you." His gaze finds me and pins me to the booth, all lightning and tension. "Alone."

I smile as if I fully expected nothing else tonight but an immortal witch rolling up to me in a crowded bar, a welcome home party in himself. Something for all the girls I hated in high school to gossip about long after I'm gone, I can only hope. I lean back against the banquette. I try on an Ellowyn-style smirk.

"That's so sweet," I coo at him. "Did you come storming in here to see if I'm okay?"

I'm kidding. Or being provocative, anyway. I don't expect the flash in that midnight blue gaze of his that makes me think, *Wait.* Is *that why he came?*

But I have no time to dwell on that possibility.

No matter how much I'd like to.

One moment I'm sitting in a booth sandwiched between Ellowyn and Georgie and the next I'm outside standing on a riverbank, a cold wind attacking my foolishly exposed abdomen once more.

Naturally, the wind appears to have no effect on his arms. Particularly not the biceps I can see are even better up close—

Focus, I order myself.

One of these days I'll learn my lesson. *Yeah, right.* I glare up at the man who thinks he can just *yank* me out of my sister's party, refusing to curl my arms protectively around myself like everything inside me wants to do. "I'm getting tired of that."

One of his impossible brows lifts. "Then stop me."

"I'm supposed to fight off a famed immortal witch who I had to read about in history class?"

"You could *try*."

And it bothers me that he's right. I could try. Yet never do.

I should probably think about why that is.

Nicholas's cut-glass voice gets even more dry the more he speaks, or maybe that's just a knock-on effect of the wind picking up over the river. Or his cold blue gaze. "Would you prefer me to give you until tomorrow morning? Make an appointment to speak with you?"

"Why not? You have all the time in the world."

"But you do not."

He's serious. There's no sardonic lift of his mouth. No hint of dark amusement in his eyes.

I want to make a crack about his immortal sense of time, and how I'm sure I have a good century or two left to go—but instead I find I have to swallow at my suddenly dry throat.

I don't think he's talking about a witch's usual lifespan. I think he's talking about the two short months I have before Litha. And my new test.

And whatever comes after that.

If there even is an *after that*.

But…why is he concerning himself about the time *I* have? Why is he here? For all to see? Yanking me out of bars so we can speak *alone*?

I spent a lot of years hating myself for the fictions I made up about him when I was a teenager. For the shameful things I did that he witnessed, that I would blame on him if I could. I've tried to forgive myself, because healing begins with mercy for past mistakes. For being young and foolish.

I won't go down that path again, no matter how different this feels. Because we may not be *equals* exactly these days, but we're on more equal footing than we were back then.

That doesn't mean his behavior actually *means* all the things I fantasized it might when I was sixteen.

"What happened this morning is not typical," he says somewhat stiffly. I want to imagine he's not liking what he's picturing as the probable result of my upcoming test, the way I am also not liking it, but telling myself stories about what Nicholas Frost thinks and feels is what got me into trouble the first time around.

I keep right on glaring at him. "No shit."

His gaze drops to my nose piercings in disdain. "Perhaps the ritual was too much to start with."

"Perhaps your ritual sucked."

"Sucked," he echoes, like in his ancient vocabulary my word choices are some kind of affront. But I don't quite believe that,

because if he was that much of a walking heirloom, surely he wouldn't be wearing jeans that I don't need to inspect for labels to know are pretty much the rage right now. And are also worn in places machine-distressed jeans normally aren't, suggesting he actually wears them a lot—when not appearing in puffs of smoke to frighten the populace.

Or this is all a glamour and he's messing with my head. Obviously that's the most likely scenario.

"As you said, in your colorful way, there is something imbalanced."

"I said something was wonky. We fixed the whole river imbalance thing." I wave a hand at the river beside us as if that was easy. Because I have a beer and a kamikaze shot in me, and last night—was it really only *last night?*—feels almost fun in retrospect.

"You took an important step, yes. But water is only one element, as you well know. There are others."

Other elements. As much as I knew facing down the Joywood would be a challenge, I figured the whole saving the town thing was done. That's kind of Emerson's whole milieu. Surely she already did it.

"What, like hurricanes and earthquakes and wildfires?" I shudder to think what might be required if we have to face all that too. For all of us, not just Emerson. Again and again and—

"Must you be so literal?" he asks. "It's distressingly human." All with that practiced condescension that I used to almost yearn for.

Because it meant he was paying attention. Expecting something from me. Even if I didn't meet his standards—then or now—it was still him *seeing* me.

It's amazing how powerful that is.

"Your visions should not be fractured," he tells me. "Scrying should not cause pain."

"Did you rip me out of my sister's engagement party to tell me what I already know?"

His cold gaze…flashes. That's not the only thing that's different about him—fire where there's normally only ice. It's like he honestly seems to care about what happened to me earlier. Enough to come here to tell us what he thinks happened.

Except he isn't telling *us*. He's telling *me*.

This feels too much like my childhood all over again. *Our little secret*.

There's still that fire in his gaze, but it's darker now. "You have special powers, Rebekah."

I stare at him. I almost laugh. All those years I would have given anything to hear him say that. Now that I don't want it…

Well, that makes all the sense in the world, doesn't it? Men being men.

"But this is not special in and of itself," he continues, in case I'm tempted to go for that big head all of a sudden, after all these years of every single person I know making sure I hold myself back from the egomania that clearly waits for me, just out of reach. "Anyone can be born with a gift, an innate talent, a power. What matters is what you choose to do with it. Ten years ago, you chose to save your sister—but only in a way that made *you* feel good. Not in a way that might have actually helped her."

I cannot believe how patently unfair that is on so many levels, not the least of which is I was *seventeen* and had just had my entire life stripped from me. The injustice of it actually takes my breath away. Of *course* I was helping Emerson. I was proving something for us both.

But Nicholas has introduced a question inside me. *Were* my

motives pure? *Is* my memory flawed? Were the Joywood more right than I'd like to believe with their accusations that the only power I've ever had is borrowed black magic?

If they weren't, would I still feel that ribbon of shame every time I think of what I did that night?

Would I still keep it secret from the people I love most?

"This morning confirmed some suspicions that what happened ten years ago did not," he's saying, like he doesn't know that he took my knees out from under me.

On the off chance he really doesn't know, I refuse to show it. "Like what?"

He does not speak. While usually that's some kind of mind game, there's something about his silence that reminds me of Ellowyn when she wants to lie. But can't.

I know Nicholas can tell all sorts of lies. If he was cursed like Ellowyn, someone would have mentioned it before now in the endless lore about him. Then again, there are all kinds of curses out there.

Isn't immortality itself a kind of curse? Who knows what other things might be holding him back?

But I nearly laugh out loud then. Surely one of the most feared witches in the universe isn't being held back by *anything.*

"It will need to be you," he tells me. In that way he has, like if there was a stone circle handy his words would carve themselves into monoliths and stand guard across centuries.

"What will need to be me?"

I'm more familiar with the look he gives me now. The one that suggests that I'm very, very dim, but he's too polite to mention it directly. "The book I gave you. It will need to be you who finds what needs to be found. You must be the one to prove what needs to be proven."

"Be more cryptic," I invite him with enough sarcastic bite to give the April wind some competition.

Nicholas lifts a shoulder that should not seem so elegant when it's also so *muscly.* "I will be what I must."

But that's a much-needed wake-up call. I stop perving on his *shoulder.* I need to start picturing the troll that is clearly beneath all his centuries of magic and misdirection.

I shake my head. "You know what? No."

"No," he repeats, as though I've begun speaking in tongues.

"That's what I said. Would you like me to repeat it? Maybe in a few different languages?"

"I would like you to explain, please, just what you think you are refusing."

I make a face. "You. This whole thing. Books and special powers I magically have now that I didn't before. I'm not interested. You want someone to save the world, talk to my sister. I am here for me and me alone, because the goal here is not dying, pure and simple."

"You are, as ever, completely off base."

"Yeah, well, my prerogative." I move to walk away, but I realize too late that I should have simply disappeared the way witches do, because he stops me.

Not with his hand—why be so prosaic—but with his magic. A cushioned wall I bump into when I turn away from him to storm off, because I can't see it. I also can't get past it.

I look over my shoulder to glare at him, and still there is no humor. Not even the comfort of his derision. Just a black seriousness that makes me…afraid.

And damn it all, I don't want to be afraid.

I *refuse.*

I'm not proud of my reaction then, because it's too much like my reaction *that* night. I let that throb of power deep within me lash out without any attempt at controlling it.

And I'm not aiming at the wall he made.

I'm aiming at him.

He blocks me—of course he does—but a lash of anger sparks back at me, and better yet, I can read it on his face. A surprise, because it is a tiny chink in his famous icy control.

In all the ways he's slapped me down over the years, it's never before been with even a *hint* of his temper.

And while, yes, as a teenager, I had a stupid, mortifying crush on the man, the myth, the legend—his many slap-downs then never once reverberated deep within me like sex itself.

It makes me angry enough to try again, even knowing full well I'll never win. He did challenge me after all. *You could at least try.*

I spit lightning at him, but not like I did the night everything was ruined. The night I left. I hold back a little, and of course that's stupid. Because Nicholas Frost knows everything, has seen everything. My pulled punch is *nothing* to the likes of him.

But Nicholas is struggling with his temper tonight. He doesn't show it on his face any longer, not after that first unmistakable flash, but somehow I know it's still there. Somehow I know…it isn't lightning that will win this war. I see it, like one of my visions.

I need to touch him.

It makes no sense, and Hecate knows it's asking for sheer disaster when this little battle of wills is less like a proper fight and more like *foreplay*.

But before I can even take a step forward, before I can even reach out to try and press my fingertips to his skin the way everything inside me is screaming that I should—

I can't.

He has wrapped himself in some kind of protection, some kind of ward, and his eyes are bluer than I've ever seen them. I feel his gaze inside me, like he's the one touching me.

When he speaks it's not out loud. Just inside my head. *You can bluster and fight all you want, witchling, but we both know what you'd do to protect your sister and your friends. What you already did. To be effective, you must have access to your full power.*

Think you can handle it? I shoot back at him.

Unwisely.

Probably.

There's more of that wild blue gaze. *The next full moon will rise on Beltane. You will meet me at Frost House at midnight.*

I want to challenge that, too, but the truth comes at me hard. Of course I'll be there. I'll meet him anywhere. I always have.

I don't know what shows on my face, but the temper in him seems to ebb then. A high tide receding, and it's not until I realize I can't do anything to stop it that I realize something else.

I'm not afraid of his temper. On the contrary, I crave it.

I threw my own at him because what I wanted was his.

What I'm afraid of is this.

This...moment between us, that swells like a song too frightening to sing. The way he looks at me. The way it *feels.*

As if all of this has been nothing more than smoke and mirrors, storms and lightning flashes, to protect us both from the quiet immensity of *this*—

He disappears then. Not dramatically. No thunderclaps or raven caws. He's simply gone. And it's *wrong.*

It's all terribly wrong.

I don't want to think about that last moment, that impossible song. Maybe I can't, though I can still feel the ache of it inside me.

What I think instead is that he's ruined my night, once again. He's very good at it. But Emerson and my friends are still in that bar and I am not a teenager any longer. What I am is suddenly far too sober and definitely too freaking old to let him keep wrecking me whenever he feels like it.

Assuming an immortal ass who is almost certainly a glamoured-up troll actually feels a goddamned thing.

I turn back toward the bar, happy that no one else is lingering around outside tonight. Points to the wind. I force myself to hold my chin up high. I take a few breaths, then a few more, until I can breathe normally. I mutter a few words to take care of the heat in my cheeks, that enduring ache deep within.

I will be damned if I walk back in there looking like he got to me.

When I push through Nix's heavy door, the one Nicholas just tossed open like it was an insubstantial screen, I shake my hair back and march to the table full of my friends.

Who are all silent, watching me with questions in their eyes that I refuse to answer.

I slide into the booth on the outside of Georgie this time, but Ellowyn leans around her, jabbing a thumb at the window that I realize—belatedly—gave them all an excellent view of Nicholas and me out there.

"That was like watching *porn*," Ellowyn whispers, making Georgie flush—but she doesn't disagree.

I do not have the wherewithal to react to this at *all*, but luckily Zander is muttering darkly from his backward chair beside me.

"That guy is the devil. Maybe literally."

"A really hot devil," Ellowyn says, sipping her drink *at* Zander. I see someone ordered me a new drink, and I don't even check what it is. I toss it back.

"You can't be serious." Zander would be clutching his pearls if he had any. But angrily. "He's *ancient*."

"But he sure doesn't look it," Georgie says with a wistfulness that surprises me.

I slap my empty glass down on the tabletop and look over at Emerson. She is resolutely mute on the subject. All she does is look at Jacob, clearly having a private discussion. But she does not rush in to demand I tell her everything that happened so she can tell me I need to be careful or more like her, and that means something.

Then I laugh. Because what else is there to do? My sworn enemy suddenly wants to help me—I guess? Presumably this mysterious Beltane meeting is about that help, or maybe it's just going to be more fighting.

Fighting. We fought with magic out there, and Ellowyn might have thought it was like watching porn, but she has no idea.

There aren't words to describe what it felt like, but I know *porn* wouldn't be one of them even if there were.

"All right," I say, calling on every last piece of magic and energy inside of me to create my bright and happy daisy smile. I beam it around the table like spring is my responsibility and I'm bringing it, hard. "Let's get serious about this engagement party."

IT IS, OF COURSE, A MISTAKE. THE PARTY. THE drinks—so many drinks. The magical fight with an *immortal witch* and then that quiet moment of something like song that I want to forget, even though it lingers inside me, like a bruise. The whole damn night that, when I wake up the next morning, gets a little fuzzy in my recollection after what happened outside with Nicholas.

There's something about the roiling stomach, pounding head, and cotton mouth that feels like the punishment I deserve.

For a few swimming seconds, I simply look up at the ceiling and count my breaths.

Perhaps you should have counted your good sense last night. Smudge's voice echoes in my head like a marching band is drumming through there. And I'm pretty sure she's purring with extra vigor, just to make the bed shake a little. She's mean like that.

I should probably have a suitable rejoinder, but mostly I just make a noise that sounds like a donkey. A dying donkey.

I try to concentrate on some tried-and-true meditations that are supposed to calm my nervous system and work a little unmagical magic. *I am made of tapestries of potential. Anything I imagine, I can make happen. Miracles are always within my reach.*

And behold, after a few rounds of this, Ellowyn appears at the foot of my bed. She's showered and dressed and looks fresher and brighter than any woman who drank and danced the night away should. But she holds one of her patented hangover cures in the glass in her hand, and that's really all I care about right now.

"You're a goddess," I say, sitting up as she hands the glass to me. I wrinkle my nose as some of the fuzzy events from last night try to come together in my head. "How many guys did you dance with last night?"

She flashes a smug grin. "As many as I could."

"How many guys did *I* dance with?" I hold my nose and prepare to take the first sip. Ellowyn rolls her eyes, then wiggles her fingers, and suddenly her little remedy doesn't smell so bad. I take a big gulp.

"That is a very interesting question," she says as I take another huge gulp. The concoction starts working almost immediately, making me feel alive again. Still a donkey, maybe, but not a dead one. "Because despite many an offer—from humans and witches alike—you did not accept *any*. When you, Rebekah Wilde, love to dance."

Because why dance with lesser witches while Nicholas Frost…exists? A question I know better than to pose to my best friend. "What are you doing up so early?" I ask instead.

"Business calls. But I can't open the shop until you tell me what *actually* happened with the immortal last night."

I wince. Not just at the last of my pounding headache as

Ellowyn's drink chases it away, or the fact she can still read me so well, but also because I have to lie—

I stop this train of thought. Why *should* I lie? This isn't about me and me alone. Facing down that flood was a group effort. Passing the pubertatum might be something I have to do myself, but Emerson will be right next to me. No doubt acing the whole thing and trying to carry me along with her... But the point is, I won't keep Nicholas a secret. Not this time. Emerson said we had to be honest, that it was a lesson she'd had to learn. So Nicholas was going to have to learn it too. Or accept it.

He won't be my dirty little secret ever again.

"I have been summoned by the great immortal for some kind of Beltane ritual," I say grandly, then swallow down another sip of her magic elixir, no longer feeling much like a donkey at all.

"Is that code for sex?" I glare at her, but she lifts a shoulder. "I wouldn't judge you. Particularly on Beltane. Beltane is a judgment free zone."

"*I* would judge me. He's a dick."

"Sure, but hot, foreboding older men are kind of your thing." She smiles slyly. "And apparently young, tattooed, and pierced witches are *his* thing if last night was anything to go by."

Heat wants to creep into my cheeks but I refuse—*refuse*—to give in to it. "He's just playing out a power trip."

"Okay, but then why you? Why *you, specifically*?"

I lift a shoulder. "I'm an easy target."

Ellowyn throws back her head and laughs. "Yeah. Right." She waggles her eyebrows at me. *"Witchling,"* she says in a deep, mocking voice.

"Condescending nicknames aside—"

This time she hoots. "Condescending? He doesn't call any

of the rest of us *witchling*, and let me tell you, Rebekah, he's plenty *condescending* to all of us."

I legitimately don't know what to say to any of this. That bruised feeling inside me seems to get deeper, uglier. Especially when Ellowyn is *laughing* like it's all a joke.

This is what terrified me, back when I was seventeen and desperately hung up on an immortal older man who only wanted to *hone my magic*. This is what kept me up at night then—worrying that he would never see me as anything other than a tool he could shape, then wield at will…

Or, worse, that it was all a *joke*.

And I'm much too aware that nothing has changed.

Nicholas least of all.

"Rebekah…" Ellowyn is studying me, a faint line between her eyebrows. "What is it you aren't telling me?"

I stare at her for a long moment. Here it is. A chance to tell her everything. All that truth I was just so righteously ready to expand on. But if I go *there*, then I have to go other places as well.

To Nicholas being my secret tutor all through high school. To how he let me fail, then let the Joywood claim all my magic was black—when I hadn't been *intending* to use dark magic at all. Then delivered me to my grandmother and told her everything I did—with absolutely no context or sugarcoating.

I could and *should* tell her.

But I don't.

Instead, I let the moment go. I crack a joke. I don't even know what I say.

Anything to escape the moment.

We go get breakfast and I hold my secrets as closely as ever. Here in St. Cyprian, where I settle into my old life as if I never left it.

I wake up in my childhood bedroom every morning. I

text Aunt Zelda every day. I tell her I'm facing down the pubertatum again, but before that, the Beltane prom might kill me. *What a nightmare*, she agrees. *I think I would throw myself in the river if I had to suffer through a school dance again—you're tougher than me!*

But she doesn't let me see that for myself. She still says she's not feeling well enough for visitors. Day in and day out.

I tell myself that's not necessarily bad news.

Some days I even believe it.

Meanwhile, I have no choice but to surrender to the déjà vu of it all. I'm hanging out with my sister and our friends again—although there's less sneaking out at night, skipping class, and other teenage shenanigans. For one thing, this time around I'm taking the study sessions Emerson calls meetings much more seriously.

Because it's life or death on the line and this time, we all know it.

I don't see Nicholas at all.

One thing I know from all my years in recovery programs is that problems don't solve themselves. You have to get up when you don't feel like it, go out there, and do the hard work of solving them yourself.

But I can't do that when it involves another person.

Particularly when that person can disappear at will.

Every morning I get up and go for a walk, down along the river that runs behind the house. I try to connect with all my Wilde ancestresses who walked this same path, all those tough women who built their lives in this place. Despite what might have been happening to them personally, or in the wider witching world.

I try not to think about my great-great-great grandfather, who woke up one morning and walked into the water, then let himself drown.

And every morning I climb up the hill to Nicholas's house, but he's not there.

I don't know how I know that. It's entirely possible that he's lounging about in his shiny mansion while I mutter spells that don't work, letting the decrepit glamour repel me on its own. I tell myself it's not just possible, but *likely*.

But somehow, I know better. He's not inside while I'm standing at his gates. He's not *here*, stuck in St. Cyprian like I am.

There's just the breeze from the river. The confluence in the distance, a melody that I would have said I forgot—though now it's in me again I understand it never left me. I know every note. Up on the hill, I sometimes find myself face-to-face with a huge raven I know perfectly well is Nicholas's familiar, Coronis.

The ancient creature who sometimes condescends to caw in my direction. Only sometimes.

I pretend he doesn't get to me either.

But I'm always a little colder when I walk back down to Wilde House.

It will need to be you who finds what needs to be found. You must be the one to prove what needs to be proven.

I think about Nicholas's words far more than I'd like. Especially when I'm up on the hill with his glamoured house looking like an eyesore before me, Coronis peering down at me from the dilapidated roof, and spring coming up green and new in the morning light.

Every night, I dream about eyes too blue, that fire between us in the dark, and a song I can't seem to help but sing.

The days evaporate quickly. *How have I not seen you yet?* I ask Aunt Zelda. *I've been home forever at this point.*

Soon, sweet girl, she texts back, the way she always does. *Soon.*

Soon never comes. But the first of May is tomorrow, and that means a whole host of terrible things are about to happen—like it or not—as the Joywood begin their campaign of humiliation.

Starting off by making a group of adults attend the hideous Beltane prom.

Which is not all that different from your average human prom. There's a little more pomp, circumstance, and magic, but at the end of the day it's just a dance to keep the teenagers busy enough that they don't go sneaking off into the adult bonfires at night.

This afternoon I head down to the river and indulge in my ongoing headache: Nicholas's ridiculous ancient tome. It took me forever to work up the magic to do a translation spell, because simple translation spells were useless in the face of something so forbiddingly ancient. I get maybe two pages read at a time before I too want to jump in the river and let it take me away.

Meanwhile, no solutions have magically appeared to me. If there's advice on how to fight the Joywood in this book, I can't find it. It's all out-of-date spells and rituals better suited for the Middle Ages than the twenty-first century.

I don't know what game Nicholas is playing, or if this book is just another smoke screen, designed to make him seem like he's helping when he's not. I'd assume that's exactly what it is, except I can't think of a reason why he'd bother. Still, I'm thinking more and more that I *won't* go to Frost House after prom tomorrow. I'll stick to one obnoxious event for the evening. I'll stand Nicholas up, and won't that be fun?

Sure. You'll stand him up. You aren't at all desperate to know what a Beltane ritual with Nicholas Frost looks like.

Since Smudge isn't around, I have to assume the voice in my head is my own conscience, not letting me lie to myself the way I'm still happy to lie—by omission—to everyone else.

Awesome.

I call it a day for the studying and send the book back home with a little spell. What I want to do is cast it into the river, so it feels deeply virtuous that I don't. I walk up the back hill toward the house, trying to get my simmering irritation under control.

I enjoy the warm sun on my face. The smell of spring, the opening of the earth. The bright yellow forsythia and deep pink redbuds have given way to the wildflowers that carpet the hill, and the last of what humans call Easter lilies—Ostara lilies for us—are still holding on, though they won't be around much longer. The dogwoods have been putting on a pink-and-white show since I arrived, though now there are more petals on the ground beneath each hardy state tree than on the branches.

I loop around to the front of the house so I can enjoy Georgie's crystals in the trees and the haphazard remains of my grandmother's garden, and I'm only a little surprised to find Emerson heading toward the gate from the other direction.

"We don't have a meeting tonight," I say to her. If I had a hot Healer waiting for me, I certainly wouldn't be haunting this mausoleum.

"Jacob had some work to do with his parents," Emerson replies. "And I realized there was an action item for Beltane we hadn't discussed."

"I cannot tell you how much I detest the term *action item*." But I hold open the gate for her and we both walk through it.

She ignores me because she's holding out that damn binder I've been tempted to set on fire more than a few times—an hour—over the past two weeks. She flips it open and points to one of the bullet points under *Beltane Prom*.

A bullet point I have read numerous times myself, usually while making scoffing noises. I think we've both been avoiding it, hoping it might go away or be rendered moot. The former being my preferred course of action and the latter, of course, being the Emerson way—especially if she does the rendering.

"'A dress approved by your parents, in the traditional manner,'" I read out loud, because that seems to be what she wants. When I look up, Emerson is giving me one of her *looks* so I hoot out a laugh. "What are we supposed to do? Track them down in the middle of their exciting and important decade of hiding in Germany and beg them to come back?"

Emerson only sighs. I realize she might have already considered this, but the fact she hasn't, in fact, flown off to Germany means she's thought better of it.

"I'm perfectly fine with them continuing to not show up for their daughters," I say with more heat than is probably necessary. "They left you here, Emerson. Literally a shadow of your former self."

My sister scowls at me. "I didn't remember magic, Rebekah. I was still *me*."

But I'm on a roll. "Mom called me like clockwork on every major holiday and my birthday, like a human, yet always managed to get my voice mail. Dad never bothered. For all they know, I spent the last decade in prison."

"I'm well versed in what they did and didn't do, thank you." Emerson magicks the heavy binder away so she can give me that big sister look of hers, full force, like I'm midtantrum on the ground. "But if this is required, then we have to do *something* to meet the requirement."

"Well, enjoy, because I have no interest in begging for Mommy and Daddy's help."

Emerson sighs heavily. "You don't have to be dramatic about it. And we don't have to flit off to Germany or *beg* them. We just have to figure out a way to send them a message that they can't ignore. They're as bound to doing what the Joywood want as we are. Maybe more."

I want to look up at the sky and yell *Fuck the Joywood* until they show up for a real fight, but there's no point in riling up the people who can literally kill me—and clearly want to—even if it's tempting.

Before I can tell Emerson her plan sucks—because nothing we could send our parents would ever rate their attention when they prefer *important magical people*, thank you—the spring afternoon changes around us as we stand there on the path in the front yard.

A certain, sadly all-too-familiar dread begins at my toes. Then it sweeps over my entire body like the echo of an old flu. The air itself is *different*.

In a very specific way.

Emerson and I stare at each other. We *feel* it.

"They can't be serious," Emerson whispers as the wind picks up.

And then...there they are. Standing on the porch, an array of luggage piled prettily behind them, because appearances matter in all things.

Desmond and Elspeth Wilde. Our parents.

12

THE LAST TIME I SAW MY PARENTS IN PERSON was *that* night ten years ago.

They look about as pleased to see me now as they did then. And they take their time with it, running their eyes all over me in a top to bottom to top again survey that takes in the whole package. They both get stuck on the belly ring and the septum below my nose, and I can see their mutual distaste. As bad as Ellowyn and I predicted. Given that I show my piercings off for the express purpose of annoying people in this town, I shouldn't care.

But it turns out, I do.

Beside me, Emerson takes my hand and I curl my fingers into hers. I remember now as I'm looking at the two of them that even she could never quite earn parental approval either. Emerson tried hard to get it anyway, however doomed her attempts were. I worked harder to live down to their censure, which didn't make any of us all that happy.

What I forgot, though, was that in the face of the Desmond and Elspeth show, us Wilde sisters always banded together.

"Well," my father says in his usual cultured tones while my mother stands beside him with her elegant arms crossed and her lips pursed. "You've both made quite a mess."

Emerson's jaw literally drops. "A mess?"

I can practically hear what she'd like to say, though she does not. *I saved the damn world, Dad. What did* you *do?*

"We're engaged in important work in Europe," my mother scolds us, as if we don't know perfectly well that while Passau is another three-river city, the power there was drained ages ago. So how important can their "work" really be? I maintain my conviction that their actual work is avoiding their disappointing offspring. "To be summoned back to St. Cyprian by the Joywood themselves to face another example of our daughters' flouting of witch society is…an unfortunate interruption."

Heaven forbid, I mutter to Emerson in our old secret language. The one our parents never could understand—or make us stop using—no matter how they tried, back when we spoke it out loud.

"You came because you were summoned," Emerson says, and it surprises me that I can hear a little thread of hurt in her voice. Like she expected them to show up for some other reason.

Elspeth stands taller, likely so she can look even farther down her nose at us. "No witches get ready for a Beltane prom without their parents. It isn't done."

This time it's Emerson's dry *Heaven forbid* in my head, and I almost smile. Snarky Emerson is always my favorite.

"We need to choose dresses and go over the etiquette for the evening," Elspeth is saying, the hint of a frown daring to mar her perfect brow. "This has to go well. The consequences are even more dire than they were last time."

"Let's not stand around on the porch, putting on a show for all of St. Charles County," my father says in an aggrieved undertone, and it's hard to say if he's scolding our mother or us. It occurs to me, in a way it wouldn't have a decade ago, that it could be both. He waves a hand and all the luggage disappears, then does it again so that the front door creaks open before him.

I have actually never seen the man open a door with his own hand in my life.

Emerson takes the first step, because that's who we are. She charges ahead, always. But we're still hand in hand, so I have to move with her or jerk away, and I can't show that kind of weakness in front of my parents.

Also, that's who I am. Always reluctant, always a little angry, and yet always connected to Emerson despite myself. I might hesitate, but I always go with her.

I wasn't really looking for that particular insight into myself the day before our regurgitated prom, but here we are, so I guess I need to make the best of it. I move in sync with my sister as we climb the steps and walk into the house.

Once we're all crowded together into the foyer—which is not small, it just suddenly feels that way—Dad does the hand thing again and the door slams shut.

It's a little ominous, frankly.

And now we all…stare at each other.

They don't look older, is all I can think. They look exactly the same and I know that's just the way witches are, but it seems unfair in this scenario. After everything Emerson and I have been through, surely my parents—who *abandoned* us, in case I'm tempted to forget that for even five seconds—should look a little crumpled.

"Well," I say brightly into the awkward silence, still gripping Emerson's hand and apparently still committed to my familial role despite the literal decade of endless therapy. "How about those Cardinals?"

But before Emerson jumps in or my father can fully commit to his scowl, Mom reaches out and snatches up Emerson's wrist. She pulls her hand closer and stares at it—or, rather, at the sparkly ring on Emerson's finger.

Clearly exactly what it is. A shiny diamond engagement ring.

"What's this?" Elspeth asks, her voice...odd. She looks over at our father. "We weren't told about this."

"You weren't *here*," Emerson points out, and I can tell she's wishing she'd kept that ring on her finger invisible just a little while longer.

"Who on earth..." My father clears his throat, cutting himself off before he says something insulting. I'd like to think it's because he thought better of it, but I know my dad. He doesn't care if he's insulting. He cares if he *appears* insulting. A critical distinction. "I wasn't asked permission," he points out instead.

"Because I don't subscribe to patriarchal institutions or the notion that I need anyone's permission to make my own decisions, and neither does Jacob," Emerson snaps back, then winces.

"Which Jacob is this?" our mother demands.

Emerson hesitates, and I can see the surprise on our parents' faces that their usually obedient daughter might not want to tell them something. Then their expressions change, as if they're sure her answer will be so embarrassing they'll wish they never came back here, and I want to shout at them. Ten years ago, I would have.

"Jacob North," Emerson says, as if she's trying to speak without using her lips.

"The Healer? Oh." My mother's voice betrays neither delight nor censure. And she looks more puzzled than anything. She blinks, then glances at our father. "Has a Wilde ever married a Healer, dear?"

"It isn't the done thing, no," Desmond replies. "Healers marry their own." He's staring at Emerson's hand, and it looks like he *could* work himself up into his trademark bluster. But he doesn't quite get there. He looks like he doesn't know if he should be pissed or if, given Emerson's prospects and recent spell dimness, he should think it's not *too* terrible that one of the Wildes—Praeceptors and Warriors all, back through the ages—should lower themselves to Healer magic.

My father loves a Healer when he needs to be healed, of course. But witches can be as snobby as anyone else. Maybe more so, because we live longer and can summon our ancestors to personally teach us what they hated. Hashtag *not all witches,* etc., but for some, there is always a divide between the more intellectual designations and what my father has been known to call the blue collar witches. Praeceptors, Warriors, and Historians tend to live in the fancy old houses in these stately witch towns. Guardians, Healers, and Summoners tend to stay closer to the natural world.

No one really knows what Diviners do, because there aren't that many.

"Marriage is an important step for any witch, and the right choice can always brighten a witch's prospects," my mother intones, giving my father what can only be called a *very married* sort of look.

"Or dim them," he mutters. "A *Healer.*" He says that as if he's struggling to find a way to make that palatable. And then, as we watch, he gets there. The same way he always does. "The Norths are very powerful Healers, of course." He says that like he's actually extending his unsought permission right now. Beside me, Emerson stiffens. And also crushes my hand. "He's Adam North's son, correct?"

"You've met Jacob, and his parents, a million times," Emerson says from between gritted teeth.

"We meet so many people. We're *ambassadors*, Emerson."

La-di-fucking-dah, I say where only my sister can hear me.

Emerson chokes on a laugh.

My mother finally goes for a smile. Better late than never, I guess.

"That means there's a wedding to plan! After we clear up this mess." She drops Emerson's wrist and waves a hand. Not to cast a spell, but to make it clear that I'm a part of the mess in question. "We don't have much time to find the perfect Beltane dresses, but don't worry. I've brought a selection." She stops smiling and gives us that *very serious* look that makes me feel all of about ten years old. "We have less than twenty-four hours to get this sorted, girls."

Girls.

We're just *girls* to her, still. Something that would be offensive if we'd spent every day of the past ten years together. The fact that we haven't and she can't recognize that we're not the same girls she left here…rankles.

I want to get into it. But instead there's a certain amount of shell shock that carries Emerson and me forward. Or it's my mother's magic nudging us along. I'm honestly too numb to tell.

"I'll handle the Beltane gowns, Desmond," my mother is saying. "Why don't you take the temperature around town?"

"Thank you, Elspeth," Dad says, his "polite" version of telling her she's an idiot. "I'm already having drinks with Festus tonight."

Festus Proctor, the Joywood Guardian. Related to Zander and his father somehow, distantly, though Festus is insufferable. Go figure him and my father would have something in common.

My mother's smile is all cut glass, as brittle as it is bright. "Wonderful."

My father stalks off toward the study in the back of the house that has always been his man cave. Emerson and I are still being herded toward the living room when Ellowyn comes in from the kitchen.

"Hey, I've been waiting for you. Weren't we going to…" But Ellowyn trails off when my father brushes past her without acknowledging her. She gapes at him, then turns back and sees my mother. And her face shows all the shock and horror Emerson and I managed to keep at bay. Well, mostly at bay. "The Wildes actually found their way back home. Just in time for a little repeat of high school. I guess that figures."

My mother goes full Elspeth. She manages to seem as tall as one of the oaks outside, as elegant as she is unnerving. Her dark eyes gleam with distaste. Even the unquestionable sophistication of her glossy dark hair in its omnipresent French twist seems malicious. "And you're still haunting Wilde House, Miss Good. Perhaps you should go home, assuming you have one, and make sure your hapless mother has approved *your* dress for tomorrow's events, as that's how my daughters will be spending their time this evening."

"Oh, she already has, Mrs. Wilde." And Ellowyn has always possessed the talent of speaking the truth she's cursed to tell, but in a tone of voice that makes it as insulting as if she was bludgeoning everyone around her with lies. "Not to draw unflattering comparisons here, but she said I can wear what I want. Since I'm an adult."

"She always did let you roam *freely*, didn't she?" Elspeth

doesn't say, *and look how that turned out*. She doesn't have to *say* it when she's raking Ellowyn from head to toe with that *look* on her face. Elspeth has always been so proud of how she married *up*—not that she'd ever describe it quite that way, but it was clear, always, she married *correctly*.

Unlike Aunt Zelda, her sister, who married a *Guardian* who was beneath her. And Ellowyn's mother cavorting with a *human*? Downright humiliating.

Ellowyn looks over at me and I know that if I look even slightly upset, she'll stay and draw my mother's fire. She's always been good at it.

But I give my head a shake. I'm good. Why shouldn't I be able to handle my own parents? In fact, it would actually be in my best interest to win them over. To get them on our side. To start them on a path toward doubting the Joywood's "good" intentions—

Let's not get delusional, I tell myself.

Ellowyn gives both Emerson and me little shoulder nudges of support as she passes and then leaves through the front door like a human. Loudly.

Mom is now unmistakably steering us into the living room. She strides before us, spine so erect it functions as another expression of her disappointment in me. In both of us. Back then she was so certain her children were on the path to glory. She used the Beltane prom to throw Emerson together with Carol Simon's doucheweasel son and wasn't happy when I engineered a chinchilla situation to distract Emerson, since Emerson never would have refused Mom's interfering no matter how little she liked it.

Back then Mom was all, *if only Rebekah would* listen. *If only Emerson could put* more *behind her power*. Maybe she thinks this is a redemption tour.

I want to tell her to wake up and smell the revenge plot.

Once inside the room where we last ate a lot of pizza from Redbrick, I see there are a parade of white dresses. They're all lined up, hanging there in thin air, a veritable onslaught of pale white and ivory ruffles and layers and, in one particular nauseating case, *fur*.

"These are—"

Emerson squeezes my hand so hard I yelp. And do not finish my sentence.

"These are very traditional," she says diplomatically.

My mother eyes Emerson. "The Beltane prom is a traditional night, as I think you know. It is when witches introduce their children to society. It is the first step of a witch's journey to his or her true place in witchkind. A tradition practiced in our communities since antiquity."

She does not point out that our failure to find our power at the ceremony following Beltane called into question not just our place in witchkind, but our whole family's. They call such things an indictment of the bloodline. *A stain that can never be wiped clean*, my father had howled at me.

As if I failed my pubertatum *at* him.

"And while it's an event worthy of all the pomp and circumstance even the second time around, Rebekah and I had some modern touches in mind," Emerson says calmly, because apparently ten years dancing around Carol and uppity people who wish they were Carol has given her even better skills at handling our mother than she used to have. "Obviously we wouldn't want to be vulgar. But we do think it's better that we make certain our dresses are appropriate."

"We wouldn't want to be *inappropriate* at *prom* at *twenty-seven*," I mutter sarcastically. Emerson gives my hand another hard squeeze. This time I keep my yelp to myself.

"We are, after all, not young girls," Emerson points out.

"And shouldn't dress like them." She tips her head to one side. "Maybe fewer ruffles?"

A few? I yelp all I want where only she can hear me. *Try no ruffles. Anywhere. Ever.*

There is nothing wrong with a well-placed ruffle, Emerson returns as our mother frowns at her precious white relics. *We've got to give her something. Like it or not, we need her approval.*

There's a lost cause if ever there was one, I return. Darkly.

Mom clearly has no idea we're talking in our heads. Or if she does, she's far more concerned with deciding whether or not to actually listen to one of her daughters for the first time ever.

"May I?" Emerson asks, indicating the dresses.

Mom gives a short nod and then watches as Emerson drops my hand, then uses magic to whittle down the monstrosities to something marginally better. Still hideous in my estimation, but at least not *completely* embarrassing. Elspeth's expression goes from distrust to something closer to amazement as Emerson magicks the dresses into different looks.

"Your magic..." Mom clears her throat, and any trace of emotion—like that moisture I thought I saw in her eyes for a second—disappears. "Well. I'm not sure this is quite right." She studies the toned-down dresses with a furrowed brow, but her gaze keeps going back to Emerson. Her hands that glow. With *magic.*

"I think this one would look good on you, Rebekah," Emerson says, pulling the simplest-looking dress toward her, so it floats across the room to us. She smiles at me, much too big, encouraging me to go along with this.

I don't want a cotillion frock, thank you.

She maintains her nearly maniacal smile. *We'll do our own last-minute alterations if we have to. Let's just get the approval over with. It's necessary.*

We clearly disagree on the definition of necessary, but I look at the dress. I suppose no white dress is ever going to fill me with joy, and though there *is* a ruffle around the neckline, it's a lot more understated.

It's not lost on me that this is likely as good as it's going to get where prom is concerned. And more, that this is a test. Mom is now watching me closely, and I know why. She's waiting for me to prove what a child I am by flying off the handle. The way I always used to. She expects it.

I will wear a dress that looks like an actual wedding cake before I play into that. There's one hanging there across the room, whispering of petticoats and nightmares.

I take the relatively reasonable dress instead and aim a smile at my mother, all happy daisies and bright blue skies. "What do you think?"

She looks at the dress, and then Emerson's hands. She does not look at me. I get the strangest feeling that she's almost disappointed that I'm not having a defiant little meltdown. Maybe I am too.

"All right," Elspeth agrees. "Then you should wear this one, Emerson."

She pulls over one that still has a fair amount of ruffles on the skirt, though it's not a full wedding cake horror. Still, it reminds me of *Little House on the Prairie*. Emerson is trying so very hard to keep the smile on her face, but her eyes are a little wild.

Hoist on your own petard, magic hands, I drawl at her.

But Emerson ignores me and bites that bullet. "All right. You approve these?"

Emerson sends the Nellie Oleson dress to the couch, then makes our obnoxious binders appear on the coffee table.

Because, yes, our mother has to literally *sign off* on these dresses.

Our mother sighs. Then she twirls her fingers in the air, a magical signature for each of us.

I should be happy about that, but the teenager inside me is spoiling for a fight. I order her to sit down.

"Now, as happy as we are to have you home, Rebekah and I did have plans this evening," Emerson says brightly. "I wish we'd known you were coming."

The subtle shade is lost on Elspeth. "You should stay in. You'll need a good night's sleep. Tomorrow will be a late night. And treacherous, given your position."

Emerson opens her mouth. I wonder if she's going to say she spends many of her nights at the North Farm. *Come on, tell her.*

I am not going to tell her that, Emerson replies, prim even in our own language.

Then she puts on her chamber of commerce voice. "While we appreciate your advice, and love you being here, I'm sure you can understand that we aren't children any longer. We have a certain amount of autonomy. As is only appropriate."

There she goes again with my parents' favorite word.

But the ferocious Elspeth Wilde is having none of it. "You're attending a children's dance and taking a children's test, girls." This time it's clear that *girls* is deliberate. She's putting us in our place—another Wilde family specialty. "Because you failed the last one. When you were actually children."

"*Did* we, though?" I hear myself ask without putting any thought into asking that question, out loud, to my mother, who didn't just betray *me* in a hundred ways, but left spell dim Emerson here alone.

My mother, who has never showed the faintest glimmer of recognition that the Joywood might be anything but benevolent and good.

I've skyrocketed past a childish tantrum straight into speaking sedition out loud in Wilde House. Go big or go home, I guess.

Oh sweet Hecate, Emerson says faintly in my head.

I brace myself for the explosion. But much to my surprise, my mother doesn't call down the Joywood upon us. She doesn't even dismiss me flat out.

She looks at me with some shock.

And then, of all things, consideration.

"WHAT DO YOU MEAN BY THAT, REBEKAH?" MY mother asks after a few humming moments of *waiting.* Still with that *considering* expression on her face. Then she looks at Emerson as if Emerson might answer for me.

Not today. "I mean it's clear Emerson had power all along. Maybe it was buried under something, but you're telling me no one could see that? No one could help her find it? And I have power too. You must know that." Since it's all she ever seemed to care about.

"But not enough," Elspeth says crisply. Pointedly. "Neither of you had *enough* power to pass the pubertatum."

"What exactly is enough?" I demand, and maybe here comes the tantrum. "And who decides?"

Elspeth draws herself up again. "You will not take that tone with me, Rebekah."

"Let's take a breath," Emerson suggests, standing between me and my mother like we're about to lunge at each other and have a wrestling match. "The important thing is that we've taken the necessary steps to move forward with tomorrow."

Always the peacemaker. But what's the point of peace when I know I'm right? When I *know* that the Joywood want to wipe us out no matter what we do?

"What you're saying is right up there with treason," my mother says, ignoring Emerson. And her dark gaze on mine reminds me of too many things I would rather forget. "Surely you've learned *something* from your ten years in exile. Like what happens when you think you're more important than you are."

I want to tell her all the things I've learned. About self-worth and emotional honesty. About living outside of their prized hierarchies and *thriving*, thank you. But I've also learned something about the pointlessness of trying to get through to people who don't want to bend.

So I simply pull out my daisy smile again. It doesn't matter if she believes me. *I* believe me. The people who welcomed me home believe me. We can fight the Joywood and their little games without my mother.

But then Elspeth surprises me, because she continues when she doesn't need to. Almost as if she's working through convincing herself I couldn't possibly be right, rather than just *knowing* I'm wrong.

That might not sound like an upgrade, but it is.

"Carol has always been...difficult," Mom allows. "But she's our leader, and she makes these decisions because we *chose* her to be in the position to make them. No one likes a leader all the time. They have to make the difficult choices that don't please everyone, because they're for the greater good. Mind wipes and exile of the spell dim *are* what's best for witchkind."

"It did not feel like the best of anything, Mother, I can assure you," Emerson says with a hint of that uncharacteristic bitterness. She flexes her fingers as if she's holding herself back from casting a spell, and my mother's gaze is once again drawn to them...as if she still can't comprehend that she saw Emerson do magic so easily.

"I'm sure it didn't, but it was necessary," she says, almost kindly, to Emerson. Then turns to me with all that ice. "It was also about excising the things that threaten us all."

But she's having this conversation. And I can't help but wonder if there's a little crack in all that ice.

If there's a little piece of her that is thinking...*maybe.*

I need to get away from her before I freeze it back up.

"I have some reading to do," I announce to no one in particular, desperately trying to reclaim some of the serenity I wear like a second skin back in Sedona.

"The Beltane etiquette—"

"I know the etiquette, Mother," I say, and at least I *sound* calm. "But I also know what *I* need. If you'll excuse me."

And then without waiting for her to say more, or for Emerson to make her own excuses, I send myself to my room. *Poof.*

I wish it felt good. I wish *I* did. I removed myself from a toxic situation before I lost control of myself. I set a boundary. These aren't things to be ashamed of. In fact, I should celebrate them. But I feel a certain kind of shame anyway.

A shame that curdles into anger when the dress appears in my room, hanging from its invisible, magical hanger there in the corner. A bright, white, partially ruffled beacon reminding me what I am to these people. Just a symbol, like that dress.

I feel that old fire rising in me. When everything feels hopeless, it seems it's all I have.

Burn it down, Smudge suggests from where she's sprawled on the windowsill.

Because she is only the voice of reason when it amuses her to be. Otherwise, she's an instigator. Because cats.

But when Emerson appears in my room a few minutes later,

I'm forced to use all my skill to tamp down the fury that wants to set the town on fire. Again.

I remind myself that I actually have these skills. To burn or to keep myself from burning, and that they're not accidents. I developed one set of skills in secret before Litha that year. And another set to survive exile.

A few weeks in my childhood home can only get the best of me if I let it.

"That was productive," Emerson announces. With more optimism than certainty, to my ear.

"If you say so." I flop back on my bed. Smudge delicately climbs on top of me and settles herself on my abdomen. I slide my palm over her head so I can rub her cheeks the way she likes. She purrs, leans in, and says nothing snarky in my head. There's not even a stray image of flames.

I eye Emerson as she wanders around my room, almost haplessly. When Emerson Wilde has never been *hapless* a day in her life. "We got her to sign off, and that's what matters. They'll probably leave the morning after the dance, once they've made sure nothing chinchilla-y happens. I can't imagine there's reason for them to stay."

I am not in the right frame of mind to discuss chinchillas of yore. "What really matters is that Mom didn't reject the very idea that the Joywood could be wrong about something out of hand. She considered it. And if Elspeth Wilde has doubts, more people will too. If we show them why they should."

Emerson nods. "They will," she agrees. "Because we're right."

I wish I could be that certain about anything. But my parents are home, and I don't have any desire at all to puncture her certainty. I want it to rub off on me.

I expect her to whirl off to tackle a few more entries on her to-do list, or tuck herself onto the edge of my bed like she used to, but she does neither. Smudge abruptly leaps off me, clawing me on the way, so I hiss a little at the sting.

Jerk, I complain.

My familiar ignores me.

So I wait, watching Emerson struggle with whatever she wants to say. She even twists her fingers together, almost like she's *uncertain*. Which I would have said wasn't possible. "So…" She trails off. Says nothing.

I wait. I say nothing in return.

She huffs out a breath and marches over to the window, glaring out toward the river. Or maybe across the river. "I know you and Ellowyn used to sneak out when we were in high school."

I consider this. "Are you going to retroactively rat me out? See if you can get me grounded? This really *does* feel like senior year."

She scowls at me. "First of all, I never *tried* to get you in trouble. You did that all by yourself."

I accept that. "Fair."

"Second of all, I just… I only wondered…"

Is she…*blushing*?

Then I laugh, because it finally occurs to me what this is about. "You want to sneak out and go have a traditional pre-Beltane make-out session with your boyfriend, don't you?"

She bristles, but her flushed cheeks turn pink, then deepen to red when I laugh even harder.

"I am going to *marry* Jacob so he's not my *boyfriend*, and since I'm not a *teenager*, it's hardly 'a make-out session,' Rebekah." She's going for a little of Mom's ice but can't quite get there with all the pinks and reds and, you know, the fact she actually has a functioning heart.

"Okay, I hear you." I'm possibly enjoying this way too much. I offer her a bland smile that I can see makes her instantly suspicious. That and my sweet tone. "You want to sneak out and have sex with your fiancé. I get it. I support it. Do you need me to give you *the talk*?"

She closes her eyes briefly as if envisioning me delivering any form of *the talk* horrifies her unto her soul, as it was meant to. "I'm an adult. It's not sneaking."

I grin at her. "Uh-huh. If it wasn't sneaking, surely you would simply leave the house when you felt like it. The way adults do."

"I would do that, happily, if it wasn't their first night home and if it wasn't the Beltane prom tomorrow," she insists, then wrinkles her nose. "It's all too high school, and the only thing worse than feeling that way would be having to explain to Dad why I'm breaking whatever curfew he imposed back then."

"You don't actually know, do you?" I shake my head.

"The curfew wasn't instituted for me, Rebekah, and I think we both know that. The point is, I want to leave the house without them knowing. I can feel the curfew spell again. It clearly came back when they did. But I don't intend to discuss my private life with our parents, now or ever, so how did you get around it back then?"

Still laughing, I take her through the specifics. "There are shadows in that curfew spell," I say, and together, we murmur a few words so we can see the boundary my father put up years ago. "See?"

She nods, and I lead her through the work-arounds. The magic we do together is bright and sweet, and we grin at each other almost involuntarily as we look at the decades-old spellwork before us. Emerson is nodding within seconds.

"They're looking for bodies in bedrooms, not necessarily *you*," she says.

"Ellowyn was fond of raccoons, charmed to build things

while we were out. I preferred cat friends for Smudge. As long as you make sure *something's* in your room, you're good."

I have no friends, Smudge informs me. *I am the night.*

Of course you are, I coo at her.

Emerson produces her planner and waves a finger so that it writes everything down as she mutters to herself.

"Just don't come back drunk. Drunk spells are sloppy and they can always tell."

"I'm not going to go *drink*."

"Oh, right, just have hot Healer sex."

She huffs out a sigh. "This is ridiculous. You were right. I'm going to walk out the front door because I'm an adult and I'm not hiding anything. I'm nearly thirty. I'm engaged. I also lived here and took care of myself, *by* myself, for years."

"Sure." But my money's on her sneaking out. Because who among us doesn't get her surly teenager on when forced to head back to high school? Complete with the return of our prodigal parents?

She crouches down and runs her hands over Smudge's luxurious black fur, which Smudge allows—clawless, the jerk. When she straightens, her expression is serious once again. Because heaven forbid she just go enjoy herself. "Whatever Frost wants to do tomorrow—"

"I can handle Nicholas Frost."

She stares at me for the longest time. "You know, it's weird. I remember everything now. Carol's obliviscor spell isn't smothering me anymore. But ever since you've come back, it feels like there are things I still don't know."

It would be an accusation from anyone else, but roundabout isn't my sister's style. She'd come out and ask directly if she had a specific question. That means she's being honest here, and, obviously, I should be honest in return. Because we're not actually teenagers anymore. We've spent years apart, and the gift of that is that I'm not choking on all the family dynamics that made things between us so complicated back then. That's not to say said dynamics don't sting, but I know better. And I can also see who she is, not just who she is in comparison to me as seen by our parents.

Meaning, I guess, that we've grown up.

And because we have, I should tell her. The years working with Nicholas. That while I was preparing to run away, like I told her I was going to do after our failed pubertatum, I *felt* her be wiped… And launched my own revenge, that Emerson would in no way appreciate.

Which means Nicholas was right—it was for you, not for Emerson.

I push that thought and all the memories away. Just like with Ellowyn a few weeks ago, I can't find the words to tell her, so I don't.

"You'll never know everything, Emerson," I say instead, all Sedona sage, but this time I annoy even myself with it. Not that I let that stop me. "The less you accept you'll ever know, the happier you'll be."

"I don't like that at all, and I'm the happiest person you know," she returns, but she laughs when she says it. She moves to the door, but hesitates, chewing on her lip. "You're sure that they won't know if I, like, kidnap a squirrel?"

"What happened to *I'm an adult*?"

Emerson sighs. "I just want tomorrow to go smoothly. I just want…" She shakes her head. "Okay, I want them to look at me and say, 'good job, Emerson.' And I know they won't. It doesn't matter to anyone except us that I dove into that flood. And I don't need it to, not really. I know I did the right thing and we saved the town and St. Cyprian thriving unawares is all that really matters." She sucks in a breath. "But just *once* I wanted Mom and Dad to think it was enough. That *I* was enough."

The words twist and turn inside me. I've been through therapy. I know all the right things to say and feel. And still, everything she says echoes inside me, the ache of knowing it's stupid to hurt and futile to wish…while not being able to keep from it.

I lived down to every expectation. I embarrassed them—fairly and unfairly. I was and am a stain on the family name. I *flaunted* being that stain. Still do.

And yet, just once, I too want them to look at me and think I'm enough.

"That's on them. Not you," I manage to say.

"I know." She looks at me. Really looks at me. "Do you know?"

I nod, a little too vigorously, maybe. "Yeah, I do."

"Good. We know it." She swallows. "So when are we going to *feel* it?" Her eyes are suspiciously shiny, and I feel mine getting there. Somehow, in this moment, I miss my grandmother more than I ever have. If she were here, she'd know what to say. What to do.

She always did. She was why we grew up *ourselves*, not carbon copies of our parents.

But she isn't here and I still can't face that, much less the last time I saw her. There's only Emerson and me now. There's only this old hurt, shoved into the middle of all this ritual humiliation, like this was the Joywood's plan all along. I can't really put it past them.

How can I possibly let them win?

I clear my throat and blink away the tears that want to fall. I meet Emerson's equally bright gaze. "Go home to your Healer," I tell her very firmly. "Enjoy yourself."

She looks around the room. "Wilde House was always home."

"Now it's not. Now it's Jacob. Nothing wrong with that."

"So where's your home?"

Something that sounds suspiciously like a raven's caw sounds within me, but I ignore it and the shiver that goes with it. "Not everyone needs a home." She looks at me like she pities me. I *hate* that look. So, I daisy smile at her in all the ways that will make her frown. "Some of us are our own home, Emerson."

Then I take it a step farther. I summon all of the deepest magic within me and do something I definitely shouldn't.

I transport her—against her will like Nicholas is forever doing to me, but that's how I know it works—and while I'm doing it, I magic in a flop-eared bunny that looks like it escaped a Beatrix Potter book in her place.

Have fun! I send her in my most cheerful inner voice.

Try consent, jerk, she replies, so grumpily it makes me laugh. I dispatch the bunny to Emerson's bedroom before Smudge can get *too* interested in it, then charm it into sitting quietly on her bed.

And then I spend the rest of the evening staring at the ceiling with Emerson's question echoing in my head.

When are we going to feel it?

14

I AM ONCE AGAIN WEARING A BELTANE PROM dress.

And while I have had this exact nightmare many times, this is not one of them. I know this because no matter how many times I pinch myself I don't wake up in my bungalow in Sedona. Like it or not, I'm heading for the prom. Up the hill to the outside door of the old high school gymnasium, set apart from the main building. I can see that inside it's packed with students and, worse, decorated. And sure, there's magic involved, so the decorations are better than a few sad streamers and insipid balloons. But it's still *the gym*. Filled with *teenagers*.

The prom might kill me this time, I'd texted Aunt Zelda earlier.

If the prom killed people, maybe we wouldn't have to suffer through them, she'd replied, and I could almost hear her funny little laugh. Sadly, you have to live through it. Again.

I'd soothed myself by imagining her saying that to Zander,

who looks as if he's attending his own execution tonight. No one else looks much happier.

I look over at my sister as we hover at the gym door, but instead of making a snarky comment I'm drawn to the necklace she's wearing—the bluebell one Grandma gave her in our eighteenth year, because Emerson was born on the first day of the year and I was born on the last day of the same year, and there were even prophecies about the power we were supposed to have, *psyche.* The necklace seems to reach out to me. I find myself thinking about my ring, hidden away in the box beneath the floorboards back at Wilde House.

That locked little safe is where I keep my last memories of my grandmother and I don't want to focus on them yet, but this feels different. As if the ring is looking for me tonight instead of the other way around.

I decide to lean into that notion, focusing on the ring as I whisper a spell beneath my breath. After a moment, it appears on my hand and the narcissus flower *does* match the whole relentlessly white Beltane ensemble, I guess. Maybe it didn't bring me luck at my pubertatum last time, but it was a gift from Grandma. It has to have *some* magic.

Even if it's just love from another time, I'll take it.

I need it, I think as we step inside the stuffy gym, because this is a living flashback—and it's disorienting because I somehow missed that the world went ahead and changed in the last decade. Even in St. Cyprian. There's new technology, music, fashion, and even the decoration choices have evolved. It's a *Through the Ages* theme, and there are different decades represented in dress and decoration—but it's a current day take on the past. I know because I remember ten years back all too well.

Still, it's the same old gym. The kids are disturbingly young and new, irrepressibly shiny in their Beltane whites and thrumming with excitement because they're gearing up for their hopefully one and only pubertatum. Their first step into *real* witch life.

Assuming the Joywood aren't gunning for them.

I feel an echo of that same old excitement inside me now, but it feels sharper than it should. Because I know how it went. I know what happened to us after our last prom.

It occurs to me then that while, yes, this is a humiliation, it's also an exquisite sort of torture. In all the recovery groups I've ever attended, we always talk about how you can't go back, you can't have a do-over, you can't change the past. No matter how much you want to do just that.

But what if I could is pure evil.

Because I can feel it snaking around inside me, giving me the kind of ideas that—if history really does repeat itself—will crush me long before the Joywood get around to it. Guaranteed.

I have to assume that's part of the plan.

As is customary, all the fledging witches have to crowd together in front of the stage set up against one wall and wait for Carol, in full ruling coven regalia, to intone the opening incantation as the sun goes down and Beltane begins in earnest. You can already smell the smoke from the traditional bonfires on the breeze outside. Tonight is supposed to be a pageant of hope and celebration, but as I listen to the old familiar words from Carol's mouth, all I feel is a creeping sense of dread.

Then again, that could be about the music that starts the minute Carol stops speaking.

In case I forgot I was at a *school dance.*

Teenagers are *everywhere.* Laughing, joking, posturing for each other. There's a cascade of those fractured visions inside of me from all the people, all the *feelings* that make the air in here immediately feel much too close and clammy. My friends and I are all standing in a horrified line, staring out at the crowd. At these children who are much, much younger than we ever were.

Ellowyn tenses beside me and I glance at her.

"I think I'm going to be sick," she says, and it's not a joke. She looks as clammy as the air around us.

I give her arm a squeeze. "I'll go grab you a drink."

She gives me a wan smile, but Zander holds out a bottle of water he clearly magicked into existence. "Here," he says gruffly.

Ellowyn doesn't look at him, but she does take the bottle. "Thanks." She takes a swig and then blows out a breath. "It's okay, Rebekah. I feel better already. The water helps."

She still doesn't look at Zander as she says that, but I take that as her releasing me from having to go find her something to drink. Which is too bad, because I actually *wanted* a task. I look around the gym a little wildly. I can't just stand here in all these *feelings*. I have to…move or something. Anything. "I'm going to walk around."

"I'll come with you," Georgie says.

I raise a brow at Ellowyn, who makes a face. "I feel like if I move, I'm going to puke, possibly in protest, but I don't want to give the Joywood the satisfaction."

Jacob gives me a little nod as I hesitate. He'll take care of Ellowyn. And Emerson and Zander are standing on either side of her like sentries.

"Go," Ellowyn says, and waves at the crowd with her water bottle. "I'm sure I'll be fine."

I feel like I'm a bad friend for pretending I believe her, but it's not puking that I'm afraid of here. I'm much more worried about an accidental spot of arson, courtesy of yours truly. So I move through the crowd of pulsing visions and chatter, Georgie at my side. My head pounds, but I don't feel *sick*. It's not that I think I might puke. I'm just…overwhelmed. Maybe a little claustrophobic.

I figure I'll step outside and enjoy some fresh air, unpolluted by teenage pheromones, when I notice Gil Redd, the Joywood's Praeceptor, standing at the door I was hoping to use as my escape. Standing there and very clearly telling anyone who ventures near to turn around and go back into the sweaty dance.

"We're stuck," Georgie tells me flatly. "The Joywood are clearly prepared to keep us here by any and all means necessary. But I do know a hiding place." She takes my arm and we weave through kids and more static, younger teachers I don't recognize, and older ones I do. Eyes seem to follow us as we go, but that could be the paranoia talking.

We get to a little corner where there's an old-fashioned silver bowl filled with red punch that can only be made entirely—and jubilantly—of chemicals. There are also little plates of cake. The sign beside the table reads *Enjoy the 1950s!*

Georgie pulls me behind the table into a little alcove where we're hidden from the crowd, currently out there enjoying a disco inferno, goddess help us all.

"Add a tiny little hiding spell and this is a good place to read," she tells me.

I study her for a second, then grin. "And maybe hide from Emerson when she wants you to parade around handing out flyers."

She shrugs, but smiles. I investigate the punch bowl, wondering if anyone's thought to spike it. "You wouldn't happen to have a bottle of gin hidden in your dress, would you?"

"Uh, no."

"Bummer." Magicking one up myself feels a bit too much to ask in my current state. Besides, I would hate to do something the Joywood would expect me to do.

We stand next to each other, not hidden by a spell but half hidden by the alcove, surveying all the sad gym pageantry. I can tell that Georgie has something on her mind. I assume that in a perfect world, she'd like to talk to Emerson about it. They've always been tight. But Emerson and Jacob are on Ellowyn duty—which, when I look over, looks to be more about being cute with each other.

I should find that annoying or maybe gross, but I don't.

"You can actually talk to me, you know," I say without looking at Georgie. Only then do I glance beside me. "I don't bite. Anymore."

Georgie looks at me, and I assume she's going to pass on my offer and wait for Emerson. Instead, she looks surprised—maybe that I could tell she's bothered by something. She chews her lip, then leans closer to me, conspiratorially. "You know what's weird? The opening spell was different."

"It's the same dumb one I remember," I say, magicking myself a cup of the punch and downing it. I'm hideously disappointed that it's just punch. What's the matter with these kids? Then again, I flush with an immediate chemical sugar high that makes me *feel* like I might actually be seventeen again, so maybe gin would be superfluous.

Georgie is shaking her head. "It's the one I remember from our first prom. But when I was doing some research in that book Frost gave you, it showed a different incantation for the Beltane celebrations that turned into proms. Not anything *off the wall* different, just fewer lines and different wording. And then when I cross-referenced, I could find no evidence that there'd been a change. No petition, no law, no nothing. Whoever changed it did it off-the-record."

"Does there have to be a record?" I ask, only half listening as I stare morosely at the teenage horror around me. The sugar high buzz can't change the fact that high school is still high school. The same peaking-too-soon guys. The same obviously mean girls. The same pretending-they-don't-care groups clustered here and there, sending longing glances into the most unlikely places—

I treat myself to more red dye forty.

"There's supposed to be a very strict record. There are rules that have been in place for centuries." Georgie is about to say more to me, but someone clears their throat. We both turn and look at a tall, slender man in a pinstriped vest and a bow tie that doesn't quite match. He's standing in our exit, blocking us into the little alcove.

We both stare at him, but he doesn't look remotely familiar to me. Georgie seems as lost as I am.

"Hello," the man offers. He holds out a hand. To Georgie. "I'm Sage Osburn. I'm a teacher. You're not students."

"No, we're agents of the demonic horde," I reply, but with a daisy smile, because that's creepy. "Behold us in all our dark glory, etcetera."

"Oh. Ah. Well." His cheeks begin to turn a little pink, but he's mostly looking at Georgie, who, it has to be said, looks good in her flowy white dress with red ringlets everywhere. Clearly *Sage* thinks so. "I...was wondering if you wanted to dance? Chaperones can, of course. It's permitted. Even encouraged."

He says that last part as if she might have been all for it, if not for the *inappropriateness* of it all. And like knowing the rules might tip her over and into his arms.

Then again, it's not like I know what Georgie gets up to around here. She's a Historian, and everyone knows Historians tend toward the duller side of witchcraft. They know everything but never *do* anything, I once heard my father bellow at a neighborhood block party.

There's a beat. Then another. I'm not sure if it's uncertainty or something else from Georgie, but it doesn't look like she's repulsed. So I give her a little nudge, and it seems to knock her out of it. She smiles, wide and beautiful, at the nervous teacher's bow tie.

"Sure," she says. "I mean, I'd love to dance. To..."

She tilts her head to one side, and Sage Osburn laughs. Nervously. "We've made it to the eighties, I believe," he says, even more nervously. "This is something of a classic."

"'Lady in Red,'" I announce as the song wails all around us, bouncing off the walls as horny teenagers pretend they're not straight up rubbing themselves against each other out there beneath the spinning disco ball. "Cheek to cheek, Georgie. Get in there."

Georgie throws me a look I can't read. Sage looks like he might fall over, possibly from embarrassment or possibly because he's too reedy to handle a breeze. Before I can say anything else, Georgie takes his hand and they head out to the dance floor.

I tell myself that the guy is just her type. He has that tweedy, academic look, right? Perfect for a Historian. And yet as I think that, something in me pulses, too fractured to read. I think, *no*.

But I don't have time to dig into what I'm picking up because the air changes. Foreboding prickles down my neck, then serpentines down the length of my spine, where I tattooed the phases of the moon to guide and keep me even when I couldn't draw the moon down the way I used to. I use my peripheral vision to get a sense of who's watching me, expecting Felicia to be hovering nearby, shooting magical daggers at me, but it's definitely not Felicia.

I turn, knowing I should be stealthier. Knowing I should at least *pretend*, but something magnetic draws my eyes, draws *me*.

The way it always has.

He stands on the edges of the crowd. The forbidding distaste in his expression is *palpable.* Many of the prom attendees look at him, whisper about him, even long for him the way I used to, but none have the courage to actually approach the notorious Nicholas Frost.

But I do.

He's here. In this same sad gym while "Lady in Red" bleeds into "Time After Time." I haven't seen him in two weeks and that shouldn't matter. I shouldn't even notice. But my heart is beating like I've been waiting for him to return to me. Pining, even.

I tell myself it's the fruit punch.

I start toward him, though I keep my walk slow. It might even be a saunter. I'm affecting a very sophisticated look of boredom.

At least I'm *trying.*

I finally reach him and I stand next to him like I belong there. Weirdly, it almost feels like I do. Nicholas says nothing. No greeting, no acknowledgment. But when I stare at him, he stares right back.

"I'm not supposed to meet you until midnight," I say.

He inclines his head. "Correct."

"You didn't need to come…chase me down."

"I assure you that I did not."

"Then why are you here? When you could be literally anywhere else?"

Nicholas only gazes at me, and something inside me… flips over.

And I know. He's here for me. The same way he was ten years ago. I understand in a flash of insight—maybe it's magic, maybe it's intuition—that if I asked, I would find that he hasn't attended these proms otherwise. Ever.

But I don't ask.

Instead, I just…take him in. He's wearing a stylish, well-appointed suit, not some relic from the 1800s. It's also not white. I can't really imagine Nicholas succumbing to something as *regular* as following a dress code, even when appearing in places where he must know his presence will cause a commotion. And not only in me.

His gaze slides down my embarrassing getup, a heat and a sizzle that centers itself where it very much should not.

"You look remarkably pure this evening, Rebekah," he drawls.

I eye his dark suit. I do not think about *purity* in this man's presence. "I thought the color of the day was white."

"Only for the uninitiated."

That can't be true, because this is my *second* initiation, but something about the way he says that word has my mind going places where it shouldn't…just like all that pulsing heat inside of me.

"I have something for you," he says, sounding as if he can barely manage to get past the tedium of his own words. "You'll want to bring it with you later."

"I was thinking about skipping our date." I smirk, as much because I used the word *date* with an immortal who I'm quite certain thinks tinder is still literally kindling as anything else. I lean in. "There are far more exciting Beltane rituals to attend at midnight. But you know that, don't you? You've been Beltaning for centuries."

He ignores my attempt to poke at him and instead holds out a small crystal. It's orange, in the shape of a perfect ball, and distracts me from imagining him haunting the bonfires back in the day, naked and wild beneath long-lost stars. The crystal hovers above his palm and I find myself…drawn to it. Enough to hold out my hand.

"What's this?" I ask as it drops into my palm.

Nicholas's gaze holds mine for far too long as something new and strange beats inside of me. "It's yours."

This isn't an explanation, but it somehow makes sense. It *feels* like mine. But I've never seen it before in my life. It's just a little sphere of a crystal. But it feels weighty and special. And yes, *mine.*

"Where did you get it? Is that where you've been?" *Wow, Rebekah, sound more like one of these sad children you're surrounded by, why don't you?*

"Don't be late tonight, witchling," he returns in that voice like silk, and I try not to think about Ellowyn's mimicry of that term as he walks away. Yes, *walks.* He executes a very mortal turn and strides off into the crowd that parts before him—and not because he's using a magic force field.

But because he's *him.* Nicholas Frost.

I want to follow, but thankfully my brain and dormant pride remind me that despite all appearances to the contrary, I'm not *in fact* ruled entirely by my old, childish desires.

Though the horned god of Beltane knows that nothing involving Nicholas feels childish in the least.

I curl my fingers around the ball and force myself to look away from him as he stalks through the gym. I get my bearings, and that takes a minute. Then I look for my people.

Georgie is no longer dancing with her teacher chaperone. Now she and Sage are standing near a wall, talking. Jacob and Emerson are sitting at a table, knees touching as they laugh at something. Nearby, Ellowyn looks better than before and is deep in conversation, but surprisingly enough, it's with *Zander.* And they don't look like they're arguing. They don't look like they're enjoying themselves either, but a duel doesn't seem to be on the horizon so I have to call that progress.

I stay where I am, alone, as images from all the excitable teens assault me. Hard. And then I hear the *last* voice I want to hear in my ear. No, not my mother or father. They would be less upsetting right now. Not even Felicia and her *sniff* of doom.

Instead, it's Carol.

"Rebekah, you look distressed," she says, while her impossible hair seems to frizz *at* me. She gives me that *concerned* face of hers that everyone seems to believe is real. But I know better. "Is everything all right?"

15

I DON'T WANT TO TURN AND LOOK DIRECTLY at the head of the Joywood, but I don't have a choice. I aim a daisy smile at Carol as I force myself to face her. "I'm actually loving this little frolic through adolescence."

"You're all alone," she says, almost like she's singing a lullaby in my ear, weaving tendrils of her power into me. "It must be hard to acclimate after ten years of isolation."

I feel her magic all over me, seeking to draw me out, but I know how to repel her. All my little rebellions in my teenage years gave me the skills to block, and all my recovery time out there in the world taught me how not to lash out with the kind of heedless anger I displayed the night I left. I hope. "Ask my parents how they're faring in the same situation," I say sweetly. "I'm sure they'll appreciate you checking in on them personally."

She only laughs. As if she's being friendly. She isn't.

I brace myself for her trademark snideness when Carol turns

her gaze back to me. And worse, smiles. "It's interesting to see that Nicholas has picked up right where he left off."

Cold dread ices right through the center of me, and there's something about the way she drawls *Nicholas* that's almost possessive. It curdles in my gut like acid. But I am daisies, I am strength. I work up a faintly confused expression. "Huh?"

"Never trust an immortal, Rebekah. I would have thought you'd know that by now." Carol shakes her head sadly, but this isn't the time to be drawn into my usual contemplation of her terrible hair. Not when her gaze feels like it's tearing into me and her magic is like a rash over my skin. It crosses my mind that the hair is deliberate. It's there to draw fire while her magic digs in. "He was, after all, one of the main voices in the case against you all those years ago. Nicholas and Felicia were very much on the same team there. I suggested *some* lenience after your volatile display of power, but they could not be convinced."

Like hell did this ghoulish woman suggest lenience. Does she think I'm dumb? Does she expect me to crumple before her?

Because I won't.

I won't lash out either. I take a breath and realize that's probably what she's really after here. But ten years has taught me that I have control of me, no matter what. Grandma's ring pulses on my finger then, like it's whispering to me.

Touch her. Touch her. Touch her.

That seems like profoundly bad advice, but my hand lifts of its own accord. I decide I've got to commit to this, whatever it is.

I reach out and give Carol a friendly pat on the shoulder. But the moment my palm makes contact with her—beneath the sweeping cape she wears, with the witch's runes marked all over the mantle—something slams into me. It's garbled, like all my visions have been lately, but at the center of it is something perfectly clear. I can't help but reach for it.

Especially when part of that clarity comes in my grandmother's voice.

Ask her about Skip.

Skip Simon. I'd nearly forgotten about him, the chinchilla incident at our last Beltane prom aside. Which seems odd, now that I consider it. He's Carol's only son, is an egregious douche, and has been Emerson's adversary forever. A constant thorn in her side. But it was like his entire existence has been wrapped up in fog until I hear my grandmother's voice. As if I didn't forget him, exactly, but couldn't quite bring myself to recall him. Even as I think that, the fog closes in again—

Ask her, urges the voice again.

"You know, Carol, I haven't even asked," I say, my hand still on her shoulder. "How is Skip? I haven't seen him around."

There's a flash of shock, a white-hot slap of power that has me snatching my hand back. It reminds me of that burning pain when we tried to do the water scrying. I look down at my hand, almost surprised at how *similar* it feels, that bright, scalding agony.

Did Carol have something to do with what happened to me at Frost House?

I look up at her, but she's locking the fury down. Or she's trying. She's pretending like she didn't slap at me, but I can see how hard it is for her. There's murder in her eyes. Carol Simon wants to eviscerate me where I stand.

It's a moment of almost unbearable honesty, because we both know it.

But she doesn't do it. She can't. Not here, surrounded by all these fledgling witches and too many chaperones and teachers and members of the St. Cyprian community, because it would be messy to clean all that up afterward.

Even so, I can tell she's considering it.

I smile at her, a whole *field* of daisies. I'm holding on tight to that realization I had back at Wilde House two weeks ago.

We are *threatening*. Something about us *scares* Carol and her cronies.

Even with the static and the fracturing, I can see straight to the heart of the matter. I can see what people don't want me to. And though my palm hurts like I poured boiling water over it, I want to reach out for her again—

But Felicia rushes up then, and Carol is saved from answering. Or I'm saved *from* her answer.

"We have an *alcohol* situation," Felicia says, tugging on Carol's sleeve, but not without sliding me a sneering look.

Carol smiles at me and I can feel that smile everywhere. It's like a slimy reptilian thing, slithering all over me, and I can't do much about the goose bumps that pop up, but I'll be damned before I cringe and cower the way she clearly wants me to.

"Excuse me, Rebekah," she says with a soft menace that I hear very clearly, though I bet from a few feet away you might be tempted to think she's being polite.

Then she dismisses me as if I'm so unimportant she's forgotten I exist before she shifts her gaze from mine. I can feel the urge in me to curl in on myself, go dark—but I fight it off the way I did that rash-y sensation. Because it's the same unpleasant magic.

The two of them walk off across the gym floor, heads together, but before they get too far, Felicia looks back at me. There's something in her gaze that's different, and it's not the flashing strobe lights from the DJ booth. It's unguarded, nearly. Then gone.

Almost like fear.

I want to grin, but my palm still feels red and swollen. I

shove it in my pocket in case it's visible to anyone, and flinch a little when my fingers brush up against the crystal Nicholas gave me. But then I wrap my hand around it anyway, sighing a little as the burning sensation fades. My skin even stops itching. As if what he gave me was concentrated cortisone, created to repel the infection that is the Joywood.

I'll have to remember to ask him about that.

I turn once again to look for my friends, feeling giddy, and this time not because of any fruit punch. That's when I see Zander is stalking toward me. When he speaks, it's in my head.

We've got to get her out of here. He jerks his chin toward the corner, where Ellowyn is all hunched over. Jacob has her hand in his, clearly trying to offer some kind of healing, but it doesn't seem to be working. Emerson is holding her other hand, whispering what looks like encouragement.

We could tell Carol she's sick and needs to leave, I offer, trying not to freak out that my best friend is *that* sick. *Here.* Of all terrible places to show even a hint of weakness. A sickness Jacob can't seem to sort out.

Zander comes to stand beside me, like we're both fiercely focused on one of those horrifying line dance situations that's unfolding before us. But he's still in my head when he speaks. *I'm pretty sure Carol would laugh and Felicia would say* good.

He's not wrong. I look past all the *to the left to the left* nonsense and peer around the gym. Carol and Felicia have collected the rest of the Joywood, but they're all standing in a circle, focused on each other. Not paying us—or anyone but one another—any mind. For now.

Georgie approaches, without her new bow-tied friend in tow. She looks worried as she glances between Zander and me. "Ellowyn?"

I nod. "Any bright ideas?"

Georgie chews on her lip, Zander stands there with his fists in his pockets—looking particularly volatile—and I…think about last night and teaching Emerson how to sneak out.

"The Joywood are busy," I say slowly, watching them. "They know we're all here, as ordered. So really all we need is the *approximation* of Ellowyn to be here until the dance is over."

Georgie's eyes widen, but Zander nods. "Jacob too, because she clearly needs a Healer."

"Okay, so we make a fake Ellowyn and Jacob and then send them on their way," Georgie says, frowning like she's wracking her brain for the right spell, which tells me all I already know about the differences in our high school experiences.

But something is poking at me. Like I haven't gotten it quite right. For some reason, I look at Zander again. Really look at him, and let myself *see.* The visions are fractured, as ever, but there's a kind of thread there. I follow it for a moment.

"You should go too," I tell him.

Zander glances over at Ellowyn and tries very hard to keep the emotions off his face. But he doesn't succeed until he looks back at Georgie and me. "It probably shouldn't be me."

I reach out and wrap my hand around my cousin's. The static is a little painful, but I get the answer I'm looking for. Immediately. "I think maybe it should be."

He pulls his hand away. He looks uncertain and reluctant, but he holds my gaze as if he's looking for permission. Like *I'd* know if it's really okay. When all I know is that it *feels* right.

"Georgie, Emerson, and I can handle things here. You go tell them the plan."

He gives me a curt nod and heads back toward them. Georgie and I stay where we are. The music changes, and I raise my brows at her. I'll admit I'm a little surprised when the *Historian* of the group looks back at me like she spends her time dancing on bars, with an expression that clearly says *bring it.*

So we do. We pretend to laugh as we fling ourselves into dancing to hometown favorite Nelly, which, even though we're putting on an act, is still more fun than any embarrassing dancing that may or may not have occurred right here in this gym way back when. Everything's better when you're not a teenager.

Meanwhile, in her head, Georgie is contacting Ellowyn's mom, off at the fires with her partner, Mina. And in my head I'm creating a block so the Joywood don't sense what we're doing. I'm good at blocks. It's how I kept myself off any kind of witch radar while out there in exile.

Georgie takes my hand and we pretend to joyfully yell with the crowd of *children*, *"'I am getting so hot—'"*

Emerson charges over and joins us on the dance floor. We create a circle, pretending to smile and dance and enjoy the song. Our ancestresses did the same around fires on this night, stretching back to antiquity, so we do what we can with "Hot in Herre." Because what we're really doing as Jacob and Zander take hold of Ellowyn and prepare to fly her out of here is creating little fake images of the three of them. So it looks like they're huddled in the corner. So it *feels* like they're here.

So the Joywood—who aren't holding a perimeter around the gym the way they have been all night for the express purpose of keeping all the teenagers and us where they want us, thanks to their little meeting—think we're being obedient and good.

And no one will know the difference except us. It takes a lot of work—energy and magic, but something about these teenage voices and *emotions* seems to amp up our power. Our abilities.

You should save your energy for Frost, Emerson says in my head. *Georgie and I can handle this*.

It feels a bit like being excluded. Like they've got this—

without me—because they've had *everything* without me for the past ten years, my best friend included.

I am responsible for my feelings and no one else can make me feel anything I don't want to, I remind myself, though it doesn't really take.

And anyway, they aren't wrong. Whatever I do or don't do with Nicholas tonight will require an energy I probably can't even fathom. Still, I'm not ready to think about what's coming for me later. I pull some of my power back. The rest of it I leave in the block I've made so the Joywood don't sense anything is amiss.

I glance over to make sure, but they're still in a huddle of dramatic cloaks, Carol's frizzy hair looking even more ugly than usual in the flashing lights. Speaking of Carol… "What exactly *did* happen to Skip Simon?"

"Oh. Well…" Georgie trails off and looks at Emerson. "I actually almost forgot about him."

"I tried." Emerson wrinkles her nose. "It's a long story, but he tried to attack us and we sort of turned him into a weasel."

"No," Georgie says gently, even as our magic weaves together to project fake Ellowyn, Zander, and Jacob into that alcove. "And yes. My theory is that we reduced him to his true form."

"That's…"

I should be surprised, or have more questions, but at the end of the day it simply makes sense. Skip Simon, Carol's son, was a weasel.

It explains a lot, actually.

"That should hold," Emerson says after a while. She squeezes my hand, and the three of us walk off the dance floor. I risk another look over at the Joywood, but they've scattered again. Standing at the exits so they can hold their circle and keep us all inside it like the creeps they are. I think about how we fed off the teenage energy and assume they do too.

Year after year after year.

"We can go with you, Rebekah," Georgie says as I hand them each a cup of awful punch from a different table. This punch is a bright yellow color, and tastes like sadness, regret, and the faintest hint of plastic. "When you face Frost tonight."

"Yes." Emerson is already nodding. "Jacob and Zander are on Ellowyn duty. We'll be on Rebekah duty."

Like I'm also sick. Or a child in need of being chaperoned. I try to smile. "Don't you think I can handle him on my own? I'm sure you've done it before."

"It didn't end that well," Georgie says into her cup, earning a slightly wounded glare from Emerson.

"It didn't go *poorly*. It was an important step in figuring out how to stop the flood. So really, it went great."

Georgie still has her face in her cup, but she looks at me over the rim. "He magicked her right into Jacob's yard, with an ancient book she could only have gotten from Frost himself, *after* she went charging up the hill alone without telling anyone."

"It was *before* I remembered everything," Emerson says with an injured sniff.

Georgie shakes her head. "Can you honestly say you would have acted differently if you *had* remembered?"

Emerson has this way of angling her chin and lowering her shoulders that is meant to look very regal, or *presidential* is maybe the better word.

But I always know what this look means: she's lying.

"I can't possibly know what I would have done in that moment if I'd remembered everything," she says loftily. "Because I didn't."

Georgie smiles and raises her cup toward me, clearly well aware that Emerson is lying too.

"You two should go check in on Ellowyn once we're allowed to leave this enduring horror," I say. "I can take on Nicholas just fine."

This is not true, on any level, but it's hard to deny the fact I want to *try*. I need to face him down alone tonight. For...a wide variety of reasons.

You could try, he'd said to me about fighting him off.

I intend to try *a lot* of things.

"And if I can't actually take him on, well, you all know exactly where I am," I continue, channeling daisies. Maybe a *little* pointedly, and at my sister. "You can rush in and rescue me."

"You know I will," Emerson tells me fiercely.

I do know that. It's more comforting than I want to admit.

Around eleven, the prom begins winding down. Teens are looking around for escapes, or pockets to make hiding spells that will allow them to grapple in the dark, away from prying adult eyes. For a second, I'm almost wistful for a time when that was my biggest worry—who I'd let talk me into their hiding place.

At eleven thirty precisely, the Joywood convene on stage and hold the closing ceremonies—after all, even the leaders of the witching world want to go get their adult Beltane on. There's the normal incantation, but I look at Georgie. She's mouthing along with every word, clearly thinking about the changes in the spell from the book.

Nicholas said it was me who had to figure out how the book could help us, but he has to be wrong. Georgie is *into* this stuff, and she knows it backward and forward. But her mouthing falters a little as the bow-tied teacher from before comes up to her. Sage, I remember. The man is a tweed-covered *herb*.

That is not nice, Rebekah, I scold myself. *Georgie did not ask what you thought of this guy.*

Emerson and I watch as Sage says something that makes Georgie laugh. Then bite her lip. She looks back at us.

"Go," I say without her even having to ask. "Enjoy some bonfires."

Sage, amazingly, blushes, even as Georgie frowns. "But Ell—"

"You know Ellowyn would be way more graphic," I say loudly to cut her off before she can mention how sick Ellowyn felt. Because I don't think anyone outside of our circle should know. "It *is* Beltane."

Georgie nods. Then she takes Sage's offered hand and they walk off together. I feel like if I was a decent friend, I would be more excited for Georgie that she found a guy she likes *at prom*, of all things. When I glance beside me, I watch Emerson frown after them. "What's wrong?" I ask her.

"Nothing's *wrong.* It's just…" But she shakes her head and turns to me, the Emerson Wilde battle light in her eyes. "I could at least walk up with you."

We walk with the crowd, filing out of the same exit the Joywood are herding us toward, and spinning out our spell as we go, so it should look to anyone watching us that Ellowyn, Zander, and Jacob are walking with us. I try to concentrate on maintaining the illusion and not on the fact it smells like sweat, perfume, cologne, and at least three flavors of that terrible punch.

I understand why Ellowyn thought she might be sick. I'm feeling a little queasy myself.

"You could come with me," I say to my sister. "But why? To keep an eye on me? To ward off more adlets?"

She shudders. "Not funny."

None of it feels particularly funny right now. It's Carol.

It's Ellowyn. It's Nicholas. It's that we're separated. It's… something around us. I can't articulate what it is, even to Emerson, but it's there.

I know it. I feel it.

We make it outside into the dark air at last. It's cool but not cold and smells of bonfires and the river and *witchcraft*. Something in me settles. Like the air itself is soothing. Like the gym was off, somehow.

Emerson grabs my hand as we walk—peeling off from the teenage crowd and heading toward Wilde House and Frost. Once we can't see the high school behind us any longer, we release the spell, and our fake friends swirl away into the dark.

I breathe a little deeper once they're gone.

"Here's what I need, Em." I swing our hands between us. "I need you to go be with Ellowyn. Hold her hand. Make her take care of herself. Make her laugh. Make sure she doesn't use her illness as an excuse to kill Zander. I can handle this."

"Rebekah—"

"I *have* to. I have to do it alone. I feel it."

Her thumb touches my ring. Then she smiles at me. "You're not alone. Even when it feels like you are, she's always with us when we need her."

I feel the usual surge of emotion when I think about Grandma. Love. Joy. Longing.

And that terrible shame that threads through all of it.

"Then everything will be just fine," I say, even though I don't think it's necessarily true. Grandma might guide us, she might be there in spirit, but there's only so much magic a dead witch can offer, no matter the depths of her love.

But if it'll get me off the hook with Emerson, I'll take it.

Emerson holds my hand until we get to the corner where we have to head in different directions. Beltane is in full swing around us. And the town has an annual May Day festival for humans that Emerson threw together in her spare time these last two weeks—because human festivals distract anyone looking too closely at why people flock to this small town on a random spring day. I can hear witches and humans alike, celebrating, and still it feels like it's just the two of us.

And we have to part. I don't know why it feels like a portentous moment—like everything changes from this choice. I smile and squeeze her hand. "Let me know if Ellowyn's doing better?"

"I will. And I'll expect a full report the minute you get home. I don't care how late it is."

"You'll probably be off farming."

It's a joke, but Emerson shakes her head seriously. "This is the beginning, remember? From here on out, this *is* the test."

I don't want that to freak me out, but it's certainly not *comforting*. Still, I don't let my bright-as-a-daisy smile falter. I know that if I do, all the witches in the world won't pry my sister from my side, not even the oldest around.

We drop hands and I turn away first, almost like if I don't, I *won't*. Then I head up the stairs carved into the hill. And I refuse to look back at my sister no matter how much I want to.

Because there's only moving forward. Into whatever this is. There's no glamour tonight. The mansion gleams in the moonlight as I approach, as unapproachably beautiful as its owner.

Or maybe the glamour is just not there for me *tonight*, I think. *As a personal gift.*

Lucky me.

But I'm not feeling *lucky* when I look up and see Nicholas Frost standing on his dramatic widow's walk, waiting for me. *Me.* To do some mysterious Beltane ritual to deal with my fractured visions and my supposedly special powers.

To do whatever he likes, that same voice in me intones.

It's not helpful, given this seems a lot like the immortal version of a date.

I'm dressed in a white Beltane gown like a virgin sacrifice, a counterpoint to the black suit he's still wearing as he stands there high above me, a part of the night.

I should want to turn around and run. Close my eyes and magic myself back to Sedona, the Joywood and their tests be damned. But no matter how many rational thoughts I have, my body moves forward of its own volition. Step by step.

Until I reach the front door, all gleaming wood and intricate carvings. Though he's given no instruction, I reach out and open the door. The knob turns in my hand, warm and welcoming.

It's all candlelight and shadows dancing inside.

The scent of woodsmoke and vetiver.

And when I step inside, I step back in time.

AS I CROSS THE THRESHOLD, I REALIZE IMMEDIATELY I'm not *actually* slipping through time. It's a vision—and it feels different from the fractured static I've been experiencing since I got back to town. I wouldn't call it *clear*, exactly, but for a moment there it really does feel like I stepped into another century. The air smells of roasting meats and is filled with chants in a language I don't know.

The door swings shut behind me, but doesn't slam, which is somehow more unnerving than if it did. The foyer I'm standing in is suitably lavish, with a gleaming hall beyond it, filled to the brim with candles. Magical candles, naturally. I would expect nothing less. And as I look around at all the stately, quiet wealth, nothing seems ancient except the statuary.

Until Nicholas appears at the top of the grand staircase. It's the kind of dramatic entrance that belongs in Hollywood movies about witches, with a swelling score and theatrics. But as he takes the stairs, moving with a glide that makes it seem as if he's *floating* toward me, *time* seems to flicker again.

Different versions of him flash in the static as he moves. I see him striding through towns that are obviously medieval, speaking in languages I can't understand, yet in the same tone I know all too well. I see him dressed like a Puritan, striding stone-faced through a hard rain. I see unidentifiable woods, dark and deep, and bonfires against the night with him moving in the shadows. I see him in a green and misty place, the hint of the sea in the air, riding a horse as if he's being chased. I see him in too many different costumes to name, though I know at once that they're not costumes at all. They're him. They're what he wore in this century or that. Immortal Nicholas Frost in all his glory.

I was never in any of those times or places, but I don't just *see* them, I *inhabit* them.

I know things I shouldn't. Who he was with. What he felt. Where he was running and who from.

In this flickering moment, I can taste the thick green mist, the smoky dark woods. I understand him, deeper than I've ever understood anyone. Including myself.

Stranger still, I don't think he has the slightest idea that I can see into him, into his past. If he knew, he would not continue toward me like this. He would *do something* to stop whatever's happening, whatever this is.

I can't decide if I want him to, or don't.

Dimly, in the back of my mind, I know I should control my breathing. Work up my trademark sarcastic mouth quirk and something obnoxious to say. But I can only stare, trying to make sense of what I've seen. What's rearranging itself inside of me. Including that glimpse I had of him as a boy, all blue eyes and heat, an unchecked force of nature even then, running wild in some stone city I can't name.

And then Nicholas is standing in front of me, that blue gaze moving from my head to my toes with absolutely no reaction showing on his admittedly perfect face.

It's like he's always been here. Waiting.

"You didn't change your clothes, witchling."

I suck in a breath, trying to remind my heart it belongs to *me* and should stop trying to escape my rib cage. I can't seem to summon either straight snarkiness or my usual daisy smile and slouch, but I do my best. "Don't worry. Just like Cinderella, I'll turn into a pumpkin the minute the clock strikes twelve."

When I can dress like myself again. I feel certain that will help.

On cue, his overwrought grandfather clock begins to bong from just inside the nearest room, visible from our spot in the foyer.

One, two, three. There's no reason for me to feel breathless. But what can I say? I'm a witch, born and bred. Even in my most human and magicless periods out there, I always felt the power of a midnight. Particularly on a festival night.

By the time I force a breath or two, we're halfway there. Both Nicholas and I are standing in this foyer, a little too close for comfort, while the clock strikes. *Seven. Eight. Nine.*

"Don't change," he says, ruining my ability to count entirely. He has not taken his eyes off me this entire time.

And something feels different. It has since earlier at the dance. It's clear to me that I'm not imagining it.

If only I had any clue what changed. But the visions I can see swirling around us still seem more past than future—which is Ellowyn's purview as a Summoner, not mine.

And thinking of her seems to conjure the message I get then, from Emerson. *Ellowyn is much better and asleep.* One of the many knots tied tight inside of me loosens. She's asleep, resting, better. With all the people who can help her.

I can't help her, no matter how I want to. I focus on Nicholas instead.

He is watching me, intently. So intently it nearly hurts. I try to refuse to do nerves, but I can't seem to keep them at bay. My own body isn't listening to me—at all. Because while this is familiar—standing in private places with this man, trying to read him, feeling things I shouldn't—tonight I'm painfully aware of the fact I'm an adult. And so is he, a thousand times over.

Everything is different, something in me whispers, and I know it to be true though I still don't know why.

"You look like you're waiting for something," I say, managing to sound as bored by that prospect as he usually looks. "Hate to disappoint you, but I didn't bring the postprom keg."

"I have been waiting a long time for you to come to me like this, Rebekah," he says, and I can't tell if he's speaking out loud or inside me. It's like both at once. Like the tolling of a new bell. "Dressed like a proper Beltane gift from long ago."

He makes that sound like a spell. Like a vision made real. Something flickers at the edge of my sight, a girl in a white dress, high on a dark hill… I don't have to turn to look. I know it's me, and more, that it's his vision of this moment, not mine.

Though up this high above St. Cyprian, in the thick dark of the most sensual night of the year, I can't quite tell the difference.

"Georgie says the incantation for prom is different than it used to be," I say to disrupt the silence that broods there between us, suggestive and deep. "Did you know that?"

He does not respond. There's the faint hint of tightening in the vicinity of his soaring cheekbones, but that's it. I don't actually expect him to launch into chapter and verse on the subject, but it seems like information *the very first* Praeceptor should know.

I keep going. "And that four-hundred-pound book you gave me may have shown *her* that, but it hasn't shown me anything." I don't want to let him know how hard I've tried with it either. That feels like weakness. I might as well fall down and show him my belly.

And you know what? That image is not helpful.

He manages to look disdainful without seeming to change a single thing about his expression or the way he stands there, languid and at his ease despite the suit he's still wearing that would make anyone else look stuffy. "Perhaps when you're finally willing to put childishness aside and come to the book without so many objects meant to dull your power, you'll find an answer."

It rankles, the words *dull* and *childishness*, when it's really about control. Still, part of me can't help but wonder... But I need the control. It's how I've made it this far. Using my piercings to ground me literally gets me through the day.

"I don't really get why you're so obsessed with my piercings, Nicholas, but if you're wondering how they feel, I'm sure there are any number of piercing studios in the greater St. Louis area that would be happy to help you out with that. Maybe a Prince Albert?"

He does not react to this invitation, though I feel certain he knows the purpose of a Prince Albert piercing. I feel equally certain that after centuries of practice, he doesn't need help finding a woman's G-spot. More things I probably don't need to think about right now.

Nicholas's eyes gleam, but all he does is gesture at the stairs. "We will do our ritual on the roof."

"Sounds safe."

"The ritual is one you should have read about in your book."

"The only ritual for Beltane in that book was all about walking through fire. All cloaks and daggers and eye of newt. No doubt originating right around the time you were born in darkness and crawled out of the primordial black ooze."

I congratulate myself on how tough I sound when the truth is, I've never had a real Beltane. I was seventeen the last time I was here, meaning no one was interested in letting me sneak off to the real, adult fires. I made do, mind you, but then I was exiled—meaning, I've never had a fully magical, adult Beltane night in my life.

I tell myself that's why I *yearn* to attempt the kind of magic this ritual promises.

As long as it's with him. Because if I die in June, I might as well go out having Beltaned with the witchiest of them all.

That might even be true. Though it's certainly not the *whole* truth.

I wonder what he can read in me. I can still see his past, cluttering up the air around us like a kaleidoscope of the lives he's led, but I don't have that kind of history. And anyway, he's powerful, but he's not a Diviner...

I'm pretty sure I'm just telling myself what I want to hear at this point.

"You'll need to work on your translating skills," Nicholas tells me in that annoyingly unruffled way of his. "There are no newts involved."

He starts toward the stairs, apparently certain that I'll follow him. I want to turn around and leave, just to make a point. But I want this more, whatever this is. A Beltane in a white dress like all the snatches of his misspent past I can see before me. Like that vision of me who's been here before, inhabiting this moment completely.

Nicholas never looks back to see if I'm following him. He leads me up the winding staircase, up and up. As I climb up behind him, one flight after the next, I think he really has a thing for stairs. But then I start to consider the fact he hasn't corrected any of my other assumptions about the ritual. Like *walking through fire*, for example.

I can't say I find that appealing in general, much less after all the metaphoric burning I've been doing lately. My repeatedly scorched hand flexes of its own accord.

There's no need to fear burning, he says, directly inside me, in case I want to keep pretending I'm anything but one more book the world's greatest Praeceptor can read at will. *You should only fear those who wish to see you burn.*

"I'm pretty sure they're the ones who fear me," I retort. Because it's true. The Joywood keep proving it.

Nicholas stops then, turning to me as I trudge up the last couple of steps and see that we're actually at the top of the stairs, at last. But I don't celebrate that as much as I should, because there's something like approval in his eyes. I wish I didn't want to see it there. I wish I didn't feel, shamefully, as if I *need* this man's approval.

But here we are. Daddy issues for the win.

At least Nicholas is hot.

He moves to open the door just there where the roof pitches, then motions for me to step through it and into the thick Beltane midnight. We're high up on the top of his magical mansion, and I hesitate in the doorway, aware of the wind against my face, this far up. I can see St. Cyprian down below me, a ribbon of light, and the rivers like dark black arteries beneath the moon. And tonight, everywhere, I see the dance of bonfires from Beltane celebrations large and small.

Up here, in the center of the maze of his widow's walk, is a kind of roof terrace all covered in candles. Clearly he's enchanted the space because the wind coming off the river does not cause even a flicker of the many flames. The moon shines down like a spotlight, landing on Coronis, who perches on a spire and gives the illusion of a living weather vane.

Not that magical, ancient raven familiars would ever lower themselves in that fashion, I'm aware.

"We will make a Teineigen," Nicholas intones as he walks out into the candles behind me. I didn't actually know I moved from the doorway.

That word echoes inside me. *Teineigen*. I know it's a Celtic term for some kind of Beltane fire, but I've never been all that interested in the correct terms and all the boring historical dates the way Emerson is.

Until tonight, I can't say that bothered me too much.

Nicholas sighs. "It's a need fire. Purifying. Clarifying. We will build it. You'll walk through it. If done right, it might solve your vision issues."

"You want me to walk *through* a fire."

"A magical fire, witchling," he chastises me, not all that gently. "You'll hardly meet your end here. I promise." Something flares between us when he says that word, *promise*. I choose not to point out that even I know better than to make vows on sacred nights. His mouth seems to tighten. "We will start the flame here with what kindling I have, then add logs in turn. You are capable of repeating after me, I trust?"

I shrug. "Debatable."

He is neither amused nor deterred. He points to a spot opposite him, on the other side of the pile of logs and kindling. "Stand there, and we will begin."

I don't know much about the Teineigen, but I know how starting a ritual fire works. "Aren't we supposed to hold hands for something like this?"

"There is no need." He says that stiffly.

Stiffly enough I see the pattern. "You really have a problem with me touching you."

"Hardly." And he begins the fire chant before I can argue. *"Heat within, flame without."*

I repeat the chant with him, then blow it out toward the pyre. Three times as the flame begins to build.

Then he adds the first log. *"Let the flames of Beltane burn."*

I add my own log and repeat his words.

"May the Old Ones now return." He adds a log, I parrot him and add another.

And so we keep on, building the fire against the night, one line at a time.

"And aid our visions strong and pure."

"To lighten what went black once more."

The fire blazes, and he's right. There is apparently no need for hand-holding. By now the flames dance high enough that they block most of my view of him.

Then, as I'm standing there, feeling parts of me that I've ignored for too long leap and writhe like the flames against the night, Nicholas walks around the fire. To me.

To me in this traditional white dress that feels less stupid suddenly than it has all night. Here in this impossible moment, trapped in the sky itself with his eyes on me, it feels right that I should be wearing a gown of white to herald the start of spring. As if I'm as new and green as the season.

So new and green it takes me a few beats of my heart to notice that he's cupping a small bowl in his palms and stretching it out toward me.

"Remove your adornments."

When I hesitate, he doesn't move or even *tsk*. He holds my gaze, and his voice seems to get impossibly deeper, darker, inside me.

Stop being afraid of what you are, Rebekah.

The way he says my name is a hit from some powerful drug all on its own. "I'm not afraid," I manage to choke out.

"You weren't. Once."

That feels like a blow and it shouldn't. Not from him. "Yeah, and look where that got me."

"It got you here. To this moment. Did it ever occur to you that now is where you were meant to be?"

Literally not once. Not in the way he means. "You, the oldest witch of them all, believe in things like fate? Destiny? In what's *meant to be*? I thought you ran around thumbing your nose at such pedestrian beliefs."

"Never."

It's a grave response. A sort of resigned acceptance that I find hard to argue against. He *has* seen it all after all.

He's still holding the bowl, like he can wait me out and more, *will*. "Try it. Just once."

We both know he could make me. He could snap his fingers and rid me of every piercing and all my ink. And it's not as if he's pleading with me instead. There's too much steel in him.

What he's demanding isn't only that I take my piercings out.

It's that I choose to obey him.

He does me the courtesy of not pretending otherwise.

And maybe that's why I find myself reaching up to take my earrings out. He's asking, in his way, rather than telling. Rather than waving a languid hand and compelling me. I can't seem to resist it.

I use my fingers to take out all my earrings, while whispering a little incantation to take out the rest, and my tattoos as well. Metal and ink float into the little bowl he holds—almost like an offering. I drop my earrings into the little soup of what I've long considered fundamental parts of my identity, then work up my courage to meet his intense gaze. "Happy?"

"We'll see." He looks me over, then gestures to my hand. "The ring as well."

I curl my fingers into my palm. "No."

Because it feels wrong. I don't *love* the feeling of losing all the metal that helps me dull everything. I made sure my piercings blocked my meridian points, deliberately smoothing away the worst of the visions that come at me, so I would never accidentally use too much magic to handle them. I feel naked without them, but I can deal. I hope.

What I can't do is take this ring off.

Nicholas studies me a moment, then frowns at the ring. He tilts his head as if examining it, though he does not reach out to take my hand or bring the ring any closer to his face, the way I feel certain anyone else would.

"Did you..." He trails off, and all I can think is that I've never heard Nicholas Frost *trail off* as if he's not sure how to proceed. Something in me goes a little seismic. "Did you bring the crystal?" he asks roughly.

I pat the little pocket in my ridiculous white dress—perhaps its only saving grace. It was something Emerson insisted upon after a lengthy lecture about pockets and feminism, and my mother relented only because it was the only way to shut her up, I'm pretty sure.

"Have you noticed anything different?" Nicholas asks with an intensity that makes the earthquake in me pick up speed and force.

But I shove that aside. I think about Carol approaching me. Skip the weasel. Ellowyn, so sick she had to leave. And yet none of that is what he means. Even the crystal doing its work to heal the burning sensation I felt after Carol isn't quite what he's after. "No."

His eyebrows turn down slightly. Is it disappointment?

Confusion? Some emotion that's so foreign to him that his face doesn't even know how to arrange itself?

I fish the crystal out of my pocket and hold it out to him. It's a tiny little thing. I'm not sure what it's supposed to do, but then the flames flicker around us as if the wind has finally pierced Nicholas's spell. As it does, the crystal pulses. Then lifts, of its own accord, out of my hand and into the air.

I feel my other hand being tugged up, like there's a magnet directly above it. It should alarm me, but it doesn't. The unseen force lifts my hand up and then out in front of me, so the ring points toward the moon. The crystal still hovers in the air, then moves until it's above the very center of the ring.

There's a pause, like the crystal is waiting for my permission. But for what? How can I agree if I don't even know what's happening? But when I look across at Nicholas, he looks taken aback, like he didn't expect this either.

I think of how he asked me for my piercings when he could have taken them, and how much more powerful I feel for having chosen to surrender. Like it isn't a surrender at all. The crystal seems to gleam at me as I consider this, and I know I'm right. This isn't the Joywood. This is the kind of magic my grandmother taught us. Choice, yes, but *responsibility* above all things. The responsibility that power breeds and can too easily stain. The responsibility inherent in having magic at all.

Grandma was all about responsibility and I failed her once. I won't again.

I look past the hovering crystal, my raised hand. To the immortal standing there, seeming to block out the world.

When his gaze meets mine, all I see are flashes of light, like a thousand stars I can feel deep inside me. A part of that seismic shift, that heat and hunger.

He feels like magic too, and not only because he has so much of it.

I honor my grandmother and myself, this man and this moment.

I focus all my attention on my raised hand and what hovers above it.

And with all I am—what I was and what I will be—I think, *yes.*

Yes.

17

THAT *YES* IS LIKE ANOTHER GREAT, OLD BELL tolling, deep within. It seems to carry on the wind, tangling with the rivers down below and the dancing Beltane firelight, making the Missouri hills and fields glow.

Up here on this widow's walk the night seems darker, the moon brighter.

Coronis lets out a low, wild croak, another kind of *yes*, as if he's singing it back to me. As if he's giving me his raven blessing.

The perfectly spherical stone lowers, then sits in the middle of the ring. And it's as if the ring absorbs it, until it becomes the center of the narcissus. Then blooms.

Like it was always meant to go right there, in the ring my grandmother made. For *me.* This crystal that Nicholas gave me at a dance that felt stupid, on a sacred night that's anything but.

There's an immediate release inside of me. The static that has hounded me, all those fractured things that flit through my brain even when I'm alone, are gone. In an instant. The instant the stone touches the ring, I feel new.

Or like myself again.

A bolt of terror slams into me. I remember, too well, what it was like before I was allowed to go out into the world, sent off into exile, and figure out what I needed to do to stop the onslaught. The constant barrage of images. The lack of control and the *chaos* that slammed into me all the time, without warning, without any of my piercings or tattooed wards that aren't *quite* spells to help.

I brace myself. I'm holding my breath.

But there is no assault, no clatter of visions. There is only a calm inner silence. It pulses with power. With connection. Yet not with all the normal *mess*.

"What did you *do*?" I ask Nicholas, struggling to take my eyes off the ring. But when I do look at him, those blue eyes blaze like flame. Not ice.

"It's a clarifying crystal. It…clarified."

It's no ordinary *clarifying* crystal, the sort of thing humans use as worry stones. It's something special, and more powerful than anything a human could get their hands on. It has fixed this static inside of me in an *instant*.

Add to all that, it is somehow mine. Meant for me.

By him? By my grandmother?

By destiny?

I look up at him as another realization comes hurtling at me.

He has been missing in action for two weeks. Not making immortal demands from on high, not whispering in my head. Maybe that's normal for him, but that wasn't how it went the last time I lived in St. Cyprian full time.

It almost feels like… "You went and found this. For me."

"There was a problem. I solved it," he returns with absolutely no emotional inflection. Not even his usual snide condescension. He sounds completely flat.

I'm tempted to imagine it means something.

Especially when his blue eyes glitter.

"If we're finished with the clarification process," he says in the same flat manner, as if I was the one running around with crystals and staircases to the sky, "perhaps we can return our attention to the ritual. While it's still Beltane."

"The ritual," I murmur, hoping I sound vaguely affirmative. "Of course."

But suddenly, what I'm thinking about is Beltane. And, more specifically, the usual activities adult witches get up to while the bonfires light the night. The kind of activities, in fact, I saw Nicholas himself getting up to in those snatches of visions earlier.

"You will walk through the fire and the ritual will be complete. Once it is, your visions should be within your control." He no longer sounds flat nor looks glittery. I suspect he might have gotten an idea of what was going through my mind just now, so I work on my blocking and attempt to look angelic.

"And what will you be doing?"

"I suppose I'll ensure you don't burn alive," he says, sounding bored.

I wish *I* could assume the same disinterest in the topic.

"Once the ritual is complete, you will not need to dull yourself with the tawdry accoutrements of spell-less humans, so desperate to feel something they pierce their own flesh and call it transcendent."

"Or, you know. They like how they look?"

"That is up to you, of course."

"Funny, I didn't think anything was up to me."

A different sort of gleam in his gaze now. "You're an adult. No matter how you act."

And the goddess knows that these tectonic *situations* inside of me are adult enough when it comes to him. This is not the sort of hero worship I had for him as a teenager. Back then he was different and dangerous enough that sneaking around to have strange conversations ripe with portent and doom felt like escape to me. My life was confinement. He felt like flying free.

This is something different.

And sure, he really is dangerous. I know that. On any number of levels.

For all I know, he's a tool of the Joywood and always has been—yet that's not the danger I'm most conscious of when it comes to Nicholas. Not even close.

Self-preservation tells me to keep my mouth shut, the way it often does...but as we've established, that's not really my strong suit. "Great," I say. "We're both adults. I guess that makes us equals, Nicholas."

Unlike back when I was a teenager who only thought she was an adult.

I don't say that part, but I don't have to. I might be the only one viewing his history tonight, but when it comes to *our* history, I know he remembers the same things I do. I don't question how I know it. I just do.

There is a weighted moment. I almost think he's about to speak—

But instead he steps back and the book appears in his hand. That damn book. I'd be happy to never see it again. Tragically, it's my experience that magical books never truly disappear. They lurk around, showing up again when it's the most annoying. With a quick word from Nicholas, the book flips open to a page I actually read the other day, since it mentioned Beltane and that seemed important. Or at least timely.

Of course, in my translation I sort of figured the walking through fire part was *metaphorical*. I should have known better.

"You will walk through the fire. You will say these words." He points to the flowing script, obviously in a cryptic, runic script that gives me an immediate headache. He looks at me as if *everyone* knows how to read it or should.

"You know, it's been a long ass day," I tell him, and I don't even know why I'm suddenly so mad. Just that I am. Or anyway, that's one way to describe all that shifting heat inside me. "I'm not in the mood to figure out impossible translation spells and then—"

The book is hovering between us now, because he's stopped holding it. Instead, he comes to stand behind me and puts his hand on my shoulder. Not skin to skin. I have the stray thought that *skin to skin* would be like taking the brakes off, and we can't have *that.* But I can feel his palm through the fabric of my dress. His hand, which is big and not in any way soft.

I'm entirely too aware that he has never touched me like this before. All those years ago when he acted as a kind of secret tutor, there was always distance. The whole thing was very hands-off.

But now it feels like he's pulsing some power into me. I want it to be as simple as heat, as need, but I know it's not that. *It's about the ritual, Rebekah*, I tell myself. More than once. So I can understand the translation without having to bother with my shaky translation spell.

It's not that I'm bad at magic, I've decided over the past two weeks, despite what Felicia and all my other teachers tried to tell me in school. It's that I've always had so much raw power inside me, all the visions and all the *knowing*, that I was always more focused on controlling that part of me. And never, therefore, all that interested in learning these staple spells that other witches find about as hard as telling time.

Mind you, that's also why I prefer a digital clock display.

And I don't have to tell Nicholas any of this, because I already did. Years ago.

It's not only that he knows. He *remembers*.

And his hand is on my shoulder, where it feels raw, like a new tattoo.

"Read," he tells me, his voice rougher than it usually is. So rough it makes me feel shivery, but I frown at the book hanging in the air before me instead of concentrating on the *shivery* part.

Fire above. Fire below. Fire within.
The wheel of the year is turning.
Beltane fires are burning.
Brand me with your clarity
Lighten the darkness within me.
Fire above. Fire below. Fire within.

"Commit it to memory," he says after I read it as I was told, his hand still on my shoulder. I know his power has translated the words for me, but now it feels like it weaves around me to keep the words in my head. To anchor them inside me.

Making them part of me.

"Now, Rebekah," he urges me then, his voice like a new spell. "Walk."

It's almost as if I'm in a trance, but I'm too aware. Of his hand. Of his breath. The way he stands behind me, dark and sure. The way I feel in my own body, somehow new and fragile yet wise and strong.

The flames rise in front of me. The moon above, the wind all around.

But there's no fear. I know what I have to do, and I do it. The words from the book dance in my head, then come out my mouth, word perfect.

And as they do, Nicholas is chanting his own.

I move toward the pyre we built and I pull my dress up with my hands. I keep saying the words, over and over.

Then I pick up one foot and put it in the fire, as if that's a rational, reasonable thing to do—

The words, witchling, comes his voice inside me, as something rolls over me, a lot like a scream.

I don't scream. I breathe out, then put my weight on the foot engulfed by flame and step forward.

Then I take another step. And I'm in the fire.

It burns bright.

But it doesn't burn *me*.

Fire above. Fire below.

Maybe I'm saying the words. Maybe I *am* the words.

What I'm not is the girl who spent ten years pretending magic is the same as cocaine.

Because cocaine can't keep a person from burning in a fire, though I suppose it might keep them from feeling it. But magic—*my* magic and Nicholas's plus these old, powerful words—keeps me safe. It's not that I can't feel the fire. It's that I *want* to feel it, and so the flames lick over me and through me.

It's nothing like the water scrying or Carol's slap of white-hot power in the gym.

This isn't something I'm *doing* or even something being done *to* me. This is something that I'm submitting to, of my own free will, and the flames of my choice tonight are…purifying.

Like the ritual says.

Whatever hisses and sizzles and turns to ash inside of me were things I didn't want or recognize in there anyway. I move through the flames, and I am free.

Light.

Whole.

Everything that isn't a strength turns to smoke and blows away.

On the other side, I step from the fire and find I am intact. Unharmed. Nothing has changed outside of me. I'm not burned. Even my dress is still the same snowy white. It's only *inside* me that everything is uncluttered and new, burned down to diamonds.

Something makes me look down at my ring, to find it on fire. I think to slap at the flame, or toss the ring aside, but I take a breath and understand…it's not hot. It doesn't *hurt.* The ring itself isn't melting or even being ruined by the flames, though it's changing as I watch. Rearranging itself, until the petals resolidify. It's still a flower, my grandmother's flower, and the crystal Nicholas gave me is still lodged in the middle, but it's all arranged in a new symbol.

I've seen this symbol. In that same damn book.

I turn to look up at him, still entirely himself, but in my head it's my grandmother's voice I hear. Just as if she's standing behind me, whispering into my ear.

Blood of my blood. Heart of my heart. First of the year, last of the year: Two sides of a coin. You are the sign. The moment. Be brave. Be strong. Believe.

I've heard those words before, not always in that exact order, but *always* from my grandmother. Emerson and I, first and last, two sides, the sign. I don't want to hear them here. With Nicholas or *anyone.*

"What the hell does this mean?" I demand of Nicholas, because now it hurts.

Not the fire. Not my ring. But feeling like my grandmother is right here, pulling these strings. When she can't possibly think that old prophecy is about *me* any longer. When I broke her heart, when I disappointed and failed her. It wasn't the way I disappointed my parents. It wasn't about the family's image or standing or *our place.*

It was about breaking promises, sacred trusts, and shirking sacred responsibilities. It was about going against everything she'd always taught me. I let the magic consume me, turn dark, and all on our sacred bricks.

It was real, my betrayal. Important. The end of...everything for me.

I look to Nicholas for answers. He points to the book, hovering before us once again.

"Read, Rebekah," he says.

Again.

I don't want to, but here I am anyway, moving against what I want. Moving instead toward the book that seems to wait for me, as if it's sentient and knows exactly how I feel about it. When I get close enough, I see it's opened to the same page, the Beltane ritual.

But on the bottom is a symbol.

Not just any symbol, but the one on my ring—an X of flower petals with a circle in the middle. And underneath, ancient script.

This time, I don't need his help translating. Something's changed. Strengthened. I know without asking that Nicholas will likely chalk it up to taking off all my metal, but I think it's something else. The fire. The stone. My embrace of both.

Or more likely by far, my grandmother.

Because if any witch could be just as powerful in the grave as in the world, it's her.

I suck in a breath and read.

This is the symbol of the Chaos Diviner. A power bestowed on very few. When the world descends into chaos, disorder, and imbalance, the Chaos Diviner finds the center of her power. This power will either destroy or heal. It will either kill, or it will birth. Destruction happens alone. Healing happens with the guidance of Who is Meant. Only then can chaos become light.

My heart is kicking at me, and I can feel it in my throat. There are earthquakes inside me, and I'm suddenly much too aware that I'm on a widow's walk in the middle of the night with an immortal witch.

In other words, this is too much. All of this is *too much.* The killing and birthing in particular, the *chaos* part when I've worked so hard for calm and control, but…*who is meant?* What is *that*?

It echoes inside of me, like it or not. I do not believe in destiny, in things that are *meant.* I was *meant* to be a powerful witch from birth, and instead I was labeled spell dim and forced into exile. And I was *meant* to die out there, I'm sure of it, but here I am.

I choose my destiny, *despite* what I'm *meant* to do. If I have a code, that's it.

Who is meant is bullshit.

And here I am, staring at Nicholas Frost.

I remember that strange urge outside the bar to put my hands on him. My grandmother's words in my head. All the ways he's kept himself physically distant from me before now—his magic might have touched me, but never *him.*

I turn to face him, once again painfully aware…of him. Of me. I'm in white and he's in black. He's centuries old, I'm relatively new. I've walked through the fire and he doesn't need to. I have none of my usual protections, and yet the ring from my grandmother and the stone from Nicholas seem all the protection I could ever need.

And it isn't protection I want.

"Let me touch you," I say.

There is the slight flicker of surprise in his eyes, not quite a jerk, but an involuntary movement in his body. I can't tell if it's some kind of flinch or *what.*

"There is no need," he says in the cold voice that might have scared me once. Might have put my back up, *once.*

"You believe in things that are meant to be," I whisper.

His eyes flare, but his voice grows colder. "Are you not concerned that you are a *Chaos Diviner*? Perhaps you ought to run and tell your little group of freedom fighters that your power might just destroy them if you don't wield it correctly."

I probably will be concerned with that at some point, but this is tonight. And tonight is Beltane. I really want to know who *is* meant, as it happens.

I step toward him. "I'm concerned that you're afraid to let me touch you."

"I do not *fear* much of anything, witchling. And neither of us has time for such childish games."

I laugh at that. At him. "You have all the time in the world," I counter.

This time, he does not remind me my time is limited. He looks at me, and there is something in that expression that makes me realize…

There is a *man* in there. Under the finery, the power, the years and years of watching the world go by and no doubt organizing it to suit him, he's still a person. Not a figure.

Not a fantasy.

A *man*.

"It won't do us any good," he grits out, and it might be the most honest thing he's said to me. *Ever.*

I could pretend I don't know what he means, but I've never been any good at pretending. I smile, and it's not daisies. "Nicholas, someone should have told you. I'm not the good sister."

But he straightens those wide shoulders and gathers himself like the warrior he once was. The warrior I saw in a vision tonight, wielding a weapon I've only seen in museums. "That will be enough for tonight, Rebekah."

An order. A dismissal.

Too bad for him I'm a woman who walks through fires

and burns herself strong. "Maybe I'll decide when it's been enough, for a change."

"No."

He tries to send me away, but it's happened too many times and I know it's coming.

And this time, I do just what he invited me to *try* back at the bar two weeks ago.

I stop him.

LIGHT SPARKS OFF THE PLACE WHERE MY MAGIC stops him, his hand extended and frozen in midair. There is a full moment of shock on his face, and it's reflected in the air. Even the fires all around us still.

I *want* to believe this is Nicholas Frost, immortal witch, being impressed.

If it is, it doesn't last. That impatient anger I saw for the first time at the bar reasserts itself across his features, and he doesn't bother to hide it. While he invited me to fight him off two weeks ago, I imagine he thought it'd be on *his* terms. When the stakes didn't matter to *him*.

They seem to matter to him now. He tries to send me away once more. I feel the yank of it, that deep inner *tug*, but I plant my feet—literally and figuratively. I use all that *clarified* power inside of me to block his spell.

Then I fling it back at him.

I nearly shout with victory when his boot scrapes against the floor of the widow's walk. Just the tiniest millimeter, like the force of my magic set him back *only that much*, even with all his magic blocking it. But he's already sending another burst of that intense energy of his directly at me, clearly intended to take me far away from here.

Far away from *him*.

Maybe all the way back to Sedona, and on some level, I should want that.

But I don't.

I refuse to go. And I refuse to stop fighting. So, the battle goes on.

And it's no joke. Nicholas's eyes blaze a blue fury. My muscles shake with the exertion of throwing it right back at him. It's magic, but it's deeply physical. It's energy and force, but unlike the spells I used to cast when I was younger or the work I did with everyone to hold back that flood, something within me is also…expanding. I've never felt anything like it before. I have to wonder if it's the whole clarifying crystal plus Grandma's magic plus whatever the hell stuff Chaos Diviner comes with.

Or, you know, him.

Who is meant.

And I can feel it then. Beneath all the power I'm expending is a new pulse beating within me. It's been beating in me since he yanked me out of Sedona to come back here and help clean up this mess. It's only gotten worse since I've been home.

Or better, something in me whispers.

Since those moments outside the bar. Since the dance earlier tonight.

Since he led me through a fire with only the sound of his voice.

It's everywhere. My temples, my neck. My wrists. And deep between my legs, as if I really am the sacrificial virgin I'm dressed as tonight.

I know, now, without a shred of ego, that I can hold him off a few more times yet. I know this with a quiet certainty, as if I'm looking at a fuel gauge instead of taking stock of the power inside me. Yet if this is a contest of endurance, he'll win. I know that too, with the same certainty, as if expending power in this way has clarified not only my own magic, but given me a frank insight into the power around me too.

Nicholas is, unsurprisingly, far more powerful than I am. But who says I have to play by his rules?

I'm an adult. We are equals, whether he wants to admit that or not. And maybe it's time I stop thinking like I'm still a teenager, no matter how many high school horror reenactments the Joywood have in store for me. The fact is, I can make some of my own rules now.

I hold up my hands in a kind of surrender, though it's not one. Not really. "You can send me away, Nicholas. Banish me if you want. Why not? Exile suits me just fine." Part of me thinks he'll just blast me back to Sedona, but another part of me—not the rebellious part, but the powerful part, and I'll have to think about why they're not the same—is still. Because maybe I know better. I watch that blaze in his eyes, and more, I *feel* it. Everywhere. Like he's part of me. I go on. "At the end of this testing period, I'll be *lucky* if I get exiled again, but I'm not giving up. Not because of them and not because of you. Something changed today, Nicholas. I won't rest until I know what it is."

He doesn't raise or lower his hands, but he doesn't fling any of that intense magic of his my way either. There is no spell to tug me somewhere else.

Nicholas looks down at me, the blue flame changed to icy condescension, but that feels a lot like a win. "You will regret it," he says.

It's not that I don't believe him. His conviction rings

through every word. It's just that regret is a choice. Life just isn't going to go perfectly or even the way you want. And if you live in all those old wishes, holding on tight to *how it should have been*, you shrivel up.

I know. I learned and I grew out there. I might be back in this place, but I haven't *shriveled* here the way I could have. The way anyone would in the face of so many bad memories and worse choices. Instead, I've stood in my power, the way those ten years on my own taught me to. You learn or you die. Sometimes that death is long and drawn out and looks a lot like fear, but it's a death all the same. You learn so you can *live.*

"I don't believe in regret," I return, somewhat surprised at how calm I sound. How at peace I feel when the night started with a prom, had a fire walking interlude, and has just now been all about hurling power at each other like we're trying to make our own thunderstorm.

But there is no peace in him. There is something like a *crack* in the air, like he's reached his breaking point, and it echoes around him. In the sky, in the wind.

And in me, over and over again.

His fine, nearly cruel mouth flattens into a shape that should scare me, but that's not at all how I feel.

"Then I will teach it to you," he tells me, like a vow.

Or a curse.

I don't get the impression he moves, but somehow he is close. So close that he could reach out and touch me—and he does. His hands wrap around my upper arms, bared to the night air, and I understand immediately why he's been so careful not to touch me before now—not when we're alone like this, and there's nothing to take the edge off the intensity or how it wallops me.

I get it then, a new level of clarity. It washes through me, bright and unflinching. That I wanted this long before I understood what it was. Who I was.

What he was then and still is now.

And this time, when his power slams into me, it isn't magic.

What I mean is, it isn't *only* magic. It's his mouth crashing to mine.

Nicholas Frost is kissing me.

But something in me rejects that. Not the fact of his mouth on mine, the fire hotter and brighter than the one I walked through. Never that—but the term itself. *Kissing.* I've engaged in *kissing* before. I practiced right here in St. Cyprian before I headed out into the world to perfect the craft. I've long prided myself on my artisanal flair.

Yet this feels like a *first* kiss.

His hands are on me. Not on my dress, maintaining that last barrier, but on *me.* His palms on my cheeks, his fingers in my hair.

And his mouth is the center of *everything*, taking me over, drawing me deeper, until longing and lust, heat and need, feel like the same thing.

This is not regret. This is the blooming of a part of myself I've never encountered before. Maybe it's always been there, hidden away, this part of me that's his. As if I have been, always and ever, only his.

This is heat, but not burning. This is magic, intertwining and turning into something so bright and bold, my knees threaten to buckle.

And while he angles his head, taking the kiss deeper, pulling me closer, there are all those visions of him again. Snatches of his past. It isn't just seeing, it's *feeling.* Experiencing it all with him.

Even when he wrenches his mouth away, I don't think he realizes all I see. If he knows this is happening. I'm not ready to let him in on it either, because the man is *immortal* and I am me, and I don't need anyone to tell me that we've just started a very different battle here.

I intend to win it.

Or at least keep my weapons to myself.

"Nicholas." My voice is as unsteady as my knees. It isn't just the kiss or the desperation for more that works in me, tying me in knots. It's all the rest of it too. The flashes of pain and longing, fear and shame, and so many other things I recognize.

We're the same, I think, and it doesn't feel like a stray thought. It feels like stone.

Coronis caws somewhere, and it echoes within me.

Something moves over Nicholas's beautiful face, and I wonder if it echoes like that in him too.

I can't tell if the kiss was something he meant to do or if it was a heat of the moment thing, but he doesn't release me. I feel certain he must want to. I can feel that part of him too.

But there is another part that holds my head between his hands, and he doesn't step away.

I think his blue gaze looks particularly tortured, like he's fighting the fact that he's the one who stepped over that line that's been between us as long as I've known him.

And I wouldn't call myself particularly gentle. I always like to slam my head into a wall instead of finding my way around or through it. It's been a long process to learn how to be gentle on myself out there, and I'm not very good at it. I would have told you a man who's been alive for centuries should have dealt with these things already, but he hasn't.

I don't question how I know that.

Just like I don't question that he needs gentleness from me. That he needs it, and more, I need to give it. I lift up on my toes and press my mouth to his, softly.

As though we have all the time in the world.

You do not.

His voice feels different inside me, now that I know how he tastes.

As if we are both brand-new here.

We have now, I tell him. *Tonight. Beltane. We don't need more than that.*

No matter how much I might want it.

No matter how much I want *him.*

This man who is myth and legend and has always felt like mine.

"Exile," I whisper, the word coming to me as his story fades in and out all around me. I can see flashes of his life, all that history he's lived through personally, and though I can pick out events here and there I don't have a clear story. I can't figure out the timeline. It's not like earlier, where what I saw was fractured and didn't make sense. I'm only allowed to see certain parts of the story. Some are blocked—which means he must know what I can see.

He knows, and he hasn't tossed me across the country already. He *kissed* me.

I feel that sparkle all the way through me, but I'm still focused on what I *can* see. The thread of it is a feeling I know. I recognize it all too well.

I blink up at him. "You were exiled."

"I've always been precisely where I want to be," he says, one hand still holding my face.

But that's not what I mean. Exile isn't just a place. Exile is a feeling. It's a distancing. It's…this house and his glamour.

He *chose* his exile. More and more with every passing century, I see, and particularly in the past ten years. Ever since my little fire show on the bricks of St. Cyprian.

I don't know what that means. What I do know is that I still haven't touched him, and that suddenly feels like more than an oversight. It feels like I won't live another moment if I don't.

Right now.

I reach out and set my palm to his heart, following an urge that I know, immediately, I've been carrying inside me *forever.* And I slide a finger in between the shirt buttons so that it's not just skin to fabric, but skin to *skin*.

I brace myself for some great insight, some new flash, but there is nothing. No bolt of truth. No harrowing look into his past. There is only his heart beating steadily against my palm, as if he's as mortal as I am.

"You will be my downfall," Nicholas says, his mouth against mine.

And then everything ignites.

Like we are falling stars, we catapult into everything and nothing.

We kiss until we're no longer content with mouths or fingertips or *clothes*. Or rooftops, apparently, because we topple into a bed too big for any one person before I'm even aware that he's moving us through the air.

I forget how to think. I'm just happy that there's a bed and there's *him* and I finally—finally—get to explore every last bit of every last fantasy I've ever had starring this man.

And there have been so many.

We are skin and bones and magic. We come together in his vast, wide bed, the moonlight pouring in through the windows all around and a skylight above. We tumble this way and that. We rush and then we take our time, teeth and curses, smiles and hands, learning each other.

Like this is the only test that matters.

We roll until I am on top, looking down. He is still and ever the most beautiful man I've ever seen. He is so beautiful that a great many choices I made, out there in the world, make a new kind of sense to me now that I've admitted that no matter how I might have hated this man, I always wanted him. No matter what I blamed him for, and still do.

But that has no place here. Not tonight. Nicholas reaches up and braces his strong hands at my cheeks, holding my dark hair back and piercing me with his gaze. The blue is a different blaze now. And the fire within me seems to reach for it. For him.

This is almost certainly a terrible idea, he says, very solemnly, inside of me.

My favorite kind, I reply, and turn my head to pull one of his fingers into my mouth.

I shift, there where I'm straddling him, bracing my hands against the fine ridges of his abdomen.

And then we are one.

I think, insofar as I can think at all, that I have never known true fire, true heat, until this moment.

I am alight. I burn, become ash, then burn again.

It isn't a change within me, so much as a change around me. There is a portent, as if witch's runes hang in the air all around us with every breath, every cry, every thrust and stretch and sigh.

As though coming together skin to skin was *meant*.

Meant.

The words in that book seem like brands inside my body, all over my skin. Like tattoos I can keep. *Who is Meant*.

I don't question it. I *am* it. It's like walking through the fire all over again.

But it gives so much more.

This isn't just *sex*—human or witch, and yes, there's a difference, because magic makes everything different—but this is bigger than all of that. This isn't as simple as pleasure, or transformation, lust or need or a bone-deep craving.

This isn't as simple as a seismic shift, tectonic plates making the world new.

I want to say it is everything. A thousand lifetimes, immortality, the universe, and all of it like a white-hot, blinding burst of *yes* inside me.

Or maybe not inside me, because I'm pretty sure I say all that out loud. Or maybe scream it.

Sometime later, I blink my eyes open. It's still dark, and though the moon is no longer filling the room with its silvery light, flickering candlelight has taken its place. If I fell asleep, it wasn't for too long.

I sit up and see I'm in this huge bed alone, though Nicholas stands by the giant window, a dark and shadowed silhouette. From my vantage point I can't see much beyond him except little pinpricks of light—bonfires in the distance and the streetlights of St. Cyprian below.

And Nicholas Frost looking down on it all. Not a dream.

A dream I've had, in one version or another, a great many times—though I never kept dreaming my way into waking up in his bed. That's how I know this is real.

That and the fact I can still feel his hands all over me.

He does not turn, or move, but somehow he must sense I've awoken, because he speaks.

"This cannot happen again, Rebekah."

He stares out the window. No, he *broods*.

It hurts, I can't lie to myself about that, but I'm also not naive enough to believe that his *cannots* are about me. I shrug expansively, like the relentlessly chill woman I'm really not, not where he's concerned. "Beltane, am I right?"

He looks over his shoulder at me, frowning, but then seems to think better of it. Probably because I'm not worried about covering myself up any more than he is. I feel his gaze move all over me before he turns back to the window. It's a comfort that I get to him too.

"There are things I cannot explain to you," he says darkly.

I crawl to the side of the bed and stand, but I can't bring myself to put the Beltane prom dress back on. Even if I could find it, given I don't remember taking it off. I want to laugh at the thought that if my mother knew what I'd done in that dress, she'd be just as horrified as when I tried to burn Felicia to the ground.

That lifts my spirits a bit. I magic myself something from my closet. I start to do the same with all my piercings and tattoos but stop. Because I love a piercing and some sick ink, like every other member of my generation, but I love my magic more. My innate power and clear visions. If I have all that back, more clear and powerful than when I was younger, why tamp it all down?

I settle for a glamour instead, so it only *looks* like I'm wearing all my piercings and tattoos. I might not need them any longer, but I still like them. A lot.

"Because you genuinely can't explain or because you don't *want* to explain?" I ask Nicholas when I feel sufficiently armored.

"Because of curses. Because of oaths." I can sense the impatience all over him, even though he's glaring out the window still. "There are reasons I act in secret, but I am also bound by promises I made long ago. In blood and with the most powerful witchcraft there is."

"Yes."

When he turns to look at me his eyes go narrow. Maybe he doesn't like that I'm dressed. Maybe he doesn't like the return of my jewelry, glamour or not. It's possible what he doesn't like is my easy agreement. Or maybe, just maybe, he's starting to clue in.

"Yes?" he echoes.

I make a meal out of my careless shrug then. "Your clarifying trick really worked. I've seen some of those oaths."

He's looking at me with concern. And not, I think, for me. "You are not supposed to see backward. Only forward, into possibilities."

That would normally be my cue to announce that I do, in fact, remember the difference between all the different designations, like every other witch who made it through kindergarten. I don't know what stops me.

It's something about that shadow I'm sure I can see in all that arrested blue. Do I imagine *Nicholas Frost* looks vulnerable? Or do I only *want* that to be true? "Maybe Chaos Diviners are different. Maybe backward and forward are the same when it's all chaotic. You know, some people believe time is a sphere."

His mouth thins, and I know what that feels like against my skin. "And some people believe the moon is made of cheese."

"And *some* people don't believe in witches at all. Even when they feel that magic inside of them. We could go around and around on what people believe and don't until the sun comes up. Bottom line is, I've seen some of your oaths. I've felt them, like I was there, chanting around the same fires."

Nicholas says nothing. His displeasure is clear, stamped on every last perfect feature. I feel like I should revel in what's happened here, but it's hard to revel when everything feels so weighty. So important and intense.

Like good can only ever be chased by bad—but that's not new. I learned that right here in St. Cyprian a lifetime ago.

"And yet you haven't run out of this house screaming. I'm not sure you've seen anything at all, Rebekah." Even when he's scathing, my name in his mouth *means* something. Like its own spell, shimmering deep inside me, like blood. Like magic.

"Not everything, of course," I agree. "Though I can't tell if you've blocked the most interesting things or they have."

"Who is *they*?"

I make myself smile. "Now, Nicholas, it isn't like you to play ignorant. Are you worried I've seen whatever you've got going on with the Joywood?"

He sighs. I'm not sure it's as condescending as it is tired.

"As I stated, there are things I *cannot* tell you." He rubs his hand over his face, and I think it's the most mortal thing I've seen him do yet. Well. Maybe the second most mortal thing. His gaze holds mine. "Let me be clear that *I* would take on Carol and her ilk, time and time again and with tremendous pleasure, but she is not an adversary *you* want. An association with me can only complicate what you and your friends are trying to do."

I frown up at him. "I'm not sure what us having sex has to do with facing institutional injustice."

He searches my face. For what, I don't know, but he doesn't use magic to try and find it. He simply looks, and something about that is almost…soothing.

"I think somewhere, deep down, you know that it all connects." Nicholas's voice is quiet, but it reverberates inside me like a shout. "That it's all a step toward what's to come."

My heart trembles. And everything else follows suit. I don't like it. "I don't believe in fate."

"Only because your definition of fate is too narrow."

"What's your definition, then, that's so broad and perfect?"

There's the hint of a smile on his hard mouth. "Fate is not the absence of choice. It is the presence of it. Each choice you make will lead you to a different fate. This did not *have* to happen. Just because a thing is *meant* doesn't make it so. You and your sister and your friends were not fated to stop any flood, but you managed it. You could all have as easily died, if different choices were made."

I think about the way he yanked me here against my will. How he involved himself, though I'm certain he didn't want to. If it was a choice and not fate, then he *chose* to help us. Align himself with us.

With me.

Just like all those years ago, he *chose* to attempt to teach me something. And I chose to thwart his teachings, and my grandmother's, and try to burn it all to the ground.

Nicholas has been here in the shadows, aiding every little step along the way. Helping me for years and Emerson more recently. Even bringing me home.

Because we are meant to choose each other. When the time is right. He has been choosing me all along, even when it didn't feel like it.

"You're helping us," I say, and it's not a question this time because he *is*. Clearly. "But I don't understand why you'd bother to help if you don't want to."

His gaze is as deep and fathomless as the centuries he's seen pass him by. "There is danger. Everywhere. You will all need to know who you really are in order to navigate it."

"Are you planning on having sex with *all* of us?"

This does *not* elicit a laugh. I suppose I knew it wouldn't.

"I do not wish harm to come to you, Rebekah. So, I offer what I can."

Which might as well be love poetry, coming from Nicholas Frost.

I tuck that away so I can get mushy about it later. "What about you? What harm might come to you if the Joywood know what you're doing? And I don't mean this," I add, pointing to the rumpled bed.

His eyes glitter, as if he's considering his words. Carefully.

"There are very few consequences that even the ruling coven can inflict on an immortal who knows as much, if not more, than they do."

"But there would be some, surely, if they knew you were feeding us hints." I step toward him. I can't help it. "They're afraid of us, Nicholas." I know he's part of that *us*. He can't seem to help himself. The good news about *that* is that I don't have to waste any time convincing him. But there is something I'm not sure I can leave this house without asking. "This whole Chaos Diviner thing has something to do with *who is meant*. That's what the book said."

I'm closer to him now. I can smell him, vetiver and woodsmoke, magic and me. I want to touch him, but I can see he expects that, so I don't. I stop a breath away from him, and I refuse to drop his gaze.

He shakes his head, though it looks like it's hard for him. Like he would keep himself from it if he could. "*Meant* isn't always what you think it is."

I'm sick of the evasion, the *I am the immortal night* bullshit. "For fuck's sake, Nicholas, you've been *inside* me. Would it kill you to be direct even *once*?"

"You want direct? All right."

I've seen this look before, in those snatches of him throughout time. With swords and daggers. *This* is the look innumerable witches and humans, monsters and creatures alike have seen before they met their bloody end at his hands.

And even now, breath caught in my throat, I can't regret it.

"I am not your destiny, but you are mine." His eyes are a blue fire, and the way he speaks isn't just ripe with emotion. It's also the endless years of power and knowledge and everything else he is. A dark certainty and whole centuries in every word. "It is a prophecy. Possibly it is a curse, but it is certainly no *choice*. And it is not romantic, despite the pleasure I have taken in you."

"Nicholas..."

I don't know if that's a protest or a promise, but he leans in closer, and there isn't the faintest trace of the lover I discovered tonight on his hard face. There is only grim fate and that same certainty, like an iron mask.

"You will be the death of me, Rebekah," he tells me, with finality. "It is written. And I can assure you that the prophecy in question is quite literal."

"THAT'S A LITTLE DRAMATIC," I SAY, HOPING he'll smile back. Assuming he ever smiles. I don't expect him to *laugh*—the fabric of the universe might tear apart. "Don't you think?"

But all he does is gaze down at me, his eyes dark and his mouth a flat line.

Until I have no choice but to believe him.

To believe that *he* believes what he's telling me, anyway. That he truly thinks that I will be the death of him. Has he always believed this? Even back when I was a kid? Was that what all the lurking and secret suggestions were about?

I can't get my head around that.

And yet the book that told me I'm a Chaos Diviner also mentioned other fun stuff like killing and death and destruction. If the right paths weren't chosen, no pressure.

Someday I'd love to hear about a happy prophecy.

But I can't just *accept* what he's telling me. "Not all prophecies come true. You've lived long enough to know that first-hand."

"That doesn't mean this one won't."

There is something very nearly like kindness in those words. Like Nicholas can see all the same possibilities I do, in the detailed way I haven't been able to for so long. Yet for all his power and magic and longevity, he *isn't* a Diviner.

So he doesn't *know*. At best, he *hopes*.

Everything in me softens at the idea of Nicholas *hoping* for anything. But… "I think if I was going to be your literal death, it would have happened by now."

His mouth tightens ever so slightly. I can tell he's trying to look foreboding and it's not that he doesn't, it's just that I know too much now. The marks on his body, scars of lifetimes lived. The way his hands feel on me, inside me. The look on his face when everything is swept away except the pleasure, almost too much to bear, of being *one*.

"There is plenty of time yet for prophecies and fate to take a hand," he says coolly. "I've lived long enough that the bloom of immortality has worn off. I do not fear my death."

"Then what do you fear?"

Again it looks as if he is trying to be kind, rusty though the urge must be. "What it will do to those who survive it."

Meaning…me.

That hits me hard, but I try to contain any reaction. If I somehow cause his death, he's worried about how *I'll* handle it?

"Are you going to…expand on that?" I ask softly.

Nicholas only shakes his head.

I know this all goes deeper than him simply not wanting to tell me things—though that's part of it. But this just confirms that there's a maze of information he *cannot* divulge, like it or not. By curse or prophesy or even maybe the freaking Joywood.

Because another thing I know is this: he isn't their friend, but that doesn't make him their enemy.

Kind of like us.

I study him now, tall and dark and covered in stars. There are so many things I want to ask him. Even though my visions of his past are clear, they aren't complete. I know he's killed men—with actual weapons, the magical flick of his wrist, even his own fists in a darker age. I reach up and touch his face again anyway.

Maybe I should be appalled, but I understand too well the mistakes we make and sins we commit. When we haven't healed what's broken within us. When the dark is too tempting.

I want to ask him everything, to go through the story of Nicholas Frost step by step, starting way back when he was born with a different name entirely straight through to now. I want to inhabit each and every moment with him.

But as my thumb drags across his impossibly high cheekbone, I understand that these would only be pieces. Hundreds and hundreds of pieces, when what I really want is a bigger picture. The why of *this* moment.

And there is only one question I can ask here and now and hope with all I am that he answers. Because immortality is not a simple spell. It's sustained magic across a great many spells and rituals and ultimately, it comes from sacrifice. It comes from giving up something to get forever.

Allegedly.

His hand rises to cover mine, there against his aristocratic cheekbone.

"Nicholas," I whisper, my gaze intent on his. "What did you give up to live forever?"

He does not pause, not even a second's hesitation, before he answers, his voice harsh. "Everything." He lifts my hand off his face, but instead of dropping it like I expect he will, he holds it in his. "There is nothing I wouldn't have done for the power I coveted. Nothing that could have stopped me from taking that final step."

There is something about the word *step* that echoes within me. That produces a stream of visions—possibilities. They are unclear, but I can see they all involve those same students from the prom this evening. Crowds of teenagers, other witches, and me and my friends. Carol holding court in all of them.

And then I know. *Litha.*

Storms. Lightning. Death. Destruction. All the things the Chaos Diviner description warned about. Or promised.

But there is light too. Possibility and laughter and hope.

I let the visions run through me. I try to let them do as they will rather than inflicting my own narrative on them. And Nicholas studies me as if he knows very well that I'm seeing the possibilities before me. He squeezes my hand, grounding me in the present rather than in my visions, so I remember that I am the one watching them—I am not lost in them.

"You must take this seriously, Rebekah," he says when they clear. "This next step rests on you."

"Not really." He sighs as if to argue with me, but I don't let him. "The book said we have to work together. Assuming that since you're the man who brought me the clarifying stone and led me through the fire and tutored me as an adolescent, you're also the one *who is meant.*"

I wait for him to argue that.

When I really don't want to hear his arguments.

Which is when it hits me. Those visions aren't just a random high school montage. When have visions ever been *random*? "The flood was Emerson's defining moment. It's what truly made her into a Confluence Warrior. So I guess that means the test at Litha will be mine."

Nicholas nods as if he's been waiting for me to get here.

"They will test you, yes. Thoroughly. But they will not let you win." For the briefest of moment, I swear, I see true regret on his face. "It is a required step in what they want."

Required step. Steps again. "What the hell does that mean?"

He drops my hand then and turns, directing his gaze back toward the world outside and the long Beltane night that still wears on. "Perhaps you should ask your Historian."

I know now that while sometimes he refuses to answer out of pure spite, or pride or arrogance or any of the other things he's full of, sometimes he doesn't give a straight answer because he can't.

Maybe he even chose this consequence of his own free will, a blood oath for immortality, never imagining how long *forever* might be or where it might lead him. Just one of the reasons most witches have a deep abhorrence of even the *idea* of immortality. Forever always comes at a price, and rarely one you can anticipate.

Read your favorite dark fairy tale if you don't believe me.

Maybe these possibilities should matter to me, make me hate this man, but they don't. Because I have lived with guilt. I have staggered around beneath the weight of the bad choices I made out of hurt and fear and yes, selfishness. I even convinced myself I was the hero, rushing in to save Emerson, when I wanted to *prove* something.

Even in exile, I make mistakes. And more since I've been back home.

I've known Nicholas forever, short though my forever is next to his. He's had a thousand opportunities to actively harm me, and he hasn't. Embarrassed me, even shamed me and turned his back on me, sure. But he's never harmed me—though he must have considered it.

There was, after all, a foolproof way to make sure I was never going to be the death of him.

I lean into him, pressing my face against the sleek muscles of his back as I wrap my arms around him. This isn't the way we touched on the roof or in the bed.

This is another way to see each other. A deeper way of seeing him.

He stiffens, but it isn't a rejection. The feeling I get is that he doesn't know what to do with this. With me. With a *hug.*

One thing we can all agree on, friend and foe alike, is that Nicholas Frost has been alone for a long, long time. I'm sure he's taken any number of lovers and has interacted with beings of all types in all kinds of ways. But through it all he's held himself apart. Immortal and *alone.*

I knew this before I saw all those truths about him.

I know it even better now.

And more, I understand. I know all about exile.

"I am not the man you want me to be," he grits out, like the words themselves torture him.

"You can't possibly know the man I want you to be, Nicholas," I return, my mouth against the skin of his back. He sports no tattoos and yet still I sense them, as if he has spells sunk deep in his skin. "But I can guarantee you I'm not looking for a saint."

He laughs, and the world doesn't end at the sound, likely because it's sharp and bitter. He turns, then holds me away from him. When he lets go, he puts space between us, but all I see is the longing to come back to me. I hold on to that.

"In too many centuries to count I have been the opposite of a saint," he says, and though his voice is rough, matching that laugh, his blue eyes burn. "I know you've seen parts of my past I would not have shared willingly. And so you know that I have killed. Not once. Not even a hundred times. There is more blood on my hands, the stain of it deep in my bones, than a thousand peaceful lifetimes could ever wash away."

I can tell he wants to shock me, so I refuse to be shocked. "We've all made mistakes. You've simply had a lot longer to make far worse ones." I don't look away. I look straight at him. Into him. Into the past I saw and the future I wish I could see. The future I can admit I want, with him. I let him see all of that. "I'm not afraid of the monsters inside you, Nicholas. I'm not afraid of your mistakes. I'm not afraid of any part of you, dark or light."

It sounds like a spell. I wish it was. Some love magic to make him melt before me, or rush to sweep me into his arms… but Beltane can only do so much.

Something else seems to crack open in me, and I breathe it out like a sigh. "Nicholas. I—"

But it's like he knows what I might say. Or fears it. He draws himself up, and he's less the lover I found here tonight, and far more the fiercely disapproving ancient who has always looked down on, well, everything.

Too bad I still find that hot.

"Go home, Rebekah," he says, infusing those words with the sort of authority that should flatten me. "To your friends. To your family."

Whatever I've found here tonight—the chinks in his armor, the truths he never wanted to tell, *him*—I can sense I've pushed as far as I can. The next step will be him claiming this was all nothing but Beltane magic, and then I'll have to hurt him.

Maybe retreat is the better part of valor here. At the very least, I need to catch up with the others. To check on Ellowyn. To tell them that my visions are restored and more, what I've seen awaiting us. Because it isn't only about *me*. It won't be only my successes or failures, my triumphs or grief. It will be all of ours. We're all linked.

We stopped a flood. We took a step toward *something.*

Nicholas too, whether he likes it or not.

Maybe giving him his immortal space is smart in this moment. But I'm not admitting defeat. "This isn't over."

He pauses so long I can't help but hold my breath. I could seek out a vision here. I could look at all the possibilities for Nicholas and me, but I…don't want to. I'm not sure any vision I could have of our future would bring me clarity or comfort.

It almost feels like the easy way out, and that's not us.

His gaze softens as he looks at me, making my unusual restraint here worthwhile. He sighs. "No. It isn't over."

I decide there's really only one way to handle this goodbye I don't really want. I give him a smile that should feel like a caress, and I see it does. Then I whisper a brief but effective spell for a twirling, sparkling exit that lifts me out of his house and into the night air, like a Disney flourish.

I *swear* I hear Nicholas laugh somewhere deep inside me, as Coronis caws through the night air. I fly back down into town, but I don't fly far. Once at the bottom of the hill, I decide to walk. I need the cool air to settle all the heat still inside me. I need to put together my thoughts.

Because there will be *questions*, and I'm not prepared to answer them. Girl talk is one thing. I'm not sure my cousin and my soon-to-be brother-in-law need to hear about my sexcapades with an ancient.

I smile to myself as I head down the dark street, the bricks beneath my feet still humming with the night's wild, fertile magic. I still can't quite get over the *intensity* of what happened with Nicholas. Walking through fires is one thing. But his bed was a different kind of pyre altogether, and I'm…not okay.

In the best possible way.

There's a difference between human and witch sex that I've

been kidding myself about for a long time. When you add magic, things change, but this was more than that.

I see Ellowyn's owl, Ruth, perched on a store sign. Her spooky eyes glow, then she unfolds her unfathomably large wings and *rises* off into the night. I see Wilde House in my head, like a vision, and I know she's telling me that's where her witch is. And I know she's still guarding over me as I head there instead of to Ellowyn's apartment. I can't see her, but I know she'll quietly watch over me the whole way, protecting me until I'm safe again.

When I let myself into Wilde House, I can sense at once that my parents are not there. This is not unexpected on a festival night. And as it's Beltane, I very deliberately don't dwell on where they might be or what they might be getting up to. No child should ever entertain such images.

Smudge figure eights around my legs as I come in. I expect scathing commentary in my head, because she always has something to say about who I choose to share my body with.

Tonight she only purrs. I don't know what to do with her *approval*, since it's so rare, and so I move toward the voices I hear coming from the kitchen.

Ellowyn is sipping tea at the kitchen table when I walk in, and it looks like Emerson and Georgie are doing the same. Zander has a beer bottle. Jacob has a glass of water.

All eyes turn to me, and I…do not know how to arrange my face. I don't necessarily want to give off *just had amazing sex with an immortal* vibes, but that is in fact what I've just done.

"Well?" Emerson prompts.

I take some time ambling over to the empty seat next to Ellowyn. "It was a clarifying ritual," I say, very self-importantly, like *what else* could I possibly have been doing with a man who has literally defined male beauty as long as anyone currently alive can recall. I sneak a little glance at Ellowyn to assess her state. She's a little pale, but she looks like herself again. And when she smirks, I feel a rush of relief, because that means she's definitely back up to speed.

What happened *to you tonight?* I ask her privately.

I should be asking you that, she replies, sounding healthy—and snarky—in my head. I slide her some side-eye and she relents. *I assume a gift from the Joywood?*

Bastards. They would pick on the half human among us.

"What the hell does *a clarifying ritual* mean?" Zander is demanding from my other side.

"It means I walked through fire." I shrug as if that's as fraught with peril as the average trip to the drugstore. "It clarified my power. My Diviner visions are clearer now. The static is gone, and I feel..." There's a certain personal nature to everything I feel, and not all of it is wrapped up in Nicholas and sex. "I'm more in control of myself."

"That's good. Right?" Zander asks.

"Very." I think, *You have no idea how good and it would kill you if you did.* But I grin at my sister. "And Em's got her special designation, so I suppose it only makes sense that I got one too."

Georgie makes a little noise of satisfaction. "First of the year, last of the year. Of course!" She claps in excitement. "You two have to balance. I *knew* it. Well, what is it? What are you?"

"I can think of a few things," my cousin mutters, but he's grinning at me.

I grab his beer and take a sip. I suddenly realize I'm starving, so I magic myself a snack and a glass of sparkling water. I don't need alcohol right now. I need... Well, I can't have what I need at the moment. I need to let him brood himself out.

I take my sweet time eating the small plate of nachos I magicked myself. I drain my glass. I let it stretch out, because Emerson's growing more and more fidgety while she waits.

When I can tell she's about to burst, I grin at her. "I'm a Chaos Diviner. Apparently."

"*Chaos?* That sounds..." Emerson trails off like she doesn't know how to make it palatable. My poor, orderly, organized sister.

"Sounds like the ancient books have met you," Zander says, and laughs when I make a face at him.

Georgie is frowning. "The amount of knowledge that's been lost *offends* me, it really does. I've never heard of that one either."

I think about what Nicholas said about steps and asking my Historian. It was offhanded, or so I thought, but maybe I'm actually *supposed* to ask her. Maybe that was him telling me what I need to do without actually telling me.

I go back over the things Nicholas said, relaying them to my friends without any *personal* details like how naked we were or how deep inside me he was for most of the night.

"Steps?" Georgie repeats, when I explain that he thinks Litha is the next *step*. "And he thinks I should know what that means?"

I shrug. "Hard to tell what *he* thinks, but *I* think he's under the impression you'll be able to find the answers."

Georgie looks perplexed, but also excited about the challenge of digging into a mystery. Especially one that likely involves whole libraries of musty books.

"Steps," Emerson is muttering. "That's a weird way of putting it, isn't it? Stopping the flood was a *step*. Passing our Litha test will be another step. But where are we going with all these steps? Shouldn't they be leading somewhere?"

I don't say that *passing* the test might not be the step. I don't tell her what Nicholas said about the Joywood making sure we fail. As much as it sometimes frustrates me, I don't want to take away Emerson's belief in a clear right and wrong.

If she believes that these steps might lead us somewhere we're meant to be, somewhere good, I want her to keep believing it. Because then I can flirt with the idea of believing it too.

"He did say, when we were dealing with Skip, that this dark magic would have many chances to win," Georgie says, considering. "Isn't that kind of like a step?"

"Dark magic would have many chances," Emerson says, taking on the slightest hint of Nicholas's particular cadence. "But we would only have one."

"Right. They get steps to beat us, and if we lose once, we're sunk." Zander makes a low noise. "Thanks for the help, immortal douche."

"I got the feeling that he genuinely couldn't tell me what it meant," I say, trying not to sound defensive.

"Because he's so benevolent?"

"No," I reply, ordering myself not turn molehills into mountains. I don't need to stand up for Nicholas to Zander. Or anyone. "Because he can't. I get the sense he *can't*."

"Like me?" Ellowyn asks, so much herself again it seems like what happened back at the gym was a dream. It's not the only thing about tonight that feels like a dream.

"I don't think he's running with a truth curse, though it could be a different sort of curse." I hesitate to bring up the other possibilities, though they seem more likely to me. It feels like sharing Nicholas's secrets, even though he didn't tell me not to. And we're trying to save our own, much shorter lives here. "A curse or a blood oath or something like that," I force myself to say.

And I kind of hate myself for it.

"In other words, something he chose," Jacob points out, with unerring accuracy.

It feels more unfair than it should. I know Nicholas has chosen all sorts of dark things.

I don't really want my friends to know it too. Assume it, sure. But *knowing it* is something different.

"Immortality doesn't come without sacrifices." Georgie sits back in her chair. She blows a red tendril out of her face. "Historians might not know the specifics, but we do know that."

"Yes, and he told me something that I…" I want to say this even less. I swallow, hard, and force myself to keep going. "It's relevant, even if I don't understand *how* just yet. He said, 'There is nothing I wouldn't have done for the power I coveted.'"

I look around, expecting them all to make the same connection I have. Instead, they nod, their expressions full of dark Nicholas Frost thoughts. I tell myself I'm impatient because they're slow on the uptake. It has nothing to do with this urge in me to protect and defend him.

"We know another group who covet power," I say, definitely *impatient*. "Who wield it without any checks or balances. Who are so powerful that even Nicholas Frost can't tell their secrets."

Everyone exchanges glances then. There's a sudden surge of electricity in the room, like we're all looking at the weeks ahead now. Wondering what's to come. What will happen. With or without visions.

I catch Emerson's gaze on me, looking every inch the big sister. Like she knows exactly what I got up to tonight.

Well, I say where only she can hear me. *It* is *Beltane.*

Magic is a beautiful thing, she replies, so primly that I suddenly understand all kinds of things about her connection to Jacob.

I love that for her.

"You guys." I make sure everyone's looking at me, because as much as I'd like to magic myself a pint of ice cream and giggle about boys with my favorite women—and I'm sure I will, maybe even later tonight—there's one key point I want to get across first. "This means that even if he can't tell us, Nicholas knows what their secrets are. If we can figure out how to access what he knows..."

Emerson's smile is slow and brilliant and every inch the Warrior she is. "Then we've got them."

20

MONDAY MORNING DAWNS FAR TOO EARLY. After a brief power struggle with Emerson over the meaning of *on time*—me going with, you know, the actual time and her insisting we need to be early—we fly over to St. Cyprian High. Early.

A million memories assault me as Emerson drags me inside. I hated high school. I always thought it was the way *everyone* hates high school. Everyone I actually find interesting as an adult, that is. But as I walk into a ten-year-old nightmare, it really hits me *how* miserable I was here. I was a hormone-addled teenager, yes, mouthy and rebellious, but despite all the drama, the truth about high school me is that I was in deep despair.

What got me through was Ellowyn sharing that despair with me and helping turn it into private jokes so it felt like we won against the demons inside us and all around.

That and my sister's unquenchable optimism. Oh, I would have said I hated it. I'm sure I did, back then. Sometimes I mocked it to her face. But she was a Warrior even then. She never cracked.

Deep down, that was what I loved most about her. That nothing and no one could *really* bring Emerson Wilde to her knees.

It occurs to me for the first time, then, that when she says she was *her* these past ten years, she means it. That she's never been anything but *herself*. And maybe that means that I really was the one who let her down. I told myself I couldn't bear losing her, but the reality is a little more complicated than that.

Because what I suspect I truly couldn't bear is this. *This*, right next to me where she's always been. The heart of her always so determined and bright and *sure*. I felt wrecked and misshapen and ruined by that night. How could she possibly *still* be *her* despite what happened to us—when she couldn't even remember the real us—when I was such a mess?

That realization sits in me way too heavily as she tows me through the arched doors out front of the main building, with a hilarious claim to educational excellence etched above them when what it should say is *Abandon hope, all ye who enter here.*

I always did.

We walk down hallways that are too glossy and new-looking, yet smell exactly the same. Everything looks smaller, and yet the glare of all that harsh industrial lighting makes *me* feel smaller. I don't know if I'm seeing the actual hallway we're walking down or my memories of *then*, but before I know it, Emerson is tugging me into a classroom.

It's mostly full, so we can't sit next to each other. The poor little teenagers look at us with avid interest as we split up. Emerson eagerly takes a seat in the front row, and I, obviously, slink over to one in the back corner.

And it takes me much too long to realize that the reedy person standing at the chalkboard in a bow tie is indeed the one and only Sage Osburn, who Georgie told us yesterday asked if he could *be her beau.* For once, I was not the only person who had to bite her own cheek to keep from responding to that with a rousing *what the actual fuck.* I swear the words hung over mine and Emerson's heads as she shared that at the dinner table. Maybe even my parents' too.

Is he three hundred years old? my father had barked at her.

Georgie had merely smiled at him. *He's age appropriate, Mr. Wilde. And very kind.*

"Settle in, class," Sage says. "Beltane is behind us, and we have a lot of ground to cover before Litha."

That almost sounds mildly interesting, but as he begins to talk he makes it clear that nothing he's going to say will rise to that low bar. I thought prom was bad, but at least there was some autonomy there. I could move around, hide in an alcove, dance. This is literally sitting in a plastic chair, listening to the most boring witch alive drone on about a test I don't want to take.

I find it hard to believe Georgie is genuinely interested in this man who could make watching paint dry seem like a great way to spend the afternoon.

Emerson, needless to say, is fully engaged. She sits in that front row seat, furiously scribbling notes and *always* raising her hand. I try to focus. I really do. But when people drone on in a monotone with no variation, my mind drifts. I can't help it. When I look down at my notes as class winds down, ten lifetimes later, I see I managed a page full of intricate doodles and one sentence:

Sacrifices can only be made by the pure of heart.

And, of course, a lot of sketches of a certain immortal witch that Rebekah of old wouldn't have *dared* commit to pen and paper, no matter how she fancied herself infatuated with him.

I asked him what he gave up for immortality. *Everything,*

he said. But that was not a pure sacrifice. It can't have been, because immortality is not *good.* It's raw, unbalanced power—corrupted power, at that.

The bell rings. It makes me want to curl into a ball and moan—clearly a trauma response.

"God, I hate this place," I mutter to Emerson as we meet in the hallway. "I can't do this every day for the next month."

She sends me a swift look. "It isn't so bad. It's not like we have to do a full day. Just this class, and then, on Wednesdays, the evening practical. It'll be good for us." She checks her watch. "I've got time to walk back to town, if you'd like. We can go over the lesson."

"I do not want to go over anything." But I do want to walk the *ick* out of me.

We get out of the building with unseemly haste, then head down the hill toward town. The day is warm and pretty. There are flowers everywhere and trees in bloom, and a hint of a good old-fashioned Midwest thunderstorm to the west. I haven't seen one in far too long.

Emerson is first to break the pleasant silence.

"Did you really..." She pauses, as if trying to find the right word. I see the determined glint in her eyes. "That is..." She clears her throat. "You made it quite clear you and Nicholas..."

I take my time smiling at her, Cheshire cat style. "Banged?"

She slides a disapproving glance at me, but there is humor at the edges. "You should tell Mother. She'd be thrilled."

"Thrilled? I think you mean *appalled*, as usual."

"Elspeth Wilde's daughter with the *greatest Praeceptor of all time*?" Emerson says that while mimicking Mom's snootiest voice.

I shudder. "That is too accurate."

Emerson laughs, but quickly sobers as we walk. Her eyes,

like mine, are on the dilapidated old house falling down on top of the bluff in the distance. "Was it serious, or just like..."

I can't wait to see where she's going with this. "Like what?"

"Like what Zander and Ellowyn do with other people. Call it lust, scratching an itch—"

"A hot one-night stand with an ancient fuck boy?"

She fights back her own shudder. "Whatever you want to call it. I just wanted to know...where it's going?"

"Where could it go with an immortal?" I say, but it's not quite as flippant as I'd like. *I do not fear my death*, he said.

Because he believes his death is coming and I will be the one to make it happen.

Emerson sucks in a breath, clearly irritated with me, but not enough to drop the subject. "I guess what I'm really asking is, are you okay with what happened?"

I would have been offended by that even a few days ago, but all these changes within me—the ritual, Nicholas himself, being home, being back in high school—give me a better ability to understand where my sister is coming from. Maybe because I'm finally understanding what I brought to the table during our separation.

Here, now, Emerson is worried, and that doesn't mean she thinks she's better and smarter than me. It just means she worries. About everything. She wants everyone she loves to be *okay*, not just like her.

I'm a little shocked at how glad I am that I can see that today.

"I'm more than okay with what happened," I say.

Emphatically. Because it's true.

"Okay."

I don't trust that simple acceptance. Not from my sister, the patron saint of flow charts. "That's it? *Okay?*"

"I may have had a lecture prepared." She gives a little sniff.

"But Jacob pointed out that I'd be the first to defend a woman's right to sleep with whoever she pleases, whenever and however she pleases, without having to explain herself to anyone."

"I've always liked that man."

"And, since he was right, however annoyingly, I had to think about what really bothered me about it. It's the power dynamic."

I shrug a little lazily. "It's a really hot power dynamic, though."

She grimaces. But she surprises me and still withholds the lecture. "If it works for you, and if you're happy, and safe, then that's all that matters."

I stare at her, eyes wide and only *slightly* exaggerated. "You *have* changed, Emerson. All because of Jacob?"

"Love is powerful and Healers are..." And it's her turn to shrug lazily, though she blushes a little while she does it. "But no. It's because of everything." She gestures to St. Cyprian around us as we make our way down one of the cobbled streets, the river playing hide-and-seek with us as we walk. "Maybe it's just growing up? We're knocking on thirty's door."

"I hate to break it to you, Em, but you've always been an old lady on the inside."

"Maybe, but that's not the same as maturing. Of course," Emerson says, tongue *mostly* in cheek, "real maturing would be taking notes for once."

I roll my eyes. "I tried. I *did*. It's just all blah, blah, blah after a while. I've got too much going on up here."

Emerson stops, then blinks at me as though I've said something terribly important when all I'm doing is waving my hand in the vague direction of my head. "You need a different kind of learning!" she exclaims, as if she's found gold.

"What?"

"You're not aural or a reading and writing learner. Maybe kinesthetic?"

"I repeat, what?"

Emerson starts walking again *with purpose* and I feel like I have no choice but to follow, at her speed, as she lectures on about *learning.*

"There are all different kinds of learning. Aural, kinesthetic, visual—well, visual and visions, maybe? I took a test to see which one suited me best. You should—"

"I'm not taking a test to see how I *learn.*"

"Your power makes it difficult for you to learn in a traditional setting, so now that you're back in a traditional setting you need to figure out how..." She trails off and comes to a stop again.

I feel why—cool fire and wild thunder and a long, hard rain—before I turn to look.

Nicholas stands in our path. We aren't that far from the bottom of his hill. Still, he's not just at the bottom of the Frost House stairs, but on the official St. Cyprian bricks.

I don't know why the sight of him on neutral ground makes me feel...so decidedly *not* neutral.

"Wildes," he greets us with the faint hint of a nod that harkens back to times of yore. Or Jane Austen movies.

I am entirely too warm. Emerson is clearly embarrassed. It should be funny. But I can't seem to look away from him long enough to laugh.

"Per your request," he says, oh so formally to Emerson, but his eyes are on me, and he seems to have as much trouble looking away as I do, "I have designed a few practice tests. If you're interested."

"I have to open the store," Emerson replies with deep, conflicted concern.

"Pity. I do live to serve."

I think of a few ways he could serve me, right here and now. And though I don't think Emerson can read my mind—or I hope she can't—I can tell she is torn between discomfort and the desperate need to use Nicholas's wealth of knowledge in any way she can. In any way, every way, that might help us win at Litha.

"Rebekah struggled with class this morning. It's just not the right setting for her to learn," Emerson hurries to explain as Nicholas's gaze changes. From cool to...considering. "She could use some individualized help with the material. Maybe more hands-on. I think she might be more of a kinesthetic learner, that is, you know, *tactile*."

Nicholas's eyebrows rise so far on his head that I think it's the most expressive I've ever seen him get. While clothed.

Emerson makes a kind of gurgling noise, as if the potential double entendre has just struck her and mortified her into a stroke.

"You okay there?" I ask. Blandly.

She sucks in a breath, straightens her jacket that doesn't need straightening, then forces her mouth into what I think is supposed to be her chamber of commerce president smile. It doesn't quite get there. "Yes, I'm just late. I hate to be late."

I'm assuming this is what you want? she asks me, without looking at me. Because, of course, she would never feed me to the wolves. Or the one alpha wolf, in this case.

Unless I wanted to be fed.

I study Nicholas. Even if he could tap in to hear us, it's our own special childhood language. Indecipherable to anyone who's not us. But I'm sure he can see my answer in my eyes.

Yes, it's what I want.

He is what I want.

I am not prepared for how fully I mean that, so I focus on Emerson instead.

"You can help Rebekah this morning, and then you should come to Jacob's house for dinner tonight," Emerson says to Nicholas, and her smile is more natural. "Give us all some pointers for Litha."

Never let it be said that Emerson doesn't grab an opportunity with both hands, regardless of any potential embarrassment.

"Across the river?" Nicholas replies, as if Emerson has suggested heading to Siberia for some winter sunbathing.

"Yes, the North farm. I'm assuming you know where it is. Either that or dinner at Wilde House." She pauses for a beat, and her smile brightens. "With our parents."

His expression freezes like he really is headed for the Russian steppes. "I would not dream of imposing on Desmond or Elspeth's brittle hospitality."

"The North farm it is, then," Emerson says cheerfully, already moving away from us in the direction of the bookshop. "Seven. Don't be late."

Nicholas takes his time looking back at me. "I did not agree to dinner."

"You've met Emerson, right?"

His mouth firms a little, but he doesn't look as harsh as usual. Nothing about him is quite as harsh as usual, I see, now that I can stare openly without embarrassing my sister.

"After you," he says, gesturing toward the stairs up the hill.

I raise an eyebrow at him. "Do immortals take the stairs?"

His only response is to stalk off in their direction, clearly expecting me to follow.

I want to rebel because I *always* want to rebel. And because he's all the things—arrogant, condescending, you name it—that my sister thinks he is. I want to stand up for the sisterhood, really I do...

But it turns out I want him more.

21

I FOLLOW, MAKING SURE TO CATCH UP AND THEN match his stride, because I'm a Wilde. And Wilde women do not scurry along behind men. The witches in our history would haunt anyone who dared shame them so.

We take the first step together, then move up the hill side by side.

If we were different people in a different time, he might have offered an arm. A hand. But we aren't, and I would refuse it if he did. So we walk with our arms only occasionally brushing, sending fire dancing through my veins every time. Just the two of us in a spring morning, with all the heat between us growing heavy, like that incoming thunderstorm.

I sneak a glance at him. His gaze is on the house, yet I felt his eyes on me.

"You chose a time she couldn't do it on purpose," I accuse him.

Nicholas shrugs negligently. "She doesn't need the help."

I try very hard not to bristle at that, but of course I can't seem to stop myself. "Of course not."

I can feel his stare as we walk—actually *walk*—up the stairs. How prosaic. Except it's making me feel less jittery, less strung out on the simple fact of him. Right here. Next to me again. I'm tempted to imagine he decided to climb the stairs like humans do to dispel some of this clattery energy.

I expect him to say something cutting. But he surprises me. "She's had more time than you, Rebekah," he says quietly.

"Or less, depending on how you look at it." Because I never lost my magic, or the knowledge of it.

He shakes his head. "If you're determined to make life a competition, you will always lose. Trust me on this."

I want to argue with him, but I recognize that he is speaking from some experience of his own. I know better than to argue with people about themselves when they've only had some twenty to sixty years so far. Not hundreds upon hundreds.

"What difficulties did you have with your class this morning?" he asks while I seethe beside him.

"Men endlessly monologuing bores me to tears, so there was that. Also, I'm not sure what ancient wars and sacrifices have to do with passing the Litha test? See also, boring."

Nicholas is apparently in full Praeceptor mode as we make it to the top. "Litha is a war itself. The light versus the dark until light surrenders to the dark."

"But there's no sacrifice, because the dark surrenders to the light again," I throw back at him, as if we're talking about something other than a planet revolving around a sun. "The planet turns. The seasons change. It's the way things are."

He makes a noise. Not exactly agreement, but not argument either. "You will be asked to show that you understand the balance. The practicum on Wednesday will allow you to work on your spells, but I can assure you Felicia will do all in her power to ensure you cannot actually do anything of the sort."

"Felicia is giving the practicum?"

"She will. To you. I would wager my riches on it." We make it down the path to his door, and he sweeps a hand through the air to open it. Inside, I swear I hear a choir sing out. It's quite a theatrical effect. His mouth curves. "And I have ample riches."

I answer that with a roll of my eyes.

"Let's go to the library," he says, leading me through the house that gleams and shines and seems to rearrange itself around us as we walk. I swear the library was in a different direction before.

There is a table set up like the water scrying day. Different bits and bobs are on it. I can hear what I assume is his pet weasel, squeaking in its cage. Something inside me almost thinks a name I know, but I focus on the table instead. I can't quite connect Sage's droning lecture this morning to this, but I also can't pretend I'm trying that hard to put any of it together.

When he is here. Standing across from me. And the moment our gazes catch, the air changes.

Suddenly, there is nothing but us. And all the magic I know we can create together. With our bodies. With who we are.

And that's what we do. With no words spoken. No excuses.

We simply meet in the middle, hands and mouths. We don't bother with a bed this time, just the soft rug below us, books all around us.

And too much magic to bear.

Until we're left, naked and panting, leaning into each other as we fight to recover. To survive what we just did to each other so we can do it again.

"Perhaps I will enjoy dying at your expense," Nicholas says lazily from beneath me, a languid hand sliding down my back.

He says it so offhandedly. So calmly. But it ties me into knots. I roll off him and frown at him from the side. "I don't find that funny."

We're stretched out on a rug that whispers of ancient looms and handweaving, all of it lush and fine. There's a fire crackling in the hearth. He stares at the ceiling in naked perfection, gleaming as much as the rest of this place, all his riches fading to nothing next to the glory of him.

No wonder he's such an asshole.

"That is because you have not lived long, *meae deliciae*," he murmurs, not sounding at all disturbed by my reaction.

"I'm not going to kill you." I am certain of it. So *close* to being certain. Because even with my visions finally working the way they should, that doesn't make my magic so powerful I could strike down a man who literally knows *all* the magic. *And* has immortality to go along with it.

He takes a very long time to speak, and when he does, he turns on his side to meet my gaze. "There are all sorts of ways to be the death of someone, Rebekah."

I frown at this. It seems like another one of those veiled, coded messages I have to untangle and unfurl because he can't simply tell me what I need to know. Why can't anything be simple?

Then I shake my head at myself. Life has never been simple, and part of healing is accepting that it never will be. You can strip away the trappings, you can get to know your soul and center. You can find peace.

But in the grand scheme of things, simplicity doesn't exist.

"We should practice," Nicholas says.

"Practice what, exactly?" I return, and I reach over to trace my way down one of his arms, with all its muscles and that sense that enchantments lurk beneath his skin.

Suddenly my clothes are on me. *His* spell, clearly, because the last thing I was thinking about was clothes. Meanwhile, he's fully dressed himself and standing above me. And instead of magicking me to my feet, he holds out a hand.

I want to lecture him on consent, but instead I take it and he helps me to my feet. And I warn the ghosts of Wilde women past to settle down. Because maybe if they'd enjoyed a little respectful chivalry here and there, so many of them wouldn't have run afoul of humorless witch hunters over the ages.

It doesn't hurt me any to accept help.

That's another thing it took me years to learn, and it feels like a kind of spell here. With him.

He keeps my hand in his as he turns me to the table. "Litha is the balance of light and dark, the sun standing still at the top of the world, or so it seems on the solstice. But the Joywood will want to use your chaos against you, Rebekah. You need to learn to balance it. So that you will only use it when you choose, and when it's time."

Still cryptic, I note.

I stand at the table, my hand still in his. I could pry into his future if I want. I can feel it tugging at me, the visions like little flashes in the corners of my eyes, trying to tempt me to look. But maybe part of controlling my chaos is *not* looking at the future of the man I'm sleeping with because I *can* control it now. His past isn't flashing before me, and maybe I need to ignore the way his futures—and everyone else's—tugs at me, unless and until they ask.

That sounds so virtuous and honorable that I'm a little nauseated by the whole thing. I frown down at the table. "If I'm named after chaos, why do I have to control it?"

"There is a time for everything. Your sister isn't out there Warrioring all the time."

It's like he's never met Emerson. "Isn't she?"

"The Healer doesn't heal all the time, the Summoner rarely

summons, half witch that she is. Even that Historian of yours isn't *always* buried in her books."

"It doesn't matter that Ellowyn is part human." I never liked the term *half witch.* She's not *half* of anything.

"It will matter," Nicholas says, but I realize it's not a judgment, like when Carol says such things so snidely. He makes it sound important.

I think of *steps* again, but it's not the time to mention them.

Because maybe I'm imagining that there's some approval in his blue gaze today. I used to imagine it when I was younger, and I know it was never really there. This is…different. "One step at a time. Now, let's practice your balance."

We do practice. Again and again, and it's much better than that classroom this morning. Nicholas explains many of the same things Sage supposedly went over earlier, according to the notes Emerson magicked into my notebook. But Nicholas explains things while we're working through the actual spells and rituals. Somehow, it makes more sense when I can see them, say them, let them flow through me and out into this domed room.

"You've done well, Rebekah," he says once I've held the light and dark in perfect balance over and over again. "Should you fail the practicum, know that it isn't your failure."

I want to believe that. I really do. "You sure about that?"

"I am certain," he says in that forbidding way that even *I* don't feel compelled to argue with.

We both fall silent. We've been practicing for hours. I feel electrified and a little burned out, but in a good way, like all my muscles—magical and physical—have been through a tough workout.

Yet we stand here, the air around us seeming to hint at all the things we don't say.

But I have my pride, and he has a thousand lifetimes' supply of his own, so I move to leave. After only a couple of steps, before I make it off the rug where I sobbed out his name and he held me in his arms like we were made for each other, his voice stops me.

"I'll see you at dinner, witchling."

I don't turn to face him. I'm afraid my smile would blind us both, and it has nothing to do with daisies. Because I know that term was once meant to create a distance. To remind us both that I was beneath him.

But I'm not now. And *witchling* has turned into an endearment. Just for us. Once I've gotten ahold of myself I give him a little over-the-shoulder smirk. "If you're lucky."

I don't stay. If I do, I might be prone to giggle or something else equally embarrassing, so I hightail it out of there. I don't particularly want to head home, because my parents are likely waiting to grill me on my first class. Maybe I'll swing by Nix, grab a burger, and check in with Aunt Zelda—still only by text, but she told me she'd be waiting to hear how high school went today—while trying to figure out the truth of her condition from Zander's general unforthcoming stonewalling. I could go to Confluence Books and curl up on one of the sofas and do some work. I could hang out in Tea & No Sympathy and make Ellowyn laugh between customers.

It warms me, all these options. All the ways this place could feel like home again if Litha wasn't hanging over my head. Not to mention other things, like my parents. Penance. Lingering shame…

As if the thought of all those things conjures the woman I least want to see, Felicia is waiting at the bottom of the stairs to Frost House. Like…clearly, creepily, waiting for me and not even trying to pretend otherwise.

The closer I get, I begin to realize she can't go farther than that little bit of bricks that dead-end into the first step. It's like there's a wall and she can't get through it.

I think she wants to. I think she's *trying* to. I know she started trying before she saw me, because I can see it in my head like an instant replay, even though I'm only supposed to see forward. But I ignore that part and concentrate on the fact that whatever power Felicia has as member of the Joywood, Nicholas has created some kind of barrier that even the most powerful witches in the world can't pass. Not if he doesn't want them to.

I feel like sobbing out his name all over again, but I don't.

Instead, I stop walking on about the third step and stand there, protected against this woman who's supposed to be the best representation of a Diviner in all the land. This mean, petty woman who made my life hell and is red in the face because she can't loom over me the way she liked to do when I was a kid forced to sit in that torturously uncomfortable chair in her office.

I make a show of sitting down, just out of reach and still above her.

Because I really do love a power dynamic.

Felicia vibrates with that temper of hers I recognize all too well. I find myself thinking the same thing I always did in high school. That she should have *helped* me. That she was a Diviner, something I could feel hum inside me without anyone ever needing to tell me we were the same designation, so why couldn't she? She's always acted like I was conceited and getting above my station to imagine I was anything like her. And yet she was and is my counterpart. Not only that, if we follow through with Emerson's insane idea to *officially* start our own coven and pit ourselves against the Joywood in an Ascension, I'll take her place.

That doesn't bother me one little bit today.

Though it does occur to me, suddenly, that it clearly bothers her. And did even back then.

"Good morning, Felicia," I offer brightly, then make a big production of looking at the sky, where the storm is now off to the east and the sun is high. "Or afternoon, as the case may be."

Her smirk should have fangs. "Nasty, dirty girls like you never know what time of day it is, do they?"

She means *whores*, I am fairly sure. I shrug as if unbothered, though it sets my teeth on edge. As it was meant to do. "Felicia. Surely you've realized by now that there are no girls like me."

"You wouldn't be the first woman the immortal used for his own ends," she continues, jerking her chin up at Frost House, her voice full of pity.

I suppose it might have worked on me as a younger, more insecure woman. Or if the man in question hadn't literally lived untold centuries already. Jealousy would be pointless in any situation, but especially in this one. I don't expect to be the first of anything for him.

But maybe the last.

I shake that thought away, particularly since it's somehow both a dire warning that I could kill him *and* a stupid fantasy that I could keep him.

"They're really *amazing* ends, though, Felicia."

"I suppose your sister found that out last month when she was cavorting up there," she says in the nearly singsong voice some people mistake for sweet. "Did she share that with you, I wonder?"

The insinuation takes my breath away. Even knowing it's not true, not in the way Felicia wants me to think, there is a weird arrow of jealousy that stabs through me anyway. Because even when there was nothing romantic between us, Nicholas always felt like he was supposed to be mine.

And even though I'm glad he helped my sister, there's something in me that wishes he was *only* mine.

That part, I think, the ghosts of my ancestresses are welcome to haunt me for.

Felicia is watching me. She's desperate for a reaction. I stay behind my protected wall, lounge on my step, and do my best not to give her one. "Is there something you wanted?"

Two can play the *I can annoy the hell out of you* game.

"Just some friendly advice," she says, intimately, as if she's ever been anything but rabid where I'm concerned. "If you think that immortal or anyone else is going to help you pass the pubertatum this time around, you really *have* learned nothing."

"That's what you all always told me, right? Stupid, stupid Rebekah. The dumb little spell dim witch, an embarrassment to her bloodline."

"If the shoe fits." She smirks. I want to slap it off her face, but what's the point?

That echoes inside me. What is the *point* of this?

Felicia keeps going. "I suppose you think he's helping you. I suppose you think your friends are truly welcoming you back into the fold. A little taste of redemption, but you and I know the truth, don't we? You don't belong here, Rebekah."

I don't mistake the threat.

I open my mouth to tell her I know what she's doing. I know that the Joywood are scared of us and what we can do, even if I don't know *why*. But there's a whisper across my mind, and the ring on my hand pulses, like my grandmother trying to reach me across spirit worlds.

Felicia *wants* me to show my hand. That's what the old Rebekah would have done. In my anger, in my hurt, I would have told Felicia *exactly* what I knew and what I was capable of.

I blink for a second, suddenly seeing the past unspool inside me in a way you'd think I'd need to be a Summoner to manage.

I see everything I was too furious, too wounded, too *seventeen* to see then.

My wild emotions, me tipping my cards so completely, was how they knew they *could* wipe Emerson with no ceremony. They *knew* they could prompt me into an explosion. Make me look dangerous. Split a wedge—memory and miles—between Emerson and me so we couldn't fight back.

I felt them wipe her—it was no accident. They made *sure* of it. And then I tried to take Felicia down to prove a point. Chaos Diviner—destroy or heal, kill or birth. They *knew* they could push me into the wrong choices.

It was my fault, but now I understand, without a shadow of doubt or any self-serving need to excuse my part in it, that they planned it. None of it was happenstance. It wasn't even because they didn't like us, though they didn't. They don't.

It was a full-fledged *plan*.

Everything has been a plot all along—not just our failure that night, but *everything*.

They used my pride and my temper to help them make it work. They want to again.

It wells up inside of me like a tide I can't control, roaring, but I think about the hours I just spent balancing light and dark. I have to control myself. This, right here, is what that dusty old book warned me about. My temper. My need to strike out. I already know where this leads.

I know the darkness all too well.

The ring on my hand pulses a warning.

The words my grandmother gave me all those years ago

ring in my head, as strong as ever: *Time is mine until time takes me home.*

Maybe my grandmother is no longer here, but I feel like I have to prove to whatever is left of her in the air, in the plants she left behind, that I can do it right this time.

I might be a *Chaos* Diviner, but I have the control.

Hecate knows I've earned it.

I feel the tide recede. I feel that balance point Nicholas and I worked on today. Where the light and dark meet. Where time stands still. Where the sun hovers before it tips back toward the night.

I will not let this woman goad me into tearing myself apart. Not this time. If she wants me in pieces, she's going to have to do it herself.

"It was nice to see you, Felicia," I say, sounding serene and very nearly sincere. "Looking forward to Wednesday's practicum."

I sweep through the barrier and brush past her to get my feet on the bricks, on my way to Wilde House where, no doubt, my mother is waiting to lecture me. I don't really want a lecture. But it's better than giving Felicia what she wants, so I sing the whole way home.

I'M THE LAST TO ARRIVE AT JACOB'S FARMHOUSE that night. The last besides Nicholas, that is, because His Ancientness has yet to grace the mortals with his presence. This does not concern me in the least. I think the only ghosting an immortal would bother to do would involve, like, actual ghosts.

I throw myself into sampling the appetizers with Zander. "How's your mom?" I ask.

This is a test balloon of a question, because I've been texting with her all day. Just like every day.

Every day is better than the one before, sweet girl, she'd texted earlier. Now tell me about your *private lessons* with the world's most famous—and most famously attractive—Praeceptor!

I did. But it isn't lost on me that her texts come at odd intervals. And she won't let me see her. Or even give me a call.

Zander shakes his head, and I see something raw in his eyes before he drops them. "Not good. Not good at all."

And it's one thing to have suspicions. It's something else to have those suspicions confirmed. It feels a lot like a kick to the gut.

I press my shoulder to his. "I'm so sorry, Zander."

"She's refusing visitors. She sleeps a lot, and when she's not sleeping, she's in pain. It's not great no matter how you look at it."

And when she's doing neither of those things, she's texting, where she can pretend she's well. I can understand that, I guess.

I nod, my eyes suddenly blind with tears. He makes a gruff sort of sound in reply. And then we handle our emotions in the tradition of our people. Meaning, we ignore them and start shoving food in our mouths.

Ellowyn stays on the other side of the room. Once the emotion recedes a little, it seems to me that there's a weirder tension than usual between her and my cousin. Not quite as antagonistic or angry, but almost…more awkward. As if she knows I'm studying her, she turns away to make a big deal out of petting Cassie, Emerson's familiar, who wags her tail happily. While Smudge makes a scene by hissing loudly from her hiding spot on top of a hutch, pretending she and Cassie aren't buddies from way back. She also spends a lot of time doing this to Octavius back at Wilde House, seconds after sharing sunbeams with him, because cats are weird.

"How did you two have time to do all this?" Georgie asks my sister, looking at the impressive spread.

"Jacob's mom has a sixth sense about these things, and voilà, a full-fledged dinner right when we need it," Emerson replies, fiddling with this and that.

And then someone knocks on the door. Very formally.

We all pause. Even though they worked with Nicholas when I wasn't here, this definitely feels like a new step for everyone involved, if maybe not the kind of step he meant.

Still, when Jacob goes to answer the door, we all trail after him like we're not quite sure who it might be.

Jacob greets Nicholas. Not the friendliest greeting, but also without hostility. Nicholas steps inside, sketches a stiff bow like it's hundreds of years ago despite the fact he's in jeans and a T-shirt again, and then we're all just…standing there.

This makes me feel a different kind of sad, so I move forward and link arms with the immortal suddenly brooding in the old North farmhouse. As if we're *pals*. Then I tow him into the dining room, but the surprising thing is that he lets me.

"Hope you're hungry!" I chirp at him, like I'm auditioning for a seat in Emerson's chamber of commerce.

This breaks the ice enough for everyone to file in and take seats around the dinner table. Maybe inspired by my rendition of her, Emerson finds her voice and natural leadership skills again. She gets most of us to laugh at a funny story about one of Happy Ambrose Ford's diatribes at a chamber of commerce lunch. Then she assigns us tasks for the upcoming German Heritage Festival, though we'll all be busy Litha-ing with her. All the while she briskly passes the bowls and platters around the table. By hand instead of by magic, for that homey feel. Zander chimes in, telling his own tales of the strange and entertaining people who show up on the ferry or in the bar. There is a clear attempt to make this night as friendly as possible.

Even though Nicholas sits there at Jacob's table, quiet and severe, seeming not to notice the way everyone darts veiled looks at him.

I wonder if mingling with mortals feels to him the way contending with all his ancientness does to me. A little breathtaking, a little sad.

He does not speak throughout dinner, but he stays into dessert. Then into a natural move to the living room, with the fire burning low and various familiars inside and out. The windows are open to the spring evening, crystals and herbs hanging at all of them.

I sit next to Nicholas on the couch and smile at him—challengingly—until he relaxes. Slightly.

When the discussion quiets, and Emerson stares at Nicholas long enough to be obvious, he inclines his head toward her. "Ask, Warrior."

"You know things we need to know."

"I know a great many things. What you need to know are but a few of them."

"Yet you won't tell us."

"Won't. Can't. I suppose it doesn't matter which." There is an aura of detachment or nonchalance around him, his words, but sitting this close to him I see that it's a mask. Armor, with something simmering underneath.

I'm tempted to imagine it's the emotion I've only seen in him when we're naked.

"Why be here if you can't help?" Zander returns, eyeing him suspiciously.

"For your scintillating company, of course."

Ellowyn and I are the only ones who laugh at that, which at least feels like old times.

"You could tell us *some* things, if we ask the right questions," Georgie says, more a statement than a question.

Nicholas's expression is almost approving. "Not all questions have answers, but there might be some."

Ellowyn studies him. "Like a troll under a bridge handing out riddles?"

"Whatever suits your impressive imagination, Ms. Good."

She barks out another laugh. Zander narrows his eyes.

"What about the illnesses?" Jacob asks, clearly not interested in laughing, or riddles. Zander gets poker-faced. "Can you tell us why so many witches are getting sick? And if it relates to all of this?"

"There's nothing to be done," Nicholas says in that quiet way he spoke to me on the stairs. And I understand now that this is his kindness. It makes my heart beat wildly in my chest, even though his answer isn't exactly helpful. "Some things, once begun, cannot be stopped. But I can give you this. Yes, it does relate."

This is not what anyone wants to hear. I reach for my phone like a text might prove that Nicholas is lying, when I know it's just a text. Zander stands up abruptly and moves to the coffee table, where a platter of brownies is waiting for him to grief-eat them. Which he does.

"There has to be something we can do," Ellowyn surprises me by saying.

Nicholas looks at everyone and no one, it seems. He stays seated beside me, but it's as if the *idea* of him grows, taking over the room. Leaving us in no doubt of his power and otherness.

But somehow I take comfort in the fact that he has to put it on, like a costume.

Like he wants to be here more than he wants to admit.

"Here is what I am able to tell you," he says, and now he sounds like an oracle from on high. His voice echoes off our very bones. "They will seek to divide you. Your power is both individual, and a unit. There are prophecies, and there is magic, all meant to help you along this road. There are steps they must take that you must stop. Quests like this are not won alone, and they are not won without sacrifice. Fate, destiny, it only goes so far. You have to choose the right paths, or we're doomed."

It takes a moment for the tolling bells to recede enough that we all seem to realize that he's stopped speaking.

Zander, who froze along with the rest of us, shoves the last of a brownie into his mouth and swallows it down. "Some speech," he mutters.

"Have faith, mortals," Nicholas murmurs with his patented drawl that I know is meant to annoy us. I look around and see it's working. "You are the chosen and the strong. Unless you lose, that is."

This time when Ellowyn and I laugh, everyone else laughs too.

"I'm not a big fan of losing," Emerson says, once the tension is broken, and even Zander sits down again. "There must be a way to avoid it."

Georgie is nodding along, but she narrows her eyes when she looks at Nicholas. "This sacrifice. It isn't one we get to choose, is it?"

Nicholas shakes his head. "No, I think your Warrior learned that the last time."

"I refused to be the sacrifice," Emerson says with some heat. "You were all there. You know that as well as I do."

"You were willing," Nicholas says softly, too much history in his blue gaze. Then it's almost as if he's quoting someone else. "It will not only be the willing who sacrifice or will be sacrificed. That is the nature of war."

"This isn't a war," I hear myself say, almost desperately.

But I know that's wishful thinking when his gaze meets mine. "It will be."

Everyone grows silent again. I don't think anyone is *surprised* to hear that, exactly. What did we imagine taking on the Joywood would involve? But it's different to hear someone else just say it flat-out.

And it ends the questions. People begin to make their excuses. When Nicholas does, so do I. Why pretend?

He says nothing. I say nothing. But he takes my hand and

we fly through the evening to Frost House. I can feel time slipping away, like the tick of a bomb. Once Litha arrives, this will be over. I feel it. I know it.

I hate it.

But it's the way he spoke of sacrifice that stays with me. Long after we've glutted ourselves on each other for the night.

I am curled up in Nicholas's bed like I belong in this mausoleum. With the moon shining down on us while he sleeps and I suffer.

I turn to face him. He looks no less dangerous in sleep. All angles and sharp edges. Beautiful, and somehow more at peace here in his sleep than I ever could have imagined.

Sacrifice.

It's not right to look into someone's future without their consent, particularly when they're sleeping. My grandmother taught me the rules, and I'm trying so hard to live up to the level of responsibility she would expect of me. The way I couldn't before.

But then it's her voice in my head. *Touch him.*

Just like at the bar, and then again at our ritual.

There are many ways to be the death of someone, Rebekah.

I refuse to be your death, Nicholas, I think at him. He shifts in his sleep but doesn't wake up.

Touch him.

I do it. I can't seem to stop myself. It's my grandmother's voice. How can I refuse? I press my fingertips to his shoulders, and with the ring pulsing on my finger, I center my power. And let it lead me in.

The visions flicker like a deck of cards being shuffled. They aren't clear. This isn't the static from before. This is more like he protected himself because he knew I'd look.

I scowl at him.

But still the word *sacrifice* hisses along my skin, and in the images that move so quickly through me I see him fall. Over and over again while the word *sacrifice* echoes within me. There is something here in these visions I need to understand.

Maybe I can't find an answer tonight, but I have found something to pay attention to. I pull my power back in. He does not stir.

And to my surprise, I fall asleep, with only visions of sunlight and laughter dancing in my dreams.

But somehow, when I wake up, I know Nicholas dreamed only of war.

THREE WEEKS PASS IN A WHIRL OF SEX AND magic, pressing worry and simple delight. The classes and practicums don't get easier. Nicholas was right to warn me about Felicia, who takes a sadistic pleasure in making sure I fail everything I try to do. My mother doesn't get any less shrill, because how can I expect to pass the pubertatum if I can't master the practicums?

But there's a delicious immortal to make up for the tedium and embarrassment. There's the sex, but there's also the classes he teaches me in his library, where the spells that somehow get flipped on me in St. Cyprian High turn out just fine.

I'm also not the only one sneaking out at night, because Emerson insists that seeming to stay at Wilde House despite the fact she's engaged will help lull everyone watching us into thinking the Joywood have succeeded in humiliating us enough that we pose no threat.

It's a bonding experience, really.

The flip side of high school, when everyone was certain

we were the farthest thing from threatening but *we* were *sure* we had power.

It's tempting to imagine we might actually win this time.

Today's Joywood exercise in embarrassment is an assembly about safe magic and responsibility I vaguely remember from back when I first dozed through it. The witchy version of a human "abstinence only" program before being sent off into the wide world to ignore everything they told us.

Even Emerson can't drum up her usual enthusiasm, possibly because it's an assembly she's not in charge of. But we're both more worried about the fact Jacob and Zander are running late. And about Ellowyn being in the gym again, when this sweaty place might have been the source of what came over her on Beltane. She's acting a little strange, which doesn't help. I try to draw her out, but for someone who can't lie, she's excellent at changing the subject.

"Did you know men account for 84 percent of lightning-strike fatalities and women only 16 percent?" she asks brightly.

"And witches none of them," I return, scowling at her.

Kids are laughing, flirting, arguing—this time in casual attire. The brownnoser from our morning class waves at Emerson eagerly. Emerson waves back.

As we make our way through the gym, we all feel the electricity of new, palpable magic filling the air. I see Georgie shiver. Emerson frowns and looks around as if she's sniffing out an attack. I feel the hair all over my body try to stand on end. I glance at Ellowyn.

She blows out a breath. "Feeling fine so far. Maybe it was the punch."

We both know she didn't have any punch, but I don't say anything. Not in enemy territory. Emerson leads the way to a row of seats and we arrange ourselves there, saving two for Jacob and Zander.

My nerves feel oddly stretched tight, when I would have said there were few things more boring than a school assembly. Georgie is the only one who doesn't seem equally antsy, but only because she's not paying attention. She's looking off to the side, where Sage Osburn is standing with the faculty. I still can't seem to help thinking that she's punching way below her weight there. Emerson and I share a glance, and I know she agrees.

But no one asks us, so Georgie keeps smiling and mouthing things at her *beau* and I look to the stage, where the Joywood have assembled themselves. Self-importantly, as ever.

I don't think it's paranoia to think they're looking our way. A lot.

Maybe that's when I realize that I haven't thought of them as anything but hard-core evil in a while now. That feels important.

But Carol approaches the podium then, and everyone hushes automatically. The assembly is starting, and Jacob and Zander still aren't here.

I'm surprised there's no point made of it. Because there's no way their absence hasn't been noticed. *Evil*, my mind keeps chanting, and then I begin to go off in a million terrible directions that are a little too close to visions—

Luckily, that's when Jacob and Zander appear at the end of our row to take their seats.

"Not good," I hear Jacob murmur to Emerson as he takes the seat next to her. *Zelda*, I think, and that same grief wells up inside me as Zander moves to take the empty seat next to me. Emerson brushes her hand across Jacob's temple. I don't have to look at my phone to know she only texted me once today.

Remember, sweet girl, she'd written in response to my usual morning text about the day ahead, *you don't have to prove anything to me. You never did.*

Yet she texted nothing else, not even when I sent her the photos of Smudge she usually loves.

I lean into my cousin, wishing I didn't hear Nicholas's words in my head.

There's nothing to be done.

But even in distress, we feel like a unit. An actual coven, even, with all the power and strength that implies. I'm not naive enough to think that will keep us safe, but it sure doesn't hurt.

"The pubertatum is an important ritual," Carol says, opening the assembly, her voice booming with the help of a microphone and magic. "It isn't just about you and what you will become, but about all witchkind. The safety and sanctity of what and who we are."

The crowd of teenagers is hushed, and mostly rapt. Sure, a few lean over to the person next to them and whisper something. And there are the occasional muffled giggles, proving they're not *all* automatons.

It almost makes me smile. Some things don't change. I glance at Zander—white-faced and stoic, when he'd usually put on a show for us—and understand, against my will, that life is nothing *but* change. You live, you learn, you lose.

I wish I'd understood that when I was as young and foolish as most of the kids here. Or maybe there's something sort of beautiful about that time. Before you know better.

"One of the most important lessons a young witch can learn before they go out into the world is how critical our rules are, for all of our own good. For our safety and our future. Rebellion isn't a joke, or a fun lark, it's dangerous. It threatens not just you as individuals, but all of us. As a whole."

That feels pointed. Even in my head Ellowyn's voice is dry.

As a knife, I reply. *And likely in the back.*

"But we don't expect you to take our word for it," Carol

says, smiling at the audience like we're all in on a joke together. "Let us give you some examples."

They drone on and on, each member of the Joywood presenting some age-old fairy tale dressed up as warning. About Passau and floods. About Salem and hangings. It's always rule breakers that lead to the loss of knowledge, the death of good witches, and the precautions we must all now take to keep our existence hidden.

Blah, blah, blah, I send Ellowyn's way, making her smile.

When it's Felicia's turn, I settle in for a long, winding diatribe about walking on the wrong side of the street or something. Maybe I can do a spell to keep my eyes open while I take a nap.

She steps up to the podium, and all the way across the gym, I feel her eyes land on me. She smirks.

Dread tightens every muscle in my body.

"These are all old stories, and likely most of you are unmoved," Felicia says, in that voice she uses when she's attempting to *relate* to the youths. She even leans on the podium, so carefree and approachable. Like a goblin. "Passau and Salem are ancient history. I know we're all more interested in moving forward."

My heart is thundering in my ears, but I still hear every word. As if it's directed at me.

Because it is.

"Let me offer a more recent example. One that threatens what we are now, and in the future." Felicia holds up her hands, head thrown back to the ceiling, murmuring the words of a spell. As she does, a screen appears and hangs in the air. A movie begins to play.

"Now we have to sit through an after school special?" Zander complains from beside me. "Wake me up when it's over and we've all learned our very important lesson."

But I can't laugh. I recognize everything about the first image. Because I was there.

It's right after Emerson's mind wipe—though they don't show that. They'd have to answer questions about how she clearly has power now and wields it.

So do I. And so did I then.

Their test was wrong about us, but who's going to remember that?

I know what's about to happen, and watching it feels like a car crash I can see coming from a mile off.

My vision has grayed at the edges, like a pinpoint, so all I see is the screen. Younger Rebekah, fury stamped on her features and fire sparking from her hands. On the bricks. Wielding my magic—not just *on* the bricks, not just *at* Felicia, two very big no-nos, but clearly mixed with black.

You can *see* the darkness in me. You can *see* me leaning into it.

My fury, my hurt, my betrayal warped me until I would have taken revenge at *any* cost. And here it is, for all to see, me pulling all that black from below and throwing it at Felicia.

Everyone who's ever done magic knows that the darkness lurks *just there.* We're all taught to be better than that. To choose good magic, always. Especially on the bricks of St. Cyprian, where it's the law.

Part of me thinks they've warped it. Made me look more like a villain, more unhinged than I ever was. But another part of me looks at that hurting, lonely, desperate girl and thinks… I was all of that. I was the embodiment of my own despair, and that black, dark magic felt like the only thing that might save me.

Because darkness lies, no matter its form.

But that's the kind of thing some people need to learn the hard way.

There's no sound. There's just me, hanging in the air on a six-foot-tall screen, clearly out of control. *Clearly* using ribbons of dark magic against another witch there on the sacred bricks. Fire erupting around me.

Clearly *this close* to causing a terrible tragedy.

It's all there. My attempt to show my grand power, the way it all got out of control, and how it would have burned down the whole town if Nicholas wasn't there to stop it.

To stop *me*.

Then we cut to the hurt and shocked Joywood, my horrified and appalled parents. They don't show my grandmother's reaction when Nicholas delivered me to her, but they don't need to. I see it in my mind's eye, my reel of shame.

And that's all bad enough. I might survive this, but Emerson is here in this gym with me, hands covering her mouth like she's watching a horror movie, waiting for the monster to jump out of the dark.

When the monster is me.

Her little sister breaking all those sacred bonds. It doesn't matter why I did it. It only matters that I could have killed people. That I look like I *wanted* to kill people. That I broke the law and *deserved* to be exiled.

If not worse.

"Shit, Rebekah," Ellowyn mutters.

And it's not the *shit, we're in this mess together again* type of mutter either. She might not look as horrified as Emerson, but she's hurt.

"You see," Felicia intones as the images fade away. "This young person tried to thwart the ruling of the Joywood. She thought because she *felt* power, she should wield it. And she almost destroyed all of us in the process."

I know it doesn't matter what the teenagers around us think. It doesn't matter what the town will think when they hear about this, and likely see the little monster movie themselves, as I'm sure they all will. This isn't for them.

This is for an audience of five, and they're all sitting around me, stunned.

Because they thought that I'd run away in exile, the same way Emerson was mind wiped. That these were things that happened to us, that we were both victims.

And I let them think that.

I *wanted* them to think that.

The Joywood close the assembly with words of "wisdom" and a rousing speech by Carol about *potential* and cream rising to the top.

I'm numb, and I can't bring myself to do anything but look forward and sit in that numbness. As the teenagers file out. As my friends get stiffly to their feet.

Emerson and Jacob file out one side of our row, Zander, Georgie, and Ellowyn the other. Leaving me alone there in the middle.

But the Joywood sit on the stage, watching us too closely. Even through all the throng of teenage bodies. I have to get up. I have to prove they didn't get to me.

Even if they did.

I wish I had it in me to think I can fix this or prove them wrong, but they've turned me into a weapon against my friends and it's my own fault.

I don't pretend otherwise.

They couldn't have used this against me if I hadn't done it. If I'd told my friends what really happened.

I walk slowly out into the cool spring night. Clouds have rolled in, so the only light out here is the fluorescent kind at the doorway and the occasional beam of light from young witches trying to light their path with weak luminescence spells.

We walk. No one flies. I follow slightly behind the group, and it's not until the teenagers have thinned out that I realize I have no idea where we're going. Somehow we're in one of the empty parks alongside the river.

My friends stop. And turn to me.

I stand there, even though I want to die rather than do this, and face them all.

Because that's the least I can do.

Literally.

Emerson is crying, though trying very hard not to. Jacob has his arm around her. Zander's hands are jammed in his pockets. Ellowyn and Georgie are gripping each other, hard.

All of them stare at me.

The ring on my hand pulses and I curl my hand around it, sure it's my grandmother, expressing her disappointment in me. Again.

When that almost killed me the first time.

Emerson looks up at Jacob, and he nods and creates a bubble around us. Meant to keep anything we say from nosy ears.

I brace myself.

"We all know that the Joywood like to play their games..." Emerson manages to say.

I shake my head, almost wrecked right there by her determination to make this okay. To make *me* okay. "No. I did it. Everything on that screen."

Isn't that what all my years in recovery taught me? That taking responsibility is about the terrible moments, the awful times. It isn't as simple as charging along, *doing* things. Sometimes it's doing the far harder work of facing up to what you did, what you can't take back. It's letting the people you love see the truth, even if it means you'll lose them.

"Why?" Georgie asks.

They're all looking at me for an answer to that.

"I knew they were wrong," I croak. The old words, the old defenses. "I *felt* them wipe Emerson. They mind wiped her without letting anyone—"

"Not why did you *do* it, Rebekah," Ellowyn corrects me. "Though on the bricks, sweet gods, what were you thinking? But that's not what's important. What's important is why you didn't *tell* us? All this time."

"They cursed you?" Emerson suggests hopefully, sniffling and wiping at her tears.

They're all looking at me, hoping for some miracle. Giving me the benefit of the doubt. Hoping there's some explanation. But there's not.

"No."

"You just...didn't want to tell us," Ellowyn says. Flatly.

I could tell her I was embarrassed. Hurt. Wounded. I could give her any number of lectures on restitution and healing and amends.

But I say nothing.

"Maybe we should all take a little break here," Georgie says gently, clearly worried about Emerson's emotional well-being. Emerson doesn't cry. She doesn't *break down*. "Let everyone calm down."

Emerson nods, though she looks lost. "I need some time to think. We'll meet tomorrow."

My sister, the queen of fixing all the things *right away*, needs *time to think*.

And she's looking at me like she sees a stranger.

She jerks her gaze away. In my head, she's silent. She and Jacob share some communication, and he nods. Then they're gone in a *whoosh*.

I feel like half of me has shriveled up and died. Again. I look at Ellowyn, but she's unreadable. Georgie's expression isn't any clearer. They're still holding on to each other.

"Tomorrow," Georgie says eventually, and then she and Ellowyn fly off.

"I've got to get to the bar," Zander says. He isn't looking at me. He's looking in the direction of the river. "You shouldn't stay here alone."

But he doesn't offer to stay or walk me home.

On some level, I knew this would happen eventually—didn't I? That everyone who matters to me would finally know the truth. And I would finally be alone. Not because I was exiled by the Joywood. But because I don't deserve to be anything but.

I broke all those rules—those sacred bonds—we were taught. And I kept everything from my friends, lying by omission.

I made sure the Joywood could use my mistakes against me. Twice.

There's no taking it back.

So I catapult myself into the sky with no fucking clue where I'm going.

Except *away from here*. I have to get the hell away.

And this time, I'm not coming back.

THIS TIME IT'S NOT MY POWER OR MY VISIONS that are fractured.

It's me.

I'm up in the air, soaring over St. Cyprian. I don't have a plan. I'm not heading anywhere. This feels like *proof* that the people I love were right to walk away from me. To leave me.

If I was worth something—anything—I would have somewhere to go, wouldn't I?

I wouldn't be *left* no matter what I did.

The real, ugly truth is what I always feared it would be, and now I know it beyond any doubt: No one wants me around. Not once they know who I really am.

That's the real reason I never tried to come home.

Maybe it's time I admit it.

I'm hovering high in the air, looking down at the miserable little town that made me and broke me, more than once. The urge that had me shoot up into the air is gone now. I don't want to go anywhere. Sedona doesn't seem like an escape any longer. None of the other places I've lived over the years appeal.

I don't want anything but to take back the last few hours. Or better yet, turn back time and do something different ten years ago.

"Time is mine until time takes me home," I say, the words falling from my tongue.

And I get it now. I had all that time, but it ran out the day Nicholas dragged me back here. I look down at the rivers, the gleaming little village, the lights that mark the ferry as it chugs across the low, brown water.

I was always coming back home, wasn't I? Sooner or later. My mistake was imagining that it might be on my own terms. That if I couldn't hide the past, I could change it or shape it, somehow.

So I spread out my arms as wide as I can. I tip myself back, like a trust fall.

Then I just…let go.

And I let myself plummet back down toward St. Cyprian.

It can do with me what it will.

Because this feels right. It feels *meant*.

And it's not like I'll *die*. I'll just crash to the ground and hurt a little. Maybe a lot.

But I'll deserve it.

All the old voices I fought so hard to come to terms with are back. It's like a faucet of shame and self-loathing, and the worst part is how well I know every syllable, every insult, every whisper—

I can't believe I thought I could actually *recover* from this.

From this place. From who I am here. From what I did.

Exile seems like more than a sentence. It seems like a kindness.

And if the Joywood take me out, well. This was all borrowed time since the night I tried to burn everything down on sacred bricks like the little criminal they always accused me of being.

Maybe, a voice whispers deep inside me as I fall faster and faster, *this is a good thing.*

I close my eyes. I spread my arms wider. I brace for impact, and with it, a little oblivion. That's what I really want.

That's what I've always wanted.

I brace myself, but I do not crash into the ground.

My wild descent stops, cushioned by something warm and soft. Like a cradle. I feel wrapped up. Held. Then I begin to move again, but more gently this time.

I open my eyes to see Nicholas standing there on the bank of the river. He's stopped my fall. His magic surrounds me, lowering me with a kindness that makes me want to cry—and then maybe slug him.

Especially when that cradle of magic delivers me into his arms. He holds me to his chest. More than anything, I want to nestle into him, press my face to the crook of his neck—but I don't.

I'm afraid if I start something like that I won't stop. He knows everything I've done. He knew that night, but he turned his back on me then.

He says nothing as he looks at me. As he sees *into* me. Then, carefully, he sets me on my feet.

I have the strangest notion that the breeze from the river might blow me away, but his hands curl over my shoulders and keep me still. *Keep me safe*, I think.

But not because he caught me.

Because he's known the truth about me all along. And maybe he once turned his back on me, but I've never had to hide. Not from Nicholas.

"I'm going back to Sedona," I blurt out. Because not hiding sounds…dangerous.

Nothing in his expression changes. But his hands fall and he steps back.

"This *is* a surprise, witchling." His voice is bored. His face is hard. It's like being shoved back in time, with whiplash. This is not my lover. This is not the man I've found underneath all those walls he's had centuries to build.

This is the forbidding, disapproving ancient I've hated all along.

Which is good. "I don't see why it's a surprise. I don't belong here. It was a valiant effort, all in all, but in the end I'm the same fuckup I always was. And it was better when I was—"

"Hiding from the consequences of your actions?" he interrupts, still sounding bored.

But his eyes flash.

So does my temper. He doesn't understand. I lost control ten years ago. And in letting my emotions take over, I behaved exactly like the people we're fighting against now. I struck out to cause pain, to get revenge, and I didn't care who I hurt.

I might as well have been auditioning to join the Joywood.

My parents were appalled at the spectacle. At what it said about our family that I would take failing the pubertatum so badly. That I would prove, beyond any doubt, that there was actually something worse than a Wilde with no power at all.

But my grandmother was disappointed *in me*. In who I was that I could do such a thing. In who I became when faced with adversity. In what that said about *me*.

And that's what I lost tonight. Not the people who already think I'm a loose cannon, an embarrassment. But the people who not only love me, but who I fooled into thinking I was like them. One of the good guys.

I want to fight with Nicholas because he's never been anything as simple as *good* or *bad*. I want to fight with him because I want to *fight*.

And because I can't hurt him. He's too powerful, too ancient, too well-trained over too many centuries.

Safe, in other words. For me, he's always been *safe*.

But I decide I don't deserve that either. Not tonight. My temper is just another hit of a drug, one I want to use to hide. To make myself feel better. I can't allow it.

I force it back down. I say nothing, even though he's basically just called me a coward. The thing is, he's right.

His dark blue gaze narrows. "It is your choice, of course."

My problem is, I still want everything. Even the things I know better than to want. Even things that were never mine to choose. Here by the river with the stars as witness and the wind stirring through the trees.

"I'd like to take you somewhere." Nicholas sounds almost formal, and that strikes me as absurd when we've spent so much time turning each other inside and out. Because he'll do anything that feels good, and I have no inhibitions at all. There's nothing *formal* here. But he continues in the same tone. "It shouldn't take long." He even offers me one of his stiff little bows. "Consider it a goodbye gift."

Goodbye cracks through me like a terrible chasm.

I've spent my whole life trying to get away from this place, then trying to stay away. This should feel like a reprieve. A stay of execution—because sure, the Joywood might chase me down, but it's just as likely they won't bother. Either way, I get to be gone.

And if Nicholas helps me leave, he's probably not going to haul me back again. I bet he'd even help hide me from nosy sisters and rampaging ruling covens alike.

I can finally stay gone for good.

It's everything I've ever wanted.

So this is the moment I realize that I don't want any of that at all.

I want to stay.

Here in this town with these people. With the weight of the past and the future. I want to fight beside my friends and build something new with my sister. I want to fulfill the prophecies and live up to my ancestresses.

I want to *stay*.

But it's too late.

Nicholas's hand is on my elbow and he flings us both into the dark night. And he flies the way he does everything else, with purpose and ferocity. Yet lands as easily as if he merely stepped off a low stair.

It takes me a moment to realize that he's set us down just outside the cemetery on the other side of the river.

The only time I've been here since I left—and since my grandmother was buried without me—was the night we fought the flood and won. Where I stood next to Nicholas and poured my magic into my sister, to help her, to save her, to defeat the black in the confluence.

I have avoided even looking in this direction ever since. Emerson visits frequently and often invites me to go with her, but I can't. I haven't. I can't bear to see my grandmother's name carved into cruel, uncaring stone. I still refuse to accept that she's gone.

Forever.

I turn to get the hell away from this place. Panic and dread and an old, familiar grief are a drumbeat in my head, my neck. Even behind my knees.

But I only run into the hard wall of Nicholas's chest.

"I don't want to be here," I say to the steel and brick that make up his pecs.

"I think you do," he returns.

So calm. So *detached.* Like he doesn't care either way.

But when I try to get past him he holds me firm—with his strong arms and his wily magic and something else I can't let myself name.

"Rebekah." And his voice is so gentle it makes tears prickle behind my eyes. Nicholas Frost…*gentle*? How am I supposed to fight that? "Face her. You need to."

He turns me around like a child and even nudges me through the black metal archway. I don't *want* to know where she's buried, but I do. Witches treat their dead better than humans do, and part of that, here in St. Cyprian, is familiarizing ourselves with our family plots. My gaze is drawn straight to the spot where I expect to see her gravestone standing next to my grandfather's.

But instead, I see…her.

Not a stone. Not even her fox familiar in his statuesque glory.

It's *her.*

I stop walking. I'm surrounded by gravestones, all of them bearing names I know. All of them marked with the small stone statues of creatures that the human population thinks are nothing but a cute little local tradition.

And my grandmother, who has been dead for *years,* is not beneath the ground. She is not floating in midair like a regular old haunt or common ghost. She is not flickering in the starlight, as she might if some medium raised her up for a brief chat.

In fact, as I stand there with my mouth open, she holds out her hand to me. The way she always did. "Come, child. I don't have all day."

I blink. It's not a voice in my head. It's the creaking, decidedly cranky voice from my childhood. Out loud in the night air.

Something like muscle memory takes over. I walk toward her because she told me to. Because I don't have it in me to disobey Grandma, especially this long after missing her funeral. She sits on a little stone bench, settling herself there the same way she did in her favorite chair, adjusting herself with a little song I find I still know all the words to.

I sit down next to her and I can *feel* her. Actually feel her body next to mine. I can smell her, the lotion she loved, the earth that was always on her hands, the flowers she grew. She smells like spring. And maybe she's not *quite* as substantial besides me as a human being filled with life, but she's not simply a spirit either. There's a sense of the woman she was—she is—as she takes my hand in hers. I can feel the heat of her papery palms.

My eyes want to close. The tears want to fall. But I don't want to miss a single moment of this, whatever it is. I already miss too much I can't get back. "Grandma," I whisper.

"My Rebekah." Her voice is soft and rough and undeniably *her.* "Finally."

As if I deserve to be here, with her. When I know better.

"I..." I don't know what to say, how to wrap my mind around this. I understand spirits and leftover magic. I understand no one we love really leaves us, and that as witches we get the great privilege of witnessing lives long after death. I have seen her before.

But only ever with Emerson, and only as a vision. A shadow of the grandmother I remember.

This is something else entirely.

"I'm afraid we don't have time to ease into this," she says, and she pats my hand the way she always used to. When the tears or the whining or the drama had gone on long enough, by her estimation, and it was time to buck up. Not one for a wallow, my grandmother. Her gaze is direct. "Things must be said, so things can be done."

But I shake my head. "I ruined everything. That night… It'll always haunt me."

"Only if you let it."

"Grandma…"

"You think I don't understand." Her gaze never wavers. Her hands are old, but strong on mine. "You underestimate me that way. But the true crime is that you underestimate yourself. Rebekah." She says my name the way she did before. Like it's the song she sings to herself. Like she wishes I knew *these* words too. "Darling child, why did you run away?"

"I was exiled."

"Yes, but also no. That isn't the why of it. Not really." I feel very small, very young. And yet aware of every one of my years, especially the ones I spent too far away from here. "You were running away before that. You were burning down everything behind you so you would never have to turn around and deal with who you are."

This part I know. This part I know all too well. "I'm so sorry I disappointed you," I tell her solemnly. "I'm so sorry, Grandma."

"This is the lesson you refuse to learn, to this day." Her frustration is familiar, but also laced with love. Always love. How did I miss that before when it's so clear to me now? "You can make mistakes, Rebekah. You can disappoint me. But you have never and will never lose my love. Or my belief that you can do better and *be* better."

"I know," I manage to say. "I don't deserve—"

"Making mistakes doesn't make you worthless, Rebekah," my grandmother tells me, her voice as steady as her gaze. As her grip. As her love, across all these years and death besides. "It makes you alive."

Everything in me shakes at that.

Grandma keeps going. "Running from your problems doesn't solve them. It can't change who you are. You take yourself with you, but leave those who would help you behind."

"It's better that way."

She looks impatient then, which is more her than any wise words or sweet, familiar scents on the night wind. "You fled to avoid any possibility of absolution, not because you were afraid you wouldn't get it, but because you didn't think you deserved it. So you left. You hid where I could only reach you with breezes and signs and the occasional crow." I think of the crow who used to sit outside my bungalow in Sedona and croak me awake, the one I used to tell Smudge was following us. Goose bumps shiver all over my arms. "And your sister couldn't reach you at all."

I ignore the goose bumps. "I was exiled, Grandma. Officially. And Emerson was mind wiped."

"Those are excuses." This doesn't feel fair, but it does sound like her. And the way I bite my tongue to keep from defending myself feels familiar too. "But you came back anyway."

"I was *dragged* back," I correct her. "Against my will. *Twice.*"

My grandmother smiles her old, special smile. The one that was just for me when she was being mischievous. "Not such a bad thing to be dragged hither and yon by a handsome man, I would have thought. Besides, you stayed."

"The Joywood—"

"At some point, you will have to take responsibility for your own actions instead of continuing to punish yourself for the actions of a girl. Actions you can't change."

I nod miserably. But she isn't lecturing me, I realize in the next moment. Because everything about her softens, and she pulls me into a hug I can feel down to my toes.

"My darling, you're never going to move forward until you forgive yourself." I feel her hand on my face. "All those recovery meetings and you should know this by now. You have to forgive yourself. To save anything, including you."

I cast around for something to say, something to encompass all the grief and sorrow, shame and longing inside me, but all I can say is, *"How?"*

"Easily," my grandmother says with gentle certainty. "Consider seventeen-year-old Rebekah as I do. A young woman who had *wars* inside her and did not know how to fight them. A girl who was never given the support she needed, even though I tried."

"You should have been enough, Grandma. It was me who—"

"My dear, no one person can ever be enough. Not for a lost child trying to find her way. Your teachers and your parents failed you. The Joywood failed you."

It's the absolution I dared not ask for, and I'm still not sure I deserve it. But I want it.

Especially from her.

"Grandma..."

"I forgave you before you left," she tells me, her eyes on mine so I can see what I always saw there in her gaze. Love. Always love, no matter what else might come.

"I disappointed you." I can barely push the words out.

Her nod doesn't help the tightness in my throat. "You disappointed me, yes. But love and disappointment aren't mutually exclusive. Because I love you, I knew you could do better and be better. Because I love you, disappointment is only a starting point, never the end." Her gaze seems to grow brighter now. "Forgive yourself."

I would have said I'd worked on that for years. I did. But now I know what it's like to see almost everyone I love turn away from me because they finally see the truth. "I don't know if I can," I say softly. "Or if I should."

"You're holding yourself to an impossible standard," Grandma tells me. "Whoever told you love comes in absolutes?"

She points past me, and I turn to see what she's pointing at.

But I know.

Nicholas.

He stands at the entrance of the cemetery, framed perfectly by the iron arch and the rising moon. He looks beautiful and unreal. Immortal, untouchable.

And he still looks like mine.

"Here is a man who's run away from the consequences of his actions for hundreds upon hundreds of years," Grandma says. "You could even argue that the greatest and saddest consequence of his actions is him. Do you blame him for this?"

The "no" is automatic. An intuitive response that requires no thought, because of course I don't. I've already told him so.

"Here is a man who has hurt people for his own selfish desires, in his time. Who sacrificed everything for a drink of power and then learned, too late, that power only seems like a reward to those who have none. Do those mistakes mark him forever, Rebekah?"

I don't want to answer, because I see her point. And I'm not sure I'm ready.

"Or," continues my grandmother, right here beside me despite the fact she's dead and I've failed her, "do you love him? *Because* he has made mistakes and those mistakes help make him who he is?"

I don't want to use that word. *Love.* But then, it stands to reason that I would fall in love outrageously, the same way I do everything else. Why fall in love with some run-of-the-mill witch who works magic in accounting and likes to let loose on Beltane with a barbecue and an extra beer? That was never going to be me.

Of course, instead, I go and fall head over heels for an immortal who lurks around in his haunted house, lives for cryptic warnings, and occasionally looks at me like I'm the only sun he'll ever need.

Not that I remember falling in love with him, exactly. There was that fire at Beltane, but all it did was clarify what should have been clear to me all along. I never hated him, I just hated that he was there that night. That he stopped the mess I made, after I'd already begun to make it. I never hated him, though I wanted to. I hated myself. The truth is, I've loved Nicholas Frost my whole life.

For as much good as that does either of us now.

"No one is ever perfect," Grandma is saying in her quietly fierce way. "Not an ageless witch. Not the first Diviner we've seen in St. Cyprian in decades. Not Emerson or your parents or even me. There is no standard you need to meet, except your own. That's how you put your mistakes to rights, Rebekah."

"But..." I'm still looking at Nicholas. And I *see*. I see so many of the things he did. I know how he felt. I know all the whys and hows, and I'm not excusing them. Even if I think he's not that man any longer. I love him anyway. Not despite what I see, but because I see it and I also see him now. But I'm used to visions. Of knowing private sorrows and secret shames. "But Grandma, they all *saw*."

And the good thing about having conversations with my long-dead loved ones is that no explanations are necessary. She knows what they saw. Just as she knows who showed them.

She slides her arm around me. "Then, child, let them see *you*, for a change. Let them love you. I'll let you in on a secret. They already do."

I turn to her then, and as I do, I let go of so many things I've held on to for far too long. They rush out of me like a river, like I'm giving them back to the St. Cyprian sky above us. Fear. Shame. Grief. I gripped them all so hard I made marks. I dug in. I called myself an addict to everything I refused to let go of. I wrapped them tight around me and built a new life on top of them and letting them go makes me feel...almost tipsy.

But free.

Grandma smiles and it is warmth personified. It is love. I feel it in all the places that I just swept clean. And I know I ran away from this because I was so afraid that I wouldn't be able to feel her—this—anymore.

I didn't *deserve* to.

"You should have come to me then, but you did not. You weren't ready." Grandma looks at me with only love. Only kindness and hope. And faith, I understand, that I might be better tonight than I was ten years ago. *Because* she loves me. "Can you come to me now? Of your own free will? And ask me for help at last?"

"Yes," I say, and it's more a vow than confirmation. "I'm sorry I didn't ask before. That I ran, when you never gave me any reason to believe you wouldn't love me, forgive me." I suck in a deep breath, and it feels like all that peace I struggled to grasp out there. All those retreats, all those yoga challenges, all those tarot cards, and it was just this. Just love. "I don't know if I'm ready to forgive myself for my mistakes, but maybe I'm ready to stay and face them. And I need your help. *We* need your help. What do we do?"

My grandmother nods, and she closes her eyes briefly. When she opens them, I can feel her magic pulsing around us. Her brown eyes glow gold, as Emerson's do with her magic, as mine do too, when I let them. "The Joywood are a powerful enemy. They will stop at nothing to get what they want."

"What do they want?"

Her eyes, so much like mine and Emerson's, cloud. Her mouth turns down. "Everything."

A cold chill snakes through me. I've always seen my end at the Joywood's hands. Too many ends, too many times to count. And I never really thought beyond that—beyond *me*.

But that's one of the lessons here tonight. It might involve me, but it's not *about* me.

I'm reminded, suddenly, of what Nicholas said when I asked him what he gave up for immortality.

Everything, he said.

The echo sits in me uneasily.

"Pain is coming," Grandma tells me. "Grief. It is not happenstance. It is not accidental. It is purposeful, Rebekah. And when it comes, don't let it change who you are. Who you *all* are. Let it bind you. Let it fuel you instead, because grief is love. And love is magic."

She sighs then, and it's like a breeze across my face. I can feel her getting weaker. It's powerful magic, *she* is powerful magic, but she can only sustain this for so long.

But I understand now. She's always here. Even when I can't feel her hands on my face, or her breath in the breeze, she is here.

With me. Always.

The ring on my finger pulses.

"Do not stand in your mistakes, seek to fix them." Her voice is getting quieter and quieter, and it's happening too fast. I knew it would happen and still, the sense of her fading into an image and then an image into mist…*hurts*. But I don't cry. I try to honor it, the way she would. She was always a gardener, and the first to remind us all that there are seasons for a reason. "Remind him, Rebekah. Don't let him…"

But she's gone before she can finish that sentence. And I'm sitting by myself on a stone bench in a graveyard in the moonlight, looking at a headstone with my grandmother's name carved in neat letters that do nothing at all to capture her. With a stone fox standing guard.

"Don't let him what?" I ask, my voice desperate.

Touch him, her voice urges me, from deep inside.

I look up at Nicholas. And even though I know she said *touch him* in my head, I swear I can hear her voice carrying on the breeze. I wonder if he can hear her too.

He stands there at the entrance to the graveyard, his long coat whipping in the wind I didn't feel while my grandmother was here. I stand up on legs that feel shaky, like they're new. Like *I'm* new.

And as I approach him, I find I feel the same.

Hollowed out. Clean. *Loved*.

It's like the Teineigen on Beltane that made me new—but that was my magic. It was a new start, but I hadn't forgiven the old mistakes yet.

I don't know what forgiveness feels like, but this seems like a good start.

"Do you still wish to leave?" he asks me as I draw near.

Because it's my choice. It always has been. There might be consequences to choices, but there are always choices.

I think of hanging so high in the air, looking down at the lights of this haunted river town I still call home. And how even then, my eyes were drawn to the place that's always haunted me the most.

And the man who lives there still. The man who's lived forever.

The man I've loved so long I never thought I was falling in love at all, until I fell from the sky. And he caught me.

So I choose. Finally, I choose.

I'm all about listening to my grandma today, so I lift up on my toes. I slide my hand up to smooth over his jaw, catching him the way he caught me, in the best way I can right now. Because if I told him I was leaving, he would take me wherever I wanted to go. He might have a few cutting things to say about it, but he would do it.

I know that as surely as I know him—inside and out, mistakes across the ages—and I do.

So I make him a vow too. "I'm not going anywhere."

25

I GIVE MY FRIENDS UNTIL MORNING.

I send off little magical messages to all of them, all tucked up in their various beds before dawn, while I fly across the river to the North Farm where I know my sister is snuggled up with her Healer. I could be in bed with my favorite immortal right now, mind you, but we spent the whole night using up our silences.

All that's left are the words we don't say, and no one wants that. Much better to head off to face and fix the mess I made, buoyed with my grandma's love and each and every one of the things Nicholas does not say to me.

I feel them all the same.

Once I land I set off toward the cozy-looking farmhouse where Nicholas actually sat and had dinner, like a regular old mortal witch. It's a cool morning, out here before the sun, and the ground is damp. Something makes me stop as I make it to the yard and I look around, a kind of awareness prickling over me. I tense—

But then I see the huge stag standing where the yard fades into the trees.

Watching me.

"Murphy," I say softly, and incline my head in his direction. I've known Jacob's familiar as long as I've known Jacob, but that doesn't mean he'll let me approach the house if that's not what the occupants want. For all I know, they told him to keep me away.

I'm not afraid of that—because I'm a little sister who's perfectly capable of getting my big sister's attention when I want it—but I realize I'm holding my breath as I wait to see.

Across the yard, Murphy dips his antlers, then seems to let the trees suck him in whole.

I blow out the breath I was holding and start moving again.

I march up to the door, but pause once I climb up on the porch. I suck in a cleansing breath. Or five. I can't change what she saw. What I did. I can't take back my feelings, or my fear. But I can be honest. I can ask for help.

I think, *I have to.*

Panic beats inside of me, but it's the same as outside the cemetery last night. I didn't want to face my grandmother. Or really, her disappointment. I was scared to see my own feelings reflected back at me, and that was wrong. Because it was wrong to think so little of her.

Just like it's wrong to think so little of Emerson now.

So, I knock on the door. It takes a few minutes, including me sending a little *zap* into the house in the hope of waking its inhabitants up.

When the door opens with a creak, Emerson is standing there in her pajamas, with a robe and slippers that I don't think are hers. Maybe she's commandeered them. She yawns, her eyes barely opened. Though she jolts when she finally sees me. "Rebekah."

I sweep in. Even now, I feel the need to lead with brazen indifference, because I might have cleared out a lot of mess within, but I'm still me.

"I called a meeting," I announce to the dim, quiet living room. Cassie is curled by the fire and only opens one eye at me, then closes it, like she's bored. Or maybe telling me to *get on with it.*

"You..." Emerson trails off. She stands there, door still open, her hair a tousled mess. Still half-asleep. "You did what now?"

I want to smile. Somehow, I've caught Emerson off guard. *I'm* the one put together, ready to set things to rights. And she is the one still struggling to pull herself out of sleep.

It's like *Freaky Friday* and I love it.

But this isn't the time for little sister goals. "I wanted to talk to you first."

Emerson squints at the pretty picture window in the living room that looks out over some of Jacob's fields. "The sun isn't even up."

"No, it isn't."

She rubs her hands over her face. "I was up late. I was worried." When she drops her hands, her expression shows hurt. "You blocked me."

My self-satisfaction fades at that. Because I didn't consciously block her or anyone, but it fits, doesn't it? Everything my grandmother said. What I did then. What I did last night.

The fact I thought I was so alone that I let myself fall from the sky, but Emerson was trying to reach out to me the whole time.

It's been a long night of facing myself and much as I'd like to, I don't back away from that now. "I'm sorry."

"For which part?"

"All of it. Everything."

She frowns, and then shoves her hands in the pockets of her robe like she doesn't know what to do with them, and I think I've never adored her more.

"Emerson," I say, and my voice cracks over her name. "I saw Grandma last night."

Her hands sneak back up to cover her mouth, like she's happy for me, but emotional about it, and I tell her everything. It pours out of me.

Not just about Grandma and what happened ten years ago. What I ran from, why I did it.

I tell her about flying so high I nearly made my nose bleed. And Nicholas catching me when I fell.

I tell her what I feel for him—what I've always felt for him. And all the secrets I kept growing up that I thought were parts of who I am, but now realize were the trophies I collected to prove I was worthless all along.

The real treasures were love, and I kept those apart, tucked away under the floorboards. Or texts calling me *sweet girl* where no one else can see them.

As I tell her these things, there are parts that don't surprise her and parts that clearly do. She's long since magicked us some coffee, and despite the fact I don't usually mess with caffeine, I drink from the mug she gives me. We're sitting on Jacob's couch the way we used to sit in our favorite window seat in Wilde House. Feet tucked up, facing each other, almost touching.

This doesn't mean we don't have things to talk out. We do. We probably always will.

But I know we're going to be okay.

It's not something I *see*. It's something I *know*. In my heart.

"It's not that I don't understand the black magic thing," Emerson says, holding her coffee mug between her hands. "Maybe it wasn't right, but I *understand*. They were determined to smack us down and they were unfair. Cheating, even. We both tried to prove them wrong in our own way. And, you know, I *was* planning treason. If off the bricks."

I laugh. I can't help it. "You didn't think of it that way, though. You were all about justice. I knew what I was doing was wrong. I can't even say I was trying to prove myself, not really. They hurt you. I wanted to hurt them. I *wanted* to do something terrible, so why not dark magic?"

Emerson looks thoughtful. "Neither of us handled it right. But how could we? How could any of us? I tried to barrel on. Jacob tried to stand in front of me, not with me. You tried to show them up, and Nicholas let you run away rather than working with you." She lifts a hand to rub at her temple. "We were teenagers, though. Well, three of us were."

"Nicholas prefers to be opaque."

She doesn't smile. "We aren't teenagers anymore, Rebekah. You should have told us when you came back. You should have told *me*."

"I should have." I keep my gaze on her. I hide nothing. "I just...wasn't ready."

Emerson sucks in a breath and studies me. And there's nothing for me to do but wait.

All those years of recovery. All that pain and fear, stuffed down deep. So much work to get back to a place that, in the end, requires nothing of me but vulnerability. And patience.

Nothing and everything, then.

I don't look into the pathways I can feel opening and closing around us, keeping time with whatever my sister is thinking through. I don't look for clues on her face. I keep my gaze on her, and I wait. I have the power to do that now.

I have come here, to her. I have trusted her with all of me, without trying to pretend—about anything. I have hidden nothing. I have made no excuses.

There's nothing more I can do in this moment, and there's a peace in that. A peace I never found in vortexes or red canyons, though I tried. No psychedelic vision quest or trip to Black Rock City could manage it. Just this.

Honesty. Love. Hope.

But what happens next is up to Emerson.

She blows out a breath. When she moves, it's to come closer. She arranges herself like we used to do when we were little, legs tangled together and heads close.

And she holds my gaze. "They want to split us apart. We can't let them."

It isn't forgiveness or absolution in her words. It's pure practicality. But she leans her forehead into mine.

And I realize… I don't need *her* to absolve me, I need to absolve myself. I don't need *her* forgiveness either. Because I've never lost her love.

"I love you, Em," I say, because I didn't say it out loud to my grandmother enough when she was here. I can say it in my head a hundred times and reach her; I know this now. But I don't want to wait until we're ancient spirits to say the same to my sister.

"I love you too. I always will. No matter what."

And there's another thing the Joywood could never understand. These are the kind of people who magic weasels into bullying sons. They don't have feelings the way we do. That means they're never going to understand the kind of loyalty that comes from love instead of blind obedience.

It's a weakness and I doubt they even know it.

"I like to think that we're learning how to work together, even if it is in actual high school classrooms," Emerson is saying. "Not as *those disappointing Wilde sisters*, but as a team. As a—"

"Coven?" I finish for her. "Not just a coven, like anyone

can throw together for a big spell or whatever, but a coven you think can take the Joywood's place?"

Her eyes get bright then. And more, *sure.* "I know what we can be. So do you. We've *already* saved St. Cyprian, which is more than anyone else around here can say. All these games Carol and the rest of them are forcing us to play makes it clear that we're better for witchkind than the Joywood. Not to mention, it's only right and fair."

Despite myself, I find I'm caught up in her vision of what we could be. The seven of us. If we're honest with each other.

Today, I actually believe it's possible.

"So, what's your agenda for this meeting?" she asks, pulling back to sit a little straighter. I can tell she's ready to adjust the bullet points she thinks I have in my head. Bless her.

"I'm going to apologize and explain. And I think if we all go through that night together, we can make sure we don't make the same mistakes this time."

Emerson nods. "I think you're right." Then she studies me carefully, as if she doesn't know how to ask. "Is Nicholas invited to this meeting?"

I smile, thinking of immortal *feelings* and all the ways that beautiful man *broods.* "I think this one's just us."

Jacob comes in from the kitchen before Emerson can say anything to that. I realize that he must have been out there doing farm things this whole time. Maybe even before I knocked on the door. "Georgie and Ellowyn are outside," he tells us, his gaze moving over his fiancée like he's looking for marks. "With the familiars."

Emerson gets up and waves a hand, magicking herself into clothes and brushed hair. She drains the rest of her coffee, then straightens her shoulders. Jacob opens the front door with his own hand wave. Georgie and Ellowyn come inside, Octavius following along lazily at Georgie's heels. Ruth is perched on the porch railing, hooting under her breath. Zander's eagle swoops in next to her, Zander appearing not more than a second later.

Smudge makes her own entrance, like the queen she is.

They all come inside. There's none of the usual chatter, but there's not really the awkwardness I was expecting either. Everyone arranges themselves in the living room, and Ellowyn mutters a little spell that makes teacups appear on the table.

She hands me one. She doesn't smile. She doesn't speak in my head. But she hands me a cup full of tea, and that says enough. Why couldn't I see this before? These people are my family. My friends. My heart. It never mattered what I did.

But I should have told them.

"You know, some of us work the evening shift," Zander says, yawning into his tea.

"I'll be quick then," I say, when normally I'd give him a hard time. But he isn't just working the evening shift. He's watching his mother get sicker by the day. Whether she can admit it or not. He's holding his father up, handling the ferry, handling the bar. He's a one-man show doing all sorts of shitty things he shouldn't have to do—not yet, anyway. While all this other crap goes on around him.

It isn't fair.

So, I dive right in. "I'm sorry about last night. All of it. I wanted to hide. I didn't want to face the mistake I made."

"I would have done the same thing," Ellowyn says with a shrug, which is both a huge surprise and exactly what I expect from her. It makes my heart swell a little in my chest. "I just would have *told* you all before a decade passed."

"Yeah, you're real good at laying it all on the line," Zander mutters.

She flashes a nasty grin at him. "I said it, so it must be the truth, babe."

The awkwardness from our dinner after Beltane has reverted to their normal antagonism. I'm not sure if that's good or bad.

But it's *normal*. I have to love it for that alone.

Still, I walk them through that terrible night. What I felt, what I did. I tell them about Nicholas when we were kids. I really do lay it all on the line. Both because it's the right thing to do, and because it matters. "The point of rehashing this isn't just that I'm sorry I didn't tell you sooner, though I am. It's that they're going to pull the same shit," I tell them while they're digesting all the secrets I kept. "It worked last time."

"But only for a decade," Georgie points out. "It wore off."

"Which means they'll hit harder this time," Zander says darkly. "They'll want to make it two decades this time around."

Or forever, I think to myself. A handful of executions, and problem solved. "That little movie last night does two things. One, it discredits me—despite the fact I obviously have power. But it goes further than that. It discredits anyone who backs me."

"But it also discredits the Joywood," Georgie points out. "They said you two *didn't* have power. Not that it was bad power or whatever."

"They'll spin it," Emerson says with a frown. "I think they've been deciding how best to handle this since I broke Carol's obliviscor. Nicholas mentioned steps, right?"

"Where is the old fart?"

I glare at Zander. "That's the second thing I want to discuss." I try to emulate Emerson's no-nonsense, presidential way of speaking.

"How good ancient immortals are in the sack?" Ellowyn asks with a grin, earning a low groan from Zander.

But I am not Emerson, and Ellowyn's joke reminds me of

that. "A discussion well worth our time, but no. He's up to something."

"Something bad?" Zander asks. "Hate to break it to you, cousin, but that's kind of his whole thing."

I tell myself this is not a betrayal. These people love me, and because they do, they will help me love him. Whether they would choose him for me or not.

All of these things are love. "I think… I think he's trying to make amends."

Ellowyn considers that. "For what?"

"Whatever he did to get him immortality," Zander says, tossing a crystal from hand to hand. "If I had to guess."

"That first lesson Emerson and I had to sit through after Beltane was all about sacrifice," I say. "But the practicums, the test, are all about *balance*."

"Sacrifice can be part of balance," Emerson says. "That's how they teach the kids."

"Yes," I say softly. "But who came up with the curriculum?"

Everyone looks at me, but it's Jacob who speaks. "You think he's going to sacrifice himself."

I nod. "I do."

Jacob nods, and he and I look at each other for a moment that seems to go on too long. Because he knows. He watched Emerson sacrifice herself and nearly succeed. *Love*, I think again. *He loves her and he almost lost her.*

And would have done anything to save her. I remember him healing her out there in the fields, how much it took out of him. How much more he would have given.

All for love.

"But…why?" Ellowyn asks.

"Whatever he's planning he doesn't want me to know." I

blow out a breath. "But I know it's for me. Or maybe even for us."

"There's a pattern," Jacob says then. "If we're thinking of the flood as step one, Emerson didn't *have* to sacrifice herself to stop the flood, to save the town. She had to be *willing* to."

"I think it's the willingness to do it that matters." Georgie is sitting up straighter, nodding. "There are lots of unwilling sacrifices, sure, but all the books make it clear that the real magic is in surrendering to the knife or the ritual or whatever it is. Knowingly giving yourself over to your end is powerful, deep magic."

I tell myself this isn't the time to think about prophecies. Or how I'll be the *death* of Nicholas Frost, like it or not.

"If he really does try, and it's the thought that counts, then we have to be willing to try to save him," I say quietly instead. "He's willing, but that doesn't mean he has to succeed."

Jacob nods. Everyone else joins him.

Except Zander. "What for?" he asks. "He's already lived longer than he should have. Longer than other people, *better* people, get."

"He's part of the coven," Emerson says before I can work up a response through my shock. Because I didn't see that coming. She looks at me. "And Rebekah loves him."

This does not seem to soothe Zander any. "I didn't agree to any immortal in our coven."

"It doesn't need agreement, Zander," Emerson returns. "This is the way it is."

"Already playing dictator, Em?"

I want to snap at Zander, but Jacob shakes a head at me. Emerson holds up a hand.

In this moment, she's the Warrior, the leader. Not our friend and family. And somehow the shift doesn't bother me the way I thought it would. "I know you're tired. In all aspects. I know all the *what-ifs* hurt. If you need a break, take one. No hard feelings."

"Fine." Zander lets the crystal fall to the table with a *clunk*. And then he walks out of the house, slamming the door behind him.

Leaving behind a heavy silence while we all decide who's the best person to go after him.

Emerson makes a move while Ellowyn bites at a fingernail and deliberately makes no eye contact, but I find myself standing. Driven by more than just the need to ease my hurting cousin's feelings. Something more intuitive, more magical, within me knows I'm the one who needs to do this.

So, I walk out. He's standing in the yard, like he meant to fly away but couldn't. I have a flash of something. Him and Emerson out here, not long ago. An evening. But it's the past again, when I should see future.

I push it away, because this is about the present.

"I'll come back in," he says when I approach. He's staring hard in the direction of the river that's not visible from this vantage point. "Just needed some air."

"You don't have to come back in. Not if you don't want to."

He shrugs. "Might as well." Then he kicks at a rock in the ground. "She's not going to make it, Rebekah."

I know he means Aunt Zelda. Who hasn't texted me today, even though the sun is up now. I know it, and I think he might be right, and still… "We don't know…"

"We do know. Your immortal said it himself. There's nothing to be done. Jacob can't fix her, and I don't know anyone who'd try harder. But we've failed."

It's not the days that matter, she texted me once. *They blend into each other. What you remember are the seasons. The sweet years.*

I want to break down into sobs, facing this thing I don't want to face, but once again, this isn't about me.

"Zander. It isn't your failure. It's an illness."

"I'm just supposed to accept she's going to die this young?" He belts that out, and then he turns on me, but he's not seeing me. "I have magic. I am a Guardian of St. Cyprian. I'm just supposed to say, *Okay, mysterious illness, you win.* My mother dies, my father falls apart, and that's what? Just *life*?"

He doesn't say it isn't fair. He doesn't have to.

"I don't think there's a *supposed to* in this situation."

"Meanwhile there are people walking around with lifetimes to spare," Zander spits out. "Lifetimes they didn't earn. How is that okay?"

I know he's talking about Nicholas. But I lean my head onto his shoulder anyway, and I tell him what I know. "Your mother loves her life, Zander. She loves your dad and she loves you, and she lived the hell out of every day she got. I think what's left once we lose her is living the kind of life that will make her proud."

"You haven't seen her in a long time, Rebekah."

I swallow until I can speak. I think of what my grandmother told me about grief. "Maybe not. But I have ten years of daily text messages that are *almost* as good as visits. I know what I'm talking about."

He breathes hard for a moment, clearly fighting with all the emotions warring inside him. And possibly the urge to storm Frost House while he's at it. I don't blame him. "I won't rest until I figure out why this is happening."

I don't tell him there might not be a why. It wouldn't be fair in this moment. But part of me wonders, even knowing Nicholas confirmed her illness is caught up in this, if it's just...life. "No, *we* won't rest until we figure this all out," I say instead.

"You *love* that guy?" he asks me, his voice rough.

It should feel odd to discuss love with all of them before I've admitted it to Nicholas himself, but it doesn't. It feels right. Even if calling him *that guy* does not. "I do."

Zander remains quiet for a long minute. Then shakes his head. "I don't know what to do," he tells me, his voice barely a whisper. And I know this might be the gravest admission a man like Zander will ever make. That he doesn't know the procedure. That he can't find his way. "She refuses to see anyone aside from Dad, me, and Healers. And even me only every so often. Dad and I have tried to change her mind, but she's so weak. It feels wrong to go against her wishes."

I want to cry. I want to rage, throw things—but I know it won't do any good. Not only because Nicholas *and* Grandma said so, but because I *know.* In that way I shouldn't. There's no changing this. "We'll do whatever she wants. If it changes..."

"You and Em will be the first to know." He tries to smile. "Hell, she'll probably text you herself."

This is the pain Grandma was talking about. There are going to be losses and some of them—this one, Grandma herself—will always feel too big to bear.

Hoping otherwise is just borrowing trouble.

"Go home, Zander," I urge him. "Be with her. Or your dad. Do what needs doing. When Litha comes, I know you'll be right where you need to be."

He looks down at me. "That a Diviner premonition?"

I smile at him, ignoring the dampness on both our faces.

And then I lie. "Absolutely."

JUNE ROLLS ALONG HUMIDLY, LITHA IS LOOMING, and the entire town thinks I'm a fire-starting, dark-magic-wielding maniac who might, at any moment, set half of Missouri alight.

My father refuses to look at me and finds reasons to forever be away from the house. My mother openly weeps the first time she comes face-to-face with me after that assembly, but as the days pass, she manages to keep the tears in check. Still, there is a lot of *tremulous gazing.*

Not ideal. But also not the worst thing I've ever gone through.

Besides, the good news about the Joywood deciding to throw the big, heavy rock of those images into the St. Cyprian pond is that I get to see not only the people who support them completely, but the people who don't. The seemingly innocuous clerk in Felicia's office at SCH who gives me a thumbs-up where Felicia can't see him. The clearly disaffected teenagers, already sporting the tattoos and piercings I was forbidden at their age, who can be heard challenging the kids who whisper about me. The random witches I pass on the street who don't cross to avoid me and my pyromania, but stay the course. And sometimes whisper things like *you go, girl* or *next time call me for backup.*

I'm gathering a list of supporters and it's not small. It's not just us.

At the very least, it suggests that Emerson is on to something with her dreams of challenging the Joywood's grip on not just St. Cyprian, but the whole of witchkind.

In the meantime, I'm studying as best I can for the test I'm going to have to take. The test we all know is going to be specifically unfair to Emerson and me. My sister's position is that because we know we're being set up to fail this time, we have to work *harder* to be *better,* and before the night of the assembly, I would have moaned about that. I would have rolled my eyes and acted like a lazy fourteen-year-old and done all the usual things I do so no one thinks I care too much. About anything.

But what's that except another form of lying?

I'm done with that. So I embrace *harder* and *better.* I do my best to pay attention in class. I read Emerson's meticulous notes. Nicholas works with me every day. And I can feel the power in me…shift. It feels less like a bomb I'm trying to avoid jostling and more like some kind of clay that I'm learning how to work *with* instead of *against*.

If I had to grade myself, it would be A+ for effort across the board.

At the high school, however, I continue to fail all the practicums no matter what I do. Emerson aces them. One week she throws one, though it about kills her, and still aces it. That makes it clear to us that this is one more example of the Joywood's divide and conquer policy. They want to make sure we feel as much like the teen versions of ourselves as possible. And they *really* want to drive a wedge between us.

So we pretend they do. We don't walk to school together anymore. If we all have to be together for an event or another assembly, we make a show of not quite looking at each other. I stick to Ellowyn's side and Emerson sticks to Jacob's. We're scrupulously polite to each other in public, but I always make sure to roll my eyes the minute my sister turns away and someone could be watching.

Anyone observing us would think we're at odds, but pretending not to be, which feels a lot like the more adult version of our adolescent dynamic. When the truth is, we're closer than we've ever been. We speak in our old language, together and apart. I even name my next theme of planner stickers after her: The Confluence Warrior Collection.

And then I break all my old rules and show them to her.

She's suitably amazed and, being Emerson, orders an entire set of *all* my planner-friendly items. Then starts brainstorming ways to incorporate my work into as many local businesses as possible. Including stocking Confluence Books with my art.

Which feels more full circle than I can even fully describe.

I try my hand at some painting, something I haven't done since I took art classes at the high school. I paint the confluence on a bright June morning, because Aunt Zelda hasn't been texting much. Every few days, if that. And because I know she loved to walk down to observe the place where the three rivers meet every morning when she was well. When it's done, I hand it off to Uncle Zack with a collection of books from Emerson.

"Until we can come and give her a hug ourselves," I say.

My uncle swallows hard, and won't quite meet my gaze. "Until then."

I come back home feeling empty, but I don't know what else there is to do for Zelda and the illness that's killing her.

Or the test I'm going to fail that's certain to kill me too.

So, in addition to all the studying and practicing, I also spend time with that book I hate so much.

Nicholas gave it to me and I know it's given us some answers, but shouldn't I be able to find a few more? Because we're running out of time. And the particular sick genius of the Joywood is that they've made certain that the lives of everyone I care about hang on me passing that unpassable test.

They've had a long time to perfect their Mean Girl approach to...well, pretty much everything.

At first I hole up in my room and give myself headaches trying to decipher the long passages of ancient text.

Remember when there was going to be less lone-wolf nonsense around here? Smudge asks testily one afternoon, when my muttering interrupts her beady-eyed concentration on the June birds singing in the trees outside.

"You're a terrible hunter," I tell her, because I don't have claws. "The birds are making fun of you."

She flattens her ears at me. *They're probably talking about you, Backdraft.*

As usual, her claws are sharper.

But I take her point. Reluctantly. Sitting around driving myself crazy, alone in my room, is giving the Joywood what they want. I can't have that. So I heave the big book into my arms and take it up to Georgie's third-floor rooms to ask for help.

Georgie sits in her attic bedroom, down the hall from her own overcrowded library, surrounded by books and crystals and lace. I have the immediate urge to sketch her space, because it's so *romantically* witchy. I'm not sure I've ever seen anyone with an aesthetic quite like hers.

But I'm not here to sketch and daydream a product line to suit a bohemian witch surrounded by crystals who only pretends to be airy as it suits her. Not today. I stand in the doorway with the book clutched to my chest and hope the expression on my face is imploring.

Georgie is sitting cross-legged on her hardwood floor, surrounded by all kinds of books in stacks and many opened before her. Others hang in the air. Octavius opens one eye, notes my presence, and then wiggles onto his back in the middle of Georgie's four-poster bed.

I force myself to actually *say* the word. "Help?"

And I watch as Georgie breaks into a wide smile. "I was *hoping* you'd ask!"

But by day three of operation *figure something out*, all I've learned is that I get grumpier with each session. Georgie, by contrast, remains unruffled.

Today, like every day, we sit on a bench in front of one of her long tables filled with crystals and lit candles and altars and go through every page. Inch by inch. Word by word—which involves spells, other books, consultations with spirit guides, and translations worked out by hand on a pad. Which looks like a lot of hieroglyphics and math to me.

"Maybe we're going at this wrong," Georgie muses. She piles her red curls on her head and jabs a pencil into the knot she makes to hold it in place. "Maybe this isn't about reading and translating. Maybe you have to *do* something."

At our feet, Smudge and Octavius, who have spent the last two hours curled up together, begin hissing at each other. I look down and Smudge jumps into my lap. Then onto the book open before us with another hiss.

Smudge flashes her claws.

"Don't you dare," I say, a knee-jerk reaction that I know is a mistake the minute the word *dare* is out of my mouth. Her yellow eyes flash at me.

Then she leaps from the page, leaving a little claw mark on the old brittle pages.

I mutter a curse so filthy I expect it to summon my grandmother to threaten me with soap in the mouth. Georgie groans and I lean in to look at the damage. Smudge's antics have ripped out a word from the passage we've been giving ourselves migraines over, and I want to scream in frustration.

I glare at her. But the irritating cat sits on the edge of Georgie's bed and licks a paw. Serenely. *Delicately*, even, as if she's done nothing terrible and should, in fact, be worshipped and praised.

You're a menace, I growl at her.

A long, slow, yellow glare. *You're welcome.*

I look back down at the book because I'm considering throwing it at my obnoxious familiar. I glare at the claw mark while frustration simmers inside me—

Wait.

I scowl down at a particular word that jumps out at me, next to the hole Smudge ripped in the page. I put my finger over it. It's not that it hasn't been there this whole time, but now I'm seeing it isolated instead of in a sentence thanks to Smudge's claw mark. *Hingeben*. In the context of the rambling spell laid out here, we thought it was instructing the spell doer to lay down, but isolated…

Something inside me…wakes up. Like an alarm has been set off.

"Georgie, what does *hingeben* mean?"

She doesn't have to consult the translation guides hovering about in the room. She tips back in her chair and stares at one of her crystals, because she *just knows*.

She repeats the word. *Hingeben.* "Well, in German it can mean *to sacrifice*..."

I don't listen to anything else she says.

Sacrifice.

That damn word.

"This spell," I say, shoving it over to her without reading through it. "Is this something we could do?"

Georgie frowns over the page, *tsks* at the claw mark, then murmurs words either to translate in her head or just because she likes reading out loud. I can't tell.

"This is a pretty old-fashioned protection spell," she says, shaking her head ever so slightly. "There's a lack of consent here that's not really acceptable these days. Even when you're doing something for benevolent reasons there should be consent and acceptance." She looks up at me, her dreamy green eyes clear and focused. "You're thinking it's for Nicholas, aren't you?"

There's no point in hedging. Not with time running out. Not with me doing my best here to be open and transparent when that's not my natural state. "Yes."

"It could be suitable, I guess. Though I'm not sure why an immortal would need protecting. I've never heard of an immortal *losing* their immortality. That kind of takes all the fun out of selling your soul, or whatever they do."

"But there aren't that many immortals wandering around," I point out. "They must lose it at some point or another."

Georgie contemplates that, and I have to give her credit. She shows nothing on her face. Not a hint of what she's thinking. She looks as airy and dreamy as ever, as if I'm not sitting here asking her if we can save my immortal boyfriend from sacrificing himself.

"Most of the immortal creatures people write about aren't

exactly the sacrificial type, you know. So, there's no precedent. But that doesn't mean we couldn't try to make one."

I tap the page beneath my finger again, like I'm taking that word—no matter what language it's in—into my skin.

I know that he's building to something. It swirls between us, unsaid, but I know it's there. And like Jacob and I discussed, it has to be the kind of sacrifice Emerson was prepared to make. It even makes sense. Litha is about balance, and he's a creature made of imbalances. Sacrificing himself with no thought of gain would be a way of righting the scales.

It would also hurt me more than I can bear to think about.

So I don't. "But this spell can prevent him from dying, right? No matter what he does. What he *wants* to do." He only has to be *willing*. He doesn't actually have to *die* to complete the sacrifice. Emerson showed us that.

Georgie's gaze searches mine. "Theoretically. But like I said, there's that ancient disregard for consent. We don't really do spells like that these days." She pauses. "I mean, and call ourselves the good guys."

I shrug, and force a smile. A wilted daisy if ever there was one. "The good news is, he *is* ancient. So I doubt he'll be offended by unwoke spellcraft."

Georgie studies me for a long moment, then nods thoughtfully. "These aren't your typical herbs and crystals for modern application. I can probably get most of what the spell needs from the museum and the archives. I'll have to be careful about who I ask about some of these things, though. Someone might put together what you're trying to do and..." She trails off. Because there are so many bad things that could happen, there's no point in listing them all.

But this has to be done. "It has to be before Litha. Before the test." That's when he'll sacrifice himself. I'm sure of it, even with all the ways he's blocked me from seeing into *his* future.

"I'll do my best. But I can't promise…" She blinks. Once. "Sage."

I try not to grimace, but I'm a bad friend, because I know she sees me trying.

"He has access to pretty much anything and everything at the school. He can certainly fill in any gaps." She begins to read over the spell again.

"Would he…" I clear my throat, trying desperately to be diplomatic. "I mean, could he keep it quiet? Is he on our side?"

Is he brave enough? Because I really doubt that he is.

"I'm not sure." She doesn't look up from the spell, too busy jotting down what I think is a shopping list. On a pad that hovers near her and writes down what she wants in an invisible hand. "But I'll find out. Carefully, of course."

I chew on my lip, fighting not to say what I want to say. It's none of my business. Georgie is my friend, but not the kind of friend I should feel comfortable assaulting with my opinions on her choice of dating partner. That would be Ellowyn, who would happily respond in kind.

But the words tumble out anyway. "Georgie, do you really think that he's…?"

She looks up at me, her gaze so unexpectedly direct that I trail off without finishing what I was going to say.

"I know what you think, you and Emerson and even Ellowyn, but I'm not like you."

Whatever I thought she'd say, it's not this. "What does that mean?"

She gestures around her adorable room as if that's an answer. "I'm a Historian."

"So…what? You have to have a boring boyfriend?"

Her mouth firms. There's something almost resigned in

her gaze, and it makes my breath catch. But then she smiles in all her usual dizzy brightness. "He's a nice man, Rebekah. And he might help."

Which is all that really matters. For now.

Because I think we need all the help we can get. Even his.

27

THE DAY BEFORE LITHA, EMERSON INSISTS WE have a party. She calls it a meeting, of course, but Ellowyn and I decide to treat it like a party. We convince Emerson there's no point in yet another practice round when all we've done for the entire month of June is practice, practice, practice.

"There's such a thing as overtraining," I tell my overachieving sister.

She eyes me over her stacks of binders and spell books as I lounge on her bed, lazily painting my toenails. I spent the last three days doing literally nothing *but* practicing balance spells with Nicholas—who I now know firsthand is a much harder teacher than any I encountered in these soft modern times, goddess help me—but I don't share that with her. It will ruin the moment.

"How would you know?" Emerson asks. Evilly.

And then laughs when I throw one of her pillows at her.

"It's about coming together as a coven," I say, trying a new tack, when Ellowyn and I begin mixing margaritas in the kitchen of Jacob's house. To Emerson's consternation.

"Alcohol is known as the great unifier," Ellowyn adds. Soberly.

Emerson only sighs. But she doesn't stop us. We make margaritas and Emerson puts together dinner, and once we're all gathered together, we do just that. Gather. We eat and drink together. We laugh, and even with tension and grief their own overwhelming entities in the room, we find ways to take a moment for ourselves.

A breather.

I'm home at last. Emerson remembers everything. And all this might change tomorrow night, but tonight we are…us.

And a better us than we were a decade ago, because we all know, now, what there is to lose.

But it can't all be fun and games and telling stories about high school shenanigans, as entertaining as that is. I need my friends' help. I'm not sure how to approach it, though. I'm not sure the best way to get them involved—much less invested. I'd hoped a margarita or two might loosen my tongue, but instead I find myself getting quieter and more tense.

Until Georgie reaches out and squeezes my hand. "We're missing one crucial piece of our coven tonight," she says. "But for good reason."

Well, there's always the direct approach. Funny how that never occurs to me.

Everyone's staring at me, making this moment feel bigger than it should. There's no reason my heart should be *thumping* at me. But I follow Georgie's lead. Direct. "I'm pretty sure Nicholas is going to sacrifice himself for us. Tomorrow."

Zander snorts. "Yeah, that sounds like him. That's why he's nine thousand years old. All that sacrificing himself."

"Is that even…possible?" Ellowyn asks.

I shrug. "I can't tell you how I know, but he knows how to make it possible. And I know he will."

"It isn't necessary," Emerson says before Zander can say anything else insulting. "We've got this."

"We don't know what the Joywood will bring tomorrow night, Em," Jacob returns, earning a scowl from Emerson. "No matter how prepared we are. That's just an unfortunate fact."

"The point is, we need to do something," I say, sliding in there before Emerson can respond in her rallying-the-troops way. "He's helped us. Repeatedly. Maybe not with a smile and an encouraging word, sure. But he's done nothing but help since Emerson killed those adlets."

"It's true," Emerson says forcefully. So forcefully that I wonder if she actually likes Nicholas more than I thought she did. Or maybe she likes the fact I like him. Either way, she's going full speed ahead and I love her for it. "I'm with Rebekah. We need to do something."

I nod, trying my best not to look *desperate*, though that's how I feel. "Georgie and I found an old protection spell we think might be the answer."

Georgie explains the spell. I fight my disappointment that Zander still looks irritated and Jacob appears decidedly neutral, like he's hiding his true response. At least Ellowyn looks curious, if cautious. For once, I'm with Emerson and Georgie, who are so eager and ready they might as well be bouncing.

I would be bouncing myself, but I feel that might be off-putting.

"I got everything we need," Georgie says. She slides a look my way, then back toward the group. "Sage was a great help. I didn't tell him what it was for, specifically, but he knows not to let anyone in on what he shared."

"Got him whipped already?" Zander asks with a laugh,

which at least means Georgie is too busy glaring at him to see the way Emerson and I exchange a quietly raised eyebrow.

But all the sniping fades as we gather in a circle in Jacob's living room.

"I'll lead the spell," Georgie explains. "But you'll each play a role. You'll each bring something, and Ellowyn, we'll rely on you to speak to the spirits and gods."

Ellowyn goes a little pale. "Is that necessary?"

Georgie holds her gaze. "Yes."

Ellowyn turns to me, eyes a little desperate. *You really want to leave protecting the guy you love up to my half magic?*

"Nothing about you is *half*," I answer her out loud, scowling.

"Control—"

"Doesn't it ever get old?" Zander asks with a smile that is *not* nice. "Always blaming things on your lack of control?"

She whips her furious gaze to him, but Emerson cuts in.

"We are a coven. We are doing something important. You can fight and bicker all you want." She holds Zander's gaze, then Ellowyn's. "But for this spell, we trust and believe in one another to be what's needed."

Wynnie, I say, just us, using her rarely used nickname so she knows how serious I am. *You helped save Emerson. I know you can help save Nicholas too.*

Ellowyn does not look convinced, but she nods and squeezes my hand. Whether she believes in her control or magic or not, she's in.

Georgie builds an altar in the center. She asks Jacob to bring her earth from outside. She has Ellowyn scent the air with the incense she makes with her own herbs. She sets out a clay bowl and asks Zander to magick in water from the river. Then she has Emerson light a thick candle.

Once that's done, we all join hands and sit in our circle.

"Listen carefully," Georgie says. "We'll call in the elements the way we always do, but we're going to do it in a very old way."

And one by one, we invite the elements to join us here. Earth, air, water, and fire.

But the invitations are different. The words we use, in heavy German and thick Latin, make me shiver. And the elements they invite into our circle aren't the ones I know. These are their older cousins, from times when they were gods.

I can tell we all feel it.

And you don't *compel* gods.

You ask. Nicely.

And very, very carefully.

As our Summoner, Ellowyn is the one who reaches out to the spirits, the beings of light, those that protect us. Nicholas once called us the chosen, and I have to believe him.

In words I hardly know, my best friend speaks to the spirits. And we all repeat their replies.

I take a small stone from my pocket. Last night, at the stroke of midnight, I dove down into the confluence, where the three rivers come together and nearly took my sister's life two months ago. I asked for a talisman and the rivers gave me this.

Tonight I take it and I place it in the earth Jacob brought in from his fields.

Together, we ask the earth to hold the wearer of the stone, to keep him solid and whole.

The stone begins to glow. We feel that glow go through us. I feel it all over me, like light.

I take the stone to the incense and bathe it in the scent, the air, murmuring the spell Georgie taught me to make it dance in the smoke until it seems to suck the smoke inside its gleaming surface.

And so, too, do I feel it fill me up.

I look around and see my friends breathe harder, as if fighting the smoke. Surrendering to it.

We ask it to take away any negative energy that might surround the wearer, to blow it away like the wind clears smoke.

And when we can breathe again, the stone grows brighter.

That, too, I feel *inside* me.

We repeat the same ritual with the river water and feel drenched as we ask it to nourish him and drown those who might come for him. Then we burn as we ask the fire to fight off his enemies and purify him.

And when we are done, the stone glows so bright it nearly blinds us all.

Then the glow fades, and it is only a stone again. We are only people once more, and there are no gods here. Only a candle sputtering on a makeshift altar, an incense cone smoking its last gasp, and two bowls of muddy water.

But this is the magic I loved. The magic I missed.

It doesn't have to look like anything to change everything. That's what makes it so powerful. And it's always better done with my oldest and best friends.

I pick up the stone we've made into a talisman and turn it over in my hand.

"It doesn't feel complete," I say, frowning down at it. There's the problem of getting Nicholas to carry it, of course. Without him being suspicious. I'm still waiting for inspiration to hit on that one.

But it's more than that. It's something…just out of reach.

"Maybe it will feel complete when it's needed," Emerson suggests brightly. "We're protecting him on Litha, so maybe it needs Litha."

This isn't a terrible theory, so I force myself to smile. We sit and talk some more, but soon it's clear that Jacob needs to recover from the day's healing. And Zander has to go to the bar. We're all reluctant to leave each other—and even more reluctant to say why—but Emerson, ever practical, insists we all need a good eight hours of rest. She even orders us off to our various beds with sleep spells wafting over us.

I wave mine away. And I don't go home to Wilde House. There's something I need to do first since I likely won't see Nicholas prior to the Litha ritual tomorrow.

In fact, if I was a suspicious sort of person, I might even say that he's going to make absolutely certain I don't see him ahead of the test. I'm okay with this, because it's so telling. If I couldn't stop him, he wouldn't care if he saw me. That means I have my window—I just need to find it and make sure to use it.

When I get to Frost House, he's standing on his widow's walk, the night dark and deep around him. Instead of cloaks and drama, he's in jeans and a T-shirt. It's no less breathtaking. I don't like thinking about the widows who paced around on rooftops like this. It all seems a little too on the nose, suddenly. But his magic pulses in the night. It calls to me, and I have no defenses against it.

Or him.

And I don't want any, so I throw myself into all that pulse and passion and let it raise me up to meet him.

"You should be with your little coven," he tells me darkly with his hands in my hair. "Celebrating your last hours before Litha."

"And yet you're not there. You *are* our Praeceptor."

He grunts. There's an edgy energy inside him he's trying to hide. It isn't working.

The stone is in my hand, shoved deep in my pocket, pulsing with old spirits and new heat. I say a little spell in my head so that the stone melds with a chain and become a kind of medal. The kind Catholics wear, especially in St. Louis.

Not that I want to think about how people become saints. No martyrs, please.

I pull the stone on its chain from my pocket and hold it out between us. "I made you a little something."

He blinks. Then again. Then he raises his cool blue gaze to mine. "I think you missed the part where I'm an immortal being of incalculable power, witchling. I do not require protection charms from minor covens."

I know him well enough by now to be touched that he feels the need to make us sound like less than we are. It's as good as a rousing pep talk from anyone else.

I smile at him until his eyes flash and his hands tighten in my hair.

"I prefer to think of it as a talisman." My voice sounds rougher than it should. I want to smile. I want to cry. I want to wrap myself around him and grow roots, deep into the earth, and hold us here forever. But the moon is high and it is nearly Litha and we are out of time. I keep going. "When I was in exile, I couldn't use my magic. I treated my visions like migraines and waited them out with a cool compress in the dark. But I could hold on to precious rocks and pretty crystals and ask them for the help they would give anyone, witch or human alike."

"And you think I require this…gift shop aid?"

"What I think," I say quietly, "is that we don't know what will happen tomorrow. But if I'm not here tomorrow night, I want you have something to remember me by. Something—" and I raise my voice a little over his scowl and the protest he begins to make "—that I made with my own magic and imbued with all four elements, to be with you if I can't."

It's not a love poem. Not quite. And yet he looks as if I reached over and tore his heart from his chest. He drops his hands, and I take that as an invitation.

I go up on my toes and loop the chain around his neck. He does not stop me. And the things I see in his gaze make my own heart hurt.

Nicholas looks at the stone as it lies there against his T-shirt, in that hollow between his pecs where I like to press my face, then back to me. The magic in him seems to pulse harder between us, around us. His hand moves to cover the stone. Then his gaze bores into me.

"You should know that if I fall—"

"No one's *falling*, Nicholas. We're witches. We *fly*."

He shakes his head, his eyes ancient, now. "We all fall, witchling. When our time comes."

Those words my grandmother taught me ring in me then, but tonight they feel less like a comfort and more like an omen. *Time is mine until time takes me home.*

"When my time comes, I will not be able to return like your grandmother," he says, very intently. Making certain I hear what he's telling me. What it means. "The choices I have made before and after becoming immortal preclude me from the kind of afterlife that would be…useful to you."

"Nicholas." And it costs me something to even attempt to get near a daisy sort of smile for him. "This sounds suspiciously like a goodbye. And we know you don't do that. You prefer the puff of smoke. The flash of light. A goodbye is too *mortal*, surely."

"These are my consequences, Rebekah," he tells me quietly, as if I haven't spoken. "Not yours."

I see it for what it is. The goodbye, sure, that I don't plan on letting him make. But he's also protecting me or reminding me. If I cannot conjure him, the fault lies with him. Not with me.

There is something else in his words, little as I want to hear it.

I could die tomorrow. I wasn't saying those things about the talisman I made him just to keep him from guessing that I'm trying to save him—and from himself, if necessary. I could be extinguished as easily as a candle flame. To the sound of applause. It would take a wave of the hand—and there are no shortage of hands in this town.

Time has run out. It has taken me home, as promised. It has brought me here, to him. This man outside time.

So, I face him. "Say it."

"What do you wish me to say?" he returns, but he doesn't pretend he doesn't know what I mean. I'll give him that. "Foolish declarations of love that mean nothing from an immortal who has no future?"

"Yes," I say, unfazed. If this is all we are, all we have, why not?

But I don't really think he'll do it.

This isn't the first time Nicholas Frost surprises me. He runs a hand over my hair. My cheek. He looks deep into my eyes. "I have loved you across time," he says. "I dreamed you when I was still mortal, too many lifetimes ago to count. I knew you before I met you, Rebekah. I spent centuries fighting it, long before you were born, but all roads led me here. To you. Where I watched you grow and let you leave and knew all the while you would come back to me, like it or not. And so you did."

There are a thousand things I could say. I want to say them all. I want the *time* to say them. Instead, I shake my head at him. "Do you have any idea how much I would *kill* to go back in time and tell fourteen-year-old me that the hot older immortal witch who's always lurking around in the shadows *really does* like her back?"

And he breaks my heart by laughing. A real laugh. It makes me ache.

His smile makes it worse. "No one likes fourteen-year-olds, witchling. Love them? Yes. Hope for the best for them? Certainly. But no more."

Then his hand is on my face, tracing patterns on my cheek. Ancient words, possibly even spells. Talismans of flesh. I can't bring myself to mind.

"You must know, *meae deliciae*, my own witchling," he whispers. "That none of this can matter in the end. What will happen tomorrow will happen."

But I don't want to talk about tomorrow.

And I don't plan on letting him do whatever foolish thing he thinks he's going to do, here on the other end of his extraordinary life. Because if it really was leading him to me, two months is not nearly enough time.

I know what people say. That it's not the time that matters, but how you live it. That a moment can outweigh a millennium.

But I think that sounds like bullshit.

I want more.

"There is no future in this," he says, though his eyes say something else. "No matter what happens tomorrow. Not the kind of future you mean."

I could take tonight to argue with him. But I've never been so conscious of time before—or how little I want to waste it when I could be marinating in it instead. There are thousands of moments between now and the morning, and I want every last one of them to live in me like his millennia.

So I twine my arms around his neck and I jump, knowing he'll catch me. He does, gripping my bottom so I can cross my legs at his back and smile down at him.

Daring him.

I watch my immortal lover's blue eyes gleam in response, though he tries to fight it. But we are past fighting it, he and

I. "Did you hear me, Rebekah?" he asks me in a stern voice that makes me shudder a little, deep inside.

Because I love a good power dynamic. I think I've made that clear.

"I heard you, oh great and glorious Praeceptor."

He grins, but it's a feral thing, as I press my body against his and move a little, just for good measure. "And?"

"And..." I draw it out. "Well..." I wrap my arms around his neck and look down at him, and love him so much it hurts. But I love that too. "I suggest you make sure that this night is the kind of memory that lasts. Long enough that it feels like a future. If you think you're up to it."

And when Nicholas Frost laughs, it sets us both alight.

LITHA MORNING DAWNS AND I AM IN MY OWN bed. I left Nicholas in the smallest hours of the night because I couldn't sleep. Too much fretting to do. And it feels weirdly right to wake up in Wilde House, just like I did ten years ago.

If you start crying now, Smudge says from where she's curled up on my head, which is as uncomfortable as it sounds, especially in the Missouri humidity, *you won't stop.*

Cat comfort is bracing, but it works.

It gets me up and on my feet and I even spend a few minutes I don't have rubbing Smudge's sulky face and kissing her on her furry forehead.

Emerson and I eat a tense breakfast with our parents, which is also tradition. We reenact all those mornings before high school together, compressed into the most fraught morning of them all. My father says nothing, his cold eyes communicating his distaste for the daughters his own mother promised would elevate the Wilde name. And Grandma isn't here to shame him into better behavior, so my mother is left to fill the gap. She tries to make conversation, but it all turns into her imparting advice.

To her two grown-ass daughters who raised themselves in her absence.

Emerson is making a show of taking dutiful notes, but I'm sitting next to her and can see that actually, she's working on her own to-do list. *Double check spells for German Heritage Festival cleanup. Foment rebellion. Save world—yet again. If live through night, pick up dry cleaning.* I almost laugh out loud, something that would only irritate my father more. I wonder if Emerson was always putting on more of a show than I thought she was. I wonder if it was little sister stuff that made me think everything was so easy and perfect for her and that *just happened to be true*, no effort from her required.

Maybe that's why I realize, for the first time in my life, that my mother's high-handed *advice* is how she expresses her own anxiety. She can't help herself from trying to control outcomes, trying to control *us*. She wants everything to be perfect—herself, her life, us, and it never has been.

And sure, I wish she could have learned that nothing is ever perfect, the way I had to a long time ago. But today I feel a rush of sympathy as I consider the possibility that maybe she's incapable of that kind of understanding. Or this *is* her version of understanding. After all, I don't know what it's like to give your whole life over to a man like my dad, who takes up all the space in every room he's in, looks down on everything, and even disapproved of Zelda's choice to "marry down" into the Rivers clan so intensely that I can't recall the last time Mom and Zelda spent time together.

Clearly Elspeth Wilde hasn't been lucky enough to have someone she loves and lost sit with her in a cemetery and help her deal with her trauma.

I almost want to give her a hug, but that would likely terrify the poor woman. Especially today.

After breakfast, I go find Georgie—whose residency in Wilde House apparently doesn't require she show up at tense family breakfasts—and we hole up with the book in a last-ditch effort to make sure we haven't missed anything. The feeling of incompleteness hounds me as the hours tick by, too long and too short, until Emerson finds me and insists we go over the pubertatum one last time.

"It's not going to be the same as what we practice, no matter what we practice," I tell her as we walk past Georgie's library—a room packed so full of books it's impossible to get in without turning sideways. Reliably, the sight of that much *mess* makes my sister shudder. "They're going to make sure we fail. Spectacularly."

"Thank you, Rebekah," she replies dryly as we hit the stairs. I make a face at her and she smiles, but her voice is serious as we walk down a floor. "I don't think the goal here is to convince the Joywood of anything. We know their mind is made up. But I have to think that if we're prepared for the way they twist things, we should be able to show the audience that we *can* perform the necessary magic to pass the test. And that means we can argue our case, which is more than we got last time."

She has a point there. We go into my room and stand together in the late afternoon light that pours into the room, lighting up the Wheel of the Year so it casts it shadows over us in blues and reds and greens.

We face each other and she nods. Together, we begin.

I conjure the light like Nicholas taught me. Then whisper the dark into life in perfect balance. Across from me, Emerson does the same.

Without discussing it, the balls of light are the same size, like mirror images of each other. The same, yet different.

Like us.

Then, as we stand there, murmuring the words to keep our magical balance, our little balls of light combine. Without having to communicate the next step, we look at each other, then meld our dark to even it out.

Over the balls we hold in the air between us, light and dark, Emerson and I smile.

My first of year. My last of year. My two sides of the same coin. Grandma's voice wraps around us. The scent of her is in my head. I *feel* her, even though I can't see her. It's like she's standing just at the edge of my vision and if I turn my head—

But I don't. I breathe her in.

I look at Emerson, tears in my eyes, to see the tears in hers. "Together," I whisper. "Maybe the trick is *together.*"

Emerson nods, full of all that marvelous certainty that makes her *her* and makes me feel safe. "I know it is."

We end the ritual together, our voices a perfect harmony as we combine all the balls before us and then turn them into light. And when they're gone, we fall into each other. Laughing, maybe. Crying, definitely. But holding each other tight the whole time.

And I know Emerson has welcomed me home from day one, but this feels as if, finally, I've *arrived.* Like I can finally see exactly where I've been standing this whole time, and better still, who's always been standing right here beside me. Waiting for me to catch up.

To *want* to stay.

A mix of all that laughter and all our tears clings to us as we head downstairs. Our last practice took a while, and that means our friends will come over soon to meet us. We'll walk to the confluence together to face the fate the Joywood have prepared for us.

That twists in me uneasily, but I take Emerson's words to heart. This isn't about proving anything to people who hate us. It's showing the people who don't that they've been lied to about who we are.

Once we do that, maybe we can live through this. And once we do *that*, we can work on doing something about the dark scourge that is our ruling coven. *So no big deal, then*, I tell myself as we all gather in the Wilde House kitchen. And I try not to laugh, because I'm afraid it will come out sounding maniacal.

We're not required to wear anything in particular tonight, so we've all come dressed as slightly more formal versions of ourselves. Georgie and Ellowyn are also wearing their traditional amulets—necklaces given to a witch by their parents the morning of Litha to ease their passage into full adult witchhood. If you fail your pubertatum, they're destroyed. If you pass, your designation is engraved in the back.

Looking at them makes me realize our friends never wear theirs. And while no witch is *required* to wear theirs all the time, many witches do.

"Why don't you wear those more?" I ask. I think of Zander's necklace with the three rivers that Aunt Zelda gave him that morning ten years ago. As far as I know, he never takes it off. "Zander always wears his."

Georgie and Ellowyn exchanged looks.

"Because you can't," Ellowyn says, almost gruffly. "Neither of you."

"And in fairness, Guardians need to wear their amulets to control the ferries on the river if there are any big storms," Georgie adds. "So Zander has to wear his. Just in case."

Emerson looks at them both, her eyes looking much too

bright. I think if she cries, we'll all cry—but instead, she performs a perfectly executed fist pump. One of her specialties.

"Every little rebellion counts," she says, as we all smile goofily at each other.

It's all sweet and wonderful and so *them*, but it also gives me a stab of pain that the Joywood took things away not just from Emerson and me, but everyone who loved us. Too many things to count at this point. With more to come tonight, if they have their way.

Anger simmers in my gut, but I know I can't sink into it. Not now. Because like it or not, tonight is all about *balance*.

I repeat that word to myself. I try to breathe.

Ellowyn glances at the clock on the wall. "You know I don't care about being punctual, generally speaking—"

"Bite your tongue!" Emerson replies in mock horror.

Ellowyn doesn't laugh the way she usually does. "The guys are running late. I'm not sure tonight's the night to test whether or not punctuality is *actually* a virtue."

We all glare at the clock, like that might help.

"Jacob went over to Aunt Zelda's this morning," Emerson says quietly. "I haven't heard from him since."

And I haven't heard from Aunt Zelda either. I check my phone, just in case, but the last text is from me to her. The day before yesterday. My stomach twists.

We all fall into silence. We watch the clock. We get more tense with every minute that creeps by, yet no one seems to want to state the obvious or come up with an alternate plan—until the side door into the kitchen opens.

Zander and Jacob stagger inside, bringing the sunset with them, and I know immediately.

Jacob is so gray he's almost transparent. Emerson rushes to his side, helping him into a chair. But Zander's coloring is worse. And his eyes are red-rimmed and wild with anguish.

I think we all know.

But no one wants to say it.

"Jacob," Emerson says carefully. I watch as she curls her hand over the chair's back to stay upright. She wants to fight the truth away.

If we could, I know we would. Isn't that the point of having magic? Of being witches? Of existing outside human rules of life and death and—

"She's gone." Zander's voice is a rasp.

I move before I know I'm going to, wrapping my arms around Zander from one side. Emerson comes over and does the same from the other side. I want to be strong, but I can't be. I'm not even sure why I want to be, but this isn't the time. I want to argue, to deny it, to tell him he's wrong—but all I can do is cry while I hold on to him and Ellowyn cries silently on Georgie's shoulder.

Zander stands stock-still, like he feels none of it.

"There are seven others," Jacob says into the silence, and though he sounds less gray than he looks, there's something else in his voice that I recognize. *Guilt.* "Eight witches died today, all with ties to St. Cyprian and long before they should have. From something no Healer has ever seen. Or was able to stop."

I understand the guilt he feels, but I also remember what my grandmother said.

Pain is coming. Grief. It is not happenstance. It is not accidental. It is purposeful. When it comes, don't let it change who you all are. Let it fuel you instead. Grief is love. And love is magic.

I only realize I've said it out loud when everyone looks at me like I've turned into an oracle on the kitchen floor.

I clear my throat, like that might help the bleakness that seems to permeate the room. "Grandma said so."

"You can't stand trial today," Emerson says into Zander's

shoulder, her voice thick. "That's cruel and unusual. This must be put off."

"They said no," Zander says, his voice little more than a scrape.

"Surely your father—"

"My grandmother came this morning. She argued with Festus herself. Dad wasn't in any shape to and neither was I."

"Good to know that the Joywood Guardian is as shitty to family as anyone else, I guess," I say. I think about my father, who seems to have Festus Proctor's ear whenever he wants it and also didn't seem to care what was happening to his sister-in-law.

I tell myself this is no time to rage against the Desmond of it all.

Zander rubs his hands over his face, but I'm pretty sure it's less about needing to gather himself and more about stepping away from Emerson and me. "Festus said Carol wouldn't hear of putting this off. Not for any reason. She's quite adamant."

"Fuck the Joywood and fuck Festus, especially," Ellowyn says very distinctly, but the heat in her voice sounds tired. It's like she's *trying* for anger because it's better than grief.

But Aunt Zelda is gone. And there is only grief in me now. Anger sounds like a luxury.

"If Zelda is dead, we aren't participating in this nonsense tonight," Ellowyn says, and though her words are harsh, they echo with the same pain I feel. She jabs a finger at Zander. "I'll damn well refuse for you."

There's a noise and we all turn to face it. Like it's a threat, but it's only my mother.

"What did you say?" she asks, her voice so very careful. She holds herself like she might break.

Zander turns to face her, and the color surges back into his face. Though when he speaks, his voice is frigid. "Don't pretend you care now, *Aunt* Elspeth."

She absorbs those words. For a moment, I think she's going to say something, maybe even reach out to Zander. But then she blinks and drops her hand. For a moment, I actually feel sorry for her. Then she pulls herself together, and I wonder how deep the need to be perfect goes.

And just like earlier, I find I can't hate her. That would be easier. Instead, I just feel sorry for her. And us. And Aunt Zelda.

How sick are you really? I asked her in one of our last text exchanges. *I'm getting worried that you're not telling me how bad it is. On purpose.*

You don't have to worry about me, Rebekah, she'd texted back. My full name and everything. *I promise you, I'm good. Whatever happens, sweet girl, I'm good.*

Maybe she'd told me then. Maybe I hadn't wanted to hear it.

I decide then and there that I can either collapse into the grief, or shove it off until later. And if I collapse, that only helps the Joywood, so I know what I have to do.

Zelda would have wanted it that way. She would have cheered us on.

Zander walks out the side door, into the backyard, letting it crash shut behind him. We all move to follow him, but Elspeth's voice stops me in my tracks. A glance tells me it has the same effect on Emerson.

"Girls." And I wonder what it costs her to sound so… politely empty. "I need to speak with you a moment, please."

Emerson and I eye each other, but everyone else is outside with Zander.

I turn back to my mother and follow her into the great room. Even in all the ways I have butted heads and more with my mother, I feel something change in me. A certain weird mix of sympathy and blame.

She's lost a sister. Even if she made mistakes for twenty years, even if they never had a relationship, that *must* hurt. I try not to think about how I might have felt if I'd come back to find Emerson dead.

My mother says something low to my father, who sits in the corner. He says nothing. I'm not sure he even acknowledges our existence.

How familiar.

Elspeth picks up two large jewelry boxes from the coffee table and holds them out to us. One box is white, one is black, and I think we all know whose is whose. "Every fledgling witch needs an amulet on Litha. The Joywood destroyed your originals," Mom is saying, and I imagine I hear something in her voice just now. Something perilously close to... not agreeing with a decision handed down from on high? "But it's tradition."

Emerson takes her box first, though her hand shakes a little. I assume we're both remembering last time. How proud we were to finally wear our amulets. And how they crumbled to ash at our necks when we were pronounced failures. "You had...duplicates made?"

Our mother shakes her head. She seems especially brittle, but she won't crumble. I doubt she knows how. "These are new ones. For this new beginning."

I take mine. Emerson and I exchange a look, then open our boxes at the same time. She doesn't gasp. Neither do I. But it *feels* like there's some gasping all the same. Because these amulets aren't like our old ones—bulky and full of Wilde symbols and crests.

These are much more understated. Much more to our taste, in fact. I instantly wonder if my mother knows this and did it on purpose to celebrate us, or if this is supposed to be a dig. That we're not worthy of the old ones.

But when I turn it over I see that mine is stamped with the symbol of the Diviner. Emerson's has the Warrior symbol. This time, Elspeth isn't waiting for the Joywood to give us a designation. And that can only mean that she believes… we are who we say we are.

I swallow at the lump in my throat.

"*I* think this whole thing is nothing more than a fool's errand," our father says, ruining the moment. "A failure is a failure."

Charming.

But I am a different person tonight. I can't grieve my beloved aunt, and I certainly won't let my father get to me. I don't need him to believe in me to be worthy of becoming a Diviner. I'm already worthy and bonus, I've always been a Diviner. I don't have anything to prove tonight.

I already know who I am.

Maybe that's why I do something I haven't done in ten years. I move forward and give my mother a hug. She's stiff, no surprise, but I feel her hand on my back for a brief second. Emerson hesitates, but then repeats the process, also giving my mother a hug.

"We'll be in attendance, of course," my mother says, and her eyes shine, but she does not let the veneer crack. She's still Elspeth Wilde. As much herself as ever.

"You're required to be," I reply, but gently.

She blinks. She doesn't turn toward my father, and that feels like a quiet little revolution. Then she smiles, and it almost feels real. "You should go. You don't want to be late. Would you…" She trails off. "Never mind, I'll pass my condolences along to Zack myself."

She shows no emotions. The word *condolences* seems so cold.

But there's something under all that control. A loss even Elspeth Wilde can't ignore.

Emerson and I walk back through the hallway and the kitchen, studying our amulets as we go.

"These are not what I expected," my sister says.

"No." I look back at the hallway. I can't see my mother and everything is silent. "Maybe she's not what we expected either. Maybe that's the lesson."

At the side door, we pause. We loop our amulets over our neck. Emerson sucks in a deep breath, then pushes it out before we get to the door. "They won't make it easy, but we're ready. I know we are." She squeezes my hand. So sure. So Emerson.

I am neither of those things. I never have been. But as I think, *I never will be*, it doesn't come from a dark place. I'm not *supposed* to be a clone of my sister. I'm supposed to be *me*. My grandmother always tried to tell me that.

We're supposed to balance each other, or none of this works.

And we need it to work.

It has to work, or all of this was for nothing—and I'm not prepared to accept that.

I won't.

29

OUTSIDE, EVERYONE IS QUIET AND SUBDUED. Because someone we all know is dead, and it doesn't make sense. Witches aren't immortal, but they live a long time. Hundreds of years on average. I try to think through every single thing anyone ever told me about the weird sickness that slowed Zelda down so much, then confined her to her bed. A sickness so odd that neither medical science nor magic nor some of the most powerful Healers in the world could help her.

I think about Zander vowing to get to the bottom of it, and vow that no matter what happens tonight, we will. We will find a way.

The sun is setting and my cousin's heart is broken. Ellowyn is holding his hand. My heart is broken too, but it makes me weirdly proud of all of us that we can share this grief the way we shared the joy of Emerson and Jacob's engagement. The ways we can hurt ourselves, each other—and still find ways to forgive, reach out, and love one another.

Without turning cold and bitter like my father.

It almost makes me as sorry for the Joywood as I felt for my mother back there, because whatever power they have, they don't have *this*. They don't have love. They don't have loyalty. Not like we do.

Jacob starts walking, and we all follow him. I expect Emerson to launch into one of her rallying-the-troops talks as she walks beside him, but she doesn't.

Maybe because we've not only said everything already—we've done this before.

I can almost see those brash, excited versions of us walking as we head to the path by the river and follow it as it winds its way toward the confluence. There are witches all along the path, coming to take part in Litha whether they have a connection to a fledgling witch or not, but I don't focus on them and the way they look at our group, then away.

We approach the confluence. Rows of chairs are set up out in the field leading to the river, like any old human high school graduation. Teenage witches stand around vibrating with nervous energy, milling about with their friends and their families in their various states of finery.

Humans walking by would see a private school graduation ceremony or a small outdoor wedding, perhaps. This close to the confluence and with this much magic in the air, everything that actually happens here is easily shielded and hidden from them. But they'd feel it. And they wouldn't know why a simple ceremony gave them such a shiver and made them steer clear.

We find our seats in our usual row with our names in the same golden scroll as everyone else's, floating serenely above our chairs. I see my parents in the family section. Uncle Zack is seated on almost the opposite side of the area, with Zander's Grandma Rivers. Ellowyn's mother, as usual, is fiercely focused on Ellowyn, and is sitting with her partner Mina in the front row, as close to us as it's possible to get. Georgie's parents sit in the middle of a pack of Pendells, looking as subdued and pinched as all their relatives look alternately bewildered or delighted to be out of their usual bookshelves.

For some reason, I notice that not one of them has red hair. Not a single one.

I don't have time to focus on that, because I'm still looking around. But Nicholas…is nowhere to be seen. I crane my neck around to search every face. I send out a little probe to find his energy in the mix of so many people, but he isn't here. I don't feel him anywhere.

I would be grateful for that, but I know better.

He should be unknowable, but I know him.

And that means I know enough to worry that I don't see him glowering from behind his own flowing cloak of doom to the left of the stage, where the rest of the Praeceptors and other non-Joywood teachers sit during these things.

"This Litha will be a little different from others, my dear friends and neighbors, citizens of St. Cyprian and honored guests from afar," Carol says by way of greeting, suddenly appearing at the front of the stage, hair a frizzy halo and her kindest—and therefore most terrifying—smile in place. "We have a very rare and sacred balance to test tonight, a bit outside the usual scope of our Litha ceremony."

Our whole row gets a little too still and much too tense. Even Zander lifts his head from a scowling contemplation of the grass beneath his feet. I suddenly feel a lot less okay with Nicholas not being here. I try not to panic.

"As we all know well, witches in their eighteenth year are asked to come before us and show what they can do. As they demonstrate their ability to balance the light and the dark, on this night of the earth's balance between both, we all see who they are. What powers they possess innately, and then, what role they will play in our community going forward." She smiles wider. "But this is not a human job fair or a college application process."

That gets the laugh she was going for. It only confirms for me that she really is pure evil, because she made that same joke ten years ago.

This time she doesn't segue into the usual tedious breakdown of the various designations. "Over time, it can grow difficult to remember why we do the things we do. Why we celebrate the same rituals in the same order, year after year, though the world changes all around us. And my answer to that is what it always has been and always will be. One thing can never change, and that is our sacred duty to protect witchkind. So it is not only the balancing of balls of magic in the air that we consider tonight. Far more important is a more fundamental question, rooted in the horrors of old world witch hunters and the tragedy at Salem. Can a witch demonstrate that they will be good for witchkind? A positive influence that furthers our aims and is certain to keep our secrets? Or, more rarely, will we be forced to protect the witch population either from a power too dull to be dependable or too wild to control? As your ruling coven—"

And there's a little stagecraft then, as the rest of the Joywood are suddenly revealed to be standing behind her, all of them in their finest robes, blowing just slightly in the lack of breeze on this airless, humid night.

"—it is always our hope that every witch we test on Litha will join our community, our collective, as one of us," Carol says warmly. So warmly.

Meanwhile, I have gone completely cold. And I still don't know where Nicholas is.

"Ten years ago, two young witches, never standouts among

their peers," Carol begins, now sounding *concerned*, "failed to show us any balance at their pubertatum."

"Never standouts!" Emerson's whisper is outraged.

Jacob slants a look her way, and she presses her lips together, but I can practically hear her temper continue to boil.

"Instead of accepting the judgment of the Joywood and living under the rules and regulations that govern the choices they made, they have instead made choices that necessitate another test. As adults. As grown witches." She pauses so we can all hear the murmur that goes through the crowd. Because witches live a long time, and no one thinks a reversion to childhood is appealing. That's a human thing. But then, grown witches have more powers than humans do. "They have involved their friends and family in these crimes against witchkind. They have broken laws and rules. Frankly, they have wreaked havoc all over St. Cyprian these last few months."

I see Emerson open her mouth, as if she's about to mount an argument, but she looks at her fiancé and shuts it. But when she looks over at me, her eyes are flashing. Matching mine, I'm sure.

"If you've missed all this, you're welcome," Carol says, and lets out one of her cheerful little titters. "The Joywood, as ever, work hard to protect you from such things. Nonetheless, these witches have displayed what they term 'power.' It is written in the old laws that any witch who claims to hold power can request the opportunity to prove themselves on Litha. Tonight, I hope you will join us as we see if they can wield it safely and positively, in a way that protects witchkind rather than risks our exposure."

That's quite a framing job, I think. Why not drag Emerson and me up to the stage in prison stripes and chains? It would amount to the same thing.

Carol leans into the microphone she's only holding for

show, since she's been happily magicking her voice directly into every ear here. "Please come forward," she intones. "All of you."

She nods to us and we're compelled to move toward her. Whether we want to or not, we're carried forward until we're all set down on the stage, and not all that gently. Emerson and I are tugged along by invisible hands and deposited slightly to the left of Carol. Everyone else is held off to the side. Their judgment will stem from our verdict and suddenly this has all gotten a little too real, if everyone else's expressions are anything to go by.

I work to school mine as I look around once again, trying not to look like that's what I'm doing.

There is still no sign of Nicholas.

But as I'm talking myself through the waves of panic moving through me, my gaze is drawn to the trees. Familiars are scattered throughout the proceedings, all manner of pets and wildlife. I see Zander's eagle and Ellowyn's owl. I see Smudge and Octavius, very deliberately sitting apart from the teenagers' familiars. Farther out, I see Murphy's antlers, and am pretty sure that's Cassie beside him, laying low so as not to call attention to herself.

It's then I see Coronis, sitting on the highest branch of the highest tree. And everything in me...relaxes.

Because I get the feeling Nicholas is somehow right there, looking out through his familiar's eyes. Biding his time. He doesn't want the Joywood to know he's here just yet. I can think of all kinds of different strategies that would be helped by his seeming indifference, and I know him now.

He might not *want* to love me, but he does.

"Emerson Wilde and Rebekah Wilde," Carol says now, as if she's sermonizing. This close to her, that gleam in her gaze is dangerous and there's not the faintest hint of the friendliness she projects out into the crowd. Not a single stray hint. "Failures of their first pubertatum. Untrustworthy hoarders of misused power."

I really feel like our names are introduction enough, I complain to Emerson in our heads, in our own language.

I wish this was a duel, Emerson replies, sounding bloodthirsty when she looks perfectly saintly on the outside.

My hero.

"Show us, novices," Carol says, finally getting to the ritual itself and the words that make it sacred, "can you balance light and dark?"

We know the responses by heart. We knew them a decade ago. "It is our honor to show you, Warrior," we reply formally.

Carol's gaze glitters, but she inclines her head. Emerson and I follow the ritual as it was written lifetimes ago—likely by the man who I last saw naked and beautiful in his bed, splayed out in the starlight.

The ritual wasn't written for sisters, and as Emerson and I go down the line of the Joywood coven, dutifully expressing how honored we are to have the chance to prove ourselves to them, I think that they've miscalculated.

Because part of why the pubertatum is so overwhelming is because you have to do it alone. It's just you, staring down the grim-faced Joywood, well aware that everyone else is watching you. It's you and whatever you bring with you—all your fear, your shame, your doubt.

Your daddy issues. Your rage.

Your dreams and hopes. Your hidden *what-ifs*.

It's the loneliest thing in the world.

But it only works on adolescents, I think now. And only if they're made to feel as alone as teenagers always feel.

Because Emerson and I are together, and unfortunately for the Joywood, we're grown.

We know we're loved. We know that people who love us are standing right here on this stage with us. We know we love each other.

We make it all the way down the line, and now it's time.

We don't turn to each other at first. We follow the rules. We face the Joywood, and we each bring forth light and balance dark. Perfectly. *Expertly.* Like we were made to do this all along.

We make our demonstration bigger than the teenagers do, partly for the metaphor of it all. And also because we want to make sure everyone can see exactly what we're doing.

Then, because there aren't any strict rules for a team, we forego the usual weak finish.

Instead, we turn to each other like we did back in my room at Wilde House. *First of the year, last of the year. Two sides of the same coin.*

A prophecy worth fulfilling. Because the prophecy is us.

The prophecy is this.

In a typical pubertatum, the dismount is a fizzle. The balance bleeds into light or dark, and sometimes the whole thing explodes. Mind you, that doesn't mean those witches fail. That seems to be just us.

So Emerson and I put on a little show. Our lights and darks grow bigger and move around, perfectly mirroring each other.

And then they meld.

Not light, not dark, but both at once. All things instead of none. And we hold them together like it's nothing, raising them up until they hang high over the confluence like our very own moon.

Then we let it shine.

I feel my grandmother's love surrounding us. I feel Nicholas's pride flow through Coronis. I can hear our friends' awe.

Out in the crowd, I hear applause. Even some cheers.

Oh yeah. They're rooting for us.

We are special. We are powerful. We are all the magic they tried to deny us.

They can't deny it now.

We let the ritual come to an end, but we do it beautifully, bringing our beautiful full moon down to the rivers, and letting it set there. First a glimmer on the water, then gone.

Emerson and I are both breathing hard, and I can see the jubilation on her face. I know I must look the same. We grip each other's hands as we turn to face the Joywood at last.

Their expressions give nothing away, and I'm not sure why this worries me. I want them to be angry. I want them to be awed. I want *something.*

But it shouldn't matter, because look what we did…

The moments drag on, and still they show nothing. Emerson's hand tightens on mine. Something in the pit of my stomach curdles. They didn't throw us any curveballs, as we expected, but they couldn't have seen *that* coming.

They couldn't have imagined we'd get the crowd going.

Carol sighs, and it's almost too believable. It tugs at me. I want to comfort her—and I hate the woman. "I know this isn't what anyone wants," she says, shaking her head so her frizzy hair bounces forlornly. "It pains me, but as the ruling coven, we must do what's right. What's best, even if it contradicts our personal feelings. I'm afraid you've both failed."

Her voice echoes everywhere. I hear her with my ears and inside my head too. But Emerson and I stand there, hands clasped tight and neither of us react.

Because it doesn't seem real. It seems more like an old memory.

Failed.

But then I remember that we're together, so it can't be a

memory. They just want it to feel that way. *They want this to feel inevitable*, I say to only Emerson. *Because they know it's bullshit.*

I feel my sister stand a little taller beside me.

"We displayed exponential power," Emerson replies, and her voice is calm. Unruffled.

Perfect.

"Exponential isn't what we need from you girls," Carol says sorrowfully. And I'm reminded of that slap of power at the dance. How it should have maimed me, but didn't. "I'm afraid it's just too dangerous."

"It's as clear as it ever was," Felicia chimes in with a smirk she does nothing to hide. "Your power is wrong. Warped. It does not help witchkind in any way—it threatens us. You melded light and dark. *We* don't do that."

But I know she doesn't mean *witchkind*. She means the Joywood. *They* don't do that.

"We balanced more light and dark together than the seven of you could," I retort, but I keep it sounding calm. "Is that the real issue?"

Felicia smiles the kind of nasty smile that invites me to fight back. She wants me to. Before, I wouldn't be able to help myself.

But I'm a new me now. So I don't take her invitation, no matter how much it hurts.

And believe me, it hurts.

"This time there will be no choices," Felicia tells me, with obvious satisfaction. "No running away." She looks at Emerson. "No wandering around like the village idiot." And she doesn't spare our friends. "And there will be no quarter given for your deceitful little collaborators."

Felicia turns to Carol, but before Carol speaks, there's a shout from the audience.

A loud, clear, *"No."*

Emerson and I turn at the same time, and I'm sure we wear twin looks of absolute shock on our faces when we see who it is.

It's our mother who does not merely stand, but has shot up from her seat to hover in the air. Cold, elegant Elspeth in all her ferocious glory.

Defiance radiating from her.

"Any fool can see that my daughters are two of the most powerful witches in St. Cyprian history," Elspeth continues in her precise, polite, and utterly vicious way. I look for my father, but he's nowhere to be found. "They always have been, yet they have graciously subjected themselves to your childish humiliations since Beltane without complaint. So the question I must ask, Carol, is why, exactly, the ruling coven has not celebrated them as such? Then or now? Is it that you find them a threat to *us*—or to you?"

I WISH I COULD TELL THE ANGRY TEENAGER I was once upon a time that things would end up like this. That Elspeth would *defend* us. She wouldn't have believed it.

"Pardon me?" Carol is so visibly taken aback she might have clutched her pearls if she had any. Or sent out one of her vicious power slaps—if she could get away with attacking Elspeth Wilde like that, out here in front of everyone.

I almost wish she would, and not because I want my mother hurt. But so we can all stop pretending.

"The power they've displayed is off the charts," Elspeth says, and for the first time, it crosses my mind that while my father likes to play at being a diplomat if it means he gets to smoke cigars in rooms where powerful people are, my mother really is one. It's the way she speaks to Carol. It's her clear expectation that Carol intends to correct herself at any moment, and possibly apologize while she's at it. I've never thought of her as a particularly powerful Praeceptor, but now I wonder. "It doesn't fit the proscribed test, but it shouldn't. They're not in their eighteenth year. It is a power appropriate for adult witches a decade on and, I'd argue, far more impressive than many witches a few hundred years beyond that."

Carol tries out a sigh. "You're their mother, so of course you want to spin this to their advantage, Elspeth."

"I didn't last time," my mother says coolly. "But this is different, isn't it? We've all seen what they've done tonight. We all remember how hard it was to achieve balance at our pubertatums, I'm sure. My daughters *played* with it." She's throwing her voice wide, making sure every last person here can hear her—and well. "These are not spell dim women. These are not dangerous women. These are *powerful* witches, and this is not Salem. We exist to lift up powerful witches, or why are we here at all?"

I still can't believe this is our mother saying these things. Our mother, who I would have sworn could never and would never set a foot wrong, openly challenging the Joywood? *In public?*

"Sit down, Elspeth," our father calls out, morbid embarrassment infusing every word.

"Desmond," she replies, her eyes hot but her voice cool—and loud, "why don't you do what you do best? And shut up."

I hear reactions to that, choked laughter and maybe a small cheer, but I am too shocked to say anything. To do anything at all but grasp Emerson's hand. Emerson, who looks as wide-eyed as me.

"You've had an emotional day, Elspeth," Carol says soothingly. "Losing a sister, and now this unfortunate judgment. No one will blame you if you need to go lie down."

I feel the push of power behind her words. And there in midair, my mother shows the first sign of wavering.

"But she's right," comes another voice. It's Holly Bishop. She shoots up above the crowd. "We all know Emerson somehow broke your obliviscor. We also know Emerson isn't warped or wrong. Everything she does is for this town, for us. This isn't right."

Ellowyn's mother shoots up too. "Rebekah showed you power that night, the one you put in your little movie. Anyone can see that."

"She used dark magic on the bricks to almost burn the town down," Felicia returns with malice. "And me with it."

"It's still power," Ellowyn's mother says, no fan of the principal who made her daughter's life hell. "You can say it was rebellious power, but that's *power.* The pubertatum was never supposed to be about having the right *kind* of power. It's supposed to be about whether or not you have *any.* Enough to call yourself a witch. They both clearly do."

"There are rules," Gus Howe, the grumpy antiques dealer and an insufferable Praeceptor in his own right, says from another seat. "These *are* the rules, like it or not."

"Really, Gus?" my mother asks crisply. "And who wrote those rules?"

That feels like a great moment for Nicholas to show up, but he doesn't. Instead, the audience of adult witches begins to divide into sides. Some support Emerson and me, but some, like Gus, are either supportive or afraid of the Joywood.

But they all break down along the lines I expect them to, just as I've been reporting to Emerson. Corinne Martin, chef at the Lunch House, stands next to Holly, while the tedious Joanne Walters sidles up to Gus. But as people move around, talking among themselves, it's not clear which side has more.

"All right. All right," Carol says, calmly zapping everyone into silence—even though this can't be how she thought this would go. The rest of the Joywood are muttering to each other, Maeve Mather shooting daggers at my mother with her eyes like she used to do to my grandmother. "It makes sense that something so…challenging, and out of the norm, would get us all worked up, but let's not forget what tonight is about." She smiles beatifically at all of them. "It's about our young people. The future of St. Cyprian."

I want to punch her, but Emerson squeezes my hand.

"We'll all take a breath, calm down, and think about what's best." Carol looks at us with mild distaste, but inclines her head in a manner that must look gracious if you're farther away. "Let's let these young ones take their tests, then come back to the thorny issue of the Wilde sisters."

Then she pushes the six of us back to our seats with a harsh magic no one else sees.

Though it stings. And I can feel her power crawling all over me, like ants.

The six of us exchange unsure glances as we sit there. Obediently. Or maybe not so obediently, but I feel a little too winded to check to see if I *can* get up. On our own channel, Ellowyn says, *Did the immortal forget what day it is?*

I don't dare look back at Coronis on his high branch. There is a reason Nicholas hasn't shown his face yet. I know this. I only wish I knew what it was.

Or maybe I fear what it is, and why he's waiting so long.

Either way, the procession begins. Young witch after young witch comes to the stage in groups of eight. One by one, they each prove they can balance light and dark to some or other extent—though some barely manage to stand upright, much less do any magic. They answer a few questions for the skills test, and then Carol awards them their designation, immediately engraved on their amulet. I watch them stagger off the stage, flipping over their amulets to see who they are.

When that's backward, isn't it? Surely you should get to decide who you are. Emerson did. I had to. We fought to earn our designations, and all the power that goes with them…

But this really isn't the time to question the whole system. Even I can see that. Especially because no one seems to be failing the test today, and isn't that just perfect? It's beginning to look like maybe this is all Wilde family sour grapes.

As the ceremony goes on without a hitch, I begin to feel something claw around in me. Words and thoughts that aren't my own begin pounding inside my head.

I poisoned them out of jealousy.

It was me and I'm not sorry.

I put a hand to my temple. What the hell are these... intrusive thoughts? I'm no stranger to those, but mine follow the same old themes of guilt and shame for things I already did. And all the things I felt when I was a lonely teenager here.

I'm suddenly grateful for all the experimenting I did out there, because it feels like I've been dosed. Like someone has planted these thoughts in me. Painfully shoved them into my brain and let them start unspooling.

"Em," I say, or try to, but my mouth doesn't move. My hand falls to my lap, and I can't pull it back up to press against the pain in my head.

Up on the stage, another set of eight teenagers march into place.

It's like that first night when Carol hexed me mute, but this isn't just a muting spell, or even a paralyzing spell. It's something more. Something much worse.

Because I can't move or speak, and these thoughts in my head are not mine.

They are not true, but they're twisting in me like they're mine.

Up on the stage, I see Felicia's mouth moving. Her mean little gaze meets mine, and a bolt goes through me. It feels like her power, but it's not. It's realization.

It's that *knowing* thing I do, though it's only just dawning on me that it's one of my gifts.

I don't have "gut feelings." I *know.*

And what I know right now is that the Joywood are framing me.

I remember that vision at Beltane, in Nicholas's house. I saw Litha, storms and destruction. The promise of hope, or perhaps the possibility…but looming over it, the far more likely possibility of ruin and despair.

I'm jealous of them, comes that voice inside me that sounds like me, but isn't. I can feel it, alien and thick, oozing into me. *It was me and I'm not sorry.*

Shock slams through me, though my body doesn't react because it's frozen into place. But *I know.* Something is going to happen to these children.

And I'm going to take the blame.

The line of students is trickling toward the end. It feels like one of those dreams, though I know it's not. The last set of eight climbs onto the stage. And as each one starts the ritual, something changes. One stumbles. One has a coughing fit. Another cries out and brings a hand to his head as if the pain there is unbearable.

In moments, all eight of them are writhing on the stage floor.

The Joywood jump into action. They are suddenly all that is comforting and helpful. They chant spells over the students who are now moaning, complaining of immense pain, crying out into the night as their parents cry out from the audience.

It looks like poison, someone says into every head here, and it's impossible to pinpoint who said it. But I can hear the word begin to be whispered all around me.

"Looks a lot like poison to me," declares Gus Howe. Because he would.

Meanwhile, I sit there, frozen into place. I wait, knowing I'm going to take the fall for this. Knowing it will only be a matter of time before they start whispering my name.

And I have a terrible feeling—I don't want to admit I *know* it—that they're going to kill off these children to make sure there's no doubt in a single mind here what my punishment should be.

Up on the stage, the moaning grows more intense.

"Stand back," cries Felix Sewell, the Joywood Healer.

Thunder rumbles in the distance then, though no storm was predicted. The wind picks up. There's another crash of thunder, far off, and yet a bolt of lightning strikes right there in front of the stage.

"This ends now."

It's Nicholas at last.

His voice booms, louder than the thunder, and he appears like a vision—or a nightmare—in midair above the stage. He looks like what he is—the most powerful lone witch in St. Cyprian, and therefore the world.

He lands on the stage and looks only at the Joywood, but I know he sees everything. Those poor kids. Me. All the familiars and Coronis in his tree.

"They will know what you have done," he says in that voice that seems to start deep inside my own body and roll through me like an internal thunderclap. "And what you seek to do."

Carol stands from where she'd been kneeling beside one of the children and glares at Nicholas. "You can't do this. You might be immortal, but you're constrained."

But her eyes narrow like she's not sure.

Nicholas does not back down. He seems to grow larger as he stands there. More dangerous. As if he really is the storm.

Gil Redd, the Joywood Praeceptor, moves next to Carol. "You know what happens if you do this."

Nicholas nods. Grimly, I think, but he doesn't hesitate. "Better than you can possibly imagine."

Carol starts to say something, but Nicholas raises a hand and she is silent.

It is, truly, one of the most beautiful things I've ever seen. It brings tears to my eyes.

It also terrifies me. Because if he can do this, it means he always *could* do it, but didn't. What did Carol say he was? *Constrained?*

What I know, without any magic involved, is that if he's decided he doesn't care about whatever *constraints* he's been wearing all this time, it can't be good.

For him.

He turns to the crowd. I can see the Joywood frantically trying to slap at him with their magic, but he is impervious.

No one looks at me in my frozen, bespelled state.

No one even hears me from the inside as I frantically try to access the usual channels we use to talk privately.

He's sacrificing himself in front of me and there's nothing I can do to stop it.

"Do not be fooled by your ruling coven," he tells the assembled witches before him. "They are not interested in the good of witchkind and have not been for some time. Ask yourself why you can't remember what coven came before them. And further, why you have no memory of the ascension rituals you are all encouraged to imagine took place. Tell me, does this sound benevolent?"

There's a murmur in the crowd, but I can't tell if it's speculative or suspicious. The Joywood are busy trying to pretend they care more about the children than the raving of a madman. I can see how desperately they try to project one thing while doing another.

I'm muted and paralyzed, but I can *see*. They've pumped

these children full of poison, and they'll blame me for it. This is showy and deliberate, but…it's not all they've done. Because what I know about them is that whatever you *see* them doing, it's what you don't see that you should worry about.

Zelda, I think, her name like agony inside me. An illness without name that shouldn't have killed her, but did. What if they poisoned her too? And the seven other witches Jacob mentioned.

Eight total. Just like the eight teenagers on the stage.

What if they're why Grandma died so early?

I try to scream out, tell anyone what I can see, prove Nicholas is right, but I can't. I can't reach anyone.

It's like I'm alone after all, and this is worse, because I'm not thinking about me.

I don't care about *me* at all.

"It is simple," the very first Praeceptor tells the crowd, his voice still thundering and no doubt rippling out across the witching world. "The Joywood have power because they claimed it. A long time ago, they discovered how they could make that power too big, too vast, to be challenged. But in order to wield that power, they would need immortality."

"You're the immortal," someone from the crowd shouts. Likely that damn Gus Howe again.

"Therefore I would know," Nicholas replies, sounding bored. I want to laugh, but I can't do anything. I can't *do* anything at all but stand here and witness this. "Understand that I am telling the truth because I have no reason to lie. What do I care if the Joywood kill you all? I have seen more witches die than many of you will ever know in your puny lifetimes. But these are facts. The Joywood seek immortality, but immortality requires a set of steps. All must be completed. And with each step, they draw closer."

"I think we all know what this is really about, Nicholas,"

Carol says firmly, with that titter of hers that makes it seem like she's embarrassed *for* him. "It's not much of a secret, is it? Your highly inappropriate relationship with the Wilde girls?"

Not for the first time, I have to admire how effective the pettiness is. Here I am, spellbound and held in place, while my lover inches ever closer to a noble act that will kill him and eight innocent kids lie about in an agony that I'm about to be blamed for. Death hangs heavy in the air.

But all I can focus on for a breathless moment is that horrible woman insinuating that Nicholas is sleeping with me *and* Emerson. And that even if he was, it would be inappropriate *or* any of her business.

Gods, she's good.

"The Joywood have planned a careful course to achieve their goals," Nicholas continues as though Carol hasn't spoken at all. As if he's merely giving one of his lectures. "They will seek even now to confuse you, shame you, scare you. In the end, they will betray you."

"Are we really going to listen to some disgruntled immortal *traitor*?" Felicia all but screeches. "He's only angry we wouldn't let his brand of evil into our righteous, good, honorable coven."

Still, Nicholas shows no anger. He doesn't react at all.

He looks out into the crowd. "I have vowed in blood that I will never speak aloud the true aim of covens that take these steps, for I was a part of one. It is the shame I live with, but that cannot change the oath. It cannot change what I have done. Just as nothing can change what the Joywood have done, or will do if you do not stop them. I am bound to be struck down by the very oaths I made to live outside time if I speak the next." He takes a breath. And then he finds me in the crowd and looks at me at last. And breaks my heart with all that dark blue resolve. "If they succeed, they will be immortal. And you will all be slaves. You are already halfway there."

On the last word, the sky cracks open and lightning flares, fire and electricity sending Nicholas to his knees. He doesn't cry out, or writhe like the teenagers on stage, but I can feel the screaming pain inside him just the same.

I can feel it in me too.

It's not the Joywood doing this to him. I remember all the things he's said about being unable to give us information. *Blood oaths.* The kind that end in painful death if you break them. And even breaking them requires significant power and spellwork. So much so, most people don't believe it's possible.

But I know anything is possible with Nicholas.

I can't speak or move. Nicholas burns. The kids on the stage are vomiting. Some lie perilously still.

Carol stands at the podium, looking smug.

"The righteous win at last, witches of St. Cyprian," she intones from on high. "We have had a deep, unfortunate scar here among us. I don't like to say it, but we've let ourselves be corrupted." She points at Nicholas, who slumps to the stage floor as if he has no bones. "It ends now."

I try to break the spell around me, I try to reach out to Emerson, to Ellowyn, even to my mother. But I am stuck. Blocked.

And Nicholas is dying. He's *dying.* I can feel it like it's happening to me.

I can't let this be the end. For him. For us. We were supposed to work together, but they've separated us. I can't reach anyone. I'm alone again—

But I'm not alone. *You're never alone.* My grandmother said she's always there. Even when I can't feel her.

I call out for her without thinking, with everything I am.

It's Ellowyn's magic that calls on spirits, but I call on my own. *Grandma. Aunt Zelda.* Please. *Help. I need your help.*

Something shimmers and shakes, but I seem to be the only one who sees it. Sees *them* as they bloom into being on either side of me—and then into the aisle.

My grandmother. Aunt Zelda. Women I don't recognize but have my grandmother's eyes or my mother's nose. The ancestresses. *My* ancestresses, who I've long asked to haunt me at will. These are the women who came before. Every woman who had a hand in making me and Emerson and the world we live in.

The world that's falling apart in front of us, though all I can see is Nicholas.

Help me, I beg.

They circle me, spirits and orbs, birds and butterflies, energy and signs. They chant.

And while they do, I push all the hot pulsing power inside of me against the bonds that hold me frozen and still.

I manage to move an arm. Then my neck.

Finally, I can see the scene erupting around me, and it's chaos.

Chaos that was dimmed for me while I was spellbound. I have to assume that was deliberate.

My friends haven't been muted and frozen solid like I have, but they all have their hands full. Jacob is working with other Healers to help the children. Georgie and Sage are arguing with Happy Ambrose and Gil—over books—while a crowd of Historians and Praeceptors press in and argue around them, yelling and shouting as well.

A group including Zander's family surround Festus, hurling angry shouts at him while he tries to create enough magic to put them off, but Zander is with Ellowyn and Emerson, creating a kind of barrier that keeps Carol's and Felicia's magic from getting through.

With my ghostly help, and everyone else preoccupied, I throw off the vestiges of the spell and rush the stage, throwing myself up to the stage floor and diving over to Nicholas.

My immortal, who sacrificed himself for the truth. For information that will allow the Joywood to be stopped. Defeated.

When I finally reach him, he's gray and motionless. I make a sound I hardly recognize, terrified he's dead already.

But he isn't cold. And there's a flicker of something in his eyes.

Touch him.

And I realize that all this time, my grandmother's voice has been urging me to touch him and it wasn't in general. It was for *this*. Because time isn't linear—hers or ours.

I put my hand over his heart, where the rock I gave him sits, cold and pointless.

"You lived forever. You can't die now," I whisper. "You *dick*."

And when I touch the stone, it blooms with heat.

Another thundering crack echoes through the air, and blistering pain scorches through me, but I press harder. My hand. His heart. *My love.*

I have loved you across time.

I feel the magic of the elements. The old gods charging through my veins. His magic and mine.

Time doesn't go one way. It isn't just the now or then. It's all things, and I am in tune with the weaving, waving nature of it all.

Chaos.

Diviner.

Me.

And us.

That's the one thing no one is ever prepared for. That we're an *us*.

I call my friends to me once more, then I press my magic into him. I give him all my love. I remind him *who is meant*.

I feel my friends around me. Chanting the words we infused into the stone. Helping heal him.

For me. For us.

Because this might be the end of Nicholas Frost, immortal witch. I might be the death of him.

Literally, just as he told me at Beltane.

But this is only the beginning.

AS IF HE HEARS ME, NICHOLAS TAKES A SHUDDERING, painful breath, but it is *breath.*

Breath means life, and I try not to sob out in relief. I try so hard to maintain my focus.

Jacob kneels down on the other side of him and helps Nicholas sit up. I never take my hand off his heart, as if I've turned myself into his talisman.

Nicholas takes another few shuddering breaths. He holds up his hand and looks at it.

"I do not understand," he rasps.

He looks around him. At my friends in a ring around him, prepared to pour their love into him though they barely trust him, because he's ours. Because he's mine.

Then he looks at me.

"You're not dead," I assure him.

He shakes his head, as if he doesn't believe me or doesn't understand. "I am not… It's different. It's…"

Life.

There is blood on his hand, and he looks at it as if it is new.

"I have not bled for many years," he says, his voice exhausted. But not weak. "This is different."

Jacob lifts his hands from him. "You're mortal," he says with all his Healer authority.

Nicholas blinks. Then again.

"You didn't sacrifice your life," I whisper. "You sacrificed your immortality."

He looks as if this never occurred to him.

"The end of your immortal life is just the beginning of your actual one," I tell him, though I'm still gripping the stone at his chest. I thump him a little, in emphasis. "You're welcome."

"Congrats," Zander mutters, but mercifully, does not choose this moment to discuss who gets to live and who doesn't. "But am I the only one…seeing ghosts?"

We all twist around, and it occurs to me that I should be wondering why the Joywood aren't all over us. But the chaos from before has subsided. The whole Joywood coven are standing together as if they're prepared to fight.

Better yet, they finally look angry. Not a smug smile to be seen or a titter to be heard.

Because our families are holding them off.

My mother is standing shoulder to shoulder with Ellowyn's mother when I don't think they've had a nice word to say to each other in their lives. Georgie's father is standing right next to Uncle Zack, who's flanked by Zander's grandmother. Much of Jacob's extended family is helping the affected children, who all seem to be white-faced but upright, and his mother and father stand there too, blocking the Joywood.

My father and Georgie's mother are missing in action, but that's all right. We have a whole line of parents, standing up for us. Finally.

And all around them are our beloved dead. Our ancestresses and ancestors, filling in the gaps. A gleaming wall of ghosts and birds, signs of the other side, gathered here for us.

Aunt Zelda turns to look at us. Her eyes find Zander's, and she smiles.

Her *I love you* seems to echo in all of us.

And then, for me alone, *My sweet girl, you have been so loved, all along.*

Because in the end, love is what matters.

It might be all that matters.

"Look at what you've done," the Joywood say in unison. To us. But they can't get *to* us.

We have so much on our side.

All they have is spite.

"Look at what *you've* done," I retort as I stand. "We all heard the truth. Nicholas gave up his immortality to thwart yours. That's powerful magic."

"I think we can all agree that what happened here today is a problem," Carol says, her tone much more neutral. Even if I can see the hate in her eyes. "No matter what accusations questionable immortals lay at our feet, we would never do something without thinking of the good of the whole. It's why we have Ascension rituals after all."

"Excellent point, Carol," I say. Interrupting what is no doubt meant to be a diatribe that ends in her manipulating us all into doing what she wants. But Carol's talk of Ascension reminds me of Emerson's plans. There's no time like the present to put them in action. "Let's have a vote."

"Ascension is in the fall, dear, is in the fall," Carol all but coos at me, but she's made the mistake of amping up her volume and drawing the attention of the crowd. Like I knew she would. "You must have gotten a little addled tonight."

I turn to the bulk of the townsfolk, all here in the audience tonight. And I match Carol's volume. "You're all witnesses here tonight. You all saw what Emerson and I can do and you can decide whether we're a danger to witchkind or not. You new graduates have been with us, in class and at events, for the past two months. And most of the rest of you have known us all our lives." I turn back to Carol and Felicia and the rest of the nasty little Joyworms and smile. "Let's put our pubertatum to a vote."

"These...*high school children* can't vote," Felicia screeches. Earning a reproving look from Carol that makes me smile even wider.

That and Nicholas getting to his feet, already regaining his color.

"They're either adult witches after passing their pubertatums or they're not," Ellowyn says with a smirk. "And if they're not, why have a pubertatum at all?"

Carol looks like she'd very much like to separate Ellowyn's head from her body. "Our job as the ruling coven is to protect witchkind. And sometimes that requires difficult decisions not everyone agrees with. Pubertatums are not up for *popular* vote."

There are murmurs in the crowd. Fear shudders through me, but I shove it aside. And I keep my hand on Nicholas's heart. Because I like to feel it beat.

"But," Carol continues, sounding like a benevolent ruler ready to offer the peasants a crust of bread, "if you all feel strongly, I would be happy to listen to the results of a vote." This time, she aims her smile at me. "By those who've passed their pubertatum, as is only fair."

Meaning Emerson and I can't vote. Because Carol Simon is nothing if not petty to the end.

"It will need to be anonymous," Emerson says, sounding every inch the head of the chamber of commerce.

Before us, Carol's mouth tightens ever so slightly. But she

can't argue. Not in front of everyone. Not after everything else that's happened tonight. She's trapped herself into being the *democratic* leader.

I think of all the students Emerson helped by leading study groups and encouraging them after failed practicums these past months. I think of the girls in bathrooms I taught little spells to so they could take a breather from the tedium of being poked at by teachers who couldn't help them.

Even the business owners who Emerson has supported over the years. People love her. They'll vote for her. And some will even vote for me. Because we have *power*, and it isn't scary if you aren't trying to wield it all yourself.

Something hums in me and I think, *We can win this.*

I say so, to Emerson.

We will *win this*, she replies at once.

"Very well," Carol says, and though her voice is clearly bitter to me, I'm not sure anyone else hears it.

"We'll need to use an impartial member to set up the voting," Jacob says, clearly anticipating tampering. And possibly Emerson's execution.

There's some discussion on how to hold an impromptu vote, and I take the opportunity to turn to Nicholas.

He is holding himself very still, but it's not his usual stillness. This is a stillness born of lingering pain. And perhaps not knowing quite how to *be* in a mortal body.

Nicholas takes his time meeting my gaze. "You saved my life. Against my wishes." But he reaches up to touch the stone, wrapping his hand around mine.

I make myself smirk, though what I want to do is sob. "Did they not teach you how to say thank you in Byzantium?"

He inclines his head, something dancing in his expression. "It was the usual thing, as I recall. If you save a life, it is yours."

"Pretty much forever, if I remember my history classes right."

We both know he's the only history class I've ever paid attention to, or ever will.

He reaches out and takes my chin in his fingers. "Forever once meant nothing to me. But I am as mortal as you are now. I could die tomorrow."

"It's a tragedy, I know," I say as a tear rolls down my cheek. "You might have as little as a couple hundred years left. Witches die so fast."

He wipes away the tear and his eyes darken. But before we can say anything else, there is another commotion.

A magical vote, ready to go.

"On the other hand," I say with a battered sort of daisy smile, "I might not make it to midnight."

But Nicholas winds his arm around me. "You'd be surprised, witchling, how much small acts of goodness can matter. Especially when no one's looking."

A magical scoreboard appears on the stage. As people begin to cast their votes, murmuring words and flicking them toward the board, the numbers change.

Life and a proper witch designation on one side.

Punishment by way of death on the other.

And a clock ticking down, because you only get three minutes to cast your vote. If you don't vote in the time allowed, you're forced to abstain.

If I wanted to complain about these things, I should have been paying attention.

I'm focused on nothing else now.

The numbers change. The lead goes to one side, then the other. The seven of us move off the stage together, holding on to each other and whispering reassurances.

The Joywood remain on the stage. And as good as they can

be at optics, they don't seem to think this one through. They look powerful, separate, and scary up there.

I have to think that in contrast, we look warm. And alive. And real.

And when the timer clicks off, the numbers stop moving.

We win.

We win.

By three votes.

I let out a shaky breath. I can't celebrate exactly. It's too close.

But we live to see another day.

In the silence that follows, Emerson steps forward and then turns to address everyone who sits and stands in the Litha ceremony seats. Everyone seems to be in various states of confusion, awe, and discomfort.

Then again, so am I.

"We want to thank you all for your support," my sister says in her usual pleasant way. It makes people lean in to hear more. Because while she always claims she isn't a politician, she's awfully good at it. "And when Ascension comes this fall, I want you all to remember what you saw here. What you felt. Who helped you and who didn't. Who sacrificed himself for what's right. Because come Samhain, the Joywood won't be the only coven up for Ascension."

That goes through the crowd like electricity.

"If you do this, Emerson," Carol hisses from behind her, "you start a war."

Emerson turns to face Carol. Our families no longer block them from us, because it's our turn now. I take Emerson's hand first, then she takes Jacob's. We form a chain from there, Jacob to Georgie to Ellowyn to Zander. I look to Nicholas on my right and hold out my hand.

His mouth firms. He doesn't *want* this. But that's what makes it special. That's what makes us right.

We don't want the power. We hate the idea of a war.

But we want to do what's right. We *have* to do what's right. And no matter how you look at it, the Joywood aren't right.

Nicholas takes my hand.

We are a coven. Together, we will defeat the Joywood.

Because we have to.

Emerson lifts her chin at Carol. We all back her up. "Then, Carol," she says quietly, but with all the power of the Warrior she is, "a war is what we'll have."

32

THE JOYWOOD SLITHER OFF TO LICK THEIR wounds, and slowly, almost accidentally, the Litha ritual turns into its normal party. A celebration of newly minted witches, poised on the cusp of the rest of their lives.

No one talks about war. Even the good guys get a minute to breathe, celebrate, regroup. And Emerson and I are two of the newly minted witches here. We earned this celebration. We didn't get one last time.

We dance. We eat too much sugar and chase it down with bubbly things that make us all giddy. We laugh too loud.

We *live*.

Not just with each other and these good people who voted to let us stay alive, but with the spirits of those already gone. Those who helped us today, including Aunt Zelda.

I dance with her to an old song I remember her singing when we were small. Later I see her with Zander and Uncle Zack, all holding each other close. She'll cross over soon, but she'll always be part of us. Here, in the way spirits are. I look farther and see my grandmother sitting near the stage, tapping her feet to the music and laughing along with a whole group of fearless Wilde women, stretching back through time.

She nods at me, looking proud.

The night wears on, but no one seems inclined to leave.

Emerson and Jacob are swaying in the middle of a group of teenagers who were eager to tell Emerson they voted for her and will support us come Samhain. Georgie and Sage have their heads together over a book. But they smile at each other as they flip pages, and maybe it isn't the kind of amazing, all-encompassing love I think Georgie's capable of, but it's nice. Sage is nice, and he helped us.

Maybe I need to remember that I used to tell anyone who would listen that I wasn't one for big emotion or high drama. For all I know, watching all the fireworks around her is what convinced Georgie that she needs someone safer. Quieter. Less…immortally melodramatic, possibly, and who can blame her?

Then again, maybe I put a lot more stock in *nice* tonight—and unseen acts of goodness, even—than I did before.

Later there's my best friend. And my cousin. There's no dancing for the man who lost his mother this morning and spent his evening with her ghost. But Ellowyn is sitting there talking to him, there's *almost* a smile on his face, and it feels *right*.

And that vow Zander made, that I made myself, doesn't sit heavy on my heart. Because some things are necessary and meant, no matter how they hurt. We will get to the bottom of what happened to the eight witches who died this morning too young. It lies somewhere at the bottom of the Joywood.

This was a battle, and there's a war still ahead.

But we'll celebrate the eight young lives we saved, and our own, and all we might save in the future.

Eventually we all congregate together while the teenagers carouse. We tell happy stories about Aunt Zelda. We make grand plans for Ascension. We laugh, we love, we grieve.

And we even choose a name.

We decide to call ourselves the Riverwood, because we're right here at the confluence, where the three rivers meet. Where we came together as a coven the first time.

Where we will no doubt fight again, in the heart of St. Cyprian's power and influence, for the right to use all that might and magic for good.

But we don't talk about the Joywood at all.

Not tonight.

Much later, Nicholas and I dance in the moonlight, until loss feels like a song someone sang long ago and fear seems a distant future, too far away to touch.

We dance and we dance, until we feel like us again.

Or for the first time.

No prophecies. No *death of me.* No pretending I'm going to leave this place when every last part of my heart is here.

Us.

"I suppose if I am indebted to you forever, my puny mortal life in your hands," Nicholas says in that lazy drawl of his that I suspect will always make my toes curl, "you will have to forego the pleasures of your childhood home."

"Will I? How will I tear myself away?" I look up at him—an immortal no more and yet still somehow *my* immortal. My immortal love. *Mine.* My life as much in his hands as his in mine, for as long as we have left.

And this time, when given the opportunity to look into all

those futures he blocked from me or I refused before, I let myself. Because *Diviner* is who I am, and we still get to choose.

No matter what I see.

The visions flow through me. Varied, intense, different. So many choices. So many paths. There are challenges ahead, sacrifice and pain, but that *is* life. And worth it, when you allow yourself to love—fully, wholly—those who love you, and even yourself.

The best kind of recovery I can imagine is love.

There are so many options winding out in front of us, but the one thing that is clear is whichever fate we find, it will be together.

"It is unavoidable," he says once he senses I have put the visions aside. "You will have to make Frost House your new home so that I may worship you accordingly, with all my many riches. All yours to use at will, of course."

"Well." I blow out a breath and pretend to think it over. "If *riches* are involved…"

He laughs. Nicholas Frost *laughs*, and the more he does it, the more easily it comes to him. The more it seems to kick up in us both. I smile up at him, so much and so hard that my cheeks hurt.

And I think, *I will hold on to this moment forever.*

Because tonight, all that matters is this. Us.

Nicholas Frost is a mortal. And he is mine.

I am a Diviner, officially. *Chaos Diviner*, if you're being specific, and you can be sure my sister will correct you if you're not.

There is darkness ahead, but I focus on the light.

On hope. And the beating heart of the people we love, who love us too.

And him.

Always him.

When he sweeps me into his arms and kisses me, there near the place where the three rivers meet, I whisper, “Take me home, Nicholas.”

And he does, my man out of time, just as I was promised long ago.

You can call it a prophecy if you like—a good one at last.

★★★★★

The magic continues in
Book Three of the Witchlore series.